BORDERING ON LOVE

Natasza Waters

Unconditional love is the best gift we'll ever experience.

CONTENTS

CHAPTER ONE

From Grayson's vantage point, the decrepit industrial warehouse on the San Diego waterfront appeared quiet. Like him, other members of the narcotics vice squad waited in unmarked vehicles hidden in key locations. Intercepting two hundred million dollars' worth of cocaine before it hit the streets would put a smile on his face, but the lack of activity indicated the anonymous tip to the task force was bogus.

He tilted his wrist to check the time. Twenty-three-hundred hours on a warm May night. Until the operation's lead officer stood them down, Grayson monitored the odd stray cat on a nightly prowl.

His cell vibrated from the center console. He checked the ID of the caller. *Second Chances.* He grimaced, recognizing the name of the inner-city shelter.

"Detective Brooks," he answered.

"Hello. This is Emma Flask from Second Chances Rehabilitation. My apologies for disturbing you at this time of night."

Maybe he'd luck out and the woman wasn't calling about Erika, but he seriously doubted it. "What can I do for you, Emma?"

"A detective by the name of Grant Warren gave me your number when he dropped a woman off at our shelter a few minutes ago."

Grant was a buddy and worked in vice as well, but his area of responsibility covered a district in San Diego known for prostitution and small-time drug trade.

Keeping an eye out for movement near the weathered,

metal-clad building with an air of abandonment and broken windows, Gray asked, "Okay, and you're calling me because...?"

"Normally, we'd make room for Erika Armstrong. She's stayed with us before but, unfortunately, we're over capacity and our policy is that our guests are not under the influence at the time of admittance. Erika is in an agitated state, and I don't want to release her in this condition for safety reasons. She said you're her boyfriend and would pick her up."

Boyfriend wasn't a term he'd use. Erika was a woman he kept rescuing every time she hit rock bottom, which was often. Grant hadn't reached out, but there was a reason he left Erika at the shelter. Grayson guessed it was that or jail.

"Yeah, all right, I understand. Listen, I'll be there as soon as I can, but I'm working a case. Give her a cup of coffee and tell her I'm coming. She'll calm down."

"Thank you, Detective."

As if the gods favored Erika's self-induced dilemma, the lieutenant soon called an all-clear over the radio. Grayson responded that he was standing down for the night.

Driving through the city, he called the detective who had dropped Erika at the shelter.

On the second ring, Grant answered. "Hey, man. Guess you got the message. Dispatch said you were on the job, and I didn't want to interrupt."

"We're stood down. I'm heading over to the shelter now. Where did you find her?"

"The Red Room. I've been working the area for the last couple of weeks. I know you and Erika have history, which is why I didn't arrest her when she approached me at the bar. She was looking to make some money the old-fashioned way, if you get my drift."

Grayson had hooked up with Erika years ago when he served in the SEAL teams. She'd been a one-night stand that evolved into a toxic union he couldn't shake.

"Yeah, I get your drift."

"I'm sorry, Gray. She's using again, that's why she wanted some one-on-one time. I figured the shelter would take her, but they were full and not happy about letting her in the door in her current condition. I know it's not your problem, but it was that or arrest her."

Erika's abusive father and negligent mother had forced her onto the streets at a young age. Extremely beautiful, she'd relied on men to keep a roof over her head, at least temporarily, but she was still a victim. That's the real reason Grayson kept answering her SOS calls and patiently listening to her vows to kick the drugs. When they were in their early twenties, her appreciation came in the form of wild sex and like an idiot, he'd accepted payment.

"Thanks for dropping her off, Grant."

Two blocks from the shelter, he stopped at a red light. A mix of restaurants and stores had grown up around an older suburban neighborhood. The shelter had converted an old apartment complex, adding a medical clinic and counseling facility.

"You bet, buddy. Not my business, but if I were you, I'd stop playing Clark Kent to her damsel in distress. Guys in our profession have a hard enough time juggling a relationship and the job. You're never gonna find a future Mrs. Brooks while Erika has you on speed dial every time she gets into trouble."

Relationship? Not likely. If nature called, he hooked up, but he'd never run across someone who made him double-time to a jewelry store.

"If I ever find that elusive creature, I'll worry about it then." Grayson was pretty sure *she* didn't exist. After ten years with the SEALs and five working for the Sheriff's Narcotics Task Force, his profession took precedence.

"Never say never, Gray. I used to think the same thing until I met Donna."

"She's too good for you, man. Say hello to the wife for me."

"You bet."

He disconnected and slipped the cell into his shirt pocket. Grayson liked Grant's wife, Donna. She was an intelligent, friendly woman. Before the wedding, the guys from vice squad had thrown Grant a bachelor party. After ten beers, the groom had admitted that falling in lust with beautiful women always ended in disaster. Donna wasn't a beauty queen but she was all heart, and he was going to love her until death did they part. Grayson had to respect that. His parents had been married for thirty years when his mom died unexpectedly.

When the light turned green, he took a right turn at the intersection.

He eased the black, unmarked sedan into an empty spot along the sidewalk across from the Second Chances shelter, a brick-faced building with green lawns and landscaped flower beds. Tired, he sighed while shutting the engine off. This record had played so many times, he could almost recite the next two hours verbatim.

* * * *

As Grayson walked into a lobby reminiscent of a hotel with calming, neutral tones, a middle-aged brunette looked up from the computer at reception.

"Detective Brooks," she greeted, rounding the desk and offering her hand for a shake.

"What gave it away?" he asked.

"You look like a cop."

He grinned. Not what an undercover detective wanted to hear. "Thanks. I think." The name tag on her pale blue nurse's uniform identified the woman as Emma. "Has she calmed down?"

She clasped her hands together and offered a professional smile. "Erika is—"

"Gray! There you are." Erika's tight tone announced her

approach. She swaggered down the hallway, able to navigate on spike heels while half cut. Wearing skin-tight jeans and a snug, red shirt that barely covered her breasts, she aimed for him then slung her arms around his neck. "Baby, I'm so glad you're here. Get me outta this place."

Her big, blue eyes stared up at him while she blinked her fake lashes. Even with all the drugs she'd put in her system, her features were stunning, with high cheekbones, soft lips, and silky, blonde hair. At five-ten, her rockin' bod was a man's wet dream. Grayson gripped her wrists and untangled her hold on him. Chastising her wouldn't work. He'd tried many times before. Talking sense to an addict fell on deaf ears until the high wore off.

Grayson nodded at the nurse. "Thanks for keeping her safe."

Emma's brow creased with empathy and understanding. "I'll have room tomorrow."

Erika's expression curled with disdain. "I'm not coming back here—ever! I don't need this place. I'm not an addict." She coiled her cold hands around his upper right arm and leaned against his side. "Gray, let's go home."

Instead of pointing out that his place wasn't her home, nor had it ever been, he put a hand to Erika's back and escorted her out to the undercover sedan, opened the passenger door, and closed it once she'd tumbled inside.

"Are you mad at me?" she asked in a sweet tone after he got behind the wheel.

Checking for traffic, then pulling a U-turn, he headed for his townhouse in Grant Hill. "You hungry?" Grayson kept his attention on the road when her slender hand slid over his thigh.

"For you, always."

When her fingers crawled closer to his junk, he placed his palm over her hand and removed it from his leg. "Food, Erika. Are you hungry?"

She snapped her hand back and crossed her arms over her

chest. "No. But I could use a drink."

He switched into the left lane and slowed for a red light. "Think you've had enough for tonight."

Erika swept her luscious hair over her left shoulder. "Guess you know the cop that picked me up."

"Yeah, I know him. That's why you're not in lock-up." She wasn't falling down drunk and could probably string a few thoughts together. "You think it's wise selling yourself for a hit?"

"That's a lie! You always think the worst of me." When he didn't respond, she said, "Grayson, I'm not a bad person."

"I know that." He glanced across his shoulder at her. "You're a victim. And you keep putting yourself in that position every time you numb the pain with narcotics or alcohol."

She was quiet for a blissful few minutes but that wouldn't last, and she didn't disappoint. "I know a part of you still loves me, Gray. That's why you come when I call. I wanted things to be different between us, but you wouldn't let that happen. Your job was always more important than me."

He didn't want to burst her bubble but he'd never loved Erika. During his time in the Special Forces, she'd find him when he returned from deployment. In those days, she wasn't smoking crack or popping ecstasy. They'd hook up, and Erika had satisfied his needs. When Grayson left town, she'd warm another team guy's bed.

"Erika, I want you to clean up your act. There's nothing but tragedy waiting at the end of the line if you don't get help."

She shifted onto her left hip. "If that's what you want, I'll do it. Even when we're apart, I think about you. I worry about you, Gray." She scrounged through her leather purse and pulled out a pack of cigarettes.

"Put 'em away. No smoking in the patrol car."

She sighed and let the pack tumble from her fingers back into the purse. "We had a lot of good times together. If you'd just give us a chance, we could build a family. I've told you that a thousand times."

Grayson hung a left and rolled into the entrance of his townhouse complex then took the first right. At the fifth driveway, he turned the wheel and opened the single garage door with the remote access on his phone. With any luck, he'd get a call-out tonight and let Erika sleep it off.

Easing the sedan past his Ford pickup, he entered the narrow garage, parked and turned off the ignition, then released his seatbelt.

Erika clutched his forearm. "Gray, don't shut me out. You've always done this whenever I've talked about a future." She shook her head; her eyes filled with emotion. "I'm not perfect. I know that. Is that what you're waiting for? Because if it is, no one will meet your lofty standards. It's easy for you to criticize someone when you come from a good home and have a successful career. You had all the chances I didn't."

He scrubbed his jaw and eyed her. "I do come from a good home, but the rest I achieved on my own. Every time you drink too much or get high on crack it's your choice, Erika. Every guy you fuck for money is your decision."

"But you never cared," she whispered.

"I do care. That's why you're staying here tonight, because I hate that a beautiful woman like you continues to destroy herself."

Erika snapped her eyes closed as if resisting the truth. "But you saved me. You come when I call. It means something."

Yeah, it meant he hated to see anyone suffer. As much as he'd love to snap his fingers and erase her demons, that wasn't possible. Instead, she kept flying into his net on purpose, hoping he'd change his mind and ask her to stay. Like taming a feral cat, she'd curl up on the couch for a rest but the call of the wild never went away. Nor the urge to party. She'd take refuge at his place for a couple of days, empty his wallet, and take off.

"It means you need to get some rest," he said, cracking open the driver's door.

Erika followed him into the modest townhouse he'd bought while serving in the Navy. A place to crash, and easy to lock and walk away from for seven months.

Grayson flicked on the kitchen light. Erika slid up behind him and pressed her breasts against his back.

"There was always one thing we were good at." She wrapped her slender arms around his waist. "You make me wet just looking at you, baby."

He turned to face her and Erika flattened her palms on his chest. The urge was there but he hadn't touched her in five years. "You know where the spare bedroom is. Get some sleep."

She huffed and stepped back, her blue eyes steely with determination. Erika gripped the hem of her snug shirt and pulled it over her head. Although his cock flexed at the sight of her perfect tits and rock-hard nipples, he'd never walk down that road again.

"How long has it been, Grayson?" She slowly unzipped her jeans and thumbed the waist, shimmying the pants and thong to her ankles, then easing the clothes aside with her foot. "C'mon, Gray. I'm not asking for forever."

The woman stood there in nothing but high heels and a seductive smile. Temptation begged him to give in. Most men would have her hanging onto the back of the couch by now. Years ago, he'd been one of those guys. Every time they'd hooked up, she'd fallen deeper in love with him.

"Erika, my cock is staying in my pants."

Her face constricted with angry creases, then she swept her clothes from the tile floor and marched out of the kitchen toward the stairs. Grayson released his tight grip on the granite counter and exhaled a deep breath.

There had to be something wrong with him. No matter what woman he spent the night with, nurturing anything outside of an orgasm never entered the picture. His cock recognized lust and sex, but his heart was color-blind. Never a flicker of light. Before Grayson left his hometown in the Pacific Northwest, he'd been a different guy. At eighteen, he'd joined the Navy, leaving the farm, his friends, and family behind. He'd served his country and now his community.

A door slammed upstairs and roused him from his thoughts. Instead of using the spare room, she'd entered his bedroom. Grayson shot a glance toward the clock above the sink. Ten past midnight. Time for a cold beer.

* * * *

The shrill ring of his cell woke Grayson with a start. He blinked and reached for his phone sitting next to his empty beer bottle on the coffee table.

"Six-thirty in the morning. So much for sleeping in." He shifted to a sitting position on the couch and forked a hand through his hair.

"Hello."

"Gray. Did I wake you?" the woman asked.

He groaned. "Ivy. Hey what's up?" he asked his sister.

"I wanted to catch you before you went to work and before Dad gets up."

"Everything okay?"

Their father had a heart attack last year. The doctors operated, and the old man ended up with a triple bypass and a second shot at his golden years. Samuel Brooks, the patriarch of the family, was tough as nails. When Grayson had watched the TV show "The Ranch", he'd laughed his head off. Sam Elliot's character and his father were like twins separated at birth.

"No, things aren't okay," Ivy said.

Grayson heard the springs of the front screen door on the old Victorian farmhouse screech open. He could visualize it so well since he'd passed through that doorway from the time he was born to the time he left home.

"What's wrong?"

"I've put off calling you for weeks, but I'm drowning here, Gray."

He'd been afraid this would happen. Their father was still able but running out of steam. Ivy, Grayson's younger sister by two years, resembled Superwoman. She ran every aspect of the farm, from the farmstead's grocery store to the livestock. Ivy had raised her son as a single mom and kept an eye on their father, who refused to admit he had limits. The Brooks farm had one ranch hand and Ivy's old friend, Arlene, helped out at the store. His sister was stubborn as hell and wouldn't be calling if she hadn't reached the end of her rope.

"You're trying to juggle all the balls, aren't you?"

"I can do it, Gray. I just need a hand this summer. To catch up, ya know?"

He grinned. This call had to be killing Ivy. "What about Cole?"

He and his best friend had met in second grade. Cole had left Bellingham after high school to attend college in Arizona. After acquiring his Bachelor of Science in Criminal Justice, he'd worked at the Tucson Sheriff's Office then returned home and joined the Skagit County office.

"He's around," she said.

"Around?"

"Yes. Around. He lends a hand all the time, after he gets off duty and on his days off. If he's not here or at the Proactive Unit headquarters, he's at Roosters picking up stray women."

To him, it sounded as if someone had stepped on Ivy's tail. Grayson chuckled. "You don't approve."

"None of my business," she said sharply.

Roosters was a favorite adult watering hole. Almost everyone had their first legal drink at Roosters bar. The food was fantastic, and if ya wanted to hook up, a guy hardly ever struck out.

"So, you want me to take a leave of absence and come home."

Ivy made a little humming sound in her throat he was familiar with. Indecision. "I know it's a big favor and I hate asking."

"I can tell." Grayson stood and stretched the kinks out of his neck.

"I'm worried about Dad. He keeps doing too much. More than he should. He's frustrated because he's not thirty years old anymore. If he doesn't slow down, he's going to keel over in the calving barn."

That was their old man, all right. He loved the farmstead that had been in the Brooks family since the 1800s. Grayson did too, but once he'd become a SEAL, he didn't visit enough. When he'd retired from the Forces and jumped to law enforcement, he remained in San Diego and left the whole operation on Ivy's shoulders.

"Are you going to make me beg?" she asked.

"If I did, I'd never hear the end of it."

She snorted. "Don't be a jerk."

A couple years younger than him and more than a hundred pounds lighter, Ivy's feisty attitude packed a punch that could knock a grown man on his ass.

"I'll talk to my captain today."

She released a huge breath. "Thank you."

He strolled to the fridge and opened the door. Inside, he had all the makings for scrambled eggs, which reminded him of Ivy's talents in the kitchen. Mom had shown her all the family secrets and when she'd gotten sick, Ivy took over cooking for the family.

Reaching for the egg carton, he said, "I'll call you tonight, okay?"

"Love you, Gray."

"Love you, too."

He hung up and turned to put the eggs on the counter. Erika stood there in one of his long-sleeved cotton shirts, hands on her hips. Her blonde hair disheveled but still sexy as hell.

11

"Who was that?" she demanded.

Before she flew into a rage, he clarified, "My sister."

Her brows shot up. "Ivy? I've always wanted to meet her."

That would go over like mixing fire and gasoline. Ivy protected her family like a lioness. One sniff of overindulgence with alcohol or the use of drugs and she'd fire Erika's ass onto the street.

"I'll put a pot of coffee on. Help yourself to a shower."

Erika rounded the center island in his kitchen. "Are you going home for a visit?"

"Longer than that." He turned his back on the gorgeous mess of a woman and retrieved the frying pan.

"Take me with you, Grayson. A new start for both of us."

Sober, Erika's colorful zeal couldn't be ignored. It's what had attracted him in the first place. Hot sex and her mind-blowing figure were an extra benefit.

"My family needs help on the farmstead. It's a large operation and my sister can't handle the work all on her own. Dad's slowing down with age. My buddy, Cole, helps out when he can, but it's not enough."

Erika palmed the edge of the counter, hopped, and sat her ass on the island while he tossed the old coffee grains into the garbage.

"I'll help."

"You don't know anything about farming."

A brilliant smile beamed on her face. "Then teach me."

In good spirits, he hated to burst her bubble, but enough with tiptoeing around the truth. He moved the frying pan from the drain rack to the stove, then turned and put a hand on either side of her hips.

"Erika, you're an addict. You know how to survive on the streets. Last night you tried to fuck a cop for money. I'm not taking you home and dropping that kind of shit on my family."

Her brow crinkled and her eyes welled with tears. "I can do better, Gray. Just give me a chance."

"I know you can do better." He thumbed the tear from her cheek. "I know you're a strong woman but until you find her, the cycle will keep repeating itself."

She sniffed and bowed her head. "Then help me break the cycle."

He'd indulged her apologies too often, always there to give her a soft landing when she asked. If he left, she'd have to find another safe haven or make her own.

"Erika, I want you to get clean, but you have to do it for yourself. Not for me."

She palmed his jaw and pressed her mouth to his lips. A part of him wished he could feel something for her but like the other women who'd quickly come and gone in his life, there was no spark. He'd never experienced a sense of loss when they walked out the door. He didn't feel a damn thing.

"I love you so much, Gray."

"I wish I could say the same but I can't. I care about you, Erika, but it's not the same as love. It's not in me. Never has been."

Her thumbs gently grazed his cheeks. "I think it's hiding behind that superhero cape you wear all the time. Your sense of duty never takes a day off. It was your confidence that attracted me in the first place. It still does. You're just afraid to fall in love."

That wasn't the case. He experienced a sense of envy when he'd seen the team guys with their wives or girlfriends.

"Not afraid."

"And now your family needs you. How long will you be gone?"

As if she hadn't heard a word he'd said, she'd do what she'd always done—wait for him. His cell rang, and he headed toward the coffee table.

"I'll finish breakfast," she said, hopping off the island.

Grayson plucked the phone up and answered without looking at the ID.

"Gray, hey, man, did I catch you at home?"

"Cole. I just talked with Ivy a few minutes ago."

"Good. I've only been telling her to call you for—" He stopped midstream and cleared his throat. "I mean, what did she say?"

He grinned. "Worried you're gonna spill the beans and have to face my sister's wrath? You're off the hook. She told me she needs help. Question is, why the hell didn't my best friend tell me this months ago?"

"You know your sister. She threatened to annihilate me if I talked."

"You carry a weapon, don't ya?"

Cole laughed. "Not even that would bring your sister down if she was angry enough. And these days she's been on edge. I'm worried about her."

Everybody was worried about somebody. "She told me you're still helping out at the farmstead. I owe you big time for stepping in."

"You're welcome. That's part of the reason I'm calling."

Gray watched Erika hustle around the kitchen in his button-up shirt showing off her long, sexy legs. If she could dump the addictions, she'd make some guy a happy man. "I'm listening."

"Ivy probably asked you to get her through the summer."

"She did."

"She needs more than that, Gray. Maybe not full-time, but available all the time. I told you about the new unit I'm working for at the sheriff's office. So happens, the brass likes what we're doing and they're expanding our department. There're two new openings. I told our lieutenant about your work experience and that you might be coming home. It's lower key than what you're used to, but the Proactive Unit is making a difference. We concentrate on gathering intelligence and infiltrating known crime rings and problem areas within Skagit County. Plus, it's mostly eight to four, which will give you time to help out at the farmstead."

"Never heard a better pitch, and all in one breath. I'm

impressed."

"Fuck off."

Grayson broke into a chuckle. "Give me the lieutenant's number. I'll call him this morning." Cole didn't hesitate and Grayson wrote the number on the corner of a day-old San Diego newspaper.

"Your sister needs you, buddy. She's working herself to death, but I think, psychologically, she'd find some relief knowing you're there to lean on. Besides, I wouldn't mind partnering up with my best friend to put some bad guys behind bars."

Grayson didn't doubt Cole would make a great partner. "I appreciate the call."

"I should have visited you in San Diego a long time ago. Just never got a break."

"We're both guilty of that," Grayson admitted. "How's my nephew?"

When his father had his bypass, Gray had gone home, just in case. He couldn't believe how big Jackson, Ivy's son, had grown. He'd been a toddler when Mom passed away, but she'd lived long enough to see her first grandson. Unless his sister remarried, Jackson would be the only grandson. The boy looked exactly like Ivy, with a mop of blond hair and the Brooks' family signature blue eyes.

"Growing up fast," Cole said. "He's quite the kid but then again, his mom is amaz—well, she's raising one hell of a son."

Grayson paused when Cole's tone held a hint of...what? Respect? Or was it something along the lines of yearning.

"I'm long overdue to play catch with the kid."

Whether he put assholes in prison here or in Washington State didn't matter. His family needed him, and nothing was keeping him in San Diego. Couldn't hurt to talk to Cole's lieutenant.

"I'm sure you don't want to give up palm trees in lieu of thirty-nine inches of rain," Cole said. "Ivy doesn't know I'm calling or suggesting something more permanent, but she can't keep up this pace by herself and refuses to hire more than temporary help, even though she can easily afford it. The situation is only going to get worse."

The aroma of freshly brewed coffee called. "I told her I'd let her know my plans tonight. You don't have to convince me, buddy. We'll talk later, and thanks for putting in a good word for me."

"As if you need one. Lieutenant Kline's waiting for your call. He was hoping I could convince you to join the team. Later, man."

Erika placed two plates on the small, pine kitchen table he rarely used. She returned with the coffee pot and filled their mugs. When he sat down, she didn't spare him a glance. After retrieving the milk from the fridge, she finally sat and looked across the table at him.

"Your life is here, Gray, but you're leaving, aren't you?"

After downing a sip of hot, black java, he set his mug next to the plate. "My sister is an army of one that will never admit defeat. She needs help."

Erika swallowed. "What you're saying is, there's nothing holding you here, but what about me? Take me with you."

Grayson looked around the sparsely decorated townhouse. He'd kept things simple. All the necessities but nothing he would care about losing, except for some framed photos in his office from the times he'd spent in the teams. He'd take those with him. If he had a job waiting for him in Washington State, he might not come back.

"Listen, why don't you stay here?"

Tears welled in her eyes. "But you won't be."

"If I decide to stay in Washington, I'll eventually put this place up for sale, but until then, you've got a roof over your head." Grayson wasn't kidding himself. Within a week, maybe less, she'd be fucking some guy in his king bed. But at least she'd have a place to crash.

"Don't leave, Grayson. I swear to God, I'll clean up my act."

He smiled at her and held her hand. "Hey, I know you can.

One day you're gonna find the strength to kick your demons to the curb. I truly hope that's soon."

Tears washed down her face and she swept her blonde strands behind her ears. "Thank you." She cleared her throat and stared toward the stove. "You've always been there for me. I don't know why, but you have."

They'd had this conversation before. She knew the answer. Although she'd had a rough start in life and doubled down as an adult abusing herself, she was still a woman with a lot of potential. She just had to believe in herself enough to walk a new path.

"You're going to be okay, Erika. You need the rehab facility to give you support, and they will if you take the first step. If you do, I guarantee you'll be proud of what you can accomplish. And you're worth it."

She snuffled and blew her nose in the paper towel she'd set with the cutlery. "You're the only man who's ever told me that. The only guy who didn't throw me away." She gazed at him with watery eyes. "I love you." She sniffed. "But this is goodbye, isn't it?"

He offered a sympathetic smile. He'd never uttered those three important words to a woman who wasn't related to him, and he never would. Gray knew there was something wrong with his hard wiring. He'd screwed enough women that it equated to a small country. The second he rolled out of their beds, his emotions went dark. He had zero urge to see them again. Erika had been the only exception he'd allowed in his bed more than once, but she'd always accepted sex was all he'd offer.

"It's time, Erika. And, yes, this is goodbye."

Fourteen days later, Grayson loaded his truck and had a job waiting for him in Skagit County. Erika had checked herself into the Second Chances rehab facility. As he heaved the last cardboard box into the bed of his pickup then closed the Tonneau cover in case he ran into rain on his twenty-four-hour drive northbound, he looked forward to seeing the family.

A new start in a familiar place.

He had no regrets. Although his captain had been shocked by the announcement, he understood and wished Grayson well. Some of the guys had gotten wind of his departure, and last night they took him out for a few beers.

Gray checked the townhouse doors to make sure they were all locked. Erika had a spare set of keys to access the place. At some point, he'd probably contact a realtor and put it on the market, but there was no rush.

Backing out of the driveway, he felt a spark of excitement. It had been an easy decision. His instincts told him to keep his foot on the gas pedal. It had been fifteen years, but he was finally going home and for some reason, he couldn't wait to get there.

CHAPTER TWO

A row of Japanese maple trees cast dappled May sunlight over the community mailbox where Holly stood while searching the great crevasse of her purse. She spent hours unraveling the mysteries of ancient languages but had ten seconds of patience playing hide-n-seek with her keys.

"Ah, there you are."

She opened her box to find a large manila envelope unceremoniously folded in half and crammed into the cavity by the postal service. She retrieved the mail and locked the box.

Holly flattened the envelope sent by the McDunlop firm on her thigh. About time it arrived.

The early summer afternoon sun warmed her cheeks, and she inhaled the fresh air. She lived in a modern neighborhood of townhouses with small, landscaped front gardens on either side of narrow roads that networked each phase of the strata's subdivision.

As she walked the cement path to her front door, Holly's neighbor, Mrs. Norman, stood up, holding a small hand shovel.

"Getting an early start on your annuals, I see," Holly said.

Widowed and in her seventies, Mrs. Norman kept herself active by taking walks and working in her garden when the weather improved.

"Hi, Holly. About time you got outside for a walk. I haven't seen you in a week."

"You know how it is. Work, sleep, repeat," she said.

"The university takes advantage of you, if you ask me."

Holly shrugged. "Self-inflicted. I love my job."

The department head didn't ask her to work until eight

p.m. most days. She did it because ancient languages never got boring, but whiling the evenings away in an empty house did. "I'm headed south tomorrow morning."

Mrs. Norman scratched her nose with the edge of her wrist. "Ah, yes. Your monthly retreat. I have a lot of friends who visit the Neon Lights resort."

"It's fun. You should come with me sometime."

The spry senior citizen grinned. "Doubt you'd meet any handsome men with me hanging around."

Holly chuckled. "I haven't met any handsome men there, ever. I go because it's a change of scenery."

Mrs. Norman's expression creased with an empathetic expression. "Dear, a lovely young woman like you deserves a decent man. He's out there. I promise."

When Holly and her husband, Kevin, bought the townhouse, Mrs. Norman was the first person they'd met. Five years later when Kevin walked out, their neighbor noticed he wasn't around. Holly had kept the explanation brief, and the kindly woman called him a foolish idiot.

Holly wasn't overly concerned about meeting anyone. "Men in their thirties are either already married or single for a reason."

The senior waved her gloved hand in an *oh-go-on* gesture. "I was completely smitten when I first saw David. Love is like being struck by lightning. When you see your soulmate, you'll know what I mean."

She smiled at her neighbor's optimism, but her belief in soulmates was about the same as believing in unicorns.

"I'll take your word for it."

Holly agreed that Mrs. Norman's husband, David, had been a handsome man when she'd showed her pictures of a twenty-year-old guy wearing an Army uniform. They'd been married for fifty years before he'd passed away.

Back in Cape Breton, where Holly and her ex-husband had met, her girlfriends thought the rookie cop was a tall, swarthy hunk of hottie. She hadn't been as impressed. No man had ever made her speechless, and she highly doubted any guy would cause that kind of physical reaction.

"I'll be back Sunday night," Holly said.

"Have a good time, dear. I'll keep an eye on your place."

"And I'll keep an eye out for my soulmate," she teased.

Mrs. Norman chuckled and went back to pulling weeds.

After dropping her purse on the kitchen counter, Holly took the envelope to her office and tore it open. Lawyer-speak was like hieroglyphics—nearly unreadable unless you wanted to spend years deciphering the terminology.

There was no unraveling the mystery behind her ex-husband's infidelity. The judicial stamp certifying the divorce made it official.

Kevin had left two years ago. Although her ex had crushed her confidence, she refused to tuck her tail between her legs and move back to the East Coast where her family lived.

She deposited the paperwork with the rest of the lawyer's documents at the back of the file cabinet. Later, she'd pack a carry-on size bag for her three-night stay at Neon Lights, a thirty-minute drive past the border. She avoided the long wait times at the popular crossing between the US and British Columbia by leaving Thursday morning.

But first, dinner for one. Another reason she liked staying at the resort—no cooking. With a choice of restaurants plus the buffet, someone else cleaned the dishes. Holly turned the light out in her office and headed for the kitchen.

Within twenty minutes, she'd built a green salad, added mandarin oranges, raisins, leftover chicken, and tossed it with homemade sesame dressing.

It was too depressing to sit at the large dining table that she and Kevin had bought together, so Holly settled on the couch and flicked on the TV to watch the six o'clock news, interrupted by nauseating commercials.

Eating alone wasn't a foreign concept. Because of Kevin's shifts, half the time she'd spent evenings entertaining herself. In retrospect, she wondered how many of those evenings he'd spent in some other woman's bed.

Halfway through dinner, her sister, Paige, called.

"Holly, girl. How ya be?"

"I be just fine. How's Mom and Dad?" Living for seven years on the west coast, Holly noticed her sister's accent, and had mostly lost her own.

Paige was the middle child, Holly the oldest, and Reagan the youngest. All were two years apart in age and all born in July, known as the McNeela sisters by the folks in Alder Point, a small seaside community on the east side of Cape Breton Island.

"They're fine but wonderin' when youze coming home."

Holly chuckled. "For a visit?"

"For good! They don't like that you're so far away. Doesn't make a lick of sense ta dem, ya know."

"I know, and I do miss you guys. Maybe I'll fly home in early September for a visit."

"You better, but be prepared for an epic guilt trip. You know Ma."

Her parents lived in a two-story home on ten acres. Her father fished commercially, like many in the region. They'd had some lean years, but their mother worked in a human resource department located in Sydney and kept a regular paycheck coming in.

"Look forward to it, but I like the four seasons in British Columbia. Plenty of rain, but while the tulips bloom here in the west, you're getting slammed with blizzards. Besides, I love my job."

Paige groaned. "Sometimes I regret not finishing my degree, especially when the kids drive me nuts."

Her sister's sons were ages seven, five, and three. "Then finish it. James can pull his weight," Holly said.

Holly's father owned four boats. Two Cape Islanders dedicated to lobster fishing and two for shrimping. James captained one of the lobster boats.

"He would if I asked. He's a sweetheart compared to that rat bastard you married."

"Received my divorce papers today. Signed, sealed and I wish him well."

"I hope the cheating ass gets an early case of erectile dysfunction."

Holly cracked up.

"Seriously, Hol, I don't know how you kept it together. Or took him back after the first time he cheated. You're a saint, girl. A saint!"

After gossiping for a while about the folks back home, it was past midnight East Coast time, when Paige said goodbye.

Holly cleaned the dishes, then headed upstairs to pack a bag for her trip to Washington State. By ten o'clock, she crawled into bed to read. Life was less complicated without a husband. The legal decree declaring her divorce was final didn't bring a sense of closure. Kevin's confession that he loved someone else had terminated their marriage.

Mrs. Norman had lucked out finding a loyal husband to share her life with. The only place Holly would find a guy with integrity who made her heart palpitate was in a book, and she reached for the paperback on her bedside table.

* * * *

The topography changed from drought-ridden fields to evergreen as the miles marked Grayson's coastal trip north to Bellingham. He'd caught some winks at a rest stop last night. With a few breaks for fuel and a bite to eat, he was on schedule for a five o'clock suppertime arrival.

Using the Bluetooth in his truck, he called home.

Ivy answered.

"Hey, I'm on schedule. Be home for dinner." Grayson grinned at the thought. The closer he got to the farmstead, the faster he wanted to go.

"Great," she said. "I'll order pizza."

"Seriously?" He'd been dreaming about a home-cooked meal for miles.

She laughed. "No, not serious. Get your ass home, brother. Dinner will be on the table when you get here."

He hit Seattle at the worst possible time. Bogged down with commuter traffic, the I-5 was a parking lot from the Emerald City to Mt. Vernon, then eased as he reached Bellingham city limits. After twenty-four hours, he'd driven from the southern border in San Diego to a few miles shy of the northern border with Canada. Grayson took the off-ramp and joined the country road leading to the family farm.

Five minutes later, he steered the truck into the Brooks' gravel drive. The line of oak trees on either side of the road were flush with leaves. To his left, the white building with red trim known as Brooks Farmstead Store, closed at five p.m. To his right, cattle grazed on shoots of lush grass. Rounding a bend in the driveway, the old house came into sight. A three-story Victorian his great-great-grandfather had built on four hundred acres he'd purchased. Gray's ancestors had made the trek from Kansas to settle in Whatcom County in the late 1800s. They'd started out in the coal industry but ended up as farmers.

Grayson rolled past the western edge of the apple orchard. Behind that sat the blueberry field. He parked next to a white Acura in front of the house and eyed the wide, wraparound porch with a swing and six white rocking chairs. A second later, the front screen door flew open and a young boy with a shock of blond hair raced from the house.

"Uncle Grayson!"

Gray stepped out of the truck and stretched his stiff muscles. "Hey, Jackson. Come here, kid." He lifted his eight-year-old nephew into his arms and gave him a hug. In one year, the boy had sprouted. A few seconds later, Ivy and Dad appeared. Arlene, who worked at the farmstead store, and her husband, Hugh, were a step behind. Ron, the farmhand, and his wife, Charlene, all poured out of the house.

Ivy squealed and ran down the steps. "You're home!"

Grayson set Jackson on the ground and Ivy jumped into his embrace, legs wrapped around his hips, giving him a big smacking kiss on the cheek. He laughed and squeezed the shit out of his sister.

Gray watched his old man, the patriarch of the family, step up with a bow-legged gait. "Dad."

"Good to have ya home, son."

After all the hugs and hellos were done, Ivy chased them all into the house for dinner. He'd gone from fast food, late-night stakeouts, and beer with the boys to a handmade, plank-top dining table with a loud ruckus of family and friends, catching up on gossip.

About to spoon the garlic mashed potatoes onto his plate, the screen door opened, and his best friend stepped into the kitchen.

"Sorry I'm late," Cole said.

Grayson grinned. "Just in time."

Wearing his sheriff's uniform, Grayson figured Cole had been delayed by a case. His buddy's swarthy good looks and linebacker physique hadn't transformed into a potbelly and bald head over the years like some of their high school friends.

"Welcome home, Gray."

Grayson got up from the table. "Good to be home."

They shook hands and slapped each other on the back.

Grayson sat at one end of the table and his father at the other. The chair on Grayson's left had been left open for his oldest friend.

"Thanks for the invite, Ivy," Cole said.

She shrugged but didn't look at him. "No problem." She held the dish of fried chicken while Jackson speared two thighs and transferred the meat to his plate.

"Sit your ass down and load up," Grayson said to Cole. "Ivy went all out. And—you made me pie, didn't ya, Ivy?"

"Do you deserve pie?" she teased.

He snorted. "Do moles in your garden drive you nuts?"

His sister was a beautiful woman, but when she smiled, it lit a room. Cole was spooning peas onto his plate when he glanced across the table at her and stilled. If Grayson didn't know better, his friend had stopped breathing. Gray lifted an eyebrow in question at Cole, who quickly dumped the peas and handed off the bowl to Arlene.

Jackson, fisting his fork like a weapon, scooped up some mashed potatoes. "Mom made my favorite. Lemon meringue."

"That's *my* favorite," Grayson said. "And I might leave you a piece."

With a full mouth, Jackson said, "It's Cole's favorite too, but she doesn't make him pie."

Cole chuckled. "That's because she's still pissed at me for something I did five years ago."

Ivy handed Grayson the gravy boat. "He's so full of himself," she said.

"What'cha do?" Grayson asked, sensing more than genial tension between his friend and sister.

Their father chuckled from the other end of the table. "He gave her a speeding ticket when he was still working patrol."

Ivy rolled her eyes. "You're my brother's best friend and you're at this farm at least once a week."

Cole grinned while chewing on a mouthful of food. "So? You were speeding. Do the crime, pay the dime."

She glared at him. "It wasn't a dime, it was a one hundred and fifty dollar fine."

He cleared his throat and glanced at Grayson, then laughed. "Don't worry, she got even. Made me muck out the barns for a month."

* * * *

With a couple of cold beers, Grayson and Cole shifted outside after dinner to sit on the porch that overlooked the side lawns and the orchard.

Grayson sighed, the green landscape easy on his eyes. "It's good to be home. I'm kinda surprised there isn't a Mrs. Sterling by now."

Cole tipped his beer and took a deep pull. "Look who's talking. You ever date a woman you didn't pick up in a bar?"

"Spent the afternoon in bed with a flight attendant once," Grayson said, watching a bumblebee land on a purple flower in Ivy's hanging basket. "By the time I got home from deployment, she'd married a pilot."

Cole palmed the beer with both hands, resting the bottle on his solid abs. "You've been out of Spec Ops for years. What stopped you from settling down?"

Grayson shrugged. "Force of habit. The hours at vice are all over the map." A boldfaced lie, but since he couldn't explain his peculiar response to a woman who wanted more than sex, he wasn't going to voice it to his friend.

"Excuses. Whatever happened to that woman, Erika? You mentioned her a few times. Sounded like a train wreck to me."

"Still around and still medicating. She had a bit of bad luck when she offered sex for a few dollars to my buddy on vice, but she's trying to straighten out. I left her with the keys to my townhouse."

Cole tilted his head in question. "You're letting her stay at your place? Is that wise? She might use your bed to earn her next hit."

"Probably is," he admitted.

"Why would you do that?"

He shrugged. "Because it's the right thing to do. Every time she sobers up, she gets a new chance. Maybe one day she'll figure things out."

Cole took a draw off his beer. "Are you waiting for that day?"

"Nah. Nothing like that."

"You mean Erika, or any woman who crosses your path?"

"I've known a shit ton of women. Never met someone who brought me to a full stop. Anyway...thanks for helping out at the farm all these years. I should have come back long before now."

"Helped when I could. It's good you're home. Maybe Ivy can take a breather once in a while."

The screen door squeaked open, and Jackson tramped out in his rubber boots, wearing a scowl on his face.

"What's the matter, buddy?" Grayson asked.

The kid leaned against the porch's thick, white column. "Todd and Jake wanna head to the skateboard park. Mom says I can't go."

"Why's that?"

"Because by the time I finish filling the chicken feeders, it'll be dark, and she says nothing good happens there after dark." He shrugged his slender shoulders and bowed his head.

Ah, the hardships of a farm kid. "Where's the park?"

"By the high school. Todd's mom said she'd drive us."

From what Grayson could see, Ivy did a great job raising the boy. "Your mom is right, Jackson. But tell ya what... I'll take care of the birds. If your mom agrees, I'll come pick you up before dark."

"Really?" His eyes lit with excitement. "Thanks, Uncle Grayson. You're the best." He ran into the house, shouting for his mom.

Cole chuckled. "Oh, man. You're gonna wear that one, Gray."

Within two heartbeats the screen door snapped open and banged against the clapboard siding. Ivy grilled him with a mom-look she'd perfected while he'd been away.

"What the heck, Grayson!"

"What? The kid wants to hang out with his buddies. I'll pick him up."

Ivy's glare shifted to Cole. "What the hell are you still doing on my porch?"

Gray arched a brow and waited for his friend's response.

Caught in her crosshairs, Cole said, "Trying my best to irritate you, I guess."

Jackson ran under his mom's arm just as she said, "Well get off it, and go pick up some hussy like you normally do."

Jackson yanked his ball cap onto his head with one hand while he gripped his skateboard with the other.

Ivy huffed. "You can go this time, Jackson. Gray, we need to talk about rules later." The screen door slammed shut with her departure.

Jackson looked mystified. "What's a hussy, Cole? Is that a new cow?"

Grayson choked on his beer and nearly snorted the liquid out his nose. He leaned forward, coughing out the ale he'd sucked down his windpipe, and then laughed his head off. Oh, fuck, it was good to be home.

"Never mind, Jackson." Cole's expression pinched with agitation. "How the hell did I end up in the doghouse when she was mad at you?"

Grayson coughed once more and relaxed in the white rocking chair. "Hell if I know." He turned his attention to Jackson. "If any teenagers try to sell you something, you tell 'em to shove it up their ass. Got me?"

Jackson tucked the skateboard under his arm. "I know. Cole told me all about drugs and bad stuff."

His old friend had done more around the farm than just the heavy lifting. Grayson could easily see Cole cared about Ivy's son. He'd been part of the boy's entire life.

"You got your phone with you?"

Ivy had mentioned she'd recently given Jackson a cell phone but restricted his usage. She didn't want him turning into a "Data Zombie."

Jackson bobbed his head and patted his back jean pocket. "Yup."

His buddy must not have lived far away. A silver minivan rolled down the gravel driveway toward the house. "Tell

Todd's mother I'm picking you up. I'll give the other kids a ride home too."

"Thanks, Uncle Gray," he said, already at the bottom of the steps and running to meet the van.

Grayson finished the beer and stood. The warm May evening at the farm brought a noticeable sense of calm. The air fresh. Birds chirped to each other from the tall cedar trees. "Guess I got some hungry livestock to take care of. I'll pick you up tomorrow morning."

Cole gripped the armrests and pushed his daunting six-foot-three frame from the chair. "You bet. I'm gonna hit the sack early tonight. I start training some rookie tomorrow."

Grayson chuckled at his buddy's jibe. Tomorrow was his first day at the Proactive Unit and he looked forward to meeting the other detectives.

"I'll be on my best behavior." Cole gave him a two-finger salute and Gray picked up the empty beer bottles. "Mind taking these inside for me?"

Cole cleared his throat and took the bottles but looked as if he'd asked him to swan dive off the San Francisco Bridge. "Yeah, sure."

Nope, it hadn't been Grayson's imagination. During dinner, it seemed every time Ivy's attention was elsewhere, Cole's was on her. And Ivy had been her usual in-charge but relaxed self until Cole walked in the door, then she'd tensed. Her off-the-cuff remark about Cole chasing some skirt added more evidence.

Son-of-a-bitch!

No way was Grayson going to let this slide. Cole had moved back to Bellingham seven years ago. He had to wonder how long his best friend and sister had been avoiding the obvious.

CHAPTER THREE

"L t. Kline?" Cole tapped on the senior officer's open office door.

A lean man about Grayson's age with short-cropped, red hair got up from his desk. "Come on in." He extended a hand. "Grayson Brooks, good to have you on the team."

"Good to be here."

Kline resumed his seat and pointed at the two guest chairs in his office. "How was the drive from San Diego?"

"Not bad. Twenty-four hours from one end of the I-5 to the other," Grayson answered.

"Thought you'd take a few days off before showing up at work."

"Not necessary."

Grayson had talked at length on the phone with Kline before putting tires to pavement. He wanted to be sure the lieutenant understood his responsibilities to the family farm. Kline didn't have a problem with his request and summed up the Proactive Unit as a department that gathered intelligence on and infiltrated known crime rings to bring criminals to justice. The officers didn't answer regular calls for service or conduct routine patrol work.

Kline clasped his hands together on the desk. "Cole's working on several cases, but the priority is finding a neighborhood crime ring that's responsible for stolen vehicles, property theft, and we suspect a couple of assaults. While he gets you up to speed and you familiarize yourself with the county again, you'll be partnered with him."

Grayson nodded. "He told me there's been an escalation in thefts at the Neon Lights resort."

"Unfortunately. Popular place. Cole's been conducting a walk-thru once a day to show additional law enforcement presence, but management is starting to lose patience."

"Ours or the resort's?"

Kline grunted, then grinned. "Both. The resort brings a lot of money into the area. Neon Lights sits on tribal land, but their guests also visit neighboring tourist sites. If word of mouth spreads that it isn't safe, there'll be a negative ripple effect."

Politics, business, and law enforcement played an important role in the county. Washington State prided itself on its natural beauty, temperate climate, prolific agricultural resources, and opportunities to raise and support a family. Keeping illegal activity in check meant safer streets. Crime rings, big and small, were like ingrown hairs; the deeper they rooted, the more trouble they caused. Bellingham, in particular, had a bad record.

Cole finally interceded. "First thing on the agenda is to get you suited up and issue you a weapon, then we'll head out to Neon Lights to meet with the resort's manager."

"Sounds good. Let's get 'er done," Grayson said, prepared to don the Skagit County sheriff tags. He'd worn a uniform since he was eighteen years old, aside from vice, where he'd dressed in street clothes to infiltrate the drug trade.

* * * *

After a long walk around the flowering gardens surrounding the resort property, Holly changed into her bathing suit and did a few laps in the swimming pool. She returned to her room, showered, and made her way down to the gaming floor by eleven-thirty in the morning.

The buffet didn't open until noon. She chose the last slot machine next to the wide, carpeted walkway that led to the east exit. On the other side of the aisle was one end of the bar. In the shape of an arc, it wrapped itself around an enclosed lounge where live entertainment and dancing happened on Friday and Saturday nights.

Slots provided a little excitement, but people-watching interested her too. A couple of guys in their thirties stood at the bar. Dressed in jeans and t-shirts, they talked and drank beer. Neon Lights employed a healthy security presence and enforced a strict policy about alcohol consumption. Drinking was permitted but with the first signs of inebriation, the beverage servers would cut you off. It surprised Holly to see one of the guys swaying a little. Not only because of the early hour, but because the bartender set another glass of beer in front of the guy.

A steady flow of people entered the casino and strolled by. Young and old filtered past her machine. Sometimes guests came in small groups, sometimes alone. Holly checked her wristwatch. Another fifteen minutes before the buffet opened.

The guy who swayed on his feet chugged his beer, then swung his gaze in her direction. Not interested in attracting trouble, Holly focused her attention on the glass exit doors. Two tall men entered the casino, both wearing county sheriff uniforms. On occasion, law enforcement strolled through the resort, making an appearance.

One of the officers was a tall, dark drink of water like her ex. The other cop radiated an air of confidence. The brim of the ball cap hid his eyes but revealed a defined jaw. With broad shoulders and thick biceps, Holly figured the man took his physical fitness seriously.

Her gaze stalled on the officer, and he raised his strong chin. Holly's pulse tripled. The term *alpha* streamed through her brain. Gawking at the officer, she didn't notice the guy from the bar had crossed the walkway.

"Hey, baby. Saw you lookin' my way."

Startled, she turned her head to see him standing behind her left shoulder. He stretched his arm out and palmed the edge of the machine.

The guy's buddy crossed the aisle. "Kyle, come back and finish your beer."

Kyle puffed noxious booze breath in her face. With deep brown eyes and trimmed brown hair, he was a decent-looking man, but when his gaze dropped to her breasts, she slid out of the chair.

"Where ya going, little lady? Just came over to say hi."

"Hi," she said and backed up a pace.

The guy's friend gripped his shoulder. "Beer's getting warm, Kyle."

Kyle yanked his shoulder free. "Just making a new friend, John."

John wasn't drunk like his buddy, and he cast a glance toward the two uniformed officers.

Not a second later, the two cops closed in. The larger of the two stepped forward with a taut expression. Close enough now, she saw his brilliant blue eyes.

"Everyone having a good time?" The words weren't aggressive, but his undertone carried a definite warning.

Kyle was too wrecked to pick up on the nuance or be intimidated by the size and obvious strength of the cop.

"I'm just leaving," Holly announced.

Kyle's hand clamped around her upper left arm. About to tell the drunk where to stuff it, the cop's large hand snapped around Kyle's wrist.

Now the drunk paid attention and turned an angry gaze on the officer. "What's your fucking problem?"

"He's had a few beers," John said, as if the excuse would stand the cop down.

Out of nowhere, two casino security guards showed themselves but remained a few steps back.

There was no mistaking the intensity painted on the cop's expression as he glared at the drunk. Kyle's fingers pinched her arm, and she did a tug test to free herself—unsuccessfully. If the cop used force, she'd end up on the ground with Kyle.

"Would you please let go?" she asked, hoping Kyle would release his grip.

"Sweetheart, I just want to buy you a drink," he slurred.

John chimed in. "Kyle, come on, man. Let go of her."

With all the male testosterone gaining energy around her, Holly put her attention on the officer with blue eyes. Waves of raw masculinity washed against her. He wasn't handsome in a polished way, his features were rugged, weathered, been through hell and back, like a warrior. Her heart ticked faster.

Instead of using force, the officer used the guy's name. "Kyle, you're hurting the lady. Don't think you want to do that, do you?"

The drunk's eye narrowed. "I think you should fuck—"

Within a blink, Kyle yowled in pain and released the grip on her arm. The cop slammed the guy against the slot machine, knocking over the heavy chair she'd vacated. Holly stumbled backward and the other officer moved in, snapping cuffs on Kyle's wrists.

Kyle struggled but didn't stand a chance against her savior's muscled physique that kept the drunk pinned with little effort. Guests stood in a loose circle, watching the excitement but keeping clear.

The blue-eyed officer said in a deep timbre, "Kyle, we're going to leave this beautiful woman alone and take a walk outside to have a discussion. You have a problem with that?"

"Yeah, fuck, whatever," Kyle mumbled with his cheek flattened against the colorful slot panel displaying the machine's name.

With one hand on Kyle's shoulder, the officer's toned biceps flexed when he wrenched Kyle away from the slot and steered him toward the exit. The security guards from the casino followed, as did John.

A third casino security guard stepped up to her side. In his late forties with silver strands sprinkled through his dark hair, Holly recognized him. He'd worked at the resort for a few years.

"Hi, Rick," she said, massaging her arm.

"Holly, you okay?"

From the way her arm throbbed, Kyle had left a bruise. "Nothing serious."

"You know that guy?"

"No. Never seen him before. Think he just had a little too much to drink."

Rick's brow creased. "You sure you're okay?"

She stopped massaging her arm and smiled. "Of course." The crowd dispersed and she was glad for that. "You think they'll arrest him?"

"Depends. I'm familiar with the leaner, dark-haired cop. His name is Cole Sterling. I don't know the other guy. He's a new face to me."

Holly righted the toppled chair. "He certainly knew what he was doing."

Rick smiled. "Yeah, that was some slick move. Either he knows martial arts or he's ex-military. Either way, I wouldn't take him on in a fight."

Holly slid over to her machine and cashed out with less than twenty dollars on the ticket. With her pulse still elevated, she needed to walk it off. "You don't mind if I go, do you?"

"I'll tell the officers you don't know the guy. Are you going to stick around here?"

"I was waiting for the buffet to open. Think I'll wander to the other side of the casino," she said.

Rick gave her a nod. "Doubt Sterling or his partner will want to ask you anything. Sorry this happened, Holly."

She shrugged. "No harm, no foul."

Rick strode toward the exit, and she strolled toward the opposite end of the gaming floor, stopping off at the washroom on the other side of the player's club card desk. After going to the bathroom then splashing some water on her face, she exited the restroom and turned right toward the hundreds of slot machines.

She wandered around, not overly enthused to play. The moment she and the blue-eyed officer had locked gazes, an unexpected rush of warmth had heated her skin. Then again, what woman alive wouldn't have the same reaction to a man like that? Although it rarely happened, she was well aware her response was attraction.

To a cop, nonetheless.

Her ex-husband had two unwavering priorities: his job in law enforcement and cheating on her.

Even jaw-dropping attractive as the officer was, she chalked it up to a momentary lapse in sanity. Thankfully, the chances of seeing him again were none and zero.

* * * *

Holly's stomach grumbled. Time for lunch. She joined the buffet line-up and waited her turn to be seated. Wonderful aromas of freshly made food filled the restaurant and stirred her hunger.

Servers on the floor delivered drinks and cleared plates. Holly watched the tables fill up around her. At least one busload of seniors had arrived, which was often the case at the resort. They usually received ten bucks of free play, a voucher for a meal, and a reasonable rate for the hotel room.

Before the server arrived to take her drink order, the two sheriffs arrived and sat at the table to her left.

For God's sake!

Her mouth dried and she needed water.

Dammit, don't look at him.

Staring straight ahead, she felt her skin prickle. *Shit.* Get it over with, she thought to herself. If they weren't looking at her, then she could relax.

They'd removed their ball caps, and her heart thumped madly with an unimpeded view of the blond cop. Yup, he wasn't just good-looking, he was the most captivating man she'd ever seen, his features intoxicating with high cheekbones, a carved jaw, and tanned skin.

With an unreadable expression, his gaze turned her way.

She cleared the lump from her throat. "Thank you." She nodded. "For your help earlier."

For a second, Holly didn't think he'd respond.

"Did he hurt you?"

His intense blue eyes made her uncomfortable. She hadn't done anything wrong, but still felt like she was being evaluated. "I'm fine."

His head tilted slightly. "He's been banned. You won't see him again."

"Never seen him before," she said. "Thank you again."

She blinked and turned her attention to the other tables, but the cops were sitting so darn close, her ears tuned in to their conversation.

The swarthy, dark-haired officer spoke about a string of robberies and a crime ring.

Holly waved over a server.

"What can I get you to drink?" the middle-aged woman asked with a pleasant smile.

Her luck was at the low water mark today, but she asked, "Is there another table available?"

"Sorry, hon, not right now."

Holly collected her purse and stood. "I'll come back later, if that's okay."

"Sure. Should thin out after one o'clock."

The server quickly strode to another table of guests, and Holly analyzed her choices. Leaving was the best option.

"Not necessary to move," the blond officer said.

Holding her breath, she ventured a look in his direction. "I feel like I'm eavesdropping on issues I shouldn't." She nudged her chair under the table.

"Are you a regular?"

His statement held the connotation that she was a low-life gambler, and it put her on edge. "I visit here once a month for a break."

He was probably the type of cop who gave a speeding ticket for two miles an hour over the limit and thought anyone in a casino had an addiction, which was the farthest thing from the truth in her case.

"Other than attracting men and causing a disturbance, have you ever seen any suspicious activity around here?" he asked.

Holly gritted her teeth. She didn't *attract* men. "I spend most of my time at the pool or the gym. In nice weather, I walk to the Coffee Hut." A gas station, located within eyesight of the resort, accommodated a drive-thru espresso shack a few steps away on the same property. The convenient, tiny java stops were located all over Washington State, a novelty you didn't find in BC. "I've never seen any trouble on the gaming floor. Once in a while, people troll the machines looking for a few cents and cash out the ticket, but nothing criminal."

"Coffee your beverage of choice?"

She blinked, surprised by the unexpected question. She spouted, "Salted caramel milkshakes. No one makes them better than the Coffee Hut."

When a hint of a smile tipped his smooth, firm lips, her cheeks heated. Holly's thoughts scrambled and the first one that landed was how many women had melted in this man's embrace.

"Is that so," he said in a low timbre.

Holly's skills in reading ancient Tamil far outweighed her ability to flirt. Sadly lacking, she'd just admitted favoring milkshakes over a full-bodied red wine or some other adult beverage to the type of man that women conjured to fulfill a sexually-charged fantasy. With firm abs and pecs, he was the entire package of ultimate masculinity.

"Should I be concerned?" she asked.

He shifted his broad shoulders, turning them in her direction. "Only if you're lactose intolerant."

She tsked, then realized he was teasing her. "I'll rephrase —should I be concerned for my safety?"

"Do you always come here alone?"

The question struck at the heart of her failed marriage. She wasn't beautiful or exciting enough to keep her husband's attention. But the cop didn't know that. Holly could have a significant other playing Blackjack. Or was it that obvious she was single?

Crap.

She swung her gaze to his partner, who remained quiet. "Yes," she admitted.

"Don't venture outside for a walk after dark."

She tucked her purse under her arm. "I'll keep that in mind."

The casino manager strolled up to the sheriff's table. He shook hands with the officers and sat down.

Holly took the opportunity to quickly depart. She couldn't quite shake his earlier words to Kyle. *"We're going to leave this beautiful woman alone."* A comment she knew wasn't accurate about her looks, but when the words rolled off his tongue, it made her smile.

* * * *

"This is my new partner, Detective Brooks," Cole said, introducing Grayson to the casino manager, Paul Gibbons.

"Nice to meet you," Gibbons said.

"You too."

Grayson's gaze remained on the raven-haired woman who quickly wove past the tables and exited the buffet. He got the feeling she'd been insulted when he'd said *"other than attracting men."* On re-examination, he probably could have voiced that another way. It had come out as an accusation, versus what he'd really meant. She hadn't freaked out when Kyle grabbed her arm. Even tried to speak calmly to the guy.

"Thanks for helping out earlier." Gibbons waved a server

to their table. "Lunch is on us."

Cole had wanted to arrest the drunk, but Grayson talked him down. Kyle's friend said the guy had lost his job after fifteen years working for a local contractor. Grayson believed him. Numbing his bad luck, the guy had put too many down. The woman with the most incredible grey eyes had gotten caught in the crossfire, but she wasn't hurt.

Cole grinned. "We'll take you up on that offer. Always good food here."

The server stopped by, and the manager let her know the casino was buying lunch.

Before eating, they discussed the recent robberies and the escalation of events. Cole had already given him a SITREP, but Grayson listened to Gibbons' plea to find the criminals and a quick recap of the incidents.

An hour later, with full bellies, he and Cole headed for the patrol car parked outside the main casino entrance. Gray surveyed the guests as they passed the table games and slots but didn't see the raven-haired woman. She'd probably vacated after being man-handled by the drunk.

Fifteen minutes later, Grayson settled at his new desk in the Proactive Unit's headquarters. Opening his office email, he found several electronic forms from the HR department. He opened the first attachment. This would eat up the afternoon.

Four o'clock struck and Cole sauntered over. "You about done?"

"Yup." He hit the send button, shooting the email with all the attachments back to HR.

"Let's call it a day, partner."

Grayson collected his laptop and locked his file drawer. This morning, they'd carpooled to work. His buddy only lived a mile from the farmstead. No point in taking two vehicles.

"Wanna grab a beer at Roosters?" Cole asked when they exited the side door and headed for Grayson's truck.

Knocking back a beer usually led to more beers, which

reminded him of the drunk they'd cuffed and dragged out of the casino this morning. Gray could kid himself and say the incident spurred a memory of the dark-haired woman, but that would be a lie. Her image kept interrupting his focus since they'd left the resort.

"You trying to get me in trouble already?" Grayson grinned. "I've got work at the farm to finish before the sun goes down. I'll take a rain check for Friday."

"Need a hand?" Cole asked.

Did his long-time friend really want to get his hands dirty, or was it a chance to see Ivy? "If you're offering, I won't refuse."

They hopped in the truck and played red light, green light until they merged into the slow-moving traffic headed north on the I-5.

Instead of analyzing the case and interpreting the muggings and thefts to find a common thread that would lead to a bust, Grayson's mind conjured an image. Grey eyes with sweeping, dark, natural lashes and a waft of silky, black curls.

"Regrets already?" Cole asked.

He shot a look over at his buddy. "Regrets?"

"Give it a couple weeks before you tell me the Proactive Unit isn't enough of a challenge compared to vice."

Grayson chuckled. "Don't think you'll be hearing that from me. Hey—umm, that woman at the casino today, the one the drunk was pawing. Ever seen her before?"

Cole shrugged. "Once or twice, maybe. I wouldn't call her a regular."

"I didn't," he shot back.

"You asked if she was, and in a tone she misunderstood as contempt."

Even Cole had picked up on that. "Not what I meant."

His friend laughed. "I know what you meant, but she didn't. She's a civilian, not an insurgent."

"That bad?" he asked.

"Pretty much," Cole said. "All those years in special ops left its mark on you, my friend. It's no wonder you can't find a woman."

"I found plenty," he barked.

"Sure, for one night," Cole fired back in a matter-of-fact tone.

"I can't count the number of times women wanted to change the arrangement into something permanent." The married SEALs always had problems juggling family and seven-month deployments, never mind the constant training. "When I left the Forces and jumped into vice at the sheriff's department, they had the same problems. Wives and girlfriends were constantly ditched because of a case, and it caused no end of grief. I didn't need the hassle."

As if Cole knew better, he said, "Nah, I think it's something else."

Gray shook his head. "Can't wait to hear this nugget of wisdom from the other certified bachelor in the truck."

"You never met a woman *worth* the hassle. Believe me, I get it."

Brake lights on the blue Prius ahead of them came on, and he eased off the gas. "Kept my focus on the job."

Most of the gals who ended up in his bed, he'd met at a bar. Sometimes the SEAL wives hooked him up with a friend, but as friendly and hot as some of them were, none of 'em had made a mark.

"Hey, buddy. I'm just pulling your leg. Finding a woman who accepts us—imperfections and all—isn't easy," Cole said.

The line of traffic ahead sped up and Gray shifted into the left lane. He appreciated Cole's observation, but it wasn't true. "Don't want to sound like a dick, but not in my case. I could have put a ring on at least twenty fingers. Call me old-fashioned, but I don't want to settle for any woman." He shot a look toward his friend. "I want to love her, like my old man loved Mom." It was a fairly reasonable excuse and partly true.

"Your folks had something special," Cole said. "Your dad

has a tough hide, but when it came to Kira, he sure loved her." He sighed and removed his ball cap. "My parents fought all the time. Probably why I liked hanging out at your place so much as a kid. I think your mom knew, that's why she always let me stay for dinner."

"She knew. I told her."

Cole's folks divorced when he was ten, and he never heard from his old man again. His mom eventually remarried, but the stepdad had a temper. They didn't see eye to eye, especially once Cole hit puberty. Maybe that's why his buddy wasn't in any hurry to tie the knot.

Cole checked his cell. "Twenty-eight years later, and I'm still eating at your dinner table." He held his phone up. "Text from your sister. She's apologizing for being rude last night."

A second text arrived with a ding. He burst out laughing as he read the message, then typed a response.

"What's so funny?"

"Ivy says if I'm not hunting for my next one-night stand, dinner's at six." Cole slipped the cell into his shirt pocket.

Obviously, his friend wasn't reading between the lines. Ivy's offhand remark camouflaged her jealousy. "Sounds like you're both making excuses to see each other."

His old friend didn't respond with a quick objection. He leaned forward and looked into the sky. "Gonna rain tonight."

Okay, avoidance acknowledged.

Heavy, dark clouds loomed overhead. "Probably."

Traffic moved along at a better clip once they cleared Burlington. Suburbia and businesses thinned, changing to open fields. Gray's pulse ticked faster when they passed the highway sign that read *Neon Lights Resort. Take next exit.*

"We got off topic," Cole said. "That brunette at the resort, I've seen her on occasion but doubt she has anything to do with our case."

Grayson didn't think so either. Cole didn't know her name, or he'd have used it. He couldn't ditch the moment he'd entered the casino and his gaze connected with the mystery woman. Everything faded into white noise, except her. She was attractive, but he'd met women who far surpassed her in beauty. Nor was it instant lust, which was something he understood. He could only define it as some kind of strange tunnel vision. Probably because he saw Kyle stagger from the bar to where she sat at the slot machine. When she quickly stood and backed away, Gray sensed trouble.

The fact they'd been seated next to her in the buffet was kinda weird. He couldn't help but grin when she'd boldly stated she loved milkshakes while her unforgettable grey eyes snapped with indignation at his previous statement about causing a disturbance, which was the most innocent but cutest response he'd ever heard come out of a woman's mouth.

CHAPTER FOUR

"**W**hat the heck, Holly? You're packing it in for the day?" Juliette asked, leaning against the office doorway. "You never leave before eight p.m., even on Fridays."

Holly shoved her laptop into the carrying case. "Actually, I took an hour off." She checked her phone. Two o'clock. "If the traffic doesn't suck, I should get to the border by three."

Juliette pushed her dark-rimmed glasses up her nose. "Border? So soon? I thought you visited that resort once a month. Weren't you there just last weekend?"

The intern was too observant, but that's what made her a great assistant researcher, especially with ancient languages. Holly shifted the case from the chair to her desk and sat down.

Juliette crossed the small office and perched on the edge of the taupe guest chair. "You've been acting a little different lately. Head in the clouds kinda stuff. Everything okay?"

"That obvious, eh?" She'd felt anxious all week. Made it difficult to concentrate in the lab. And particularly difficult to make any headway on a beautiful 9th century BC slab with Hittite hieroglyphics.

"I don't mean to pry."

Holly rested her elbows on the maple desk. "Lately, the townhouse seems claustrophobic with memories of my ex-husband. I received the finalized divorce papers last week. It's official."

"Did you get rid of everything that rat bastard left behind? I'll gladly bring the lighter fluid if you supply the barrel, and we can burn any favorite shirts he forgot."

A couple months ago, a guy Juliette had dated for three years dumped her with the audacious claim that the brilliant intern was too smart. Holly had to wonder what kind of jackass would be intimidated by a woman with a brain.

"Nothing left of Kevin's. It's not like I miss him, but we bought that place together. At one time, I loved the townhouse. Now it reeks of failure."

Juliette removed her glasses and slipped them onto the top of her head. "His failure, not yours, Holly. Maybe it's time you find a new place to live."

At twenty-five, Juliette carried a very sensible head on her shoulders. Holly hoped that once the woman's internship ended, the university would hire her as an ancient language researcher.

"I've considered selling."

The young intern crossed her legs, clasping her forked hands around her kneecap. "You need a new perspective. Take me up on my offer to come out for a girl's night. You'd have fun. I have great friends."

That's how she'd met Kevin. The small fishing town in Nova Scotia where she'd been raised couldn't support a bar, but there was a favorite watering hole only twelve minutes away. Everyone, including herself, tipped a few at the *Shanty Shack*. Kevin had shown up one Saturday night with a friend. He'd flirted with her. They'd danced. Talked. At the time, she didn't know he was an RCMP officer and had just transferred to their area. Their relationship advanced quickly and the next thing she knew, they were married and transferring to the west coast.

"I'm thirty-two. The bar scene isn't for me. Been there, done that, ya know."

Juliette's brown eyes narrowed. "But a casino is?"

"It's not the casino, it's the resort as a whole. The grounds are beautifully landscaped. The hotel suite is huge and comfortable. Sometimes I curl up in front of the fireplace and just read a book. Other times, I exercise at the indoor pool or take a long walk. The atmosphere is uplifting, and I guess that's why I'm going back so soon. I need a pick-me-up."

"Kinda sounds relaxing."

"It is. And I usually venture out to see the sights. The Daffodil Festival in La Conner during March or the Spring Fair in April, and the Washington State Fair in September. It's so much fun to wander around."

"By yourself?" Juliette asked as if she didn't believe Holly.

She sighed. "Yeah, well, I guess that's the way it is."

"Don't guys hit on you at the casino?" Juliette asked. "I mean, you're gorgeous. I can't believe no one has ever tried to pick you up."

Holly snorted. She certainly wasn't gorgeous. "Thanks for the compliment, but I barely wear makeup. My shopping sense leans toward conservative, and I can't remember the last time I put polish on my nails. Besides, I'm not exactly the approachable type." Staring at a five-thousand-year-old tablet for hours topped shopping for current fashions any day.

"And whose fault is that?"

"I admit I'm a comfort-over-fashion kinda gal. On the weekends, the lounge at the resort brings in live entertainment and the younger crowd shows up to party, but I never go in there."

"I think you should ask a friend to come with you sometime."

She grinned. "Perhaps a certain research intern I know?"

"Perhaps," Juliette chirped.

"Sounds like a plan." Holly collected her laptop. "I better get moving. Lineup at the border is only going to get longer. Have a good weekend."

* * * *

By three-thirty, Holly had crossed into the US, stored her luggage in the suite and wandered down to the gaming floor. The one thing she hadn't admitted to Juliette was the unforgettable sheriff whom she'd had the misfortune of seeing last week. What was it about a man in uniform? Especially one that carried himself with a boatload of natural confidence.

Holly chose one of her favorite slot games and slid one hundred US into the bill validator. If she were totally honest with herself, which she didn't particularly want to face, the cop might be the reason she was back so soon. She'd been completely stunned by her attraction to the man. Not only was it a stupid reason to return, because a guy like him had to be married or dating a model, but the chances of seeing him again were improbable.

Nonetheless, she kept her eyes on the people roaming the colorful carpet, versus her slot. Visitors moved from machine to machine, looking for Lady Luck. Two hours later, angry at herself for fantasizing about a man so far out of her league he might as well be from a different planet, she smacked the shit out of the play button on the slot.

Was she having fun? No. Was she relaxed? No. Should she give up and go back to her room? Definitely, yes.

What the hell was the matter with her? Acting like a sixteen-year-old with a crush on some elusive guy she'd seen twice was stupid. She was a grown woman, for God's sake.

Fool.

Smack.

Dumbass.

Smack.

"Should I put that slot machine into protective custody?"

The recognizable, deep timbre of his voice made Holly's nerves pop with excitement. Afraid to turn around but needing to make sure she wasn't hallucinating, she swiveled in the seat. Decked out in his sheriff's uniform that reminded her more of camouflage than police garb, the man who'd invaded her thoughts all week stood there. Up close, his rugged features filled her with crazy joy. The cop with broad shoulders, thick biceps, and a chest that could stop a 747 from taking off, rested his blue gaze on her face.

When his serious and seemingly unfriendly expression broke into a slow grin, her cheeks heated with embarrassment at the ludicrous thought of running into the man's arms.

Keeping her voice level, she said, "More than likely, I should be arrested for assault."

Invisible waves of raw sexuality pulsed from the man and scattered her normally calm sensibilities.

The officer tipped his head to the right. "Don't think I'll arrest you today. Why are you back so soon?"

"Unwinding," she answered. "Catch the bad guys yet?"

He crossed his thick arms as if in no hurry to leave. Either that or if body language was a real thing, he was protecting himself, but against what?

"Not yet."

She arched an eyebrow. "I'm not under suspicion, am I?"

The officer's carved jaw clenched and only proved to make him more appealing. She had to stop reading romance novels. Since her divorce, she'd tripled her consumption.

"Something you'd like to confess?" he asked.

His intense blue gaze intimidated and thrilled her. Other than a couple of fleeting murderous thoughts when she'd caught her husband cheating, Holly didn't normally react spontaneously. She grinned. Not because the officer teased her in a professional manner, but because she was happy.

"You mean about the bank I robbed earlier? Nope. Nothing to confess."

It was like the sun breaking through dark clouds when his full lips parted, and he laughed. She couldn't stop staring. Didn't want to stop. She'd probably never see him again. This was her one and only chance encounter. Not as romantic as Cinderella—a lost slipper and a prince—but a rare, rugged man who eclipsed her life for a few short seconds then dispersed, leaving only a memorable sensation.

The handsome sheriff took a step back. "No walking to the Coffee Hut after dark for a milkshake," he warned.

Hard to believe he remembered she'd admitted loving the cool, creamy refreshment, and felt foolish all over again. "I'll keep my fixation to daylight hours."

One of the cocktail servers stopped by and asked, "Something to drink?"

"Coffee, please," Holly answered.

The girl in the skin-tight, short skirt flashed a look at the sheriff, smiled and moved on. Holly expected his eyes to target her retreating perfect ass, but he didn't. Did that mean the sizzling, hot sheriff also maintained a strict sense of conduct?

He narrowed an eye, which made her smile again.

"So, you lied," he said.

"I beg your pardon. I did not. You asked if coffee was my beverage of choice. It's not."

The grin on his mouth slackened. Was he surprised she'd remembered what he'd said too?

His lips parted as if to say something, then thought better of it and cleared his throat. "You must have a hectic job if you need a break so soon."

Could he tell she was fibbing just a little? As a cop, he probably had reasonable instincts. "I get the distinct feeling you're questioning my veracity."

"Am I?" He removed his ball cap and ran a slow hand through his blond hair, then replaced the cap. "Kind of my job to interrogate people."

"Uh-huh. Criminals, but not innocent guests."

The officer he'd been with last time rounded the bank of slots. "You coming, Gray? Manager's waiting."

Gray? Last name perhaps? Then her gaze slid down the snug, moss-green shirt stretched across his muscled chest to the name tag. Brooks.

"Be there in a second." Officer Brooks' index finger tapped the brim of his ball cap in a friendly salute. "Have a good evening, ma'am."

She smiled, even though her heart ached with his farewell. Holly hadn't won anything from the hungry slot machine, but she considered herself lucky to have seen him again. Her gaze followed his departure. At the last second before he disappeared from view, the sheriff turned his head toward her, and their eyes met.

As if her heart knew something she didn't, it thumped madly.

Holly was a thousand percent certain that the chemical reaction stirring her emotions into a frothy mess was one-sided. Men like Officer Brooks were a fantasy to science geeks like her.

* * * *

"What the hell was that? I thought you were right behind me. I looked back and you were gone," Cole said as they strode across the gaming floor toward the security desk.

Grayson had spotted her out the corner of his eye and his feet changed direction, pulled toward the raven-haired woman. As he closed in, his pulse increased. Friggin' crazy. When she'd turned to face him, his stomach clenched with excitement as he gazed into her extraordinary grey eyes. It was her, all right.

He and Cole stopped to allow an old man using a walker to cross ahead of them at a turtle's pace.

"Something going on?" Cole asked.

"What? No. Why?"

His partner eyed him. "Wasn't that the woman we saw last week? The one in the buffet."

Once the old boy cleared the aisle, he and Cole cut through the heart of bells and whistles toward the east entrance. "Yeah, that was her."

"Your instincts pinging?" Cole asked. "She looks like she's about our age. Maybe we went to school with her."

Nope. Grayson had never seen her until a week ago, that was for damn sure. "Don't think so," he muttered.

The casino manager, wearing the same grey tie, pink shirt, and grey suit he'd worn the week before, waited for them at the security desk.

Paul Gibbons shook their hands. "This is starting to be a regular thing," the manager said.

Early that afternoon, a couple at the resort reported their car missing from the parking lot. The individual or individuals responsible for the thefts were increasing their activity at the Neon Lights. Bad for business and the pressure was on the sheriff's department to catch the perps.

Grayson begrudgingly put his concentration back on the case. "What did your security team find on the surveillance video?"

"The incident was recorded but not clear enough to identify the guy," Gibbons answered. "He wore a ball cap and a dark hoodie. These bastards know what they're doing. We had our early summer celebration giveaway last night. The place was full. The guest parked at the far end of the east lot. He ended up staying overnight but didn't move his vehicle into the hotel guest parking closest to the hotel."

Grayson and Cole followed the manager as he led them to the security surveillance room. Several men watched a raft of monitors overlooking the gaming floor, exterior parking lots of the resort, and the cameras located within the hotel.

While the manager asked one of the employees to pull up the video feed from last night, Grayson's eyes slid to a cluster of monitors covering the south side of the casino. Even among all the guests, he spotted her walking toward the glass doors closest to the hotel. There was no interior access between the casino and the hotel like most resorts had. Grayson continued to track her movement as she exited the casino and the next monitor picked her up as she walked along the covered sidewalk to the front entrance of the hotel.

"Here it is," the manager said.

Gray reluctantly shifted his attention as the replay of the theft, which occurred around zero-three-hundred hours, showed a guy jogging across the empty lot, doing his best to keep to the shadows and stopping at a newer model Lexus. From his pocket, the guy used a handheld device and opened the door without the alarm activating. Not more than thirty seconds later, the vehicle drove out of the lot.

Cole nodded. "Has the tools and knows what he's doing."

"Yup," Grayson agreed. "Someone must have dropped him off." A gas station and espresso shack, the one Grayson's grey-eyed mystery woman liked to visit, was less than a quarter mile from the resort, which sat on Native land. The tribe had their own police force and the county sheriff's office worked with them in cases like this. The gas station was owned by the resort as well. "What about the gas station? Are you linked to their video system?"

Gibbons shook his head. "No, it's independent of the resort, but I asked the manager to review the feed. They didn't see the guy on their video. Someone dropped that asshole off, and he walked in."

Cole continued the questioning, "Is the guest still at the hotel? We'd like to speak with him."

Grayson's gaze slid to the monitors to his right, and he suppressed a grin. She'd made it into the hotel elevator. The guy responsible for monitoring the feeds in the hotel also watched as she waited to reach her floor and tucked a waft of dark hair behind one ear. He'd never seen a woman with silky, loose black, natural curls like hers before. Or eyes of shimmering grey with flecks of green. He liked her witty comebacks. People on the West Coast didn't always have an identifiable American accent. The elevator doors slid open, and she exited, turning left.

"Gray?"

He jerked his attention back to Cole and the casino manager. "Is the guest a local?" he asked.

Gibbons shook his head. "Canadian. We're so close to

the border, I'd say half our customers are from Canada. According to our regulars, we offer a better experience here at Neon Lights, but word of mouth will kill our reputation. If these thefts continue, people will find somewhere else to take their business."

He and Cole shared a look. Grayson understood the predicament the manager was stuck between. "I appreciate that you don't want to scare your patrons, but it might be prudent to warn them to take precautions until these incidents are resolved. What about your security team? Are you fully staffed?"

"Hired two more men today. The vetting process takes a while. They appear to be solid guys with security backgrounds." Gibbons ran a palm down his grey silk tie. "I skipped a few steps for the sake of risk management. We're doubling up on our exterior patrols. Both hotels are fully booked this weekend."

Two separate hotels belonged to the resort, one attached to the casino and a second hotel behind the gas station. So far, there'd been two reports of broken vehicle windows and minor theft, but no vehicle thefts or assaults had occurred at the second site. Grayson hoped it would remain that way.

"Cole, why don't you talk with the vic? I'm going to check out the gas station video to make sure they didn't miss anything."

His partner nodded. "Good idea."

CHAPTER FIVE

G ray, Cole, and Gibbons exited the security monitoring room. While Cole followed the manager to the hotel, Gray headed for the south entrance where they'd parked the cruiser. Didn't take more than twenty seconds to drive from the resort to the gas station.

Time on the cruiser's console read five-thirty. So much for the eight to four schedule Cole had mentioned, but that was police work. The PU, *Proactive Unit,* was an easy fit and he liked the other detectives. All of 'em seemed like solid guys and had years of experience.

So far, he didn't miss the hectic pace he'd left behind in San Diego, nor the constant pressure of the narcotics task force, and Ivy's cooking was better than he remembered. Sitting on the porch after supper and talking with his old man was irreplaceable. This week he'd worked till after sunset every day doing chores around the farmstead. Not only did it feel good working with his hands again but it was second nature to him.

Grayson locked the cruiser and headed inside the gas station to review the surveillance video. Thirty minutes later, he'd seen all he needed. Nothing suspicious caught on their system.

About to open the door of the patrol car, Grayson glanced over the roof and grinned.

She really did love those milkshakes.

His mystery woman sat at a two-person outdoor patio set situated on a small patch of grass in front of the drive-thru espresso shack. The sun was still high on the horizon, so he couldn't give her hell for venturing out by herself.

Cole was probably finished questioning the victims and

waiting for a pick-up. The family usually ate around five. Hopefully, Ivy had kept a plate warm for him. He gnawed on his bottom lip. An intense pull from the middle of his cortex urged him to jump on the opportunity.

Taking long strides, he crossed the paved station lot. She looked up, saw him, and jumped to her feet, surprise widening her eyes. He laughed when she *not* so eloquently shifted the arm holding the plastic cup behind her back.

"Is that what I think it is?" he asked when he got within eight feet.

"Noooo," she drawled, still hiding the cup as her smooth cheeks tinted with a rosy hue.

"Ya know, they sell wine in the convenience store."

Her little nose crinkled with dislike. Okay, definitely not a drinker.

"Aren't you off the clock, yet?" she asked.

If he was, he'd consider joining her just to satisfy his curiosity and the unexplainable tick in his chest.

"Not yet."

She pursed her lips. "You're investigating something specific, aren't you?"

"Good guess."

She grinned as if hiding a secret. "More like compiling information and analyzing results."

Attractive as she was, something in those grey eyes was weighted with undeniable intelligence. "You're correct. That's why I'm driving you back to the resort."

She blinked her long, dark lashes. "It's such a beautiful evening. It's not even close to nightfall."

Grayson closed the distance between them to five feet, partly to get out of the drive-thru lane, but also to satisfy the odd sensation in his chest that urged him closer. He and Cole had stopped at a Mexican joint for lunch. Probably indigestion.

He lowered his chin, sizing her up. "Are you arguing with a law enforcement officer?"

Her sleek, dark eyebrows popped with surprise. "Did you know that you have a way of making someone feel guilty even when they're not?"

"Everyone is guilty of something," he shot back.

Slowly, she moved her arm from behind her back and revealed the milkshake. He smothered a grin, almost certain the movement was an unconscious act.

Her gaze slid past him toward the cruiser. "Do I have to sit in the back seat?"

Jesus, she was cute. It was the unexpected comments she made and how she said them that intrigued him. A grin ripped across his mouth unhindered.

"No," he drawled. "Unless you want me to handcuff you and toss you back there." Mentioning handcuffs and her in the same sentence elicited something other than humor. And he was pretty fucking sure it didn't belong in a professional situation. "Listen—" He lowered his tone and altered course to a more serious note. "There's been some incidents at the resort. Mostly theft."

She dumped her unfinished milkshake in the trash can. "Mostly?"

"An assault as well." Grayson wasn't going to sugar coat the truth because he wanted her to take him seriously. "It occurred late at night to a senior leaving the resort. We suspect it's a small ring of criminals but they're pretty good at what they do. It's a short walk between here and the resort, but that doesn't mean much when you're alone."

The spark in his mystery woman's eyes dimmed. "Yeah, I am." Her gaze shifted to the large, pie-shaped field that sat between the road leading to the I-5 and the access road to the resort. Everywhere else you looked, freshly mowed lawns added to the pristine surroundings. "I hope you catch these guys. There's something unique about this place."

"Unique?"

A slip of a smile crossed her pillowy lips, yet her eyes held another emotion he couldn't read but wished he could.

"Special," she added as her eyes scanned the rich, green landscape.

His cell rang, invading their conversation. Pissed they'd been interrupted, he retrieved the phone from his pants pocket. It was Ivy.

"Hey," he answered. "I'm running late on a case. Keep a plate warm for me. Shouldn't be too much longer."

"No problem. I have some accounting work to do at the store," his sister said. "I'll leave dinner in the oven."

Before he got a chance to say thanks, his mystery woman was already thirty feet away and walking at a fast clip. "Appreciate it, Ivy."

He disconnected. Strange. Why had she suddenly put it into high gear? An incoming text had him digging out his phone again.

Finished at the gas station?

It was Cole. He responded.

Leaving now.

The petite brunette had made it to the crosswalk and trotted across the road, her soft curls bouncing against her back. He retraced his steps to the patrol car and left the gas station but got stuck at the red light. Luckily, the road ahead was relatively straight, and all the brush had been clear cut on either side. By the time the light turned green, she'd reached the lower end of the resort parking lot.

Grayson steered the cruiser toward the main casino entrance and Cole hopped in when he came to a rolling stop.

"Find anything?" he asked.

"Nothing. What did the vic say?" Cole didn't know it, but Gray was stalling to make sure his mystery woman made it to the hotel entrance.

"Not much. He's seriously pissed. Brand new Lexus. Bought it as a retirement gift for him and the wife. Their daughter is coming to pick them up."

Finally, he thought. She'd slowed her pace but made it to the overhang of the hotel's main entrance. Satisfied, Grayson drove toward the main exit road.

"Stolen car is probably already in pieces."

Cole snapped his seatbelt into place. "More than likely. Ready to call it a day?"

"Yup. Dinner's waiting for me back at the farm and about four hours of work."

Cole grinned, showing a line of perfect white teeth. "Aren't you glad you're back?"

Grayson flicked a look into the rear-view mirror. His mystery lady was still a mystery, but at least she was safe.

"I am. No regrets whatsoever."

* * * *

Mid-morning, Holly waited near the registration desk of the hotel as the sun beamed through the automatic sliding glass doors. Both customer service clerks busied themselves with other guests. The young couple in front of Holly finished checking out, and she stepped up to the brunette wearing a blue suit blazer and white blouse behind the granite-topped counter.

"Morning, Melody," she greeted.

"Morning, Holly. What can I do for you?"

"I'm looking for a tip," she said. "I usually visit the local sites while I'm here. I was thinking you could steer me somewhere I haven't been. I've hit all the well-known places, like La Connor, Fairhaven Historic District and Chuckanut Drive."

"Hmm. Well, what about a hike?"

Holly definitely loved a short hike, but she was feeling kinda lazy today. "I was thinking somewhere nice to have lunch."

The other clerk jumped into the conversation. "What about Brooks Farmstead?"

"Oh, yeah!" Melody said, "I shop there every week. Love that place."

Holly liked the idea. "Sounds promising."

The phone rang and Melody put the caller on hold. "It's a working farm that grows organic vegetables and raises chemical-free meat. They have a grocery market, but you can also grab a bite to eat there."

The other clerk added, "Try their bacon, onion, and apple jelly. I love that stuff on cheese."

Sometimes Holly missed living on the acreage she'd grown up on. "Is it easy to find?"

"Should be easy with a navigation app, and it's less than twenty minutes away. Nice drive through the country, too," Melody said.

"Thanks, then that's where I'll go. Take it easy, you guys."

Sitting in her car, the leather interior already hot from cooking under the sun, Holly found the farmstead on her phone and transferred the address into the navigation system.

The relaxing drive wound its way east of Bellingham and into open farmland. The sky was crystal blue and the outside temperature, according to her vehicle, was eighty-seven degrees Fahrenheit.

She didn't have to worry about getting lost because she'd seen two Brooks Farmstead signs perched on the edge of the road. Holly passed picturesque farms with lush fields and grazing cattle. Barns, some large and modern, others weathered and old, colored a hodgepodge mural of rural living.

Holly met a few cars on the road but mostly the traffic remained light. Urban sprawl hadn't tarnished the land with crowded neighborhoods. Telephone and electricity poles serviced the area. If you wanted to snoop on your neighbor, you'd have to use binoculars, unlike her place, where stepping out the back door meant the people in the townhouse behind her could see her every movement.

"Turn left in fifty meters," the nav system said.

Holly slowed.

"Turn left," the male voice stated.

She turned off the verbal commands. A large, colorful Brooks Farmstead sign and an arrow pointing left was perched on the corner lot.

The farm had to be large because she drove for at least a minute past white fencing and grazing cattle before reaching the driveway and a sign welcoming guests.

Holly parked in front of a one-story white and red produce market surrounded by mowed lawns, barrels overflowing with colorful flowers, and picnic tables. Beautiful oak trees lined the gravel drive that continued past the store. She couldn't see beyond the bend in the road but surmised the family home was somewhere back there.

She wasn't the only person who'd journeyed out on the warm afternoon to shop. About twenty other vehicles were parked in the gravel lot, some with Washington plates, but several with Canadian.

As she slid out and shut the door, the sun stroked her shoulders. Wearing a tank top, jeans, and flip-flops, she tossed the long strap of her purse over her head and across her chest then locked the car door. Several picnic tables dotted the manicured lawn and visitors sat under the warm sun or in the shade of mature trees.

Holly weaved her way past plywood bins of fresh produce that fronted the entrance and walked into the store decorated with modern country flare. Chalkboard signs hung over display areas of veggies and open shelving. She stooped to grab a handbasket then took her time browsing.

Pausing in front of the refrigerated cheese section, she investigated the vast variety.

"Finding everything okay?" a woman asked as she stopped beside Holly.

About Holly's age, the gal wore a t-shirt with the Brooks Farmstead logo: woven brown baskets filled to the brim with fresh vegetables and a caricature of a cow, a sheep, and chickens doing a little jig.

"I am," Holly answered. "Just tough trying to decide."

"I'm Ivy. Shout if you have any questions."

"The selection in here is incredible. Is everything organic?"

"Sure is. And all locally made, raised or grown. No pesticides or chemical preservatives."

"I was told to try the bacon-onion-apple jelly."

Ivy grinned. "One of my favorites." She pointed to Holly's left. "All the jams and jellies are over there. The one you're referring to is made here on Brooks Farmstead, but there're others and they're just as good."

"Thank you."

The pretty blonde who wore her hair in a ponytail strolled toward the deli display near the checkout counter.

Holly's stomach grumbled, telling her to stop looking and start eating. Her basket was already half full, some of the food she'd take home. She had a fridge in her suite to keep everything fresh until she left on Sunday. But for now, she needed sustenance and sunshine.

She paid for her groceries and found an empty picnic table next to an apple tree. Ivy had given her paper plates and plastic cutlery. She opened a package of cheese, crackers, and the jelly jar, then added some smoked deli meat. Holly built her lunch, then tilted her head back to soak up the sunshine and closed her eyes, listening to the calming sounds of the country.

She lifted a loaded cracker to her mouth and bit down at the same time the low, recognizable timbre of a man's voice shocked the heck out of her. Holly opened her eyes and the cracker exploded in her fingers, the contents tumbling against her top.

What the heck was he doing here?

* * * *

Grayson parked his truck on the far side of the parking

lot. He wanted to let Ivy know he'd cut out early from work and would help the old man in the tractor shed. His feet came to an abrupt halt before his brain caught up to his eyes.

No way! For an instant, his naturally suspicious mind analyzed the odds that his mystery lady was following him, but she wasn't looking for anyone. She tipped her pretty face back to pay homage to the sun as she closed her eyes and a blissful smile touched her lips.

The woman's raven-black hair glistened under the sunshine and a waterfall of loose curls rained down her back.

Until two weeks ago, he'd always favored leggy blondes. In no hurry to unglue his gaze from her moment of absolute surrender, he leaned against one of the wooden light poles that lined the walkway to the store.

He considered leaving her alone but just like at the gas station, his instincts gave him a shove to get closer. Finished praising the sun, she dug into the snack she'd picked up from the shop.

With her eyes shut, she didn't see his approach. Standing on the other side of the picnic table, he asked, "Enjoying your lunch?"

Her gorgeous grey eyes flashed open. Startled by his presence, her fingers pinched the cracker and it shattered. She quickly swiped the crumbs off her shirt while her cheeks turned a pretty hue of rose and she squared herself off.

"Hello, Sheriff."

"Taking a break from the bells and whistles?" he asked, basking in her eyes. Her gaze strayed to the name tag on his uniform.

"Is that a coincidence or…"

"No, not a coincidence. My family owns the farmstead."

Without an invitation, Grayson threw a leg over the picnic table bench and joined her.

She blinked those gorgeous, thick lashes a few times. "Don't tell me there're bad guys around here too?"

He chuckled. "No bad guys. You're safe."

"Just to be clear, the ladies at hotel registration suggested I visit Brooks Farmstead."

He grinned and pounced on the opportunity to tease her. "Uh-huh. And you mention this to clarify what?"

Holly cleared her throat and darted a glance at their surroundings. "Just...well, because they said the produce was amazing." She pushed the paper plate of premade crackers in his direction. "Hungry?"

Her nervous explanation sounded reasonable enough, and he was hungry. Not for food but hungry to know more about her. He popped one of the offerings into his mouth.

"One of our neighbors makes the majority of the cheeses we sell," he explained.

Holly tipped the paper grocery bag sitting next to her left elbow so he could see inside. Four different varieties of cheese sat on a bundle of carrots, a bag of new potatoes, and other fresh vegetables.

"I couldn't decide," she admitted. "How long have your family run this business?"

"Farm's been in our name for several generations. Started out as a cattle operation, then expanded over the years to include sheep, pork, and poultry."

Holly cut more slices of firm cheese and added them to the crackers. "I love the grocery. The woman inside told me you support the local farmers by selling their products."

He nodded. "Blonde, about five-seven?"

"Yes, I think she said her name was Ivy."

"That's my sister. She's the brains behind the farmstead store. The family built the grocery seven years ago."

Adding small slices of deli meats to the cracker combos, she nudged four crackers to his side of the plate and three to her side. "You and your sister have the same color eyes."

She smiled, and the tick in his chest increased to an uncomfortable level. "Family trait."

"The store must be popular by the number of visitors I see. Reminds me of a hidden treasure." She inched the plate toward him. "Please, help yourself."

It occurred to Grayson that she often used polite terms. Noticeably so. "Don't want to take your lunch."

Her gorgeous gaze landed on his face, and that odd tick in his chest began to hum.

"You're not. I'm sharing my lunch."

If he wasn't in this damn uniform and had a heap of chores, he'd consider doing something he had never done before—ask her out for dinner. Certainly wasn't his usual approach, but that's because women he met in the past hung out in bars, not in his front yard. Then it occurred to Gray that they were sharing a meal. Right now. Here.

"Glad you found the place," he said.

Gray liked her natural beauty. She wore a little mascara, but that was all. No brilliant lipstick to distract from her pillowy lips. Sitting this close to her, he literally had never met anyone with mesmerizing eyes like hers.

"On my way here, the white fence stretched back to the turnoff. How big is the farm?"

"Four hundred acres."

He glanced around and realized he'd been so enraptured by his mystery woman that everything else had faded into the background. Children played, laughing and shouting. A Lab and a Poodle strained at the end of their leashes and barked at each other. Vehicle tires crunched on the gravel lot, but he'd blocked it all out. For a guy like him, trained to be aware at all times, her presence eradicated something deeply ingrained in his conscious. How the hell had she done that?

Completely unaware that she'd rattled his cage, she said, "You must have a lot of cattle."

"We usually run two hundred head of cow/calf, grass-fed, pasture-raised beef. Years ago, we switched part of the land to rotational grazing because you can raise more cattle on less land. That's when we added, pig, sheep, and poultry. Plus, farther down that driveway are two large sheds for the laying hens."

While he talked, she nibbled on a cracker, then said, "I'm not familiar with rotational grazing."

The fact she was interested at all kind of surprised him, but then again not. It wasn't the first time he sensed she was an intelligent woman.

"Lots of benefits to rotational grazing. We send the sheep through the pastures first because they're more selective than cows about the type of grass they eat. The cattle graze after the sheep. We have a specially designed system that protects the laying hens that forage the area five days later. They scratch through the dung and spread it out. This breaks the manure down and the grass absorbs it for fertilizer. The hens eat the parasites and fly larvae and leave their own manure. After that, we let the meat birds come through before the grass rebounds and gets too tall to re-fertilize."

"So this process keeps the parasites in check." She unscrewed the top on her water bottle.

"So far, and we don't have to use de-wormers on the beef."

Ivy strode up to the table. "Hi. Sorry to interrupt. Gray, Dad's having a bad day. He needs help in the tractor shed. Any chance you can knock off early and help?"

"That's why I'm here. Took the afternoon off. I'll change and give him a hand."

Ivy gazed across the table, then at Holly. "I didn't know you two knew each other."

Holly shook her head. "We don't."

That wasn't completely true. "Yes, we do."

"Not really," she quipped.

His sister chuckled. "Okay, then. Enjoying the jelly?"

"It's wonderful."

Ivy glanced at the other picnic tables. "It's our mother's recipe."

"Blue ribbons all around. It's all very tasty."

"Glad you're enjoying it." Her eyes slid to Grayson. "I better get back in the store. Arlene should be here in a few minutes. I'll be in the office doing the books." She nodded at

Holly. "Thanks for stopping by."

Holly watched his sister as she retreated toward the store. "I bet your mom has a hundred delicious homemade recipes."

"She did. Ivy keeps her memory alive by making them for the store and the family."

Holly turned her inquisitive eyes his way. "I'm so sorry. When did you lose her?"

"Several years ago. Breast cancer."

"You must have wonderful memories of her everywhere you look around this beautiful farm."

"We definitely miss her, especially our father."

"I can only imagine. Losing a parent is an eventuality we all have to face, but losing them early is a tragedy. I'm sure it helps that your dad has you and your family to support him."

"He's a tough old bird. He'd never admit it, but it makes a difference."

Holly gathered the empty disposable plate and cutlery. "Well, sounds like you have to trade that revolver for a shovel."

He carried a .40 Glock pistol, not a revolver, but she didn't know that. He'd bet a sweetheart like her had never touched a weapon before.

"Stay as long as you like."

She stood and walked a few paces to the green bin and dumped the garbage. Returning to the table, she collected her grocery bag. "Although I could spend the afternoon here, I better go."

Grayson realized he didn't know her name. Pretty pathetic for a detective not to at least know that, but it really had squat to do with his badge.

"Thank you, again," she said, and turned to leave.

"Aren't you going to tell me your name?"

She peeked over her shoulder at him, her eyebrows arched as if surprised that he'd ask. "Am I under arrest?"

She certainly was responsible for disturbing his peace.

"Not unless you've got contraband in that bag I don't know about."

A smile lit her face, and his pulse went into overdrive again. What the hell was going on with him?

"My name's Holly."

Pretty name for an interesting woman. "Grayson," he said, wishing he didn't have an afternoon full of work ahead of him. The few minutes he'd had with her, they'd spent talking about the farm. He'd learned nothing about Holly. If she lived locally, maybe she'd come back to the store but if she lived around here, there was no reason for her to stay at the hotel. "You know my last name."

Clutching the grocery bag between her arms, she grinned. "That, I do."

He chuckled. "Worried I'll run you through the criminal database and find something I don't like?"

"You won't find me at all, Sheriff," she said walking backward.

Wait a second. She kept referring to him as Sheriff, which he plainly was not. There could be a couple reasons for that. "Holly, are you hiding something?"

She laughed. "No, sir. My last name is McNeela, but you won't find me on any Wanted poster."

Maybe not, but she had a driver's license. His pulse beat with unexplainable excitement, watching her walk away in a snug pair of jeans.

"Miss McNeela, feel free to stop by any time. My sister likes repeat customers."

Holly waved. "Thank you, Sheriff."

Why, when he was blessed to run into her again, were they interrupted? At least this time they'd had more than a two-minute conversation.

Parked at the other end of the gravel lot, he saw her hop into a red Audi. The chances of seeing her again were remote. As he made his way to the truck, she headed out the driveway. An odd sensation slithered through his veins. He

couldn't call it anything other than what it was.
    Regret.

CHAPTER SIX

By three o'clock, Grayson rubbed the grease from his fingers with an old rag and wandered to the open entrance of the tractor shed. Another warm, summer day graced the farmstead. A gentle breeze rustled the maroon leaves of the old Japanese maple to his right and a myriad of birds created a chorus of sound.

It had been a week since Holly had visited the farmstead's store. He'd been sorely tempted to drop by the resort last Saturday, but Cole showed up with four tickets to a Mariners game. Didn't take much to convince Jackson and Dad. They piled into Gray's truck and drove to Seattle. He loved spending time with his nephew, who'd lost his mind watching the game live. They'd sat in the stands eating hot dogs and popcorn and had a great time.

Between police work and chores at home, Grayson didn't have idle time until his head hit the pillow at night. Curious, he'd run Holly's name through the national police database. The search resulted in no records found. Nor did he find anything in vehicle registrations. He should have checked her vehicle's plate when she'd left.

His cell dinged with a text from Ivy.

Wendy's here with a delivery from Mingles. Could you help unload?

He responded.

Be there in a minute.

Wendy Mingle. He hadn't seen her in years. Her family owned a farm a couple miles away. Grayson hopped on the Honda ATV he'd just finished servicing and headed for the store. A white GMC truck was parked next to the side entrance. Ivy stood beside a tall blonde.

71

"Thanks, Grayson," Ivy said, when he shut off the ATV and joined his sister. "You remember Wendy."

The slender gal turned to face him. "Grayson. Oh my God, it's good to see you."

This was Wendy? Fifteen years and about a hundred and fifty pounds lighter.

"Hey, Wendy. Wow, been a long time." The change shocked the hell out of him. She'd always been a pretty girl, but also a very hefty girl.

Wendy grinned. "I know, big shock, huh?"

He shot a look at Ivy, who popped her eyebrows at him, then mouthed *"single."*

"You look great," he said. "How's the family?"

"Everyone's good." She rested her forearm on the side wall of the truck bed. "We expanded our fields and added ten commercial greenhouses. We're harvesting year-round. No end to the work."

Grayson surveyed the boxes mounded with ruby strawberries and dark, red-skinned cherries in the truck's bed. "Bumper crop."

"Definitely a good year. Thought Ivy might want some for the store," she said dropping the tailgate.

Ivy plucked one of the strawberries from the pile and popped it in her mouth. "Wow, sweet. I'm going to have to keep some of these for jam. I'll send out an email tonight to our customers. They'll probably be gone by tomorrow."

"If they are, just give me a shout. I'll bring another load." Wendy pinched a plump berry between her fingers and held it out to him. "Try one."

He grinned and took the fruit from her. "Thanks." The sweet, juicy flesh exploded with flavor in his mouth. "Tastes great. I'll get these into the storeroom." Grayson slid one of the wooden crates off the bed while Ivy opened the garage-style side door, and he muscled the produce inside.

"Please tell me he never married," he heard Wendy say from outside.

"My brother? Doubt that'll ever happen," Ivy responded. "He's an even bigger manwhore than Cole."

Nothing like hearing your sister call you a womanizer. Thought family was supposed to stick together. Grayson grabbed the hand truck and steered it outside. He loaded the deck with Wendy's fruit and thumbed the button to activate the battery-powered cart, maneuvering the load into the storage area.

Ivy and Wendy followed him inside.

"Hey, I've got nothing going on tonight, Grayson. Why don't you call Cole and we'll have a drink at Roosters," Wendy suggested.

And there it was, he thought. Booze, bars, and women. Did he really want to start that cycle all over again? Wendy was a nice gal. Her platinum blonde hair, tanned skin, and lean figure definitely fit the bill, but making a neighbor's daughter moan couldn't end well.

"What do you think, Gray?" Ivy asked, surprising him.

Did his sister want an opportunity to spend time with Cole, or was she helping Wendy out by trying to hook her brother up with a friend? With nothing planned tonight, he'd intended on heading to the resort. Didn't hurt to scope the place wearing civvies. If Holly happened to be there, then...then what? Talk for a few minutes. Maybe have a drink.

Ivy unloaded the wooden crates and stored the boxes on the empty shelving.

"Or," Wendy said in a bubbly tone, "have you guys ever been to the lounge at Neon Lights? They bring in a band on the weekends."

"Yeah, why not," he said with the mention of the resort. "I'll call Cole and see if he's free." Grayson returned the wooden crates to Wendy's truck.

The blonde winked at him. "See ya later, Gray."

"Ivy, I'm heading in to take a shower," he said, and strung a leg over the ATV's seat.

Thirty minutes later, he walked barefoot out of the upstairs bathroom with a pair of jeans on while towel drying his hair. The towel was ripped from his fingers and Ivy glared up at him.

"What?"

"You do realize I'm doing this for you and Wendy, even if I have to put up with that insufferable ass, Cole."

He smirked at his sister. "Huh. Didn't realize I needed help finding women."

Her pretty features tightened into a scowl. "Wendy is super nice. She's not like some of my other slutty friends."

Suppressing a grin, he said, "Slutty friends. Maybe you should introduce your manwhore of a brother to them."

Ivy slapped her hands on her hips and the wet towel draped down her leg. "Don't be a jerk. And make sure Cole knows I'm not his plus one for anything other than..."

Gray chowed down on his upper lip. His sister had put herself into a position she couldn't get out of. He was going to enjoy watching this unfold. "Other than what?"

"To fill a chair," she spouted.

"Chair filler. Okay. Got it." The only reason he'd agreed to go out tonight was to make a few patrols around the gaming floor. If Holly wasn't there, he'd have a couple beers and head home.

Ivy flicked the towel and folded it once. "I have to shower and get changed. Wendy wanted to know if you'd pick her up."

Hell to the no on that. "Cole's closer. He can grab her on his way by. I'll drive you to the resort."

"Why doesn't Cole just drive all of us?" she asked.

"If you intend on ignoring him, he might find other company and I'm not waiting around for him to score some chick. Can I have my towel back now?"

Ivy tossed it over his head like a bratty younger sister.

"If he does that, then he's a bigger dick than I thought,"

she said.

Grayson dragged the moist towel off his head. When he'd called Cole, his buddy didn't hesitate to accept the invitation. "Ivy, I have no intention of hooking up with Wendy. We're old friends going out for a drink. That's all."

Ivy sighed and her shoulders drooped. "Wendy's had a crush on you since grade school. And now that you look like that," she said, sweeping her hand in a "Z" pattern at him. "She's totally in love. Why don't you try dating a nice woman for a change?"

What the hell! "Is it mating season around here or something? What's with everyone thinking I need to walk down the aisle?"

Ivy bowed her head and hooked her index fingers in her front jean pockets.

"What?" Everyone seemed to have an opinion on his bachelor status. He was thirty-four, not sixty.

She raised her head and looked him square in the eyes. "Because we've all missed you so much and don't want you to leave," she said quietly.

Gutted, he closed his eyes. "I'm sorry, Ivy. I should have come home after I left the teams, but I wasn't ready. I needed time to acclimatize to civilian life." He draped his arms over her slender shoulders. "I'm glad you called and asked me to come home. It's where I belong now, so don't worry, sis. I'm not leaving."

Tears filled her big blue eyes. Ivy pressed her tanned cheek against his chest, wrapped her arms around his waist and squeezed. "I hope not."

Grayson kissed the top of her head. There weren't many people who'd seen Ivy's gentler side. To most, she had a vibrant, take-no-prisoners personality. His sister had her weak moments too, but only with family.

"Take your time getting ready," he said. "I'll feed Dad and Jackson."

She sniffed and backed away. "I put a casserole in the

oven. Just listen for the timer."

"You bet."

Ivy scooted down the hall and into her bedroom.

They all deserved a night off and a few laughs. It would be a dick move for him to abandon his sister and friends to go looking for Holly. And if he found her, then what? Miss McNeela wasn't a Frog Hog or some chick in a bar waiting for him to buy her a drink and take her home.

Change of plans.

He'd text Cole and tell him they were going to Roosters.

* * * *

By six p.m. on Saturday, images from a dig in northern India covered Holly's dining room table. Remnants of an ancient Brahmi script had been found in a set of newly discovered caves.

She sighed and leaned back in her chair, rubbing her strained eyes. Dhaka University staff had carbon-dated the manuscript to the first century AD. The animal hide had minimal damage. She'd deciphered texts older and in worse shape.

When the doorbell rang, she eased out of the chair, stretching the kinks from her neck before answering.

She gaped at the six-foot-two, dark-haired man standing on her stoop. "Kevin."

A half-hearted smile lifted her ex-husband's mouth. "Hey, Hol. How are you?"

"Confused," she answered. What could he possibly want?

"Mind if I come in?"

Holly stepped aside and for the first time in two years, her ex-husband crossed the threshold of the townhouse they'd bought together. In the divorce settlement, Holly had applied for a mortgage and bought Kevin's share.

"I never expected to see you again." Holly closed the door, then followed him into the living room. "How's Natalie?"

Kevin took a seat on the leather couch. "She transferred to Alberta."

Two years ago, he'd fallen in love with his strawberry-blonde partner. Guess the relationship hadn't worked out. Shocker, Holly thought.

"How's work at the university?"

Mentally tired from concentrating on the ancient script, she wasn't in the mood for an idle chat or deciphering why Kevin had dropped by.

"Busy." Holly sat on the overstuffed lounge chair across from her ex. "I received the divorce papers. I suppose you did as well."

"Yeah, I did." He folded his hands together and stared at the coffee table. "Sometimes a guy doesn't realize how badly he's screwed up until he's punched in the face with the truth."

Cryptic talk for Kevin, who usually didn't beat around the bush. He'd always had a cocky attitude but on closer inspection, Holly noticed he seemed more subdued. Stubble coated his lean jawline and cheeks, and he looked tired.

"Was it Natalie who punched you in the face or someone else?" she asked.

Kevin's dark gaze flicked toward her. "I never told you, but after Natalie and I moved in together, I screwed up." He paused, then sighed. "My department did an initial investigation, and I was put on leave. Natalie left me. Said she didn't want to tarnish her career by association."

Whatever Kevin had done, it must have been bad.

His gaze strolled across the ceiling, then returned to Holly. "We'd been living together for over a year, so we were considered common-law. Natalie sued and wound up with three-quarters of the equity that I'd put into the house in the first place."

Oh, the irony, Holly thought. She and Kevin had worked equally hard to pay off the mortgage on their townhouse. When he'd left her for Natalie, she'd given Kevin half the equity in the divorce. Now the woman who'd screwed Holly's husband had the money.

"That all sounds tragic, but why are you here, Kevin?"

"To apologize," he said, his gaze settling on her. "I had a good life when we were together and I threw it away, hurting you in the process."

"You did that more than once. You had a good life while lying to me and screwing other women. Natalie was just the last straw, but I appreciate the sentiment." She stood up. "I have work to do."

Kevin jumped to his feet. "I've been renting a basement suite in Chilliwack, but the hearing is on Monday in Vancouver. I was wondering if I could stay here until it's over."

A hearing? What kind of trouble was he in? "Stay here? What about your friends?" He had a tight group of buddies he'd always hung out with.

Her ex shook his head. "Guess you find out who your real friends are when you're at your lowest."

Translated, that meant he'd done something unforgivable. Was he that tapped out that he couldn't afford a hotel room? "What did you do, Kevin?"

Staring at the gas fireplace, he said, "I was charged with impaired driving, causing death. I'd been out with the guys from work. Bachelor party for Schneider. I don't know why I got behind the wheel. I was hammered. Stupid. Anyway, the provincial court hearing is on Monday. If I'm lucky enough to avoid a prison sentence, I'll lose my job for sure." Kevin palmed her arms. "You're the last person who I should ask for help, but I'm broke from all the legal fees between our divorce, Natalie and my separation, and now this. I just need a place to land until it's over."

Holly couldn't understand how a smart man like Kevin could end up facing a prison sentence. He wouldn't have come to her doorstep unless she was the last option.

"You can stay until your hearing is over."

Relief washed over his features. "Thank you."

"I'll pack a bag," she said, heading to the dining room table to gather her work.

"You're not staying?" he asked with surprise, following her.

He could sleep in the spare bed, but she wouldn't be his soft shoulder and sounding board. Kevin was her past. He'd already caused her pain, she wasn't going to carry his too.

"I have a place I can stay."

Kevin followed her to the dining table and rested a hand on her shoulder. "Hol, you don't have to leave."

"Actually, I do." She left her ex downstairs while she took the stairs to her bedroom and called the resort, booking two nights.

Holly's current work project could be done from anywhere. She threw a change of clothes into a carry-on bag, and a few minutes later, returned to the kitchen.

"I'll be back Monday afternoon," she said, placing her bag next to the door that accessed the garage. She retrieved a spare house key stored in the china hutch and gave it to him.

Deep creases indented Kevin's brow when he accepted the key. "I thought you'd stay. I wanted you to stay."

Memories of living here with Kevin hadn't left when he did. To Holly, the townhouse was just walls instead of a home, every room void of warmth. With his presence, the shadows darkened, and if she stayed, she couldn't concentrate on her work.

She gazed at his attractive, dark eyes. "I don't think you know what you want. I certainly wasn't enough. You left because you didn't love me, remember?"

"I was wrong, Holly. What I did was stupid."

She shrugged. "At the time, you were sure." Wishing him luck in the court case was ridiculous. Someone was dead because of him. His recklessness had left a family grieving. He'd been reckless with their marriage too. "I want the key returned on Monday before you leave. This is *my* house, Kevin. It better be standing when I get back."

* * * *

The border traffic sign notified travelers of a five-minute wait time when she arrived at the crossing. With nothing to declare, the border guard waved her through. It was a gorgeous evening, the sun hovering above the mountains.

Filled with a sense of angst, probably from Kevin's plight, she veered off the I-5 and drove east for a while, then headed south on rural country roads. She wasn't in any hurry to reach the resort. Taking the scenic route with the window rolled down, the sweet smell of the countryside helped to diffuse her uneasiness, but not all of it.

Farmhouses dotted either side of the road and fields of hay swayed in the light breeze. Some farms had swing sets or trampolines in the yards. Dogs rested on front porches, guarding their domains.

East of Bellingham, she turned west to intersect with the freeway. When the Audi bucked as if it was going to stall out, she checked her dash. A service engine light glowed amber. The car bucked again.

"What the heck!" Up ahead she saw a few business signs. "Come on, don't die on me."

The Audi coughed once more as she reached a gravel parking lot on her right and turned in to get off the road. Her car gave a final cough and stalled. Holly steered the vehicle with the last bit of momentum she had and cleared the entrance.

She shoved the door open and released the hood latch. Her knowledge of engines was restricted to checking fluid levels. Nothing smoked when she inspected the engine compartment. That had to be a good sign. She propped the metal rod in the notch to keep the hood raised. Taking a second, she surveyed her surroundings and studied the cedar-sided building to her left. A luminous pink sign over the entry read, *Roosters*. A chalkboard to the right of the door with an image of a cocktail glass and a beer bottle said half-off happy hour, 3-5 p.m. indicated Roosters was a bar. At least she wasn't stranded in the middle of nowhere.

Holly retrieved her phone from inside the vehicle and called the resort, telling them she had car trouble and would be late. The last thing she needed was for them to give her room away. Next, she fingered through her wallet to find the Automobile Association card, then dialed the emergency number.

She leaned her butt against the front of the Audi while the automated voice said there was an influx of calls, and her wait time was ten minutes. Tall cedars surrounded the area, laying long shadows across the ground with the ebbing sun.

Listening to Beatles music while waiting for an agent to answer, she never expected to hear her name called out, or the familiar low timbre of the man calling.

CHAPTER SEVEN

"**H**olly?"

She turned sharply, the gravel grinding under her heel. "Sheriff Brooks?" She blinked with shock.

He crossed the gravel lot with long confident strides. Instead of his uniform, he wore a light blue t-shirt, pair of loose fitting jeans, and cowboy boots. The man weakened her knees in a uniform but dressed in civilian clothes, her heart palpitated with a strange beat.

The sheriff approached with an expression of surprise and concern cemented on his brow.

"What are you doing here?"

"My car—"

"Automobile Association," a woman answered on the cell.

"Yeah, hi. I need some help," Holly said, snatching a look at the sheriff. "I'm east of Bellingham. My car started to cough and buck then stalled out."

As she explained the situation to the AAA, Grayson rounded the vehicle and bent over the engine.

Holly wandered to the driver's door as she gave the woman her personal details and where she'd broken down.

"Ma'am, I'm not familiar with Roosters. Do you have a street address?"

"A street address. Yes, please hold on for a sec—"

The sheriff's head appeared from the side of the hood. "2418 Billowy Road."

She parroted the address to the woman on the phone.

"'Kay, be about an hour before a roadside assistance vehicle can attend."

"An hour. Well, I'm not going anywhere." She

disconnected.

Sheriff Brooks straightened and turned his brilliant blue eyes on her. Each time she'd seen him, her heart flapped like a trapped beast in her chest.

"You're Canadian," he said, glancing at her license plate.

His demeanor seemed strained. "You say that as if it's a bad thing."

The officer swallowed and eyed her suspiciously, or angrily, she couldn't quite tell. Maybe it was just her, but she felt tension all around her as if Kevin's bad luck had hitched a ride.

"Grayson!"

A gorgeous blonde wearing a tight, black miniskirt and pink, silk blouse, carefully traversed the gravel parking lot in high heels. Holly had been right. A beautiful wife.

The blonde stepped up to Grayson's side. "Problems?"

Sheriff Brooks hadn't cracked a smile yet. "Holly's car broke down."

The woman's eyes widened. "You know each other?"

Holly's cheeks heated with her question. Guilt rippled under her skin. Experiencing the butt end of adultery in her own marriage, she felt terrible because of her intense attraction to the American officer.

"Holly, this is Wendy. She's an old friend. Her family has a produce farm close to the farmstead. My partner, Cole, and sister, Ivy, are inside Roosters. Bit of a reunion," he explained and slowly rubbed his jaw.

"Is it serious?" Wendy asked, turning a look over her shoulder at the raised hood.

Holly got the distinct feeling that Wendy didn't see herself as just an *old friend* the way she stood so close to the cop. "I don't know, but Triple A is sending a service truck."

The sheriff shifted away from Wendy. "Why don't you go back inside," he said. "I'm going to look at Holly's car, see if I can't get it started."

Wendy's gaze swept back and forth between Holly and

Grayson. "Yeah, sure. I'll let the others know."

The weight of the day, especially the crappy parts, settled in her chest with a sour twist. At the moment, even with these people standing here, Holly felt disconnected. "No. Sheriff, you don't have to get your hands dirty and ruin your evening. Roadside Assistance is on their way."

Wendy's smile brightened. "Well, if you need anything just—"

"I'm staying with Holly," Grayson said in a flat tone.

A rusty Ford pickup roared into the parking lot and came to a quick stop in front of the bar, sending dust flying everywhere with its arrival. Three guys in t-shirts, ball caps, and jeans jumped out. One of them shouted, "Yee haw, first one's on me, boys!"

The pretty blonde crossed her arms. "Holly, why don't you join us while Gray works on your car?"

Grayson didn't wear a wedding ring, but Holly was almost certain he had to be married. Maybe Wendy was the wife's close friend and sensed trouble. She didn't have to worry about that. The sheriff had never been anything but polite and professional. And Holly would never involve herself with a married man.

The lot was nearly full. Loud music blared from the bar every time someone opened the front door.

"Must be a popular place," Holly said.

Wendy kept glancing in Grayson's direction. "A local favorite. Come in for a drink."

"Thanks, I'll pass."

Holly wasn't in the mood for music and booze. She stared at the engine compartment. Traitor. *How could you break down on me?* The Audi was only three years old.

The sheriff said something to Wendy in a low voice, and the woman rolled her eyes and headed inside.

Grayson joined her at the front of the car, and he palmed the grill. Her pulse beat quicker when his aura brushed up against hers.

"Well, let's see if we can get this lump of foreign metal to start." He tilted his head to look at her and a smile slid across his mouth.

"Hey, now. This lump is reported to be very dependable."

He raised an eyebrow. "Yeah, I can see that."

She laughed despite feeling awful. "Don't be a wise guy."

Her gaze slid down Grayson's right arm, covered in a myriad of tattoos that disappeared under the short sleeve gripping his thick bicep. Ropey muscle flexed under his skin. She found herself reading his tattoos as she would an ancient text. An eclectic portrait of images: a small, crouched frog, a skull, a frothy wave and anchor. There were vines and webs. A rose and an old pocket watch, mainly tattooed in black ink, except for the red rose. Her heart stirred with the thought he'd got that done when his mother had passed.

Her gaze crept up the story on his arm, but when she glanced at his face, her skin heated because he watched her with interest.

"Sorry."

A friendly, low chuckle emanated from his chest then he leaned over, tugging and wiggling wires. "What are you doing all the way out here?"

She wondered how many other tattoos he had that she couldn't see. Visualizing Grayson naked had been a common theme for the last three weeks. She'd certainly tried to keep him out of her thoughts, but he kept strolling back in as if he belonged there.

"Taking the scenic route."

"Coming or going?" He removed the oil stick and read the level.

"Coming. It was a last-minute thing," she said, reminded of Kevin's unexpected appearance.

The officer wiggled the oil stick back into its slot, then moved on to check the transmission fluid. He unscrewed the cap and drew out the dipstick, then backed away from the car. She leaned closer to read the level.

"I do regular maintenance," she said.

"Level's good." His gaze shifted from the stick to her eyes. "Is it just me, or is it strange we keep running into each other?"

She dragged her gaze away. "Unintentional."

It *was* odd. At least, running into him at the farmstead and breaking down in front of a bar where he was enjoying a drink with his friends and sister.

When he didn't respond, she glanced at him to find his gaze riveted on her.

The fine creases on his forehead tightened. "Are you okay, Holly?"

The tone of his voice was like a comforting caress, releasing girlie hormones she didn't expect.

"My car isn't." She quickly walked away with a well of tears threatening to release.

She opened the driver's door and rummaged around in the middle console until she had control of herself again. A couple tears leaked out, but she swept them away with the back of her hand. She grabbed the wet wipes container in case he needed to clean his fingers.

"Try to start it," he said.

After a couple attempts and failures, he rounded the vehicle. "Your dependable car is a paperweight. You'll need a tow."

"It's still under warranty." She held up the wet wipe dispenser and he pulled a moist tissue.

The sheriff squatted next to the open driver's door. "The Audi dealership is on Iowa Street, but it's closed this time of night."

She sighed. Even with the hassle of her car breaking down, she'd rather be stuck in a parking lot than back at her place, listening to Kevin's woes and staring at the man who'd deceived her.

"Are you staying at the resort?" he asked.

"I have a room, yes." Sitting behind the wheel, she stared

at the dash with her stomach in knots and nodded. "Thank you for your help, but you should be inside with your friends."

She turned her head to look at him, and the knot tightened. There was something exceptionally alluring about Grayson Brooks' masculinity. Last Friday, when they'd spent a few minutes together, electricity had crackled through her blood. All week, she'd berated herself for having an unhealthy obsession with a married man. If he wasn't married, he certainly had someone in his life.

Instead of leaving, Grayson's gaze skated over her face. "How long are you staying?"

She offered him another wet wipe, but he shook his head. "Two nights. I suppose it depends on how long it takes to fix the car. Hopefully, it's not serious." Sitting this close to him unsettled her nerves. "How did you know I was out here?"

"We're sitting at the table next to the front window. I noticed the Audi and thought I was seeing things when you got out of the car." A tender smile tipped his far too kissable lips upward. "You'd tell me if something was wrong, wouldn't you?"

No, she wouldn't. She cleared her throat and opened the storage console between the seats to store the wet wipes inside. Kevin's reappearance had brought back memories. Not only her ex's infidelity but the reason he'd cheated. When Kevin walked out, he'd admitted that he wasn't attracted to her and called her boring. Definitely not something she'd share with the man crouched next to her.

"Nothing's wrong." She turned the key in the ignition, wishing it would start, but all she got was *tick, tick, tick*. A profound sound that resembled the dead car and her pulse whenever she looked at the sheriff. "There's no reason for you to stick around."

"When you lie to me, there is."

She quirked a brow at him. "I'm sorry, what?"

Gray shrugged a broad shoulder. "Were you planning on

visiting the farmstead?" he asked, changing gears.

Without a car, she wasn't going anywhere. "I don't mind a walk, but the store is a little out of my range."

Thankfully, the Triple A truck didn't take an hour and pulled into the parking lot. Grayson stood and waved the driver over, and she got out of the car. After ten minutes of poking around, the mechanic had the same diagnosis. He called his operations center and told them to send a tow truck.

It was nearly dark when Grayson's partner came out to check on things as the service truck left the parking lot.

"Thanks for your help, Sheriff," she said. "I'll wait out here."

Both men shared a look between them, and Grayson said, "Cole, I'm going to follow the tow truck to the dealership, then give Holly a ride to the resort."

"Yeah, sure," his partner said. "Think Wendy's ready to leave."

Grayson nodded. "Drop her off first."

It was like the two men were speaking English, but cryptic English.

"Sheriff, please. I'll call a cab."

The officer shook his head. "If you think I'm leaving you here in this parking lot with drunk men pouring out of that place, or in a deserted commercial area of Iowa Street at this time of night, think again."

Cole, also decked out in civilian clothes, agreed with a nod. "He's right. Standing out here by yourself sends the wrong message."

"What message?" she chirped. "There's no message." She wasn't dressed in a mini with high heels. *That* was a message.

Grayson covered his mouth as if hiding a smile and eyed his partner.

Cole made an odd sound in the back of his throat and nodded. "Ma'am."

He headed back to the bar and moments later, he exited

with two women. Holly recognized the sheriff's sister, Ivy, who crawled into the back seat of a black Mustang, then Wendy hopped into the vehicle and slammed the door.

"She's mad," Holly said more as a comment to herself.

Grayson chuckled. "We'll catch up some other time."

Cole drove slowly, avoiding the potholes, and waved as he passed. Wendy had her head turned away as if purposely shunning Grayson, and Holly couldn't see Ivy behind the tinted glass of the back window.

Grayson shifted her luggage to his pickup when the tow truck rumbled into the parking lot. The sheriff took charge and told the driver to take the car to Iowa Street and that they'd follow.

On their way, Holly checked the dealership's hours on her phone. "The service department is closed on Sundays."

"Unfortunate," he said, but a smile crept across his mouth.

"It's not funny. I feel abandoned without my car."

He grinned and tossed a look across his broad shoulder that made her heart flutter all over again.

"You hungry? Because I'm starving," he said.

On cue, her stomach grumbled. "Me, too. I haven't eaten since breakfast."

"Then let's find something to eat after we drop off your vehicle."

"You've done enough. Truly. You can leave me at the dealership, and I'll call a taxi to take me to the resort."

"Thought we straightened that out already."

"But—"

"Bellingham has one of the highest crime rates in America. I'm not leaving you on the side of the street!"

Chastised, she said, "I wasn't aware of that."

He cleared his throat, and his hand squeezed the steering wheel. "Guess you lost your appetite now."

The heavily forested area shifted to neat suburban neighborhoods that lined either side of the double-lane road.

"No, but I insist on buying dinner for torpedoing your evening."

Eventually, they turned left and entered a commercial district. At this time of night, the streets were empty. The tow truck turned left again, and Holly saw the dealership sign. Grayson followed and waited while the driver backed her Audi into an empty spot and unhooked.

"I probably have something to sign," she said and opened the door. "I'll be right back."

* * * *

His cell rang and he answered through Bluetooth.

"Just checking in. Everything all right?" Ivy asked.

"Yup, we're at the dealership, dropping off her car. You at home?"

"Yes. I have to admit, tonight wasn't as awful as I thought it would be. Wendy moped for a while. Think she was hoping for a different ending. Anyway, about tomorrow—"

"Nope," he stated sharply. The gods had spoken, as far as he was concerned. For Holly to break down in the very spot where he'd planted his ass, nothing would stop him from spending tomorrow with her. He didn't give a flying fuck if a nuclear war broke out. "I'm taking the day off."

His sister paused. "Um, okay," she drawled. "Gray, that woman you're helping. Was she the one here at the farmstead last week? The one you sat with?"

"Her name's Holly."

"Right. Something you want to share?"

Gray watched as the tow truck driver handed Holly a clipboard and pen. "Yeah, we're both starving. I'm bringing her to the store and we're raiding the pantry."

Ivy laughed. "Why don't you just bring her to the house?"

Honestly, he didn't know why he kept thinking about Holly, or why he wanted to spend time with her. Didn't make any damn sense. "We keep running into each other. I hardly know her, but she's...hungry."

Ivy laughed. "Hungry?"

Shit. "She's interesting," he clarified.

"And here I thought you were a lost cause," she said. "Do you know where the switch is for the exterior lights at the store?"

Strings of small patio lights ran through the trees and circled the picnic area next to the entrance. At night, it added ambiance. "Think so. Why?"

"Then turn them on, raid the store and have a picnic under the stars."

Holly shook the guy's hand and headed back toward the truck. "That kinda sounds like a date."

His sister's warm laughter came through the speaker. "Okay, don't call it a date, but you want to spend time with her, don't you?"

There was no question that's what he wanted. Wining and dining women wasn't his thing. Picking up a gal in a bar for mutual orgasms was more his pace. "You think she'd like dinner under the stars?"

"I know I would."

Grayson wondered whether Cole had chickened out, and by the sounds of it, he had.

Halfway to the truck, Holly stopped and answered her phone. Her body language changed. Stiffened.

"Ivy, I gotta go."

He disconnected. Something was wrong. Holly paced in a circle, then covered her forehead with the palm of her hand. After shoving the phone in her purse, she took a few hurried steps toward the service center, then stopped and turned as if confused about which way to go. Holly stood under a light post. He watched as her pretty features crumbled with distress.

Something was definitely wrong, and he jumped out of the truck.

CHAPTER EIGHT

"**H**olly, easy now. What's going on?" Grayson asked, taking long strides to reach her. Tears gushed from her eyes. "It's my dad. His boat."

He closed the distance and stopped a few paces away from her. "Take a breath. Tell me what's happened."

"My father's boat. It's gone down. He sent a distress call that they were taking on water. Take me to the airport. I have to go home."

"I'll drive you across the border. You don't have to fly."

She was crying so hard, her breaths came in big, stuttering gasps. "Nova Scotia. My family is in Nova Scotia."

That explained a lot. Without hesitating, he wrapped his arms around her slender shoulders and drew her against his body, protecting her while she came to terms with the news. Holly melted against his chest, her hot tears seeping through his shirt. He rubbed her back to calm her down.

When her tears subsided, he stepped back and thumbed the wetness from her cheeks. "Listen, Canada's Search and Rescue teams are outstanding. You have to give them time. You can book a flight for tomorrow, either from Bellingham to Vancouver and then onto Nova Scotia, or I can drive you home and you can leave directly from Vancouver. There's no point waiting for hours at an airport for a flight. Either way, you'll probably be halfway there when they rescue your dad and his crew."

She nodded quickly and swept the backs of her hands against her face. Holly took a couple deep breaths. "My car."

"I'll take care of it. You can call the dealership on Monday no matter where you are. Leave the keys with me."

"Thank you." She sniffed and her pretty grey eyes welled looking up at him. "What if—"

He shook his head. "No, Holly. Until you know for sure, you have to believe everything will be fine. Now, resort or home?"

Twenty minutes later, he waited while Holly registered in the lobby of the resort. He'd been kinda shocked with her answer. Most people in a traumatic situation would go home. On their way to the resort, they'd stopped at a drive-thru and picked up food, though he doubted she'd eat.

When she unlocked the door to the suite, Holly quickly turned on the lights then unpacked her laptop, setting it on the round two-person table. He joined her and removed their take-out from the paper bag. Her fingers clicked across the keyboard and her eyes raced across the screen as he plucked her drink from the tray and set it next to her computer.

Her cell rang. Holly retrieved the phone from her purse and hit speaker, then answered.

"Holly."

"Reagan," she said. "What? Talk to me."

The woman took a couple deep breaths as if trying to stop herself from crying. "They're still searching Da's last known position, but there's no sign of Paige. Sis and I are here with Ma. Our aunties brought a good scoff, but she won't eat, and the uncles are all right out of 'er. Are youze comin' home?"

The woman's strong accent was quite different from a Bostonian or American east coast accent. Holly clamped her eyes closed while she listened, and Gray covered her balled fist.

"Yes, I'm looking for a flight. I'll get there as soon as I can."

There was plenty of background noise with people conversing and the *clank* of dishware. "Ma is a mess. We all are."

"Does anyone know what happened?" she asked.

"It's been some cold around here. Early summer storm blew in. Came up quick and fast. Y'know yerself, right. Da was always careful. He'd spoke with Ma only an hour before the distress call. Said they was headin' back for shore."

Holly's fist loosened and Gray removed his hand, only to have her fingers curl around his as if she needed his touch for confidence.

"Keep the faith," he reminded her quietly.

She nodded. "Raegan, I need to find a flight. You'll call me if you learn anything, right?"

"I will," she promised. "Pray, Holly girl. We're all prayin'."

The call disconnected and her weary eyes zoned out, gazing distantly at the laptop. She looked shell-shocked.

"Find a flight, and then you need to get some sleep," he said.

She was too upset to eat, but she had a sip of soda.

"Paige is gone," she murmured.

He surmised that from the conversation. "Is that the name of your father's vessel?"

"Our father has four boats." Her brow squeezed tight as if struck with a bittersweet memory. "He said he named them after the girls he loved. The first Cape Islander he bought, he called Kayleigh, after our mother. The other three are named after me and my sisters: Holly, Paige, and Raegan.

Mariners were a superstitious lot, himself included. He was struck with a selfish thought, thankful it hadn't been *Holly* that had gone down.

"You're the oldest," he said.

She nodded as her gaze slid back to the laptop.

"Here." He unwrapped the chicken sandwich she'd ordered. "Have a bite."

"I'm not hungry."

"You said you haven't eaten since breakfast. You're running on empty. One bite."

She eyed him for a second then picked up the sandwich and did as he asked. Food in her belly would help.

After searching for a few minutes, and two more bites he'd coaxed her to eat, she found a flight that left Vancouver just past noon the next day with only one stop between there and Sydney.

"It's done," she said.

Grayson reached across the small table and closed the laptop.

"Time you turned in." He stood, knowing he should leave, though he wanted to stay with her. "I'll pick you up tomorrow morning and drive you across the border."

"Thank you for holding my hand through everything. You hardly know me, yet you've been so kind."

"It's my job to serve and protect." Once again, he'd hidden his motivations behind a badge, and something had stepped in to keep them apart. Tears welled in her eyes all over again. He couldn't fucking stop himself and wrapped her in his arms. When Holly's head rested against his chest, Grayson took a risk and lightly rubbed his jaw against her silky black curls. Soft as they looked. "Get some sleep. I'll be back by eight."

She nodded and her glistening eyes looked up at him. "I'll be ready."

"Let's see your cell." She collected it from the table and handed it to him. They had identical android phones. He added his number to her contact list. "If something changes, call me. I don't care what time it is, all right?"

"I will."

She escorted him to the door, but he didn't turn to say goodbye until he stood in the hallway because the irrational temptation to kiss her had him by the throat.

"Everything is going to be fine, Holly."

Tears welled in her eyes. "You don't know that."

"I can't promise, but I hope it's the truth. I'll see you tomorrow."

"Goodnight, Sheriff.

* * * *

He didn't sleep well, bothered by a nightmare. Holly stood on the bow of a ship, clinging to the guard rail as the vessel sank into cold, dark waters. Against the fierce wind, he swam hard, his arms stroking through the icy sea, but he couldn't reach her in time. The scene kept replaying and no matter how hard he swam, he always lost her. *He* failed her. Suddenly, her voice cut through the storm, calling his name. It was so crystal clear and close, as if she was lying right next to him. Panic swarmed through his thumping chest, and he woke with a start.

He blinked and glanced around his bedroom, his eyes adjusting to the darkness. The house had been built during the Victorian era, each room extremely large in size. The old wood-burning fireplace in his room had been converted years ago to gas, with a river rock face and a thick, cedar mantle. Situated on the top floor, with vaulted ceilings and exposed wooden beams, it was three times the size of a modern master bedroom. Ivy and Jackson's rooms were similar, plus there were two other guest bedrooms on the third level. Dad slept downstairs near the kitchen, originally three bedrooms when the family had servants, then combined into one master room years later.

Grayson listened to the familiar creaks of the old house while blowing out a breath of relief that it had only been a dream. He laid back against the pillow. The clock on his nightstand showed a little after three in the morning. Not even the roosters were up yet.

He wondered if Holly had gone to sleep or if she paced the floor of her suite. Maybe he should have stayed with her. The search for her father could go on for hours if they didn't find the crew. Gray closed his eyes, hoping for Holly's sake that didn't happen.

By six in the morning, he was showered and dressed. Shuffling aside some papers and a motorcycle magazine in his desk drawer, he found his passport and stuffed it in his chest pocket. The aroma of coffee wound its way up the stairs, and he knew someone was up.

"How'd it go?" Ivy asked, washing a handful of strawberries under the tap.

"Not as I expected. I'm driving Holly across the border this morning." He poured a cup of coffee and sat at the kitchen table.

Ivy poured her own cup and joined him. "So, no picnic under the stars," she said, adding milk to her mug.

"Nope." His phone vibrated on the table, and Gray saw Holly's name on the screen. He hesitated. After the second ring, he connected the call and put the phone to his ear. "Did you get some sleep?"

"They found him," Holly said in a rush of words. Before he asked the obvious, she continued. "They found all of them alive."

He smiled. "I'm happy to hear that. When did you find out?"

"Three in the morning. They were all in survival suits. Search and Rescue recovered them and they're already home."

"Good news. So, what's the plan?" he asked. "Are you still flying back east?"

"I talked to my dad. He said to wait and come for a visit in September. No sense flying all that way for a few days." She exhaled a deep breath. "I'm so relieved, but I don't know what to do."

He certainly understood the loss of a parent. When his mom was dying, those were dark, dark days.

Holly didn't have to face that yet. "Are you asking for my opinion?"

"Hmm. Would you like to offer one?"

He lifted his gaze and winked at his sister. Grayson didn't recognize himself. Selfish as hell, and with her father safe, all he wanted was to spend a little time with Holly.

"Okay, here's my thoughts. You should change your flight to September, then go back to bed and get some rest because you probably got none last night. I'll come by around noon, and we'll grab a bite to eat."

"It's Sunday, you should be with your family. Besides, I owe you so much more than lunch, Sheriff."

He really needed to straighten her out about the sheriff thing. "I'll see you at noon."

"You're sure?"

He was damn sure, the desire completely foreign to him. He refused to seduce the woman, but nothing would stop him from seeing her today.

"Yeah. I should check in with the resort's manager anyway, so I'll see you at noon."

He rested the phone on the table after they said goodbye and eyed his sister.

Ivy shook her head at him. "That was all very...platonic of you. What happened last night?"

Grayson gave Ivy a summary.

"Wow, that's definitely not what you'd planned. But why didn't you suggest picking her up and bringing her here? You could give her a tour of the farmstead while trying to convince yourself that you're not falling for this woman."

The coffee hit the spot and so did his sister's remark. "Why do you think I'm falling for her?"

Ivy snorted. "It's written all over your damn face, Gray. But that's because I know you. Otherwise, that stone-faced expression you normally walk around with is undecipherable. My guess is she doesn't have a clue what you're feeling, either."

"That's good, because I don't know what the hell I'm feeling. I've always kept things simple with women. It's not like I'm looking for a relationship. That's not what I want." He tapped the table with his fingertips. Or was it? "We could...be friends."

Resting her elbows on the table, she steepled her fingers

around the outside of her coffee mug. "Sure. Do that."

He chuckled. "You think I can't?"

Ivy wrinkled her nose at him. "I think God is trying to tell you something. Up to you whether you want to pay attention or not. Cole told me you two keep running into each other."

"Yeah, well, maybe she's a Russian agent and it's all a set-up."

Ivy's mouth gaped in shock.

"I'm kidding," he said. "Holly's a nice woman. Funny. Polite. Smart. But other than being friendly, she's never given me a sign that she's..." He cleared his throat. "Well, I'm just used to a different kind of woman."

"You mean sluts?"

He rolled his eyes. "No, I mean mutual, no-strings-attached, one-night stands. Uncomplicated." He drained his cup. "Anyway, I'm going to kick start that old tractor and move the chicken coops to a new location before breakfast."

"Thought you were taking today off?" She raised a brow at him.

Their father wandered into the kitchen.

"Morning, Dad," Grayson said while setting his cup in the sink.

"Morning," he drawled and retrieved his favorite mug from the shelf. "Did I hear you're moving the coops?"

"That's the plan."

The old man settled himself at the head of the table. "After church, I was thinking of shifting the herd into the east pasture."

"Can we tackle that tomorrow? I've got a lunch date." He stammered, "Well, not a date...date. Just lunch."

"Do ya now?" Dad said, the tips of his moustache twitching.

Ivy laughed. "He's in love." She genuflected. "Save us, Jesus. The end of the world is nigh."

Grayson snorted. It was unwise to share his thoughts with Ivy. She'd get a few miles out of this for sure. "I'm not in love. And I don't think the lady in question is interested. She keeps calling me Sheriff Brooks."

Ivy strolled back to the sink and set her cup on the counter, then shook the extra water from the strawberries in the sieve. "Well, why don't you take her for a walk in the forest and show her little Grayson."

"Jesus, Ivy!" He groaned, grossed out hearing his sister not only mention—but insult his junk.

Their father roared with laughter.

Jackson scampered down the stairs and headed for the fridge, pulling out a pitcher of orange juice. "What's so funny?"

Instead of telling his nephew that Ivy ranked in the top ten of evil sisters, he said, "I'm moving the coops. Wanna help?"

The kid poured half a glass of juice and guzzled it. "Can I drive the tractor?"

"Sure."

Jackson raced outside while Grayson shoved his feet into cowboy boots. Dad was still chuckling and so was Ivy.

Opening the screen door, he said, "Hard to believe I'm related to you people. You're both twisted."

* * * *

By noon, he and Holly sat on a bench in the resort's garden with lunch that he'd brought from the farmstead store. He was so tempted to pull out his phone and take a picture of her with the azalea covered in dazzling deep, red blossoms as her backdrop.

Although she loved the meal, she put up a stink about not buying him lunch. He didn't mind that Holly thought she owed him one. She was the type of woman who'd keep trying until she succeeded. With tact, he'd keep evading her mission just to see her again.

"I wonder how long it will take to fix my car," she said.

"Depends. Could take a couple hours or a couple days." He hoped it was a week, because he could come up with enough excuses to visit each day. Friends did that. They hung out. "Call the dealership tomorrow. I'll drop your keys off at the service department on my way to work."

She scrounged around in her purse until she found the keychain and offered him the keys to the Audi. "Thank you."

When he reached out to take the key, his fingers swept against her soft hand at the same time their gazes locked. He'd held her when she'd cried but this was different. Electricity sizzled through his nerve endings. Grayson recognized the feeling as desire, but it was cradled in something he couldn't define. Instead of raw lust, he sensed a need to protect her. He'd never been a fan of kissing one of his hook-ups. Wasn't needed when he used his mouth to pleasure more important parts of a partner, but he'd never wanted to kiss a woman as desperately as he did now.

A wisp of a smile tightened Holly's lips. She withdrew her hand and placed it in her lap. "I'll forget if I don't give them to you now," she said and looked away.

The moment had passed, but Gray had to wonder if he shredded the camouflage he hid behind with a kiss, whether he'd find she was hiding something from him too.

An older couple strolled by, arm in arm, enjoying the gardens. The seniors both smiled at Holly and him.

"Beautiful day," Holly said.

The couple slowed their step. "Good for these old bones," the husband said. "The missus insists I take a walk every day."

Holly beamed. "The gardens here are beautiful this time of year."

The wife with a neat bob of white hair said, "It's our sixtieth wedding anniversary today. Thought we'd have a little fun and stay at the resort, even though we only live in Marysville."

"Awww, congratulations," Holly gushed. "I hope you're

having a good time."

The old boy grinned. "She's having a good time spending our money on those slots."

"Oh, pooh." The wife grinned. "Honey, I bet your husband doesn't complain when you waste a few dollars on Lady Luck."

Holly's complexion turned beet red. For fun, Grayson smiled and slid his arm around her shoulders. "I don't mind one bit. She could empty my bank account but as long as I've got her, I've got all I need."

Holly coughed and offered a cheesy smile.

"See, Gabe," the old girl said, "these young people know how to have fun."

The husband winked at Grayson. "I'm sure they do. You kids have a nice day."

"You too," Grayson said as Holly waved.

When the couple trundled off, Holly slowly pivoted her head and narrowed an eye at him. "You're such a convincing fibber."

"Am I?" Need lowered his voice by a few octaves.

Literally inches from her tempting mouth, his heart thudded, wanting to sip the sweet fullness of her bottom lip. When her mouth opened a slice to inhale, his pulse fired to a thousand beats per minute.

Kiss her, you idiot. Drop the act.

Inside, he trembled like a racehorse waiting for the gate to spring open. His gaze skated to her brilliant eyes. Had time stopped? Because it certainly felt like it to him.

A cell rang and Holly jumped to her feet, retrieving her phone from the outer pocket of her purse.

"Hell—" She cleared her throat. "Hello." She paused to listen to the caller. "Mom, how is everyone?"

Grayson listened to the one-sided conversation between Holly and her mother while he gathered his scrambled wits. Collecting their empty plates, he crushed the cardboard and shoved it in the paper bag. What was he doing? They had two distinct and diverging lives. She wasn't American. A border stood between them. Most importantly, Holly was definitely not the casual sex type, so why the hell was he here?

A couple minutes later, she said, "That was my mother, just giving me a guilt trip on changing my flight."

He blinked. "What? Yeah, um, when was the last time you saw your family?"

"I went home last Christmas."

Wasn't that another reason to put the brakes on before he started something he sure as hell wouldn't finish? Her family lived on the other side of the country. Wasn't like they could spend half of Christmas day at the farmstead and half with her folks. *Shit.* Why the hell was he trying to coordinate holidays with her in his life?

"Everything all right?" she asked.

Grayson balled the paper bag and stood. "Yeah, everything's fine."

Except his common sense. He lost that every time he ventured too close to this woman.

Holly's watered-down smile and six feet of distance seemed to signal the *"almost kiss"* had unnerved her too.

"You said you needed to talk with the resort manager."

That had been an excuse, but he might as well since he was here. "I'll find him. What about you?"

She shoed away a bee with a gentle swish of her hand. "I should put in a couple hours of work, but I can do that by the pool."

They followed the bricked path until they exited the lush gardens close to the hotel lobby. "I'll come find you before I leave."

"Sure. Thank you for lunch." She waved and turned for the entrance.

In seconds she'd be gone again.

"Wait!" he barked. *Goddammit*, it was a gorgeous Sunday. She wasn't on a plane flying to her father's funeral. "Holly, you seemed interested in the farmstead. Would you like a tour?"

The smile that lit her face made his heart bounce all over his chest cavity like a ping pong ball.

"Seriously?"

"Absolutely. Besides, the first strawberries are ready. We'll pick some to take home."

"I'd love that."

The sun shone overhead, but it was her smile that lifted the dark clouds from his soul. Spending time with her felt as if he finally had something to look forward to versus just existing.

"Then let's go!"

"Now? Don't you want to talk to the manager?"

Grayson dumped the bag in a garbage bin by the sidewalk that ran between the hotel and the casino. "I'll see him tomorrow."

"Then let's do it." She retraced her steps and they strolled across the parking lot to his truck. After opening the passenger door for her, he rounded the front of the Ford and quickly typed a text to Ivy.

Bringing Holly to the farm for a tour. Leave us alone. I mean it.

He fired off the text and got into the truck.

* * * *

By seven o'clock that evening, they rolled up to the entrance of the Neon Lights resort. He and Holly had walked their legs off touring the farmstead and eaten so many berries they should have changed skin color. When dinner came around, they raided the farmstead store for supper. He'd grilled two steaks, and they'd sat at the same picnic table they'd sat at before.

He'd never talked so much in his life, but it was always about the farm, his work, or just living in the US in general. Any time he'd ask Holly something about herself, she'd always defer back to him.

His family had given them space, but they did see his father from a distance, who waved and carried on. Jackson wasn't around, spending the day at a friend's place.

Sitting in the passenger seat, Holly wrapped her arm around a grocery bag filled with her favorite things from the store and a two-pound carton of strawberries.

She opened the door. "I don't know how yesterday, which was close to the worst day of my life, transitioned into one of the best today. Thank you so much for the tour."

He'd enjoyed every second with her. "You're welcome." She yawned and covered her mouth. "Country air will do that to you."

She grinned at him. "Think I'll check in with the family one more time. I'll call the dealership first thing in the morning. Good night."

The urge to lean over and kiss her beat a relentless drum in his chest but doing that would open the floodgates to his mounting attraction to the woman. Desire swelled dangerously close to cresting the walls he'd erected to keep things friendly but platonic. Kissing her would crack the dam for sure.

"Night, Holly."

She closed the door after sliding out of the truck, waved, and strolled into the hotel.

Grayson shifted the Ford into drive and headed home. He'd spent hours with the woman, and she'd never flirted with him once. No signs. No signals. Nothing. They'd laughed and teased each other without one sexual innuendo.

Yet, there'd been moments when she'd stilled his heart. Standing next to a big old oak, the wind had teased her soft, dark curls as she gazed across the pasture, and he'd captured her image in his mind. When she'd held a squealing piglet in her arms and her beautiful eyes lit with warmth, he wondered what looking into those eyes for the rest of his life would be like. Holly had gently rubbed the head of one of the steers, and her lower lip pouted when he explained the butchering process. He'd asked if she'd quit eating steak and she'd grinned then said, *"Heck no,"* which made him laugh.

It occurred to Grayson that she was the first woman in literally years who didn't end up in his bed. Holly wasn't model perfect or sexually charged, but he'd had more than one intense urge to lay her down in the long grass and make slow, blistering love to the woman.

There was an unsullied beauty about Holly that Gray didn't want to tarnish. Or maybe it was more about him. Once he left a woman's bed, the walls came crashing down. His emotions evaporated, which meant never seeing her again. That's not what he wanted.

Sitting at his desk Monday afternoon, he received a text.
My car is repaired.

His pulse ticked with an uneven beat as he stared at those four words. He had to respond, but how he responded could change everything between them. Her life was in Canada. His was in the States. Their paths wouldn't cross again.
Are you headed home?
Yes. Thank you for all your help.

He swallowed thickly, his finger hovering over the keypad.

As he typed, *You're welcome*, he told himself that keeping his distance was the best thing for her.

He stared at his cell for the longest time, waiting, maybe even hoping she'd drop the smallest hint that she wanted to see him again, and he'd pounce.

But she didn't.

For the first time that he could remember, the term "no-strings-attached" hurt like hell.

Holly was gone.

As the week passed, and then another, a deep, hollow void settled in his soul. The ache in his chest intensified each day. He'd done an exemplary job of keeping his distance and remaining friendly but professional.

For reasons he couldn't fathom, he regretted his choice.

There hadn't been a single woman who inspired him to look past an orgasm. Holly McNeela had proven he wasn't the cold-hearted bastard he'd been accused of so many times. He'd thought the beating organ in his chest was color-blind, only able to see things in black and grey, as if it were half dead. But Holly had made his heart drum with a frantic beat. The woman with beautiful *black* curls and *grey* eyes.

The woman he'd likely never see again.

CHAPTER NINE

$\mathbf{S}$ unday evening arrived with a balmy sunset. Cole had come over to the farmstead and they'd worked all day, shifting the herd and clearing brush off the fence line at the back of the acreage.

Sitting on the porch, enjoying the cool night air, Cole's cell rang.

"Go ahead, Lieutenant," he answered, then put the phone on speaker.

"Evening, Cole. I just received a call from Neon Lights. There's been an assault. EMTs are on scene. I'd like you to take a run out there. I got a feeling this is connected to the case you and Brooks are working on."

When Cole's gaze shifted to Grayson, he nodded. "I'm sitting next to him. We'll be on the road in fifteen minutes."

Within a short time, both in uniform, they drove south toward the resort in Grayson's pickup. They didn't bother overshooting the resort to grab a patrol car from headquarters.

Gray parked as close as he could to the hotel entrance. A crowd of people congregated around an ambulance situated in front of the lobby. The tribal police force were already on scene.

Grayson cut through a line of onlookers and surveyed the incident. "Jesus Christ!"

Cole shot him a one-eyebrow lift that asked *say what*?

"It's her. Holly."

"Who?" Cole narrowed his gaze toward the ambulance. "Oh. Her. Damn. I'll speak with the tribal police."

"I'll check on her condition."

A blue blanket was draped over Holly's slender shoulders. Burning the distance, he took quick strides to reach the ambulance.

"How is she?" he asked.

The EMT working on her head said, "Refuses to go to the hospital. She has a serious injury to her left knee."

Holly wore a skirt, allowing him to see the knee was swollen to double the size and scraped bloody. The EMT applied a butterfly bandage to a minor cut over the large goose egg on her forehead.

"Concussion?" he asked the EMT, fingering her bangs aside and inspecting the injury.

"It's not a concussion," Holly piped up.

"Nobody asked you," he snapped at her.

The EMT finished working on her head injury and turned his attention to her leg. "The knee is in worse shape and needs an x-ray. Head wound came from hitting the curb, but she took most of the weight falling on her left knee."

Holly shook her head, then winced. "No way."

"Why not?" Grayson barked. "What the *hell* did I tell you about walking outside after dark?"

As the EMT cleaned the wound on her knee, she gripped her thigh with both hands. "I was going to my car."

"And it couldn't wait till morning?" *Jesus.* His temper didn't creep, it shot to the red line. This could have been a lot worse.

"I was leaving. I didn't see the guy until he hit me from behind like a linebacker and I went down." She gently pressed her fingers against the lump on her head.

Finished filling out his paperwork, the second EMT on scene handed Holly's driver's license to Grayson. "This is probably why she won't go to the hospital."

He swiftly surveyed the license. Holly was thirty-two, same age as Ivy. "I know, she's Canadian."

Sitting on the edge of the ambulance, she scowled up at him. "It's not that bad. I just need an hour to sit and apply

109

some ice."

The EMT kneeling next to her leg turned his attention toward Grayson and shook his head.

Lookie-loos stood a few feet away, watching the activities. Cigarette smoke spiraled above their heads and polluted the summer evening air.

Cole eased through the crowd with Gibbons, the casino manager, in tow.

The guy was a straight shooter from what Grayson could tell.

Gibbons crouched in front of the resort's latest victim. "Holly, I am so sorry this happened. Don't think you're in any shape to drive home tonight. I've arranged three nights for you in the Presidential Suite. All your food and room service are on us."

Holly smiled. "Thanks, Paul. It looks worse than it is, but I think you're right. I better sit tight for one night."

When Gibbons stood, Grayson asked, "Did the video catch the attack? Can we use it to identify the assailant?"

Gibbons frowned. "No, unfortunately not, but we're reviewing the video again and we did retrieve her suitcase. Guy must have dropped it to make a faster getaway."

"Well, that's a blessing," Holly said.

The EMT cleaned the wound on the knee and applied a gauze bandage but didn't wrap the joint. The guy knew what he was doing, Grayson thought, watching him work and ready to step in if he made a wrong move.

Gibbons straightened his red satin tie. "I'll have the luggage brought to your room, Holly."

Gray scanned the full guest parking lot. "Where was she parked?"

"Third row to your right. They've never come this close before. The incidents have always taken place in the lower parking area."

The EMT stood. "Ma'am, that knee is fractured. I highly recommend you have a physician take a look if you're not willing to come with us to the hospital."

"No, I'm not going with you." She put weight on the right leg and stood up, then planted her left foot as if to take a step. She hissed and retracted her foot from the ground.

"Don't think you'll be standing on that any time soon," the EMT said, picking up the scraps from the bandages and rolling them into a ball.

Gibbons handed the EMT his business card. "Any costs associated with your assistance, please send them to me. The resort will take care of the bill."

Cole had been hanging in the background but stepped up. "Need to get a statement from you, Holly."

Grayson turned a warning glare on his partner. "Later," he said sharply. He unfurled his crossed arms and leaned toward Holly until she finally turned her gaze up to him. "I'll take you to the hospital myself."

"I don't want the hassle of dealing with an American hospital. So, no, thank you." Showing a stubborn streak, she took a step toward the hotel doors, but it ended up more as a hop, a gasp and a wobble.

Gibbons swept in as if he was going to wrap an arm around her waist and give her a hand. Ta hell that would happen!

Grayson intervened and scooped her up, one arm under her legs and the other around her back. "I've got her," he stated, lifting her into his arms.

The hotel lobby doors swept open automatically, and he strode toward the registration desk.

The young guy working registration said, "Here's the key card, officer."

Grayson veered course and Holly reached for the cardboard holder that held the keys. Presidential Suite was penned next to the room number.

"Can I sign the registration card later?" she asked.

"We'll have it sent to your room, Holly. Are you gonna be okay?"

"I will be, Clark. Not a big deal."

Grayson eyed her leg, the inflammation at her knee worsening. She needed more than one bag of ice.

"If you have ice packs, send them to her room. Otherwise, bring a large bucket of ice and several towels. If you have both, bring both. And I want it now," he ordered.

"Yes, sir," the hotel clerk said. "There's two elevators. One just around the corner and one at the end of the hall. Presidential Suite is on the fourth floor."

Holly wrapped her arm around his neck and eyed him as he strode toward the end of the hallway to take the elevator closest to the suite. "Why are you mad at me? I didn't ask to be attacked."

"Because I warned you, and you didn't *listen*. You got away lucky. Damn lucky. What if he'd had a weapon? I could be kneeling beside a corpse."

Her eyes rounded. "I did listen, and you're being a little over-dramatic. Put me down. I can walk if you give me a hand."

"Do I look like I can't carry you?" he snapped.

"No, but that angry scowl makes you look like the Incredible Hulk."

"That's because I'm *pissed off*. You should have asked security to escort you to your car." Maybe the real reason he was fucking angry was because she'd been here, and he hadn't known.

"It's less than a hundred feet from the lobby to my car. What are the chances?"

"For you, obviously pretty damn high."

He strode down the hallway decorated in subdued earthy colors. At least this place was a five-star accommodation. Extremely clean and well-cared for.

He hung a left at the end of the hall. "Hit the button," he ordered, standing in front of the elevator.

She reached out with her index finger and selected the call button. "Give your arms a rest and put me down."

"No." Pissed at her as he was, he also enjoyed the hell out of holding Holly in his arms.

"Am I your workout session today?"

He sure as hell wouldn't mind Holly doing a few push-ups on him—naked. After he'd smacked her ass for being careless. Not exactly an acceptable thought in his role as law enforcement, but it was the fucking truth.

Aside from her injury, although not a tall woman, he noticed Miss McNeela had one helluva nice set of legs. Sleek yet toned.

The elevator door slid open with a clunk, and he stepped in sideways, careful not to strike her feet against the wall. Holly selected the fourth-floor button. The door slid shut and with a slight buck, they rose, not stopping on any other floor.

"Sorry for being a pain in your ass," she said in a sober tone.

If she were a pain in his ass, he would have let Gibbons help her. They reached the fourth floor and the door slid open.

Holly pointed to their left. "That way."

A few steps brought them to double doors with a gold plaque on the wall identifying the Presidential Suite. He bent his knees a little so she could slide the key card into the reader. The lock clicked and Holly opened the door.

They entered a pitch-dark room.

"Lights have to be here somewhere," she said, touching the wall.

Holly flicked the switch near the door and the lights revealed a luxurious suite decorated in tones of muted beige, gold, and greens.

To their right was a kitchen/bar combination. Straight ahead, a sizeable living room with two couches and accompanying chairs sat near a stone-faced gas fireplace. Four large picture windows with arched tops overlooked the forest outside. A few paces to the right of the living room was a large dining table.

"Wow," she said.

"Yeah, nice digs, but you need a hospital not a five-star suite."

He carefully set her feet on the low-pile carpet, and she balanced on her right foot while he investigated. To the left of the living room was a large bedroom and ensuite bathroom. He retraced his steps and investigated the room to the right of the kitchen, which was an even bigger bedroom-bathroom combination. He switched on the bedside table lamp.

"That's the master," he said, returning to Holly, who stood on one foot next to the open kitchen with a wraparound counter.

Thinking she could hop her way to the bedroom, she found out pretty quickly that wasn't the case and hissed her discomfort.

"Geez."

"It's going to get worse before it gets better."

Grayson swept her into his arms, not thinking about her injury and still plenty pissed off.

She gasped when her left knee flexed.

"Sorry," he grumbled.

He carried her to the master and laid her on the bed. Reaching over Holly, he grabbed one of six pillows on the king bed and lifted her injured leg, sliding it underneath while she tucked three pillows against the headboard and sat up.

A few seconds later there was a knock at the front door.

Grayson retraced his steps, and a woman smiled up at him when he answered.

"We found some ice packs and brought extra ice and towels," she said.

Grayson stepped out of the way and the hotel employee pushed a room service cart into the suite. "Thanks."

"Security will be right up with her luggage," she said. "I'll be back shortly with some bottled water and juices."

The woman backed out of the entry, and he pushed the cart into the bedroom, depositing the trolley within reach of the bed.

Draping a hand towel from the bathroom over her knee to protect from direct contact with the cold, he applied three ice packs and tied a bath towel around the injured joint to keep the bags secure.

Holly watched him work. "You're pretty good at that. Maybe you should have gone into medicine."

Taking a seat on the edge of the mattress, he finally raised his gaze. The glow of the bedside lamp amplified her soft features. His heart had ticked at an elevated rate since he saw it was her who'd been attacked, and it hadn't subsided.

"I've got a little experience dealing with injuries."

"With the sheriff's department?"

"No. As a medic."

Her slim eyebrows rose. "You never told me that."

There was plenty he hadn't shared. She only knew he'd worked for law enforcement.

"Military?" she guessed correctly.

He wanted her leg elevated more and reached for another pillow. "Special Forces for ten years."

"Navy?" She grimaced when he lifted her leg and eased another pillow underneath.

Among the many tats on his right arm, the anchor probably gave that away. "Navy SEAL."

Her peach-colored lips formed a slight "O" of surprise before she nodded. "Wow, that's ah—dangerous line of work. Glad you came out unscathed."

"Define unscathed."

He liked watching her eyes, and they'd softened with empathy.

"I'm sorry. Of course, that was a stupid thing to say, but I hope you did."

She blinked and unlike American women, who often got a dewy look in their eyes when he revealed his previous service, Holly's response seemed reserved. Restrained, even.

"It really is a thing with you Canadians."

"Thing?"

"Apologetic. Polite."

Seemingly amused by his comment, she said, "That would be like saying all Americans are obnoxious and loud."

He certainly knew a few people like that. "Sometimes we are."

"Do you have something against Canadians, because you scowl every time you say the word?"

"No, I don't." But evidently, he disliked that she lived north of the border. He remembered when he'd seen her license plate at Roosters, and it felt like the rug had been pulled out from under his feet.

"Are you lingering because you're evaluating my head injury, or do you just want to bawl me out some more?"

He leaned closer and inspected her head wound. The bleeding had stopped. The butterfly bandage the EMT applied would suffice. "You never told me what you do for a living."

"You never asked."

True, he hadn't. The more he knew about her, the more he wanted to know. Obviously, she didn't give a damn about him because she hadn't called to say she was here over the weekend.

"I am now."

Holly adjusted her position and nestled against the pillows behind her back. "Research."

Why the fuck did she only give him bare bones when he asked about her? He paused to look in her eyes with only a foot between them. Well, that bullshit was over.

"If you weren't Canadian, I'd think you worked for the CIA with your cryptic explanations. Researcher of what?"

He heard the sharp edge in his tone, but he was having a hard time tempering his mood. Knowing he was well within her personal space and probably made her uncomfortable, he shuffled back by a few inches.

"Ancient texts. Linguistics. I work at the University of BC."

Huh. Although he hadn't expected her to say cocktail waitress, he didn't see that one coming. "How many of those have they dug up in BC?"

"Some, but not my area of expertise."

"So, you're a college grad."

"We call it university, and I have a degree in Anthropology and a Masters in Ancient Languages, but I specialize in archaic religious texts."

Checking the ice bags around her knee, testosterone filled his brain with a sexy image of her wearing a lab coat with nothing but a red thong underneath.

"Educated gal, huh?"

"Are you going to turn this into another verbal spanking about me walking out to the car alone?"

He clenched his jaw against a grin. She wasn't off the hook, damnit. "Smart enough to cut me off at the pass, too."

For a second, they stared into each other's eyes. Warmth bloomed in his chest. Telling Holly he'd missed her sat on the tip of his tongue. He didn't care that Cole was downstairs twiddling his thumbs. The only excuse for a delayed departure was monitoring her condition, which wasn't his job.

"I'm sorry I pissed you off," she said, breaking eye contact and staring at the gas fireplace.

There wasn't a fucking chance he'd admit he was in a bad mood because he'd missed her or because she hadn't called him. "You have to understand that I've seen what people can do to each other. The worst things." Her gaze shifted to his face. "I've had to deliver news to people that their loved one isn't coming home. I don't like it. And I sure as fuck couldn't stomach telling your parents their amazing daughter and my...friend, wasn't coming home ever again."

Holly bowed her head and nodded.

Friend? Jesus. Who the hell was he kidding? He sighed.

"Do you feel groggy or sick to your stomach?"

"No. Head throbs and my knee hurts. The ice will help."

He glanced at the bedside table and the TV remote sat within her reach. "I'll get the front desk to deliver some pain meds. Keep changing the ice every twenty minutes."

Begrudgingly, he stood and shifted the room service cart next to the bed.

"Thank you, Sheriff. You've been more than kind."

Nice of her to omit he'd been a jerk. "I'll be back to get your statement."

"Don't you want it now?"

A loaded question he couldn't answer honestly. Did he want her? Apparently, he did because he couldn't stop thinking about her. "It can wait till tomorrow." About to leave, a thought registered. Maybe she didn't want him to go. He analyzed what that felt like to him. Good—it felt good. "How's your family?"

Holly graced him with a smile. "Thankful that no one was lost in the accident."

A lengthy, tense pause built as he considered asking why she hadn't called him. Asking intimated he'd wanted her to call. In the past, women who'd tried to entice him into something that smelled like a relationship meant he had to politely lay down the law. Apparently, those rules didn't apply to Holly, not that she'd asked anything of him. But why the hell hadn't she?

"Do you think the guy who attacked me is behind the thefts at the resort?" she asked.

"Probably part of the local crime ring I told you about. I noticed you still have your purse."

She hadn't taken it off. The long, thin strap crossed her torso. The guy hadn't seen it camouflaged behind the light, button-up sweater she wore over her white blouse.

"Guess I'm lucky after all." She leaned forward and slipped the sweater from her shoulders and lifted the strap over her head.

When a knock landed on the door of the suite, he figured it was Cole. Instead, a portly guard who'd enjoyed a calorie-doused diet stood at the entry.

"Here's her bag," the guard said, wheeling in a small suitcase. "We found this too. Think she was carrying it at the time." He laid a paperback down on the kitchen counter. "Resort manager wants to make sure she's doing okay."

"She will be. I've got her iced. The hotel have any over-the-counter meds to help with the inflammation and pain?"

"Yes, we do," he said. "I'll have housekeeping bring some up. Anything you need from security?"

"Did you take an initial report from her?"

He adjusted his belt, but it had a permanent home under his bulging belly. "Tribal police did. I got a copy and gave one to your partner downstairs."

"Sounds good. Listen, do you have a female guard working the night shift?"

"Yes, sir. Barb Painter. She's been with us for over ten years."

"Good. Holly can't walk on that leg, but she also has a head injury. Have Barb look in on her a couple of times to make sure she isn't showing serious signs of concussion."

"Absolutely," the guard said.

Security left and Grayson gripped the suitcase handle. About to roll the bag into her bedroom, his gaze settled on the book. The cover caught his attention...a ripped, half-naked guy with low-slung camo pants and dog tags around his sinewy neck. Looking closer, he realized it was an erotic romance novel featuring a Navy SEAL.

Well, well, well.

Flipping open the book to a random page, he hit on an extremely steamy section and briefly read the scene. Man, talk about teasing tits and thumbing clits. This was some explicit stuff.

If there was a man in Holly's life, he certainly wasn't satisfying her if she needed to read this shit. She sure as hell wouldn't need these books if she was his.

For fun, Grayson decided to pull a few of Holly's strings and get her mind off the attack.

"Want your bag in the bedroom?" he called out.

"Please."

He deposited the green bag beside the guest chair next to the bed. "Security is going to send up one of their female guards a few times tonight to check on you. They'll let themselves in."

"That's fine." She opened the cardboard sleeve that registration had given her and offered him one of the key cards. "I'm probably won't be able to answer the door when you come back for a statement."

He accepted the card and tucked it into his shirt pocket.

"Need something to read?" he asked, lifting his hand and revealing the book.

Holly gasped and slapped her hands over her face, then shook her head. Grayson's entire body heated with her response. He almost forgave her for not calling him while she'd been here. Chuckling at her embarrassment wasn't an option he could avoid. He shifted to her bedside, placing the book on her lap.

"Here I thought you're the kind of woman who reads the classics and finishes the New York Times crossword in under five minutes. You're full of surprises, Miss McNeela."

Holly dropped her hands and cleared her throat. "I read the classics too."

"Uh-huh."

"I do," she crooned.

"Sure," he said adjusting his ball cap, biting down on a smile. Patrol officers wore the recognizable campaign hats with the wide brim, but normally Proactive Unit members didn't. "From that bookmark, it looks like you're almost finished. Can I pick you up another one?"

She rolled her eyes at him. "You're enjoying this, aren't you?"

"Just a little." He scrubbed a hand over his mouth to hide a grin. "Got a thing for Navy SEALs, huh?"

Holly's cheeks bloomed a deep red. "These stories have really good plots."

This was just too damn much fun. Not only had he learned she was a scientist but also that she loved naughty romance.

"Is that before or after he binds her hands and eases into her?"

"Lord tunderin' Jeezus," she blustered. "You looked!"

Ho! And there was the east coast accent. Exactly like her sister's. So, when she got flustered, her roots showed. He'd keep that little nugget in his back pocket. Man, he'd missed her.

"Can you blame a guy?" He winked. "I'll find something you like. Just one thing…is there a dedicated smut section in the bookstore?"

She pointed toward the bedroom doorway. "You can go away."

Jesus, he loved teasing her. "Yes, ma'am." Grayson pulled a business card with his info at the PU's office from his wallet and laid it on the bedside table. "Here's my card, just in case you have questions." He paused on purpose. "About anything."

She choked and faced the window but from his angle, he saw her cheeks were still flaming red. He hadn't been referring to the attack, and she knew it.

* * * *

Cole waited near a thick turquoise and beige-painted support column when Grayson walked out the entrance. The ambulance had departed, and the bystanders had dispersed. After a quick survey of the parking lot, he figured the perp who'd attacked Holly was long gone.

"Not much more we can do tonight," Cole said, walking

beside him toward the truck.

"Might as well head for home." Grayson unlocked the doors and they hopped in.

Traveling north on I-5, Cole said, "Looks like you got another close encounter with one Holly McNeela. How is she?"

Well past eleven-thirty, the headlights washed across the dry but dark highway. "Not happy about the knee. Or the head injury, for that matter."

"Why didn't you insist the EMTs take her to the hospital?"

"She didn't want to go." He grinned. "Wasn't prepared to deal with our medical system."

"Who the hell is? Did you get her statement?"

"Nope."

Cole eyed him, then turned his attention back on the road. "Why the hell not? You were up there long enough."

He stretched the kinks out of his neck and rested his left arm on the driver's side window ledge. There was always traffic on the freeway that dissected the country from north to south. At night, semi-truck traffic increased substantially. He passed a line of five trucks, then it was clear sailing.

"Oh, I get it. Opportunity for a second close encounter," Cole said.

"Eighth," he stated, staring out the front windshield.

"What?"

"Twice, the first day I saw her. Third time was when we returned for the Lexus theft. Fourth when I went to check the video at the gas station. Fifth when she showed up at the farmstead. Sixth when she broke down in front of Roosters. Seventh when I spent an entire Sunday with her at the farm. And tonight, is the eighth."

"You're not keeping score at all, are ya?" He laughed. "Coincidences."

He heard the question in Cole's word. "You mean her showing up at the farm and Roosters? Yeah, a coincidence. She had no idea the farmstead belonged to my family. We talked for a while, and then Ivy interrupted us."

Cole snorted. "Interrupted, huh. Buddy, remember in third grade when you fell in love with Karen Lister?"

Grayson notched the volume down on the country radio station in the truck. "What about her? To a seven year old me, she was sugar and spice." Probably where his penchant for blondes started.

"Back then you denied you had a crush on her, just like you're denying you got the hots for that little Canadian."

"Nah," he lied. "Holly was shaken up from the attack but doing a great job of hiding it from me. The report can wait until tomorrow."

"Who the hell do you think you're talking to, Gray? Never seen you get ruffled over someone thumping their knee before. Shit, you nearly knocked the resort manager on his ass when he tried to give her a hand. What's going on?"

"Nothing, man. If I were you, I'd worry about your own love life, ya gutless bastard."

Nearing the exit for home, Gray activated the right signal indicator.

"I told ya, I'm not gutless," Cole stated. "Your sister thinks I'm her second brother."

"Aww, yeah. That must be why she's darting glances at you when you're not looking. My sister spent two hours getting ready for drinks the night we went to Roosters."

Grayson took the off-ramp and turned right at the intersection, headed east.

"She didn't do that, did she?"

Passing the last subdivision, the long stretch of road was pierced by the odd yard light from a farm. Tall trees and thick brush lined the shallow ditches. With his window cracked open, the familiar scent of country living drifted into the truck. If Grayson had known Holly had been assaulted, he would have told Cole to drive his own vehicle and stayed longer with her at the hotel.

"Hey, man. Does Ivy really do that when I'm not looking?"

Grayson grinned at his buddy. "Well, look who's standing at attention all of a sudden."

"Seriously, is there a chance in hell Ivy would...you know."

Grayson kept his eye on the edge of the road. Deer and other critters roamed at night and liked to dart out in front of a vehicle.

"A chance in hell? Probably." He didn't understand the big deal. His best friend had the dark and dangerous good looks women mud wrestled over. "Why haven't you hooked up with some gal and started making babies?"

"I hook up plenty. Believe me, no problem finding a chick who wants to fuck a guy in uniform. They're just not—"

"My sister," Grayson finished for him. "How long you been carrying this burden on your overworked dick and weary heart?"

"Fuck you."

Grayson laughed at his friend's frustration.

"You got nothing to laugh at. I get why you didn't settle down when you were serving Uncle Sam, but you were a detective in San Diego for five years. What's your excuse?"

"Don't have one." He shrugged. "Don't need one. San Diego is in my rear-view mirror." Nearing Cole's street, Gray turned on the right blinker. "If you've got the hots for my sister, then step up, man."

Cole sighed. "I don't know why you're my best friend. You're a dick."

He couldn't argue there. Enough women had called him exactly that. He'd been accused of being married to his job and a heartless bastard when he wasn't interested in painting a white picket fence. Job always came first, except when Erika had routinely dropped into his zone, begging for his help and locking her lips on his cock. For a long time, he hadn't refused because she was so damn good at it, but with distance between them now, he grimaced at the memory.

What the hell had he been thinking? Mostly an alcoholic,

but at times Erika was lit on narcotics while he busted guys for distribution in San Diego.

He reached Cole's place and turned into the driveway, rolling to a stop in front of the one-story rambler. "Hey."

Cole opened the door and then turned his head to look at him.

"Ivy's like our mother. She'll work from sunup to sundown unless she's got a reason to stop. Why don't you try being that reason?"

Cole removed his ball cap and ran a hand through his jet-black hair. "Think she'd believe I want more than just a one-nighter?"

"Not at first. She knows your track record with women. Start thinking with the head above your shoulders before you make a move with the other one."

His partner's brow wrinkled. "The topic of making love to your sister is one you and I should avoid."

"Agreed, but if all you want is a roll in the hay with Ivy, be upfront and let her decide. She's a grown woman, but I know for a fact she hasn't dated anyone since her husband died."

Cole strung a long, hard look in his direction. "I know that too. Believe me."

By the sound of Cole's tone, it was a concern. "Seriously, how long have you been hiding your attraction to her?"

He sighed. "It's a lot deeper than attraction, Gray." He stepped out of the pickup. Cole turned and gripped the door then gazed at him. "I'm in love with Ivy. I have been for a long, long time."

"Then why didn't you make your move the night we went out to Roosters?"

"Because she was too busy consoling Wendy when you chose to stay outside with the Canadian."

Cole's comment sounded a little too much like disrespect.

"That *Canadian* has a name." Grayson yanked the ball cap from his head and tossed it on the empty seat beside him. "I didn't mean to toss a wrench in your plans that night, but

Holly needed me. The only reason I went in the first place was for you and Ivy to have some time together."

Cole waved him off as if it wasn't a big deal.

"Ivy ever been to your place?"

He dug in his pants pocket for his house keys. "Yeah, few times. Usually, to drop off some vegetables or berries."

"Did you invite her in?"

"Course, but she always had somewhere else to be."

"You're a patient man, Cole, but I wouldn't stand on the sidelines for too long."

With the door open, cricket and frog song came from every direction. Tall standing trees encompassed the two-acre property. Cole had cut some of the forest back to give himself extra evening light and laid a large brick patio behind the house.

"I'll keep that in mind. See ya tomorrow, partner."

He gave his old friend a two-finger salute. "Mañana, buddy."

CHAPTER TEN

Around three in the morning, Grayson woke up. Not unusual for him, he hadn't slept through the night since BUD/S training. After downing a glass of water, he returned to bed and called the security desk at the resort and asked for Barb Painter.

"Yes, I just checked in on Miss McNeela," Barb said after he'd identified who was calling and why.

"Did she wake up?"

"Hasn't gone to sleep yet. Can't blame the woman, I guess. Probably running the attack over and over again in her mind."

"You're probably right. How's her injuries?"

"She's got a severe headache and her knee is terribly inflamed. I asked if she wanted help getting to the hospital, but she declined. I urged her to at least take some pain relievers."

His temper rattled to a boil. "She hasn't taken any?"

"No, sir."

"Thanks for checking on her." He disconnected then without a second goddamn thought, called the hotel front desk and asked for her room. Holly picked up in one ring.

"Hello."

"Miss McNeela, you want to explain why I just got a less than stellar report from Security?"

"Sheriff?"

He was definitely going to have to teach her American law enforcement hierarchy. "I'm not a sheriff."

"Oh, sorry. Why are you up at this hour?"

Her tone sounded tight, and he was acutely aware of what caused it. "That would be my question. Did you take the pain relievers?"

"Umm…"

"Why not?" he growled at her.

"Somebody's cranky and needs his beauty sleep."

"Question is whether someone needs another verbal spanking."

As soon as he said *spanking*, an image of Holly's bare ass draped over his thighs sprang to life, the fantasy so clear, it caused his cock to stiffen with record speed. *Shit.*

"I'll take the pills," she grumbled.

Why did he like it so much when she acquiesced to him? "Good. Now you're being reasonable. Finish the book?"

"Stop teasing me about my literary choices. It's a guilty pleasure, okay?"

"Looks like I'm not the only cranky person in this relation —conversation."

"I'm not cranky!"

After missing her for two weeks, he wanted to show her a few dozen guilty pleasures of his own. "Nothing wrong with taking your mind off the attack, which is probably on loop in your head."

"How did you know that?"

He leaned back against the pillows and stared at the ceiling. "Because it's natural in the case of an assault. I had the same response after my first mission with the SEALs. Much as we know that people have a primitive side, violence is corrosive to all of us. If it persists, I can hook you up with someone…" Shit, no he couldn't. She was Canadian. "I'm sure you have therapists north of the border. And if the memories start interrupting your sleep or other regular patterns, then you should make an appointment."

"Sheriff—ah, what should I call you?"

"Grayson," he said, smiling in the dark room.

"Seriously, what's your title?"

"I'm a detective." As much as he loved sitting here talking with her, she needed to get some sleep. "I'll explain when you're feeling better. Until then, get some rest."

"I can't. You're right, the attack is like a loop in my head. I tried reading but kept repeating the same sentence over and over again. Normally, I fall asleep with the TV on but that's not working either."

He had half a notion to get dressed and head to the hotel, but that would be stepping over the line for sure. "Take the pain relievers. They'll help you sleep."

She sighed. "There's a problem."

"Problem, as in?"

"One I can't discuss."

He sat upright, the comforter sliding off his bare chest. "You can discuss it with me. Out with it." She didn't answer. "Holly, what's the damn problem?"

"It's embarrassing and something you don't talk about in polite company."

If she considered him polite, he'd hate to see her definition of abrupt. "Can't be worse than catching you reading those erotic books."

"I have to drink water to get the pills down."

He wasn't following. "Yeah, and?"

She sighed. "I'm dying of thirst."

"Didn't the hotel bring you the water and juice?"

"Yes, they did."

"Then drink something!" *What the hell.*

Holly huffed. "Easy for you to say. You can walk to the bathroom."

Shiiiiit. It never even crossed his damn mind. She couldn't walk after the attack, nor hop. The pain had to be far worse now with the swelling. She could have asked Barb for help, but no, not Holly. She'd suffer in silence.

"Jesus, give me twenty minutes. I'll be there."

"What? No!"

Ivy had broken her ankle when she was a teenager. The

crutches were in the basement. He tucked the phone to his ear and vaulted from bed, swiping his jeans from the chair beneath the window and pulling them up his legs.

"Take the meds right now and drink as much as you can. I'll be there soon."

"That—is not necessary, officer."

"It's Grayson," he growled, then hung up.

* * * *

Fifteen minutes later, he strode into the hotel, took the stairs and ran down the hall to the Presidential Suite. He didn't bother knocking and used the key card she'd given him.

"You're crazy," she said as he stormed into the bedroom and placed the crutches on the guest chair.

"I am so damn sorry. Let me see the leg."

The lamp illuminated the room in a tranquil glow, but he halted mid-step. Holly had managed to get her clothes off and wore a see-through black negligee. The suitcase sat on the bed beside her. She must have asked one of the hotel staff to move it there so she could access the contents.

Holly swept the bedsheet aside and he got the adult version of her gorgeous legs. From her luscious hip to her fucking cute toes.

He ignored his raging pulse and placed his palm over the knee. Hot. Very hot. "Have you been icing it?"

"I did but the ice melted. I didn't want to bother anyone."

Surprised? Not. He growled and reached for the phone.

"This is a hotel, *Holly*. You're supposed to bother them." When the registration desk answered, he ordered more ice.

"Did you take the pills?" He saw the bottle of ibuprofen sitting on the bedside table and two empty bottles of water.

"I did, but if you don't mind, I need..."

He could have just as easily given her the crutches, but instead, he slipped his hands under her warm body and picked her up, then turned for the bathroom. This time, he needed more oxygen than his chest could produce because that damn negligee was a piece of fucking art as far as he was concerned. And what lay beneath were amazing breasts that would fill even his large palms.

He settled her near the toilet and switched on the light as he exited and drew the door closed behind him.

"Thank you," she said quietly.

Holly didn't need to be grateful, he did. Seeing her pretty features, her mussed curls and gorgeous little body in that nightie, rocked him to the core. His heart raced like he'd run the O course at N.A.B. Coronado.

While she was in the bathroom, the hotel staff delivered the ice and he exchanged it for the bucket of water. He considered dropping a few cubes down his pants to cool his throbbing cock. All the ingredients for making love to her were present: a hotel room, king bed, low lighting, and a woman that fired him up like none he could remember. Except he wore a badge, and she was an injured victim.

Grayson heard the toilet flush, and the tap go on and then off a few seconds later. He retraced his steps and opened the bathroom door. He found her palming the vanity for balance next to the toilet with her brow scrunched.

"Don't worry, the meds will kick in shortly." He took a step toward her, and Holly lifted her hand in a gesture for him to stop. "What's wrong?"

"Woozy." She blinked. "It's the head."

"Do you feel nauseous?"

His answer came quickly enough. Holly clutched her stomach, leaned over the toilet and heaved, expelling mainly liquid. He wrapped his arm around her hips to stabilize her, then held her hair back. Another violent round gripped his girl. Pills on an empty stomach, and the dehydration didn't help.

"I've got ya, sweetheart."

Holly groaned and gripped the toilet seat. After four

more harsh bouts, her shaky fingers flushed the toilet. She straightened and leaned against him.

What if she had an internal bleed? "I don't like this. I should take you to the hospital."

"No." She pointed at the sink.

He couldn't force her to go. Then again, he was far bigger than her. She wouldn't be happy with him if he manhandled her into the truck. Grayson helped her shift to the sink so she could rinse her mouth.

"Let's get you back to bed."

Holly wrapped an arm around his neck as he lifted her into his arms. This time, he didn't support the left knee properly. It flexed and she cried out.

Grayson carried her to the bed and gently set her on the mattress, propping the pillows behind her back.

After applying the ice, he said, "I'll be right back."

He quickly left the suite and found the snack vending machine, purchasing two granola bars. She needed to keep the meds down.

Gray returned to the suite. "Here," he said, unwrapping the soft granola bar and broke off a piece. "Eat some of this."

"I'm not hungry."

He sat on the mattress next to her hip. "Holly, you expelled the meds. I can't give you more unless you can keep this down. You need something in your stomach first." He lifted the bite-sized piece to her mouth. "Down the hatch, sweetheart."

Holly eyed him as if he was trying to feed her poison. "I thought we were friends."

Gray shook his head at her and grinned. "We are. Now open."

She gave him a wary stare but took the piece of granola bar and popped it in her mouth. As she chewed, he broke off another piece.

"Zero to ten, how's the headache?"

"Two."

Bullshit. "Holly," he drawled, knowing she was lying.

She crossed her arms over her chest. "Eight." She paused for a second. "Ten."

"Here. Another bite."

She plucked the piece from his fingers and tossed it in her mouth. "Detective, were you injured during your service?"

"Nothing serious." The AC in the room clicked on, interrupting the peaceful ambiance. "Few torn ligaments and a broken wrist."

"Why did you leave the Navy?"

He unscrewed the cap from the water bottle and offered it to her. After she had a small sip, he handed her another chunk of the granola bar.

"Felt like the right time."

Holly tilted her head a little as if analyzing his generic answer.

He cleared his throat. "I didn't want to leave. I would have easily signed up for another three years but in the back of my mind, I knew one day I'd have to return to the farmstead. Mom had died. Jumping from military life to a civilian takes some time, so I left and joined the sheriff's office."

He offered her the last piece of the bar. Instead of taking it from his hand, she opened her mouth. His heart thumped wildly and he held his breath, their gazes locked as he placed the food between her pretty lips.

Time seemed to stand still. Why had she done that? Instead of backing away, he softly trailed his thumb along her delicate jaw. The need to kiss her raged through him like a ferocious storm.

Holly's dainty fingers slid around his wrist and her lips lifted with a faint smile. "I'm sure your family is grateful you're home. That you're safe," she said barely above a whisper.

"Yeah, they are." To disguise his moment of weakness, he placed the back of his hand to her cheek as if checking her temperature. "How do you feel?"

"Nausea is gone."

"Good." He dumped two tablets in her hand, and she swallowed the pain relievers with some water. "They should stay down this time."

Holly cupped his hand between hers and innocently held it between her full breasts. "You would have made a great physician."

Like she'd done before, her actions and words reflected her honesty. There was no sexual ploy or intention to flirt. How long could he ignore the way his heart ached in her presence? He loved being near her. The closeness. The intimacy of their contact. She was the only woman who'd ever affected him this way. He could hardly believe it.

Holly's lids drooped with exhaustion. She needed rest. "I want you to lay down and roll onto your right side."

She followed his orders and muffled a groan when her knee shifted.

Her pain should be his priority but his damn mouth dried. He'd seen plenty of his team brother's asses, but day-um. The negligee's thong didn't cover a damn thing on his little patient's sweet, smooth butt.

Keeping his mind on the task, he lifted her left leg and placed a pillow between her knees to alleviate the stress. "How does that feel?"

"Better," she whispered.

"Holly, you probably have a patellar fracture. At least they'd give you stronger meds for the pain at the hospital." He placed his palm on her hip, not to grope but because he wanted to comfort her. This woman ignited a fierce possessiveness in him that he didn't think existed. There was no question he wanted to protect her, but it was far deeper than that.

Holly hugged the pillow and shoved her face in the downy center. "Thank you for bringing the crutches."

He figured she'd ignore his request. Grayson turned off the lamp on the bedside table then sat on the edge of the mattress. "You're not scared, are you?"

"No," she said. "I always feel safe here."

Interesting choice of words. Did that mean she didn't feel safe at home? This wasn't the time to chase that lead down the rabbit hole.

"Close your eyes."

"I feel guilty for tearing you away from your family."

"They're farmers, they sleep like the dead until the rooster crows."

There was a long pause before she mumbled, "Are we really friends?"

"Yeah, of course, we are." The question reminded him that she hadn't called while she'd been here. If nothing else, he wanted her to know he'd come if she needed him. Although the sentiment made him think of Erika, there was no comparison. "I'm a phone call away, Holly. Any time."

"You're just like them."

He gently caressed her curvy hip. "Like who?" he asked quietly.

She took a few deep even breaths, then said, "Unforgettable."

The cadence of her breathing told him she'd fallen asleep. Grayson carefully covered her with the blankets, then moved to a chair on the other side of the bed so he could see her face. He sat in the dark while she slept to make sure her nausea didn't return and progress to vomiting. Least that's what he told himself to stay a little longer.

He wondered whether she thought about him as much as she was on his mind. Grayson watched her sleep and dozed off with her voice repeating "unforgettable" in his mind.

When he opened his eyes, the sun lightened the horizon, and he closed the heavy drapes to keep the room dark. Holly slept soundly. It was probably safe to head home. Family would be up soon. He could get some chores done in the barn before he headed to work. He wandered into the living room and scooped the notepad with the resort's name and logo from an end table and wrote Holly a note.

When you wake up, order some breakfast. Eat it, even if you're not hungry. Then take some more pain medication. I'll be back later to check on my patient.

Grayson

He returned to the bedroom and left the note under the pills, plus added two bottles of water and an orange juice within her reach. Holly looked so small in the big king-sized bed. An overwhelming sensation to cradle her against his body scratched at his conscience.

"I never thought I could miss a woman, but I've missed you so damn much, sweetheart."

* * * *

As Grayson drove north on the I-5, the sun breached the Cascade Mountains under a clear, blue sky. There was nothing more beautiful than a Pacific Northwest summer morning. Within a short time, he steered the pickup down the gravel drive then parked in front of the old Victorian. Taking the front steps two at a time, he inhaled the scent of tilled earth, cedar trees, and manure.

"Love it."

Ivy stood in the big country kitchen painted in a cheery yellow. His mom had liked the color, so Dad spent a weekend changing it from the dismal blue to yellow when Grayson was around eight. His grandfather had built the large, square island topped with a thick hardwood counter. Ground zero for baked goods, family meal prep, and dozens of jelly jars over the years.

"You get called out?" she asked, standing next to the stove, bacon crackling in the cast iron pan.

"Something like that."

"I thought I heard you come home around midnight. When did you leave?"

"Around three-thirty." He toed off his cowboy boots and

changed into his barn boots, aka rubber boots.

"But you're not in uniform," she said, facing him and holding nine-inch tongs.

"Follow-up. When's breakfast?"

"Another twenty minutes. Jackson's collecting the eggs. Let him know, would ya."

"Will do." During summer, the main door, made of a gorgeous slab of red oak, was never closed once they were all up. The screen door squeaked when he edged it open to leave.

Dad wandered into the kitchen and collected the morning newspaper from the counter, tucking it under his right arm, then headed for the coffee pot. "Morning, Gray. You get a call out last night? Heard you leave around three-thirty."

One thing was for sure, Jackson had zero chance of sneaking out of this house when he was seventeen. "Yeah, just a follow-up on a case I'm working on."

He sure as hell wasn't going to admit he jumped out of bed to help a woman pee in the middle of the night.

"Cole with you?" Ivy asked, turning the strips of bacon.

"Nope. Pretty sure he was at home having wet dreams about some woman." He grinned, knowing which woman that was, but his sister had a different response.

The scowl on Ivy's face was priceless and told him a lot.

"I'm sure he wasn't just dreaming about it," she snarled.

He eyed their old man, who didn't say a word but grinned while he poured the dark roast into his favorite morning mug. Dad might be a senior with a bad ticker, but he wasn't senile.

"Yeah, you're right," Grayson said, adding a little fuel to his sister's fire. "Maybe this one will make an honest man out of him."

Ivy abruptly turned toward the stove, her long, blonde ponytail lashing out like a horse tail slaps at flies. "I highly doubt that."

The bread popped from the toaster and his sister

buttered the slices with vengeance, the crumbs jumping ship to save their lives.

Grayson hadn't been around to witness the torment his best friend must have gone through, hiding his feelings from Ivy.

"The farmstead would be a great place for a wedding."

She slammed the knife on the counter and turned, her blue eyes snapping with jealousy. "We don't do weddings. Who is this woman?"

Dad took a seat at the head of the old maple kitchen table they'd all been reared at. "I'm sure she's a sweet gal, honey." He glanced at Grayson and winked. "Cole turned out to be a fine man. Surprised it took this long for some woman to put a ring on his finger."

The anger melted from her brow, and she blinked a couple times. "I didn't know he was serious about anyone." She plated the toast and stuffed it in the oven to keep warm. "Good for him," she said weakly.

Grayson felt like a dick, but Ivy had to experience the loss before she'd admit she had feelings for his best friend. Cole and his sister needed to get on the same page and stop wasting time. If it meant stirring the pot a little for their sakes, he'd gladly use a shovel.

As he walked across the lawn toward the barns, the grass glistened with fine dew. The cattle called in the fields, and he heard a racket from the chicken shed as Jackson collected the eggs.

Grayson used to think palm trees and babes in bikinis were heaven when he'd return to San Diego from his deployments. At thirty-four, he'd come home and realized the Brooks farmstead, where six generations had tilled the earth and raised livestock, was paradise.

Holly slid into his thoughts. As a victim, she was part of an active investigation. Eventually, he'd catch the douchebag who'd attacked her. It would probably happen sooner rather than later. She'd thank him. He'd say, *"You're welcome."* Case closed. Their connection severed.

Grayson strode past the big old oak Holly had stood next to at one point when they'd spent the day together. An image he couldn't shake but needed to, because a woman like her would never trust a guy like him if she knew his track record. He didn't trust himself. Keeping his conduct professional but friendly maintained a healthy separation.

Maybe he'd slid close to the line last night, but she'd needed his help. He'd never refuse her that.

Grayson knew his shortcomings. If he stepped over the line and tried to kid himself that he was capable of a relationship, he'd only fuck it up.

CHAPTER ELEVEN

Around noon, Lt. Kline stood in the doorway of his office. "Brooks. Sterling."

Grayson and Cole shared a look then headed for the boss' cave. Like Cole, the lieutenant had joined the sheriff's department at twenty-one and worked patrol for years. According to Cole, he had great rapport with the community, always involved in local groups to make their corner of Washington State safer.

Grayson followed Cole into the lieutenant's office.

"I just got off the phone with the manager of Neon Lights," Kline said. "The latest attack got picked up by the media. This is the type of press we wanted to avoid. It's not good for the resort or any local business. What do you have so far on the case?"

Cole took the lead. "We believe the muggings and thefts at the resort are part of a bigger operation, but we don't have any strong leads yet."

Kline pursed his lips. "I don't see a victim statement from the latest incident. Where is it?"

That was on Grayson, and he jumped in with an explanation. "Miss McNeela was injured in the attack. She's staying at the resort for a couple days to recuperate. I'm going back there to collect the statement today."

Kline sat in his office chair. "We need to stick a fork in this ring, and soon. The Neon Lights manager is willing to back a reward for any information associated with the incidents at the resort. I'm going to launch a social media blitz from this office."

"No honor among thieves," Grayson said. "A reward could

open a few leads."

The resort wasn't the only place the snatch and grabs were happening. Although it wasn't confirmed the muggings and burglaries were associated, he and Cole had mapped out all current incidents.

"We're dealing with a ten-mile radius," Cole stated. "Gray and I plotted the crimes by similarity but there isn't a clear indication of a hub. Victim statements have identified younger male assailants, but not the same description. Whoever is running this operation has a handful of guys working for them."

Kline rested his forearms on the desk. "I want to see the latest victim statement, Brooks."

Grayson nodded. "I'll head out and talk with Miss McNeela."

As he and Cole returned to Gray's desk, his partner asked, "Sure you don't want me to interview her?"

Grayson retrieved his cell from the desk and closed his laptop. "Yeah, I'm sure."

Where some cops got lazy when it came to routine fitness, Cole worked out every day. He crossed his arms over a buff chest and grinned. "Guess you don't want me tagging along, so I'll drop by the farmstead store to grab a bite and meet up with you later."

"You might wanna get lunch somewhere else today."

Cole's dark features tightened with suspicion. "Why?"

Gray shrugged, retrieving his ball cap from the desk. "Ivy's not in a good mood."

"Any particular reason?"

"Beats me," he said grinning.

Cole gritted his teeth. "You sonofabitch. What did you do?"

Grayson slapped his partner on the shoulder and winked. "I—didn't do a damn thing. You, on the other hand, seem to have a reputation as a guy that women like my sister don't approve of."

His best friend's jaw slackened. "What does that mean, exactly?"

"Sorry, buddy. You're gonna have to find the answer to that yourself."

* * * *

Cole parked the patrol car between other vehicles in the gravel lot fronting Brooks Farmstead Store. The summer sun boosted the temperature to eighty-five degrees and guests ate at picnic tables scattered on the manicured lawn.

A few years ago, Ivy had the foresight to include the farmstead on the state tourist sites. She didn't offer a sit-down restaurant service. Guests could purchase a fresh loaf of bread, locally made cheese and deli meats, with a couple of different salads made fresh each day. Two tureens of soup, recipes handed down from her mother, steeped on a serve-yourself counter next to the till. The Brooks' farm grew apples and berries, vegetables, and raised organic meat, but they relied on other farmers to supply cherries and other fruit that Washington State was famous for.

Tourists and locals alike shopped at the farmstead because the food was pesticide-free and tasted great, but it was the little blonde powerhouse known as Ivy Brooks that added to the family's business success. Cole still thought of her as a Brooks, although she used her married surname, Perez, as her legal identification.

Cole stepped aside as an elderly couple exited the shop with groceries and a bottle of white wine sticking out the top of the paper bag. He recognized the label from a local vintner.

"Must be a good place to eat if law enforcement comes here," the old man said with a grin.

Cole nodded. "You won't be disappointed."

Wearing a short-sleeved uniform shirt, the cool air struck Cole's skin as he entered the market that Ivy kept at a lower temperature for the produce.

"Hey, Cole," Arlene greeted, smiling at him from behind the cash register.

Arlene had worked full-time at the shop for five years. Ivy relied on her more and more as popularity of the store grew. Sporting a huge belly, her third child was due in under a month.

"Your usual?" she asked.

He surveyed the shop. "Thanks, but not yet. Where is she?"

Arlene thumbed a direction over her shoulder. "In the cutting room. Samuel butchered some chickens this morning. Ivy's cleaning them up and packaging them for tomorrow's special."

"Mind if I—"

"Nope. You know the way," Arlene said, smiling.

He pushed through the swinging doors at the rear of the shop, passed through the cool storage area with a line of fridges and cold storage shelving, then walked into a stark, white room.

Ivy stood behind a waist-high processing table. Butchered chickens and plastic bags were lined up neatly for packaging. Most men would probably back out quickly at the sight of a woman wearing a plastic apron smeared with blood, a meat cleaver raised in the air and a random chicken feather clinging to her hair. But not him.

"Cole?" She lowered the cleaver, giving the carcass in front of her a brief reprieve. "What's up?"

He walked around the table and plucked the stray feather from her blonde hair. "Dropped by for lunch."

"Noon already? Huh. Guess I'm behind schedule as usual. I have to finish packaging these birds." She'd already bagged and tagged twenty chickens that sat on a metal cart against the wall behind her.

"Take fifteen minutes and join me."

She had a tendency to avoid looking him in the eyes. He'd always thought it was because she didn't like what she saw.

If Grayson wasn't jerking his chain about Ivy watching him when his attention was elsewhere, he'd been wrong. Gray's sister didn't have much choice this time, because he invaded her space, standing only six inches away.

Slowly, her gaze strayed up his chest and locked on his face. "I'm not done yet. After this, I have to send out a notification to our mailing list about the sale tomorrow." She stepped back a pace. "Did you come alone?"

"Gray's working on a case."

She glanced toward the cart. "I should get those into the fridge." She swiveled, snapped the gloves off her hands and threw them in the garbage. "Dad mentioned you were coming over this weekend to help with the cattle."

He didn't mind helping out at the farm. He'd done it for years. "Yeah, that's right."

"You shouldn't feel obligated to help out around here. Grayson's home and he, Dad, and Ron can handle things."

Ron was the only hired full-time farmhand. Like Arlene, he'd been with them for several years.

"Is there a particular reason you don't want me around?"

She gave the cart a shove. "No. I mean, you probably have places and people you want to spend your time with."

People? What people, he wondered. Ivy was acting edgier today than she normally did.

He followed her into the room where refrigeration units lined the left wall. She pushed the cart in front of one of the units and he slid the glass door open, then she piled the bagged chickens onto the shelves. Once she was done, he slid the door closed.

"What's going on, Ivy?" He gripped her upper arm, stopping her from running away. "You won't have lunch with me. You won't look at me, and now you're telling me I should stay away."

She crossed her arms and tilted her chin upward. "It's none of my business, but if you're getting serious with someone, you should spend time with her, not waste time here at the farm. I need to get back to work."

"Hey, I don't know where you got the idea I'm seeing somebody."

"Kinda shocked me too. When Gray got home this morning a little after five, I thought you'd been working a case with him. I should have known better. You're the king of one-night stands. But when he mentioned the farmstead would be a great place for a wedding, I figured you'd been talking with him. You should bring her around sometime."

Unpacking everything she said took him a second, but he addressed the most important issue first. "You misunderstood. I'm not getting married."

She shrugged. "Like I said, none of my business."

He followed her back into the processing room. "Let's get one thing straight—"

"Don't give me that *cop* tone, Cole Sterling." Ivy grilled him with an angry look once she'd rounded the table. "Who you screw is none of my business."

"You're acting like it is."

She quickly worked her hands into a new pair of gloves, picked up the cleaver and cut a carcass clean in two. "Don't care."

Standing on the opposite side of the table, he took the chance of losing a digit and placed his hands on the sterilized surface. "Then why do you look like you want to cleave me in two?" He'd never seen her this agitated before. "Put that weapon down so we can talk."

"Don't worry, wouldn't think of cutting off something that brings so many women pleasure."

She lifted her arm in the air for another killing strike on the already deceased chicken, and he clenched her wrist. "Since when do you give a shit about the women I see?"

"I don't. Get out, so I can get my work done."

"No, Ivy." He gently lowered her arm. "We're overdue for this conversation."

"About what?"

145

"Why the hell do you think I've been hanging around this place for so fucking long?"

Her brow creased into fine lines. "Because Gray couldn't be here."

"Really?" Granted, he'd kept his desires to himself out of respect. She'd always been friendly to him but in a platonic way. She filled her days with raising a son and running the farmstead. She was the last woman on the planet who'd dump her kid in someone else's lap just to hook-up for sex. "I came back because of you."

Ivy released the cleaver, but he didn't let go of her wrist.

"Me? I know I've begged for your help a handful of times over the years when we were buried in work, but I didn't expect you to keep donating your time to us."

"I'm not talking about lending a hand around the farm. I'm saying I wanted to see you."

She snorted. "Yeah, sure."

He couldn't help but chuckle at the doubt slathered across her expression just like Grayson said she'd respond. "I kept my distance out of respect. By the time I came home after college, you'd lost your husband and had your hands full with a baby. I'm not that much of a womanizing dick that I couldn't see you needed space and time to figure things out. Once you'd found your stride, you treated me like another brother."

Her nose wrinkled a little like she always did when something ruffled her feathers. "Because you treated me like a little sister."

He joined her on the other side of the table. "Believe me, I've never thought of you that way."

Ivy's pretty blue eyes sparkled under the fluorescent lights. "You never *saw* me at all. You were too busy screwing random women. Some of them were my friends, ya know."

He rubbed his jaw and groaned as if she'd clenched her fist and served an uppercut. Guess he deserved that. "I'm not a monk."

"No kidding."

Tension built not only with her prickly response but below his belt. "I'm sorry that screwing your friends made you jealous."

Ivy's eyes narrowed to slits. "I didn't say that."

"Grayson's right. I have been gutless. Now I have to admit to your asshole brother that I've been sleeping with surrogates instead of going after the woman I really want."

Her brows arched so high they formed pyramids. "You're on crack if you think I'm like those sluts." Ivy pressed her palm against his chest and shoved, with little result. "Go catch a criminal or something."

He cupped her gloved fingers with his hand. "If you want to play a few rounds of catch and release that's fine, but that's not what I want."

Ivy rolled her eyes. "Cole, I don't know what's gotten into you, but I'm not stepping in just because your steady stream of weekend sex kittens has dried up. If you want someone to talk to, fine, I'll listen—"

"Great. This Saturday after I'm finished working with your dad. Six o'clock. I'll bring a change of clothes and shower here."

Rattled, she glanced around like she'd been cornered in a small cell with a wild animal. "What?"

He wasn't giving her an inch. Not a single, fucking inch. If he was barking up the wrong tree and she didn't want him, then she could look him in the eyes and tell him.

"You and me, Ivy. No Grayson. No Wendy. No distractions. Just you and me." And he headed for the exit.

* * * *

Ivy stood with a loose jaw and tingling nerves, watching the handsome Cole Sterling leave the room. His long gait and broad shoulders made her knees weak, especially in his darn uniform. His hard jaw, piercing eyes, and jet-black hair boiled her blood any time they bumped into each other, which was too often.

What the hell had just happened? After all these years of secretly lusting over her brother's best friend, suddenly she'd agreed to a date?

This morning when Grayson intimated Cole might be serious about someone, jealousy had gripped her by the throat. She'd always had a crush on Cole. When he'd returned from college and the teenage hormones were long gone, replaced with an overabundance of masculinity, her fantasies always placed him in the starring role.

She grasped the edge of the table for balance. How the heck was she supposed to keep her wits about her? Maybe Cole was going through some crazy phase, and if that were the case, she needed to keep her priorities straight and a clear head.

Shaken but on a deadline, she bagged the whole chickens until her nerves stopped jumping before daring to pick up the boning knife and cut the remainder of the birds into breasts, wings, drumsticks, and backs.

Ivy quickly washed her hands after storing the poultry and sanitizing the prep table. Before heading to the office to email their clients, she checked in with Arlene.

"Everything okay out here?" Ivy asked.

The curvy brunette stopped unloading the shipment of parsley they'd received this morning. "No problems." She tilted her head in question. "You look a little out of sorts."

"Me? No, I'm just behind schedule, that's all."

"Cole seemed like he was on a mission when he walked in here. When he left, he didn't even stop for lunch. You two have a fight or something?"

Arlene wasn't just an employee, they'd been friends since grade school. Ivy sighed. "No, not a fight. He asked me for a date, Arlene. I mean, what gives?"

Her friend laughed. "Hugh and I had a bet going when that would finally happen. Guess I lost."

Hugh and Arlene had married five years ago and were

expecting their third child.

"A bet. What kind of bet?"

She chuckled. "When he'd finally make his move. Pretty obvious to us he had the hots for you, honey."

Ivy crossed her arms. "As if. He wasn't exactly moping while screwing Millie, Barb, and Kate."

Arlene scoffed at her. "Gimme a break. Everyone's screwed those three. They're like a lemonade stand. Throw 'em a quarter and they'll juice a guy, no questions asked."

Ivy choked at her description, then burst into laughter. "Oh my God, that is so true."

Arlene leaned over and grabbed the last two bunches of parsley from the box, setting them in the display case. "They're our friends, and I'm not judging. I mean, you can't blame them. Cole kinda falls into the upper hottie echelon. He turns heads. A little booze, a little flirting. What single guy is gonna say no to sex?"

"I suppose, but what does that make me if we're seen together?"

Arlene palmed her very pregnant belly. "That's the whole point, isn't it?"

Ivy shook her head. "Not following." She picked up the empty box from the floor so Arlene wouldn't have to bend over again.

"He's not picking you up in a bar and whisking you back to his bed of sensual sin, then ignoring your calls the next day like he did with them. Cole asked you out on a date. He wants to be seen with you. Listen, you've always liked him, and I think he's carried a flame for you for a long time. You just didn't want to see it."

"Or maybe I didn't want to get involved with someone who's not interested in anything more than an orgasm."

"You're about to find out, but if I were in your shoes, I'd have one helluva hard time refusing that rockin' hard body. So, do all of us happily married women a solid and follow your heart. If it leads to the bedroom, then ride that cop until he's breathless because as I understand it, he really knows what he's doing."

A couple in their thirties wandered into the shop and Ivy lowered her voice. "The last time someone tried to rock my world, it was totally anti-climactic, and I got pregnant. I'll throw this in recycling. Be in the office if you need me."

Crazy talk. Reality couldn't possibly be as amazing as her vivid fantasies of Cole. She'd stripped that man so many times in her mind, it was indecent.

But why now? Why had Cole suddenly decided to make a move?

She retrieved her cell from her back pocket and Grayson picked up on the second ring.

"What's up, Ivy?"

"Same question. What did you say to Cole?"

He chuckled. "He come by the store for lunch?"

"No, ya big jerk. He came by to ask me for a date. Out of the blue, and the only thing that's changed around here is you."

"Hmm. Good for him."

"Graaay. You're involved in this somehow."

"Guilty as charged. Love ya, sis. I gotta go. Talk later."

The call disconnected. She'd skin the truth out of her brother if she had to, but for now, she needed to send an email to her clients, then make a quick trip into town for a new panty and bra set. No way was she going on a date with Cole Sterling wearing cotton, waist-high undies.

CHAPTER TWELVE

G rayson knocked on the door of the Presidential Suite. A muffled "Come in," sounded from inside the room.

Holly sat lengthwise on the couch, a pillow propped under the injured knee. The crutches lay on the carpet next to her. Part of him was sincerely relieved the black negligee had been exchanged for a yellow tank top and white jean skirt.

"Afternoon, Miss McNeela. How's the leg?"

She waved him closer. "See for yourself, Dr. Brooks."

He chuckled and crossed to the coffee table, sitting on the edge, then revealed what he carried behind his back. "Thought one of these might cheer you up."

"Are you kidding!" She grinned and accepted the salted caramel milkshake from his hands.

The look of bliss on the woman's face when she slid her lips around the straw and sucked had him shifting uncomfortably to relieve the pressure behind his zipper. Watching her pure, simple pleasure made his goddamn day.

"This is way above and beyond civic duty," she said.

"Yeah, well. It's my job to remember small details."

She cleared her throat and smiled. "Of course."

"Did you eat breakfast?"

"Wasn't very hungry, but yes. And I took the pain relievers. To be honest, without them it's unbearable."

Grayson removed the ice packs around her knee and found what he suspected. "Not much better than last night, Holly."

"Were you expecting a miracle?"

He shifted his gaze to her face. *Jesus, he was on one hell of a slippery slope.* She held the plastic cup in both hands, grinning at him as she sucked the goodness through the straw. *Fucking adorable.* Something in her eyes nailed him square in the heart. He reminded himself to remain professional but the more he committed to keeping his distance, the more he felt a distinct weakening in his willpower.

"How was the knee when you moved to the couch?"

The straw slid from her mouth, and she licked the cream from her lips, causing him to swallow thickly. He had a lot of experience with women who knew how to flirt with a guy. Holly wasn't giving him any cues. Her action was meaningless but struck the target, nonetheless.

"Ten out of ten on the ouch-o-meter, but the good news is I'm hungry now and thought I'd go downstairs for some fresh air and eat lunch in the restaurant while the ibuprofen is at its peak."

"Sounds reasonable, but first I need you to write me a statement of what happened during the attack."

Holly shifted onto her right side and reached behind her. "Like this one?" She offered him a pad of lined paper.

He took her pre-written report and quickly read the contents. She'd covered all the bases from the time she left the hotel lobby to when and where she'd been attacked. Although dark, she'd given a description of the guy, including height, approximate weight, and hair color.

"He had shoulder-length blond hair?" he questioned.

"It happened so fast. I'm sure there's more, but that's all I can remember for now."

He tore the sheet from the pad. "It's a start. This might match up with another witness or victim statement. What about a vehicle?"

"I heard one as I got to my feet, but I can't swear to a make or color."

"Did he say anything to you?"

Her gaze turned inward as if fingering through her memories. "He bowled me over. I went down and lost my grip on the suitcase. When I hit my head on the curb, things got a little fuzzy. He grabbed my hair and yanked, then asked, *'Where's the purse?'* I remember saying, *'My bag,'* hoping he'd just leave, which he did. He grabbed my luggage and ran. Security came from every direction. I guess that's why he left it behind."

Grayson nodded and gave her back the report to add what she'd just told him to her statement.

When she was finished, he stood, tucking the paper in his shirt pocket. "Okay, let's get you downstairs."

Holly blinked up at him. "I was a little out of it last night and embarrassed this morning."

"Why's that?" He grinned, seeing her squirm and color flood her cheeks.

"After serving in the Special Forces, you must think I'm a big baby."

He didn't see her as weak. Just the opposite. In fact, he wished she'd rely on him more. But if she did, his past experiences proved he'd shut down and step away like with every other woman he'd encountered.

He didn't consciously make the decision to feel that way. The spontaneous reaction became glaringly evident while he was in the teams. The idea of belonging to one woman irritated him. Sex was fine, but the second a woman tried to initiate anything more, he cut them off.

He couldn't risk that happening with Holly.

"No, I don't think that at all," he stated flatly.

He wondered for the hundredth time whether someone else loved her. Wouldn't he be here? Maybe he worked out of town. Holly didn't wear a ring. Nowadays, that didn't mean much. But if there was a man in her life, why the fuck wouldn't he put a ring on her finger to tell every other guy to stay the hell away? That's what he'd do.

Holly stared at her legs. "You intervened when that drunk

bothered me. Stayed with me when I was stranded. Let me lean on you when Dad's vessel sank. Brought me crutches in the middle of the night." Her gaze slid to his. "I hope you know how grateful I am, Detective."

He didn't need her appreciation. "They say bad things happen in threes. You're over the limit. Unless you want to keep meeting like this, keep your ass out of trouble."

She rolled her eyes. "I promise I'll try not to get mugged again."

Holly's sassy, smart, and attractive characteristics appealed to him, but she was also gentle, thoughtful, and maybe a little naïve to the dangers of the world around her. The idea that no one looked out for her gnawed at his gut.

A pair of white flip-flops sat on the floor next to the sofa. He picked them up and palmed her ankle as he slid them onto her feet.

"You sure you want to head downstairs?"

She shifted her right foot onto the floor and eased her wounded leg off the couch, then sat up. Each time Holly moved the injured knee, she winced.

"Yes, because I'd like to buy you lunch if that's allowed."

This woman never failed to impress him. Her knee had to be throbbing, but she was going to bite the bullet. "You don't owe me anything. If that's the reason, then you can keep your ass on the couch."

The sweet smile melted from her features. "It's not the only reason."

Jesus, he hadn't meant to sound like an asshole, and he hated that he'd wiped the smile from her face. "Holly, I just meant I don't want you to put extra strain on that knee for me."

"I understand," she said in a serious tone.

No, she didn't understand at all. Grayson wouldn't refuse lunch if it meant spending a few more minutes in her company. He'd been on a Holly-free diet for the last two weeks and didn't like it one bit.

"All right, let's see what happens when you stand."

Holly collected the crutches and leaned them against the couch. Putting her weight on her good leg, she stood up.

"I could use some fresh air," she said, then bit her lower lip to stop herself from yelping with pain.

Yup, just as he suspected. With the shift in gravity and blood flowing past the inflammation, it caused a lot of pain. Enough was enough. He'd done it her way, now he was taking the helm.

"You'll get some fresh air while I drive you to the hospital. This is no longer negotiable. I will deal with the paperwork, and I'll call your medical insurance provider. All you have to do is sit still while the doc takes a look."

"Thought you were my doctor," she said, narrowing her pretty eyes.

No more stalling. "Miss McNeela, you can come peacefully or…"

"Wait!"

"Sorry, but we're going."

"My milkshake."

He grinned and picked up the shake from the coffee table while she adjusted the crutches under her arms. "Think of it as a hostage situation. You get the ice cream back when you're in my patrol car."

Her gaze flicked from the plastic cup to his eyes. "That's playing hardball."

"You can report me later. Lead the way." He opened the suite's door, and she crutched her way into the hall, then paused and lowered her head.

"Holly?" He placed a hand on her back, but she wouldn't look at him. Without stabilization for the knee, the motion on the crutches was too much.

"I'll go to the doctor tomorrow," she said weakly. All the color drained from her face.

"Fuck that!"

Her head snapped up and her eyes rounded.

"Here." He handed her the to-go cup. "Hold the crutches in one hand."

She did as he asked, and he scooped her into his arms.

"Oh my, God," she choked out as her knee shifted.

"We need to stabilize that joint first."

"Please. One more day with ice packs will help," she said when he swung around to go back inside.

"Holly, cut this shit out! You're going to the damn hospital."

Tears welled in her eyes, but she opened the door, and he carried her back into the room and placed her on the couch.

He had an emergency first aid kit in his car with splints and wraps. "I'll be right back."

Within a couple minutes, he returned with the kit and sat on the coffee table. She didn't say anything while he used two C-curves and wrapped the splints to secure the knee and stop the joint from flexing.

Now she was ready for transport. "Okay, we're going to do this again but I'm going to carry you."

He slid one hand under her thigh, but her fingers gripped his wrist.

"No," she said, staring toward the kitchen instead of him. "You've done enough, Detective," her tone deadly serious. "I've taken up way too much of your time. This isn't in your job description."

She was mad at him. He slid his hand down her bare arm and folded his fingers over her hand. "Sweetheart, I'm sorry I snapped at you. You need that knee x-rayed at a minimum." He paused because he wasn't quite sure whether she was listening. "Holly, if you resist, it means me spending the night, taking you back and forth to the bathroom. Do you want that?" he asked, making sure to keep his tone light.

She glanced at him then put her gaze back on her lap. "I have the crutches."

"You nearly passed out from the pain a few minutes ago."

Her nose twitched.

"Holly, don't lie to me."

"A brief second of light-headedness."

"Yeah, okay. Call it what you want." This little lady wasn't exactly a pushover. "All right, well, let's get some room service and settle in." He looked around. "Got a deck of cards?"

She tilted her head and crossed her arms. "You're being a smartass again."

He shrugged. "Not really, but if you're going to dig your heels in, I don't have a choice."

Maybe she'd agree to strip poker. He'd be up for that. "There's a Seattle Mariners game on tonight."

"I don't watch sports."

Damn. She didn't like sports? *Shit.* Not even that was good enough to divorce her from his future. "You're Canadian. You can't tell me you don't like hockey."

She grilled him with a punitive narrowing of her eyes.

Gray became aware of where he rested his palm on her thigh. Instead of removing his hand, his hidden attraction decided to take the wheel, and he slowly brushed his thumb against her soft, warm skin. "Holly, I'm asking you to go to the hospital for me."

"Okay, I'll go. Don't get cranky again," she grouched.

Gray removed his hand from her leg and forked his fingers to stop himself from cupping her neck and kissing her delicate jaw until he reached the tender flesh below her ear like he wanted.

"Oh, come on. Don't be mad at me." He handed her the crutches, then slid his arms under her legs and behind her back. "Hey, we can always stay, and you can read me a few chapters of your SEAL romance. Apparently, we're pretty hot in bed."

"Very funny." Holly wrapped her arm around his neck. "Lift with your knees."

He snorted. "My kit was heavier than you, and I used to hump that thing for miles."

"Since you mentioned it, did you pick me up a new book?"

Grayson groaned. She was a healthy, attractive woman. His perverted mind went straight to how she relieved her sexual tension. Then, for a cherry on top, wondered what it would be like to watch. He was damn sure it would make his cock hard as fuck and just watching would be torture.

"It'll be a cold day in hell when I buy you a book like that," he said, lifting her off the couch. She only winced this time. Good. The splint was helping.

"You suggested it," she reminded him as they headed for the door.

"I was kidding."

"I think you're curious."

"I don't need to read a book I already know is full of bullshit."

She tipped her shoulder with a little shrug. "How would you know, you've never read one?

"They call it fiction for a reason, Miss McNeela."

They reached the elevator, and she pressed the down button. The teasing twinkle in her eye made him nervous.

"What's the chance of making a pit stop at a bookstore?" she asked.

Was she tormenting him on purpose? "Do I have to?"

"I can only spend so many hours unscrambling the mysteries of ancient languages. Those books are a great distraction."

She could distract herself in a thousand different ways but for some reason, his sensible, level-headed Holly liked books that exaggerated the truth about SEALs, threw in angst, hot sex scenes, and ended in a love story. That wasn't anywhere near the truth. At least it wasn't common. Sex? Definitely. Angst? For sure. Fear? For the wives and girlfriends, it never ended. Divorce? Plenty. Living with a SEAL? Tough. Dealing with combat trauma in all its forms? Fucking brutal.

He'd walked away relatively unscathed, but so many of

his teammates weren't nearly as lucky.

"Why the hell do you like those books, anyway?" he asked as they passed through the lobby. "And don't tell me they have great plots."

A sweet smile touched her lips. "Because they're seductive and the hero never deceives the heroine. No matter what they have to endure, there's always a happy ending."

Grayson reached his cruiser parked by the entrance and set Holly on her feet. He wanted to tell her that life with a special operator wasn't easy. Bursting the bubble of joy she received from her favorite genre served no purpose, but it certainly reminded him that SEALs weren't saints.

Him, most of all.

He opened the passenger door, but she didn't get inside. Instead, she balanced on her right foot and gazed up at him with a thoughtful smile.

"Detective, I realize the novels are a far cry from reality, but they're loved by millions of readers because the heroes are irresistible, flawed but noble, and unforgettable."

Unforgettable. That's what she'd said last night. She'd been exhausted and he doubted she remembered saying it. Ever since she'd parted her lips and let him feed her, a question kept grinding in his gut. Had she slipped up? Sapped from the pain, had she dropped her guard?

All morning that moment had invaded his thoughts. Seductive but sweet.

He saw an opening and took it. "Unforgettable, huh."

"Absolutely."

"Funny." He placed a totally contrived curious expression on his face. "That's what you called me last night."

By the way her eyes rounded, and her jaw loosened, he had his answer.

"I'm sure you misunderstood," she said and quickly piled into the cruiser.

Gray's breathing labored as he shut the passenger door. *Holy fuck!* His pulse roared with excitement. For a split second, he saw it. Desire. Truth.

He wasn't sure if he was truly fucked or truly blessed. His heart seemed to know the answer, because it beat with impatience.

* * * *

While Holly was in the examination room at the urgent care clinic in Mt. Vernon, he called the number on her healthcare card and worked with the receptionist at the clinic's front desk. He gave the Canadian rep a summary of what had happened to Holly and who he was. Grayson had to admit it went down smooth as silk, then he turned the phone over to the receptionist, who discussed details. Everything was covered by the time the gal hung up.

"Detective Brooks?" Grayson turned and a man in his forties said, "I'm Doctor Corning. Orthopedics. If you can join us for a moment."

He followed the doc down a wide hallway and into an examination room. Holly sat on the bed, a nylon support brace with a breathable knee wrapped around her leg.

"Is the patella fractured?" he asked.

Dr. Corning flipped a switch and two x-rays showed on the backlit screen. "It's a fracture. She's lucky the bones aren't displaced. Doesn't require immediate surgery but knee injuries cause plenty of swelling. We also checked her head injury, and I don't see a cause for any long-term issues."

"How long does she have to wear the brace?" he asked.

"Miss McNeela should check in with her regular doctor when she gets home, but I suspect it will take three months for the patella to heal completely. Until then, she can use the crutches. I offered her a prescription for pain relief, but she's refused."

Gray turned his attention to Holly, who shook her head.

"Don't give me that look," he warned. "Doc, write the prescription. It costs pennies, Holly."

"It's not the cost. I don't want opioids. Dr. Corning gave

me a steroid injection. I barely feel the pain."

"The injection will wear off within a few hours." Dr. Corning scribbled on his pad. "This is a mild prescription. Don't take it if the pain is manageable."

Wisely, the doc handed Grayson the paper.

"We'll get it filled on the way out."

"I'm not taking those," Holly said, sitting with her hands folded in her lap.

He got the feeling she didn't like anything that meant losing control. He already knew she wasn't fussy about alcohol. Grayson didn't get the sense she was a prude, but she didn't get her kicks from popping pills. Convincing her to take the ibuprofen was a challenge.

The doctor slipped the prescription pad back into his lab coat pocket. "You were smart to bring her in, Detective. She needs to keep the weight off that leg for at least two weeks. The brace will stabilize the knee. She shouldn't drive. I suggested she take a bus or taxi home."

Grayson didn't understand. "It's her left leg that's injured."

"I drive a standard, remember?"

A standard? She drove an Audi. What the hell was a standard? "You mean a stick?"

Now, she looked confused. "A stick of what?"

The doc chuckled at their conversation. "I can definitely tell one of you is American and the other is Canadian. Reminds me of the old *Who's on first* skit."

"Not my fault he doesn't understand proper English," Holly said, sliding off the examination table and landing on her right foot, then adjusting the crutches under her arms.

"I understand English," he spouted. Gray glanced at the physician. "She says weird shit all the time. Looks like I'm gonna have to upload a translation app."

Holly snorted. "Maybe you need a copy of Canadian for Dummies."

Yeah, she was feeling better all right, her snappy

responses back on full power. "You know it would have done my heart good to see the doc inject your ass with a needle. Sorry I missed it."

"Think you saw enough of my ass this morning to last you a lifetime."

He bit his inner cheek to stop himself from admitting he'd love to smack her ass and make love to her so slowly she'd lose her goddamn mind. Desire heated his blood at unprecedented speed. When she got lippy with him, he wanted to bind her hands and teach her a lesson with his tongue. Then they'd see how good her English was!

Gray turned his back to her so she couldn't see the swelling erection behind his zipper.

"What happened with the insurance?" she asked completely oblivious at how she affected him.

"All taken care of," he said brusquely. "Thanks again, Doc."

He nodded pertly. "Holly told me you were a medic in the Navy SEALs before joining the sheriff's department. Think it's me who should be thanking you. If there are complications, don't hesitate to bring her back."

Holly crutched her way out of the room and Grayson followed. "We're going to make a quick pit stop at my headquarters before we get you something to eat."

"Don't worry about me. If you have to go, I'll call a cab."

Like hell she'd do that. "I told my lieutenant I'd submit your statement today. Won't take long."

"It's almost four o'clock. You've wasted the whole afternoon on me, Detective."

He opened the door to exit the clinic and gently steered her to the right, where the pharmacy was located two doors down.

"You're not listening," she said when they reached the pharmacy.

True, he wasn't, because he didn't want her to hop in a cab and end up at the border. At least, not yet.

"I'm listening, Miss McNeela. I just don't happen to agree." He opened the door to the pharmacy and swept his arm, indicating she should enter.

She sighed. "I don't think this is wise."

Debatable. "You said you have a Masters in ancient languages, not a medical degree. I, on the other hand, have years dealing with combat injuries, so get your ass moving."

Her cheeks inflated with a little puff of exasperation. "You don't understand. If something goes wrong, I have no one to call."

And there was the answer to his burning question of whether she had a significant other. As for him—he'd drop everything to help her. Hadn't she figured that out yet?

"Then call me. I'll come."

"As if! And take you away from your family again? Not a chance. I did that already and feel awful."

Grayson took a step to the right, allowing a customer to leave the pharmacy. "You feel awful because you have a fractured knee, as I suspected. It's wiser to have the prescription on hand if you need it, than not at all. We're blocking traffic here, so stop arguing with me, Holly."

"I understand what you're saying, but drugs are a slippery slope."

"Don't have to tell me that." He pointed at himself. "Narco division."

Holly's little brow rumpled. "Narco?"

"After leaving Special Ops, I worked five years in the San Diego Narcotics Task Force. I only moved home at the end of May."

"Why did you move home?"

Inquisitive creature. Always questions. "Let's fill the prescription, and I'll explain myself over lunch."

"It's almost dinner," she pointed out.

He clenched his jaw in frustration. "It's going to be tomorrow fucking morning if you keep stalling."

"Fine," she said, followed by a big sigh.

Suddenly an echo of Erika bounced around in his head. She'd swallowed opioids like candy then sent out a distress call, and he'd answered begrudgingly. Holly refused medication that she needed, and Grayson didn't want to leave her side.

He wanted to be with Holly, not avoid her. In the past, the idea of belonging to one woman never stuck. Had he changed? Or was it possible Holly was the exception to every reason he'd used to reject so many others?

After spending an evening between the sheets with a gal, he distanced himself immediately. If a woman suggested dinner and a movie before sex, he walked away like a ruthless bastard. Instead of feeling trapped by Holly, he had a savage craving to keep her that was getting damn hard to ignore. The constant drum in his chest always loudest when they were together.

Twenty minutes later, he rolled into a parking spot in front of headquarters. She offered to stay in the cruiser, but he helped her out of the vehicle, and she followed him inside. A few heads turned as he planted her ass in a chair next to his desk.

Cole was on the phone, but Kline looked up from his office and immediately stood.

Grayson entered Holly's statement into the electronic file, then added the original to a folder with the police incident number.

"I'm Lt. Kline," he said, introducing himself to Holly.

"Holly McNeela."

"You were the woman involved in the assault at Neon Lights. Appears you got some medical help."

"I didn't have much of a choice. Detective Brooks, insisted."

When it came to stubborn, Grayson was pretty sure they were on equal footing. He handed the folder to Kline, who quickly read her statement then nodded.

"This will help our investigation." He closed the folder.

"Are you returning to Canada today?"

"I can't drive. I need to make some arrangements for my vehicle first."

"Do you have family or a friend who can help you out?" Kline asked.

"No, but I'll manage."

"Thanks for cooperating. If there's anything else, we'll be in touch."

Holly shook the lieutenant's hand. "You have all my details. Call any time."

Finished scanning her statement into the system, Grayson said, "I'll take her back to the resort."

The lieutenant nodded and returned to his office.

Cole strode up to Grayson's desk. "We've got a lead. Guy wants to talk in person. Sounds like a kid, actually. He wouldn't give me his name but said he wanted to meet in fifteen minutes."

Now! Grayson clamped his jaw in frustration. Was there a reason for this karmic assault? He just wanted to eat a meal with Holly. What the hell was wrong with that? So what if he'd promised to keep his dick in his pants. It didn't mean they couldn't be friends. Hell, they were friends.

Aside from one precious Sunday, each time he'd had a shot at spending a few minutes with her, work, family or circumstance intervened to keep them apart.

It was starting to really piss him off.

CHAPTER THIRTEEN

Holly felt completely out of place surrounded by the uniformed officers. "I'll call a cab," she said when Det. Sterling, Grayson's partner, mentioned they needed to interview someone who called in with a tip.

Gray's aqua-colored eyes shifted to her. "Wait here. It shouldn't take long."

The ibuprofen had worn off and her temples pounded with an epic headache. She wasn't going to argue with him. "Sure."

His left eye narrowed as if he could read her lie. "There's a couch in the break room."

"Thank you."

Grayson slapped on the ball cap he'd taken off when they'd arrived, tugging the bill down, which made his sharp jaw, rough with afternoon shadow, even more enticing. His partner headed toward the exit, but Det. Brooks leaned over, tilted his head and stared straight into her eyes.

"You had better be here when I get back." He paused, then said, "And...I want to hear a good reason why I didn't know you were at the resort in the first place."

She cleared her throat and met his gaze. "Because you're a busy man." With his amazing, firm lips only inches from hers, Holly's heart raced. Easy to figure out why. She wanted him to kiss her so badly her skin flushed hot. The crush on this man was getting out of hand.

Grayson grilled her with a look of disapproval. "Not that busy."

Holly appreciated his commitment to public service but

from the conversation he'd had on the phone when they were at the gas station, someone kept dinner warm for him. Grayson Brooks was a wonderful guy and the woman who owned his heart was more than lucky.

"You have a criminal to catch, and I have to make arrangements."

"I'll drive you home, Holly."

Two weeks ago in the resort's garden, she'd thought for sure he was going to kiss her. Twice. But he didn't. When they'd spent the entire Sunday afternoon at his farm, she'd almost convinced herself that he might not be married. But if that were the case, wouldn't he have tried to kiss her when he'd dropped her off at the hotel? But he hadn't. There could only be two explanations. He was committed to someone, or although friendly, Grayson's concern for her was in an official capacity.

Gazing at his rugged, handsome features made her heart ache. "Goodbye."

Grayson's jaw clenched, his eyes riveted on her. She smiled but didn't receive one back and averted her gaze to her lap, just in case he could read her ridiculous emotions.

Last night, even with the pain, his masculinity had created a swell of desire. When he'd carried her into the bathroom, she experienced an irrational desire to hang onto him so he wouldn't let her go. When he'd rested his palm on her hip after putting her back to bed, the warmth of his touch had soothed the angst and stopped her mind from repeating the attack.

The man had integrity and a strong sense of duty. Her attraction to him was misguided. If she didn't put distance between them, she'd spill her feelings and have to face his polite refusal. That...would be mortifying.

"Holly," he said in a low voice, and crouched so they were at eye level. "Wait for me."

She took an enormous risk and placed her palm on his firm shoulder. Being rejected by her ex was one thing, being rejected by Grayson would truly hurt.

"Thank you for everything."

His shoulder deflated a little under her hand and he looked away. "You're welcome."

She watched as he followed his partner out the exit. Holly gave it an extra minute, and then called a taxi.

Thankfully, the cabbie wasn't talkative. The urban sprawl of Mt. Vernon shifted to green countryside. Lulled by the scenery, her mind recalled her moments with the detective. A dominant but considerate man.

It didn't take long before the vehicle arrived at the hotel entrance. Holly stopped at registration and asked for a casino host to contact her while she waited in the high-backed chair next to the gas fireplace with its soaring river rock face. Oak paneling covered the walls, and the soft, green carpet created a tranquil setting like a large, comfortable den.

She didn't wait long.

"Holly." The host, wearing a friendly smile and a dark blue suit, sat in the high-backed chair across from her. "I heard what happened. How you feeling?"

"Hey, Doug. Fractured patella, but it'll heal. I was wondering if I could leave my car here for a couple weeks. The doctor says I shouldn't drive. I'm taking a taxi to the border, and I'll walk across. I'll be back to pick up my car when I'm able."

He smiled. "No problem at all. What are you driving?"

"Red Audi. The front desk has my plate number."

"I thought you were staying a couple more nights."

She considered that too, but her instincts told her to head home. If she saw Det. Brooks again, she wasn't sure she could continue to ignore her attraction to the man. So far, she'd managed not to make a fool out of herself. In a way, he'd been a balm to her soul, proving that not all cops were like her ex.

"Home is always a better place to heal."

"Tell ya what—if you give me the keys, I'll have security move your car to a safe spot within sight of the exterior cameras."

She retrieved her key ring from her purse and removed the car key, handing it to him. "I'm going to grab a bite to eat and then head out."

"We'll cover the cab and get you all the way home, okay?"

For a situation that hadn't been the resort's fault at all, they were bending over backward to help.

"Thanks. You've been more than accommodating. I've always loved coming here. What happened last night wasn't the fault of anyone at the resort. Just bad luck."

"We appreciate that." He checked his watch. "It's four o'clock. Restaurants aren't open yet. I can send your meal upstairs."

"No, thanks. I'll pack my things and then head into the casino for an hour."

"Sure. When you're ready to leave, I'll have the front desk call you a taxi." He stood. "Thanks again for being so understanding."

* * * *

Gray drove the patrol car into the alley behind a row of shops in the historic district that butted up against a neighborhood of post-war era homes. Visibility was good as the summer afternoon waned on. Weathered fencing lined the right side of the road and backed onto low-income rental homes.

"I don't see anyone," Cole said from the passenger seat.

Grayson steered the vehicle to the right side of the back road. The caller said he'd wait behind Hermes Coffee. When a reward for information was offered, it wasn't always someone who wanted a few extra bucks in their pocket. Some guys got off or made their mark by targeting law enforcement.

"Think that's the guy," Cole said, pointing.

A guy wearing a black apron with Hermes Coffee in white

printing exited a back door and stepped into the alley. Gray approached at low speed with his window down.

The kid's head kept swaying left and right as if looking for someone or making sure no one else was in the alley to witness their meeting.

He stopped the cruiser and eyed the teenager. The guy looked half-starved with bony arms and sported a bad case of acne.

"You call the tip line?" Grayson asked.

"Yeah, do I have to give my name?"

"If you want the reward, you will."

The guy kept darting glances down the alley.

Grayson turned the vehicle off. "Listen, we don't need your name now. If your tip leads to an arrest, you can claim the reward. No one is going to disclose your identity."

The kid pulled a pack of cigarettes from his apron pocket and lit one with shaky fingers. "You sure about that?"

"Yup. The longer we're here, the higher the chance someone will see us, so tell us what you know about the thefts."

"It's not my brother," he said quickly. "He has nothing to do with it."

Grayson nodded but didn't interrupt.

"My older brother's been hanging around this group of guys. I heard them the other night talking about hitting the Neon Lights resort again. A guy named Rory is kinda like their leader, but I think he's the muscle, not the guy behind the robberies."

"Why's that?"

"Too stupid."

Grayson appreciated the kid's observation.

"My mom hates it when he comes around the house. She's scared of Rory and afraid my brother's gonna get into trouble."

"Got a last name?"

"Rory Hannigen. Blond guy. He's about six feet. Early

twenties. You can't miss him, he's got a star tattooed next to his right eye. I think he's into selling drugs too."

Wouldn't surprise Grayson. "Did you hear any dates or times for their next job?"

The end of the kid's cigarette crackled when he took a long drag. "Nah."

"What about the merchandise? Any idea where they're unloading it?"

The kid shrugged.

"You know where this Rory guy is living?"

"Not an address, but my brother told me he's been hanging out at a house in the Clayton neighborhood."

That made sense. Fledgling crime rings usually used a house for their operation. Clayton was one of the poorer districts around. "Anything else we should know?"

"If they find out I talked to you guys, they'll hurt my mom for sure. Maybe my brother too. They're cranked out on drugs most of the time, and dangerous. One of the other guys is a real prick. Heard him say he followed a chick from a bar the other night and raped her. Might have been talkin' smack to impress the other guys, but I don't think so."

"You know his name?" Grayson asked.

Cole wrote the details down as the kid talked, but the cameras they wore also recorded sound.

"Think it's Rob Downing." The kid smoked the cigarette down to the filter and dropped it on the ground. "My brother's only twenty, but he gets into a bar they go to on Fifth Street. That's all I know. I gotta get back to work."

There were two watering holes on Fifth Street that Gray knew of. Both were dives. He wasn't surprised they served minors.

"Thanks for talking with us. My name is Det. Grayson Brooks. If you hear anything else, call the tip line and ask for me."

The kid quickly scurried inside, and Grayson started the cruiser.

Cole tucked away his notepad in his shirt pocket. "Looks like we have something to work with."

At the end of the alley, Grayson turned left and joined the main crossroad. Close to five o'clock, he headed toward headquarters. "I'll run the names through the system tomorrow. If we can ID the guys, we should check out those bars on Fifth."

Cole grunted his agreement and stared out the window as if his mind was elsewhere.

"Ivy called me this afternoon," Grayson said.

Cole broke his staring contest with the road as they took the onramp to the I-5. "I asked her out on a date."

Ivy hadn't shared any particulars. "Good. So why do you look like you've got a watermelon stuck in your throat?"

He grunted. "Maybe this is a mistake."

They passed a silver minivan and the boy in the backseat waved. Cole waved back and the boy bounced and gestured to his mother behind the steering wheel.

"Getting cold feet already?" Grayson asked.

"What the hell are we gonna talk about? We've known each other since we were kids. I was going to take her to Roosters for drinks, but that seems pretty damn lame."

Grayson chuckled. "Then don't. You still got that ten-foot runabout. Take her to the lake. Bring dinner and a cooler of beer. Give her a change of scenery."

Cole's forehead creased. "Then what?"

"Thought we were going to avoid that convo." Traffic on the highway was heavy with people headed home from work. Going with the flow, he stayed in the slow lane.

"You should have seen Ivy's face. She was totally blind-sided. Accused me of screwing her friends, which I'm guilty of. And another reason I should steer clear of Roosters. Don't think she's going to forgive me for that."

Pretty much everyone they knew had hooked up at Roosters at some point.

A few miles down the road, Grayson exited the freeway.

"Can't help ya there, but I wouldn't worry about it too much."

When headquarters came into sight, his thoughts turned to Holly. After parking the cruiser in the back lot, he headed for his pickup.

"Aren't you forgetting someone?" Cole asked, closing the passenger door.

"You mean Holly?" He shook his head. "Nope, she's gone."

Cole looked perplexed. "How do you know that?"

Yeah, how did he know that? Good question. "She probably left minutes after we did." Although useless, he followed Cole inside, just to be sure.

Lt. Kline was heading out as they came in. "Hey, men. Get anywhere on the call-in?"

Gray surveyed the office. All but one of the officers had gone home for the day. "We got a few leads. We'll follow them up tomorrow. Where's Holly?"

"She didn't stay long. I looked up from my desk a few minutes after you left and she was already gone."

Grayson pulled his cell and called the hotel while Cole filled in their lieutenant on what they'd learned.

"Sorry, Detective," the registration clerk said. "Miss McNeela checked out. We hired a cab to take her home."

Of course, she was gone. "Thanks."

He scrolled through the list in his phone and stopped on her cell number. Did he have any official reason to call her? Not really. Did he want to ask why she left when he asked her to wait? Hell, yes! He was done for the day. The farm work could wait. She had two nights at the resort, but she'd left.

Cole finished the debrief and Kline headed for the front exit.

"Guess you were right," Cole said.

"What?"

"About Holly."

Grayson tucked his phone back into his pocket. "Yeah, she's on her way home."

Cole crossed his arms and eyed him. "You look bummed

about that. Wanna share with the class?"

"No," he said sharply. "Got all I need on the case. There's no reason for her to stick around."

"Okaaaay," he said, reading Grayson's abrupt response correctly and not drilling him with questions. "Wanna stop for a beer?"

"Got things to do at the farm." He marched toward the hallway leading to the front lot where he parked his pickup.

His buddy followed him outside. "You'll see her again."

Instead of responding to his best friend, he aimed for his truck. Holly's smile and pretty eyes landed dead center in his mind as he unlocked the vehicle. By the time he parked in front of the house, he was in a seriously shitty mood.

He understood why she'd left the office, but why leave the country? She had two more nights at the resort. They could have spent them together. Gone out to dinner. Hell, he'd buy her a milkshake for breakfast, lunch, and dinner.

Why had she left? Grayson palmed his phone.

If he called her now, he might take his frustration out on her. A tight ball formed in his chest. Why was he frustrated? What the hell could he say other than making sure she got home safely? Once the cortisone shot wore off, who'd take care of her? She'd mentioned living in a townhouse. What if she fell trying to get upstairs? He squeezed the steering wheel in frustration.

Gone.

She was gone.

"You gonna sit in your truck all night?" Ivy asked, jerking him out of his thoughts.

He shoved the door open, and she stepped out of the way. "If you've got anything to say about Cole, stow it. Don't want to hear about it."

She blinked. "What crawled up your ass?"

"I've got work to do." He headed inside the house to change out of his uniform. A few minutes later, he passed through the kitchen on his way outside. Ivy leaned against the island, drying her hands on a dishtowel.

"Dinner will be ready in an hour." She placed the towel on the wood counter. "Should I invite Cole?"

His sister and best friend had to be the two *stupidest* people on the planet. He palmed the edge of the doorway for balance and yarded a boot over his foot.

"I don't understand you two. You've been ignoring the obvious for years. You're in each other's front yard for fuck's sake. But instead of grabbing happiness with both hands, you've pissed away every minute. If you'd given him one little sign, the man would have chased you across six state lines to put a ring on your finger. Women who open their legs after a few drinks are familiar territory for guys like us. But that special woman, the one a man wants to keep, is totally oblivious. She doesn't give us a damn clue. How the hell are we supposed to know if a decent gal burns hot and wants us to make the first move?" By now he was shouting. "Can't you tell when a guy wants you so bad, he's losing his fucking mind?"

As he railed at his sister, her eyes widened, and her mouth gaped. "I'll—I'll set another plate," she said weakly.

CHAPTER FOURTEEN

Crossing the US-Canada border went smoothly. Instead of having the cab drop her off at home, Holly directed the driver to a rental car agency relatively close to her house. The taxi waited while she filled out the paperwork for an economy-sized automatic vehicle. After tipping the cabbie, he put her bags in the Toyota and she drove home.

The townhouse greeted her with a dark and empty ambiance.

After Kevin's court hearing, she'd only seen him for a few minutes. The jury had found him guilty of driving intoxicated and causing death, but there were mitigating circumstances. His sentencing would come later. Her ex had asked if he could stay at the townhouse until then. Holly felt bad for Kevin but couldn't let him stay. Pissed off, he'd packed his bag and left.

Rolling her luggage at the same time as using her crutches took some finesse and oddball gymnastics to get inside.

The steroid injection reduced the pain by ninety percent, at least for now. After showering and changing into her robe, she carefully made her way down the stairs with the help of the brace around her knee and entered her little office. Scrounging through the file cabinet, she selected the folder she was looking for. She kept all types of greeting cards on hand, from sympathy to get well. Fingering through the pile, she chose a thank you card.

She wrote a quick note and addressed the envelope to Det. Grayson Brooks with the Sheriff's Proactive Unit address. Surfing the Web, she found a pub in the detective's area that sold gift certificates online and bought enough to cover two meals and beverages, then added the print-out to the card.

Tomorrow, she'd drop it in the mailbox.

By eight o'clock, exhausted, she crawled into bed. Holly turned the TV on low for a little background noise and reached for a new paperback on the nightstand. One of her favorite writers had released a new military romance. She stared at the cover with a hot guy, rippling with muscles, then set the book down. Reading the story would only remind her of Grayson. The detective had found his happy ending, but the heroine wasn't her.

She swallowed two pain relievers, avoiding the prescription meds, and turned the light out. Laying back on the feather pillow, staring up at the white ceiling, she wondered how she could miss a man she barely knew.

The reason she hadn't stayed in the US was simple. She and Grayson had a few chance encounters. After the attack, he'd been professional and courteous. He'd gone above and beyond, lending her the crutches. When he'd come back today to get her statement, he probably felt it was his duty to take her to the urgent-care clinic.

She left the States holding a precious piece of a silly dream that couldn't be shattered if she'd stayed at the resort and he didn't show.

Holly turned onto her right side and slipped the extra bed pillow between her knees, reminding her again of the detective. He'd stayed while she'd fallen asleep last night. Although the pain meds helped, it was his nearness that eased her mind.

Holly closed her eyes and tried to remember a time she'd missed her ex so badly that her heart hurt but couldn't. The only moment that came close was the evening Kevin had come home and said they needed to talk.

Still in his RCMP uniform, he asked her to join him in the living room. She had no clue what was coming.

He looked her in the eyes and said, "Holly, I'm moving out."

Dumbfounded, she blinked like an idiot not comprehending. "What?"

Kevin never minced his words.

"I thought I could make our marriage work, but I can't."

Her mind whirled. He'd cheated on her again. This was the third time. "You're sleeping with someone else, aren't you?"

"I'm sorry. I can't change how I feel. She's everything I want."

Holly wasn't a complete idiot. For months now, he'd sung the praises of his partner. "It's Natalie."

He shrugged. "Yeah, it is. I don't want to keep stringing you along. It's not fair to either of us. We both need to get on with our lives."

Several emotions had run wild at that moment, but the one that hurt the most was her inability to keep her husband's eyes on her.

"Why did you marry me in the first place?"

He'd been assigned to the detachment near her hometown when they'd met. She'd finished her degree and was visiting her parents for a few months while she looked for a job.

Kevin mulled his answer over for a few seconds. "Honestly, I don't know. Small town. Pretty girl. We were both young." He shook his head. "Should have never happened. I hate to say this, Holly, but you're boring."

She managed to keep her tears in check until he packed a bag and left the townhouse. Kevin made her heart ache that night, but it was betrayal, not loss, that fed the pain.

Kevin taught her that love didn't always mean forever. Trusting a man with your heart was a gamble. Over the last two years, she'd focused on her job and found her happily-ever-afters in the pages of the romance books she read. The heroes, unshakable in their commitment, never walked away, and the women's strength and passion forged an unbreakable bond.

The irony that Grayson had been a SEAL made her grin. At least she could say once upon a time she'd crossed paths with an incredible man.

* * * *

Grayson arrived at the office before six in the morning and worked on Holly's case. Not because he was eager, but because he couldn't sleep worth a damn last night. Every time he'd closed his eyes, he saw her smile at him as she said goodbye. The way she'd said the farewell with finality chilled him to the bone.

When Cole walked into the office by eight, Grayson said, "I've got a hit on Rory Hannigen and Rob Downing."

"Makes finding them easier."

Cole strode over to take a look, and Grayson handed his partner the rap sheets. "They've both been charged for felony theft, residential burglary, with a side of possession and distribution of narcotics. Several counts."

Cole scanned the sheets. "No current address for either of them. Least we know where they like to tip one back. Did you check for sexual assaults reported in the last month?"

"Found ten but none reported in the area of Fifth Street."

Cole palmed his jaw. "Ya kinda look like hammered shit, buddy. Everything okay?"

"Yup." Grayson scrubbed his forehead. "We need more intel to solve this case. I don't want to wait. I'm going to head out for some recon."

His partner eyed him. "At the bars on Fifth?"

"Once they open. I might get lucky."

"You mean 'we'."

They'd have to nurse a few beers while undercover and watch people come and go. Hannigen and Downing might show. If that was the case, they'd follow to locate the house the ring was using as their base.

Cole sat on the edge of Grayson's desk. "Did she make it home all right?"

"Who?" He slowly raised his gaze to meet his partner's.

His friend swayed backward with mock surprise. "Okay,

guess by that deadly look in your eyes, the subject is closed."

"Holly isn't a subject," he grouched. "When I have a reason to call her, I will."

Cole rolled a nearby chair to the desk and sat. Forking his fingers, he rested them on his abs. "Why are you pissed? You mad at her for going home? Or mad at yourself?"

His best friend had a bad habit of always wanting to burrow for the truth of the matter. Probably why he'd chosen law enforcement. "Drop it. I'm not pissed off."

"Yeah, ya are. I've known you long enough. Something's eating away at you. Maybe you haven't figured it out and that's why you've gone all Nasty Nancy." He leaned forward and slid Grayson's cell closer to his hand. "Call her."

With a grimace, he took the phone and shoved it in the pocket of his jacket that hung on the back of his chair.

"Before we hit the bar, I'm going to patrol the Clayton area. Know anyone from that district who might be willing to talk?"

"Come to think of it, yes. Had a case a few years ago. A B&E at the residence of an elderly woman. If she's still there, we could talk to her."

Grayson had done all he could, digging for details in the police information systems. "Good. I'm going to ditch the uniform."

"Right behind ya."

In the changing room, he and Cole switched into street clothes. Grayson transferred his wallet and cell into his jeans and shut the door to his locker.

"I'll drive," he said.

Cole followed him down the hallway, but he wasn't finished with his fishing trip. "What'ya gonna do if she calls you?"

He halted and glared at his friend. "Answer her questions."

"And?"

"And what?" he said, frustrated as hell with this

conversation. "Holly was assaulted, and I did my job."

"Did you now?" He pursed his lips. "Ivy told me that you left the house at three in the morning. Told her it was a follow-up, which is strange." He cocked his head to the side. "I don't remember a call-out."

Damn, his sister had a big mouth. "I had hotel security check on Holly. By three-thirty, she hadn't fallen asleep nor taken anything for the pain. I'd left her there and forgot she couldn't walk, which meant she couldn't get to the bathroom and hadn't had anything to drink. I found Ivy's old crutches and took them to the hotel. Satisfied?"

"Uh-huh."

"What the fuck does *uh-huh*, mean?"

"You're thick as rocks if you can't admit there's something you like about that woman. Ya did a Super Bowl-worthy interception to carry Holly to her room. You take her crutches in the wee hours of the morning, and then you drive her to a clinic, take care of the insurance, and stand by while she gets an examination. Sounds to me like you'd walk across hot coals in bare feet for her."

"Jesus, you're a pain in the ass." He continued to walk down the hallway toward the front exit.

"Wendy was an easy score, but you dumped her the second you saw Holly out the window at Roosters."

"She needed my help."

Cole snorted. "Wendy wanted to open her long legs and let you fuck her six ways to Sunday. That was pretty obvious to me, and I'm sure you figured that out as well."

"Wasn't interested," he said, reaching the end of the hallway.

"Holly isn't like the Frog Hogs you told me about, and that's got you scared. You don't know what to do with a woman who's finally crossed your path and means something to you."

Gray donned his sunglasses while pushing the door open. "Wrong." He wasn't scared of Holly whatsoever. His friend's assumptions were way off course. "Get in the truck."

Last night, after the dishes were done, Grayson saw Cole and Ivy go for a walk on the farm. At times, his sister had a stubborn streak but mostly she was a level-headed woman. Maybe his rant had given her something to think about because Cole was holding Ivy's hand as they strolled back to the house.

Gray turned the key in the ignition as his partner jumped in the passenger seat. "If you're finished dissecting my motivations, can we concentrate on the case?"

"Listen, bud." A sincere wrinkle of concern formed on Cole's forehead. "I think you're pissed because she's gone, and you miss her. You've never missed anyone before, have you?"

Backing out of the parking spot, he slammed the brake pedal, then glared at his partner. Presented with the truth, his denial dissipated.

After a deep inhale, he said, "It's more complicated than that."

Cole pulled the seatbelt across his chest. "Guys want to figure everything out. That's why love messes with our heads. It's not meant to be dissembled or analyzed. Believe me, ignoring her isn't going to make it any easier."

Grayson gripped the steering wheel and sighed. "I snapped at her yesterday. Not because I was angry, but because I was frustrated."

His buddy laughed. "Well, if you're frustrated then call Wendy. That woman rides a man's dick like she's on a mechanical bull."

Gray jerked his gaze toward Cole. "You and Wendy?"

Cole realized his mistake and narrowed his eyes. "Don't you fucking dare tell your sister. She doesn't know about that one."

"Is this a recent development?" Grayson asked.

"Recent enough. We'd both had too much to drink. In the morning, we agreed to bury the incident. One-time thing."

Concerned for his sister, he asked, "How recent?"

His buddy shrugged. "I don't know, somewhere around the six months ago mark. Why?"

Fair enough. "Because if it was last week, I'd have a fucking problem with it."

Cole shook his head. "Give me a little credit, man. You've always been protective of your sister. That's part of the reason I never told you I loved her."

The truck's diesel engine rumbled while Grayson contemplated how Holly had turned his sensible world inside out.

"Gray, please don't tell Ivy."

"No, of course I won't. She considers Wendy one of her best friends."

Cole laid his arm along the passenger window's ledge. "Yeah, Wendy feels the same way about her. We actually talked the other day. She told me she values Ivy's friendship and what happened between us is buried."

"Wendy's good people," Grayson said.

Cole nodded. "Yeah, she is. I don't know if it's my place to tell you this, but she kinda has the same feelings for you as I do for Ivy."

He watched three officers from the PU exit the building. "I know. My sister told me."

"Gonna do anything about it?"

Wendy was a gorgeous, vibrant woman. They both came from the same roots. She had a great sense of humor. As far as Gray knew, there weren't any negative aspects, and she lived down the road. If he was going to take a stab at having a real relationship with a woman, Wendy made sense.

"Maybe," he answered.

* * * *

Grayson sat on the front porch, watching the sun disappear on the horizon and listening to the tranquil sounds of the farm as night approached. It had been two weeks since he and Cole investigated the bars on Fifth Street. The perps didn't make a showing and the old woman who lived in Clayton had passed away.

Eventually, they'd get another break and find out where the crime ring was holed up. A few more people had called in on the tip line, but none of the reports panned out.

The screen door opened with a squeak and the string of lights that ran the length of the porch blinked on. Ivy stepped outside carrying two glasses of lemonade.

"Interested?" She set them on the small patio table and sat in the other cushioned rocking chair.

"Thanks."

"Worried about you, brother." She sipped from the glass, then set it down. "That was quite the bawling out you gave me a while back."

He gripped the dewy glass and downed half the contents. No one made lemonade as good as Ivy. "Sorry, I was outta line."

"No, you weren't. Sometimes a girl needs to listen to her big brother."

"Sometimes," he said, clearing his throat. "But I didn't need to say it at a hundred decibels."

She grinned. "Not like I haven't heard it before." She covered his hand with her dainty fingers. "Thank you for coming home, Gray. It makes a world of difference. Not only for the farm, but to me."

He was lucky to have the family and friends he had.

"I needed a change too," he admitted. "Tomorrow, I'm contacting a realtor and putting my place up for sale in San Diego."

The crickets and frogs serenaded the night with their ballads. The aromatic scent of the cedar trees and fresh-cut grass went a long way to ease his tension.

Ivy crossed her legs and stared out over the side lawn. "I'm glad to hear that. Dad will be happy too. Jackson thinks you're a hero. He tells his friends his uncle is like Superman."

"That would be the farthest thing from the truth."

Holly popped into his mind. He wondered whether she thought SEALs walked on water because he sure didn't. Separating from the teams hadn't been easy. Gray remembered feeling untethered. He missed his brothers and the challenges of the job. By joining the sheriff's department, he'd resolved most of his issues. Law enforcement gave him focus and time to transition from the high-octane lifestyle of spec ops to civilian life.

But something was still missing. He just didn't know what it was. Some Frogs turned into powder kegs after leaving the teams, and the blast didn't happen for years. Then one day—boom. He didn't want to be that guy. He didn't think he was, but he wasn't certain. Aside from his inability to maintain any emotional commitment to one woman, Gray wondered if that's what really stopped him from taking a chance with Holly.

Holly had mailed a thank you card to the office and now it sat upstairs on his bedside table.

Detective Brooks,

I can never repay you for your kindness and concern, but hope you'll enjoy lunch from a very grateful Canadian.

Sincerely

Holly McNeela

He'd read it often, the cursive handwriting neat and the message polite. He'd intermittently trolled the Neon Lights parking lot to see if her car had moved. The place was packed seven days a week during the summer months. He and Cole had strolled through the casino, showing a law enforcement presence like they usually did, but honestly, Grayson only looked for one face.

When Holly resurfaced to collect her vehicle, she wouldn't call him. Not a woman like her.

Ivy left and returned with the pitcher, refilling their glasses. "You've been a little distracted recently."

"Busy with a case at work. Like to put it to bed but we

haven't caught the guys yet."

"Well, maybe the farmstead's July Fourth celebration will break things up."

Brooks Farmstead hosted three parties over the summer. They'd become a tradition for locals. Customers of the farmstead store, tourists, and farmers attended. The Independence Day party was the most popular and literally hundreds of people showed up. It was only five days away.

"Guess tomorrow we start setting up," he said.

Ivy released the band from her hair and shook her head to loosen her straight, blonde locks. "Weatherman isn't forecasting any rain. That's a blessing. The celebration is so much work, but it's my favorite."

He'd be around this year to enjoy the festivities. "Make a list."

He had seating, canopies, and tables to set up in the coming days. They opened a portion of the front field for parking, and the neighboring farms all pitched in the day before the party, then claimed their tables. According to Ivy, by ten o'clock on the Fourth, people were tasting wine and food, talking to neighbors, and by dinnertime numerous barbeques with slabs of beef, pork ribs, and chicken made people's mouths water.

"You remember my friend, Debra? She was in the store today and asked about you."

He slammed his eyes shut for a second then turned his head to face his sister. "Please, don't try to set me up. I'm not interested."

He kept calm but even he could hear the abrasive tone. The thought of anyone else but Holly near him raised his hackles.

She lifted a hand in peace. "Okay, okay. Don't get upset. But she really was in the store today and I'm sure she's coming to the celebration. I have nothing to do with it. Just a friendly heads-up that you have an admirer. Two, if you include Wendy."

He didn't need an admirer. Tomorrow was Saturday. He wanted an early start to get the chores out of the way, and then begin working on the layout Ivy used each year for the party. "I'm going to turn in."

When he rose, Ivy hopped to her feet. "Gray." Her tone was tight with excitement. "Things between Cole and me are moving pretty fast." A slip of a smile quirked her lips. "I have a feeling he's going to ask me to marry him."

Grayson grinned. Yeah, he was pretty sure too, since Cole had dragged him out to three different jewelry stores to pick the engagement ring, and he'd already asked their old man for his approval. To anyone else, their engagement might seem quick, but really, all Ivy and Cole had to do was face the truth. They loved each other, and had for a long time.

He leaned over and kissed her on the cheek. "He better ask me to be the best man."

Ivy cinched her arms around his waist, and he hugged her back. "I'm still scared to death. Is that wrong?"

He chuckled and palmed his sister's upper arms. "No, but you've got nothing to be scared of. You two are going to grow old together. He's a good man, Ivy. You've always known that."

Her face literally beamed. So that's what they meant by a blushing bride.

"He loves Jackson, but he also wants more children, and so do I."

Gray collected the pitcher and two glasses. "I got room for more nephews. Have you talked to Jackson?"

"Actually, yes. He wants a baby sister." Ivy held the screen door open.

"I'm happy for you, sis. Happy for you both."

He deposited the glassware in the kitchen sink, ready to hit the hay and hope that Holly wouldn't invade his dreams. During his SEAL training, he'd learned how to ignore pain, endure the worst conditions, but he couldn't push her image aside.

His sister clasped his hands, her eyes the same color as his, staring up at him. "I want to see you smile again, Gray. I know you're not happy, and I know why."

Bloody Cole. Guess he'd have to watch what he said from now on. Bro bonding had been relinquished to second place.

"I'm good, Ivy. I have plenty to be grateful for."

Her creased brow deepened. "Being grateful and being happy are two different things. I had so many sleepless nights while you served with the SEALs. Then I worried all over again when you joined vice. You're home. You're whole. But you're not happy, Gray. I know you have feelings for Holly, but I don't understand why you don't act on them."

He exhaled and closed his eyes. "She's not my type, Ivy. I don't do relationships."

His sister smiled sadly. "God, I love you, brother, but you are so full of shit. That might be your excuse, but it's not the real reason. The other night when you gave me a wake-up call, I heard your fears as well. It's safer not to have her at all than risk losing her. You've convinced yourself that a relationship with Holly will fail before you've even tried. I don't understand why that is."

Ivy was partly right. He'd didn't want to hurt Holly.

"There's too much stacked against us. I have to be realistic. Starting something I'll likely screw up will only hurt both of us." Gray shook his head. "Of course, I want her. I'm all about the chase, but I don't have staying power. I already know that about myself." He winked at his sister to relieve her concerns. "Thanks for worrying about me. See you for breakfast."

* * * *

Saturday morning, Holly woke up to the sun seeping through her plantation blinds. Like every day for the last two weeks, she strapped the brace around her knee. The other day, she'd ditched the crutches and found she could walk without any pain.

She puttered at home, doing the laundry and some light cleaning, and then curled up in her favorite chair in the living room to review some images of an exciting new find that had been sent to the university from a dig outside of Jerusalem. The images were crystal clear and the researchers on site had done a great job of cleaning the slabs. The script was not considered part of a living language and that's what created the stir over the two stone slabs. When it came to archaic languages, there was a lot of controversy. With six thousand languages spoken today, their roots were a tangled web. The oldest known language, Tamil, dated back thousands of years. Specialists from several universities had already espoused their theories, but Holly questioned those findings. The slabs were located in a buried structure outside of Jerusalem, four thousand miles from the roots of the Tamil language.

Holly ran her finger down the image and paused on what looked like a star.

She blinked.

A star!

The face of the man who'd attacked her popped from her brain cells. He had a small star tattooed next to his eye.

She quickly set the images aside and collected her phone. Nervous, she highlighted Grayson's number. This was about the case, not an excuse to hear his voice. She heard him every night in her dreams, anyway. Every encounter they'd had, she'd replayed over and over again in her mind. Connecting each event into something special, knowing it wasn't healthy to keep rehashing those events.

Taking a breath of courage, she dialed.

It rang five times. Any second it would go to his voice mail.

"Hello."

Definitely not the detective. Sounded like a young boy.

"Hi, this is Holly. I'm looking for Grayson. Did I dial the

wrong number?"

"Nope," the boy said. "He's outside. Do you want to talk with my mom?"

Holly's pulse roared to a hundred beats a minute. "No. No thank you." Of course, a man like Grayson was married with a family. She knew it, but her foolish heart kept trying to give her false hope. "Sorry for bothering you."

"Bye," the kid said and disconnected the call.

Det. Brooks teasing and goodwill gestures were simply acts of community service. *You're an idiot, Holly McNeela. Now smarten up and stop thinking about him.*

* * * *

Any family who farmed knew that Sundays meant you could sleep in. A huge joke, considering everyone was up at six instead of five. Grayson liked Sundays. Chores, church, and then a big lunch. Ivy usually threw a roast in the oven before they left for the Lutheran service a mile from their place.

The aroma of fresh-brewed coffee met Grayson as he descended the stairs while tucking in his t-shirt.

He patted his back pockets. Empty. Where the hell had he left his phone?

Dad read yesterday's paper at the table and Jackson shoved waffles smothered in strawberry sauce and whipped cream in his face.

"That looks good," Gray said, grabbing a mug from the shelf and pouring a coffee, then joining his dad and nephew at the table.

Jackson nodded with enthusiasm and shoved another forkful in his mouth.

"Kid's gonna choke," Dad said from behind his paper.

Grayson chuckled. "We'll just have to hang him upside down and beat it out of him. Hey, anyone seen my phone?"

"On the island," Ivy said, setting a heaping plateful of

waffles on the table next to a bowl of strawberry sauce.

Grayson grabbed his cell and set it next to his cup then clicked on the history. Wait a second. He received a call yesterday from a number he recognized, and it kick-started his pulse. Someone had answered the call.

"Ivy, did you answer a call on my phone?"

"Nope." She sat down and handed a napkin to her son because his mouth was covered in whipping cream and his fingers were sticky with syrup.

"Dad?"

"Nope." His father lowered the newspaper, folding it and tossing it on the china hutch next to the table.

After an exaggerated wipe of his mouth, Jackson said, "A lady named Holly called yesterday. I told her you were outside and asked if she wanted to talk to Mom, but she said no."

Grayson choked on his coffee. "Did she sound upset?"

Like any kid, Jackson shrugged and forked in another massive bite of waffle. Replaying the scenario from Holly's perspective, a boy answers his phone and then asks if Holly wants to talk to his mom.

"Shit!" Drawing both his father's and Ivy's startled attention. Even Jackson stopped chewing. "What else did she say?"

"Nuffin," the boy answered, his lips glistening with syrup.

"Are you sure, Jackson?"

The boy's eyes rounded with worry. "Did I do somethin' wrong, Uncle Gray?"

He scrubbed his forehead. "No, kid. Ya didn't."

Ivy looked perplexed. "What's the big deal? Call her back."

Gray's gaze bounced to the old clock mounted above the sink. "It's six-thirty in the morning. I can't call her back now."

His sister laughed. "Okay, so wait an hour or two. Is this something to do with your case?"

He vaulted to his feet. Maybe, just maybe, she'd sent him

an email. He took the stairs two at a time and opened his laptop and signed in to the office server.

Sure enough. He highlighted the email and selected enter.

Dear Detective Brooks,

You said if I remembered anything else about the night I was attacked to let you know. When the man grabbed my bag, I saw his face for a split second. He had a star tattooed next to his right eye.

I called your cell today. I'm very sorry for disturbing your family but thought I should share what I remembered. No need to return my call. I hope this helps in the investigation.

Sincerely

H. McNeela

Grayson flopped back in his chair. *Family*. She'd mentioned his family many times. Missing time with his *family*. Interrupting time with his *family*. He closed his eyes, rehashing their conversations.

He bolted up in his chair. The gas station! Ivy had called. What had he said? He was on a case, and he'd be home soon and to keep a plate warm. By the time he'd hung up, Holly was practically running back to the resort.

Shit! She'd never met Jackson. Didn't know he was Ivy's son.

Did Holly think he was married? Was that the reason she'd kept her distance every time they'd crossed paths? He'd spent an entire Sunday with her here at the farm. He swallowed thickly, remembering how he'd conducted himself. Kept his distance. She probably surmised he was in a committed relationship with someone.

"Uncle Gray, are you mad at me?"

He turned to see Jackson in the doorway, his boyish features taut with concern and near tears. "Come here, sport." His nephew sluffed across the woven rug in his stocking feet. Gray pulled the kid onto his lap. "I'm not mad at you. Not at all."

He sniffed. "You looked mad."

"I'm just sorry I missed someone's call."

"Then call her back like Mom said."

"Miss McNeela sent me an email. It's all good." He brushed the blond bang from the boy's eyes. "You leave me any waffles?"

Jackson grinned, showing his toothless smile. "A couple."

"Then let's go get 'em."

Walking to the door, his nephew held his hand. "Uncle Gray, Mom told me that Cole wants to be my dad."

"So I hear. How do you feel about that?"

Jackson squeezed his finger. "I like Cole, but do you think he'll die too?"

Grayson picked up his nephew and tucked the boy to his hip. "No. And you know how I know that?" He passed through the doorway and headed downstairs.

"How?"

"Because Cole is a superhero. He's going to protect you and your mom forever."

By the time they reached the kitchen, Jackson was smiling again. "Did you protect that lady on the phone?"

He plopped the kid in his chair. "It's my job to help people, and I helped her."

The boy stuck his fork in a waffle and dropped it on his plate. Grabbing the syrup with both hands, Jackson flooded the pockets to overflowing. "I wanna help people when I grow up."

"I'm sure you will."

Ivy deposited a fresh waffle on Grayson's plate and filled his mug with coffee. Had she heard their conversation upstairs? The answer lay in her smile.

CHAPTER FIFTEEN

After working in the calving barn, Grayson slid the cell from his pocket. It was noon already. In order to charge Rory Hannigen, they needed Holly to confirm his identity.

Cole strode into the barn, wearing a black t-shirt, Wranglers, and a pair of cowboy boots.

"We got our break in the case," Grayson said.

"What'ya got?"

"Holly sent me an email. She remembers seeing her attacker's face. He had a star tattooed next to his right eye."

Cole grinned. "Rory Hannigen, step right up. Did you make arrangements for her to come in and identify him?"

"Not yet."

"Waiting for an invitation? If we want to charge him, she needs to pick him out of a photo line-up."

"We don't know where he's hiding."

A cow in the stall next to Cole nudged her head through the bars and sniffed his hand. He scratched the white, diamond-shaped patch on the Jersey's forehead and she twitched her tagged ear, then nibbled at the hay in front of the stall.

"That's why I came to find you. I just spoke with Kline. The kid from Hermes called this morning. He gave the lieutenant an address in the Clayton district. Says it's the place his brother has been hanging out. We'll find Rory there too. We can hold him on temporary detention until Holly gets here."

"Let me call her. If she's willing to come in, let's go pick him up."

Cole grimaced. "Now? Your sister won't be happy."

Gray chuckled. "You're not even married yet and you're worried about getting kicked to the couch already? We got plenty of time, and Ivy has plenty of help. Police work comes first. She knows that."

"Yeah, okay. I'll let her know."

Grayson walked into the sunshine and dialed Holly's number. Now, he had a reason to call her. When she answered, his pulse ticked faster.

"Holly, it's...Grayson."

A lengthy pause ensued. "Afternoon, Det. Brooks."

"How's the knee?"

"Better, thank you. When I pick up my car, I'll drop the crutches off at your headquarters."

Her polite but direct answers bothered him. He grappled for something to say. Asking if she enjoyed the warm weather would be lame as shit.

"No rush. Keep them as long as you need."

"Thank you, but I'm walking without them. So, what can I do for you, Detective?"

There'd been more than a few times he'd considered jumping the border and showing up at her house. The more he thought about Holly, the more the excuses he'd voiced to his sister seemed like bullshit.

"We've identified the guy who attacked you. We can detain him for questioning but in order to charge him, we need you to make an identification."

"You mean a line-up."

"Photo line-up. All you have to do is come in and we'll show you several pictures. If you can identify the guy, we'll charge him."

"Yes, I can do that."

"Great. I'll pick you up." In the background, he heard what sounded like a dishwasher.

"Thank you for the offer, Detective, but that won't be necessary. When do you need me at your headquarters?"

Talking with women had never been a problem for him,

but this conversation was going down as the worst on record. Her strained responses bothered him. He needed to clear the air. Make sure she knew he wasn't married or committed to anyone.

He wanted that conversation to happen in person. Uncertainty needled him in the gut. She had a profession and his responsibilities kept him anchored to the ground where he currently stood. Maybe that was the reason he felt such a strong draw to her, because it was hopeless. In some fucked up way, he saw her as the grass is greener on the other side of the fence, causing him to want her but knowing he couldn't have her. Basically, keeping his old habit of not getting involved intact.

"Detective? You still there?"

"Yeah, sorry. Is it possible for you to come down tomorrow?"

"Tomorrow is July first. It's a holiday here. The border will be jammed, but I can walk across and call a cab on the other side."

"Holly, at least let me pick you up in Blaine."

"No, thank you," she said quickly, her voice a little shaky. "I'll be at your headquarters around noon, if that's all right."

Hell, no. Nothing had been all right since the day she'd left. "Noon is fine. You don't have to see this guy in person. We haven't arrested him yet. If we do, he'll be locked away and I'll be there."

"Of course. I'm running late for an appointment. I better go. Goodbye, Detective."

She disconnected the call, but worse, she'd disconnected from him.

Grayson palmed his chest, the ache bleeding into his veins. Every time he thought of Holly, the pain worsened. He wasn't that thick in the head. He couldn't date Wendy or any other woman. Miss McNeela was the elusive creature he'd convinced himself didn't exist.

But she did.

An attractive, unassuming, intelligent woman with a gorgeous smile, unforgettable eyes, a penchant for romance books and milkshakes. He wanted her, plain and simple.

* * * *

Grayson and Cole drove to the PU headquarters and exchanged Gray's truck for a cruiser, then headed for the address the kid from Hermes had given the lieutenant. One of two things would happen: Rory would either make a run for it or agree to come in for questioning, thinking like most punks, he'd walk free.

He wanted to arrest Rory for Holly's attack, but he and Cole needed to bring down the entire ring. In order to get a warrant and raid the stash house, the punk had to spill his guts.

"How's Holly?" Cole asked as they drove through Saturday shopping traffic toward the Clayton district.

"She's fine. Says she'll be here by noon tomorrow to ID Rory."

"That's all good, but how is she?"

"Confused, I think."

"About what?"

Grayson explained the call Jackson took.

"Easy enough to clarify," Cole said.

Gray came to a stop at a red light and watched a woman push a stroller along the crosswalk.

Cole leaned forward and looked his way. "You did clarify, didn't you?"

The light changed and he rolled through the intersection. "No."

His buddy shook his head. "Well, guess there'll be plenty of good old *American Pie* women at the celebration. If things go our way, we could have this case wrapped up by the Fourth. Good reason to celebrate."

Celebrating was the last thing he wanted. As they

drove into the outskirts of Clayton, the newly built homes transitioned into older ramblers with unkempt yards. The city hadn't bothered to fix the broken cement sidewalks, and litter lined the drain gutters.

"If I tell her the truth, it means I want her to know I'm not married. What then? There's a border between us. What's the point of chasing the impossible?"

Cole chuckled. "Until a few weeks ago, I sounded like you. Don't sweat the details." Cole sat forward. "Jackpot!"

"What?" Gray looked out the passenger window. "Well, well. Hello Rory."

The guy stood outside of a corner store, smoking a cigarette. Life just got a lot easier. Gray cranked the wheel and eased the cruiser into the small parking lot in front of the store.

"Easy does it," Cole said.

They both got out as if making a pit stop and not interested in Rory Hannigen.

Flying high on some drug, Rory didn't struggle much when Cole slapped the cuffs on him and told him he was being brought in for questioning regarding the assault at Neon Lights.

The kid yanked his arm, trying to escape Grayson's grip. "What the fuck, pig!"

Without a lot of fanfare, they shoved his ass in the back seat of the cruiser.

Sitting in a small interrogation room, Cole and Grayson spent two hours asking questions. The asshole was too high to make any sense. He needed to come off the drugs.

"You're being detained for twenty-four hours," Grayson said, looking at the punk with a star tattooed next to his eye. He wore a silver ring in both ear lobes and one through his columella.

"Whatever, man. You got the wrong guy. I didn't do anything."

Once Holly ID'd this guy, Grayson had enough evidence. "I got plenty of proof and tomorrow you'll be charged. The question is, how long you want to spend in prison? If you feel like sharing some information, the judge might take that into consideration."

"I'm not telling you shit." He stared at Grayson through his greasy, blond bangs.

"Get up."

Rory put his hand against the wall in order to stand. Grayson snapped the cuffs back on the guy's wrists and led the punk to a holding cell. He'd let the idiot stew and give it time for the drugs to wear off before they put him back into interrogation again.

It would be a long night, but Grayson would keep the guy awake and uncomfortable until he got what he needed.

He had a lot more experience with interrogation than Cole. His training in the SEALs had given him the skills to make Rory's life miserable. He'd cave.

All night long, Grayson kept the punk awake, switching techniques, keeping the asshole off balance. By oh-nine-hundred hours the next morning, Rory broke. He didn't admit his part in Holly's attack but spilled enough about the burglary ring that would allow Cole to get a warrant to search the house.

Relieved but tired as hell, Grayson's cell rang. Ivy's name came up on the caller ID.

"Hey," he answered.

"Gray! It's Dad. He's had another heart attack."

He jumped to his feet. "Are you at the hospital?"

"Yes, the EMTs just brought him in."

"I'll be right there." He hung up. Cole had just brewed a new pot of coffee and crossed the office to his desk. "Buddy, Dad's at the hospital."

He set the coffee aside. "What happened?"

"Ivy thinks it's a heart attack. I've gotta go. Holly's

supposed to be here at noon."

"Yeah, go. I'll wait for her. But let me know what's happening."

"I will."

* * * *

Sunday morning, Holly packed a small knapsack she could sling over her shoulders with a change of clothes, then returned the rental car.

A taxi dropped her off at the border by ten-thirty. As long as there weren't too many people like her walking across, she was way ahead of the game since the vehicle wait time was over two hours. Pretty typical for a long weekend.

With no one waiting in customs, she stepped up to the counter where a US Border Patrol agent waited and handed the guy her passport.

"Reason for entering the US?"

"Visiting the sheriff's office."

The agent gave her a slow blink. "For what?"

"Identify the man who attacked and robbed me."

"Where did the incident occur?"

"Neon Lights resort." Holly had found it was always good to keep her answers short and to the point when dealing with the American border agents.

"Who's your contact at the sheriff's office?"

"Det. Grayson Brooks." She slid his business card onto the counter.

The border agent glanced at the card, then shifted to the computer and used the keyboard. "How long do you intend on being in the US?"

She wasn't certain. "Two days at most."

"What's in the bag?"

Holly pulled the knapsack from her shoulder, set it on the counter and unzipped the bag. "My laptop, a change of clothes and my wallet."

The agent didn't even bother to look and handed back her passport. "I read about the incident in the newspaper." He finally locked gazes with her. "I also happen to know Grayson. We went to the same senior high. Played football together. Last I heard, he was a Navy SEAL."

She smiled. "He left the Navy five years ago."

"Is he picking you up?"

"He offered, but I told him I'd take a taxi. I had to leave my car at the resort. Fractured my knee during the assault and couldn't drive. I'm going to pick my vehicle up today."

"Good luck. And tell Gray to give me a call. I wouldn't mind catchin' up with the team quarterback."

The agent reached into his shirt pocket and gave her a card with his name and contact info. Of course, Grayson Brooks was the high school quarterback. He'd probably married the head cheerleader and the boy Holly spoke to on the phone was only one of his five children.

"I'll do that," she said.

Only a few steps from the customs office, a local road wove behind the building and that's where the cab picked her up. For a change, she watched the scenery go by, leaving the driving to someone else. The I-5 skirted open fields until the highway reached the city of Bellingham with its Pacific Northwest flair. Shops, malls, hotels, and restaurants. All of which she'd spent time visiting on her previous trips.

Today was about business. A lump formed in her throat. Only business. She'd face Det. Brooks with a friendly smile and keep her focus on identifying the man who'd attacked her.

Twenty-five minutes later, she spoke to security at the resort. They handed over her car keys and she limped her way to where they'd stored her vehicle.

She loved her Audi. Sitting behind the wheel felt good. She gave the clutch a few pumps, with no crazy pain shooting up her leg, then started the vehicle.

The clock on the dash said 11:45. She'd make it just in

time.

As she parked out front of the Proactive Unit's office, she had her nerves under control.

Stepping out of the vehicle, the clouds blotted out the sunny day the weatherman forecasted. It matched her mood.

Entering the building, she heard footsteps and gazed down the hallway. Grayson's partner, Cole Sterling, waved her forward.

"Miss McNeela, nice to see you're walking again."

"Thank you. Do I follow you?" she asked as they met in the hallway.

"Det. Brooks wanted to be here but there was a personal situation he had to deal with. This way."

Although fueled with disappointment, she hoped nothing bad had happened to a family member. The detective led the way into the area she'd been to before. Det. Sterling passed the officer's desks and veered to an empty table with a chair on the right side of the room.

"Have a seat."

Det. Sterling strode to his desk and returned with a folder. "There are several pictures of individuals in this file. Take your time, and if one of them is the man who attacked you, please point to the image."

She nodded. The detective placed the open folder in front of her and she looked at each face but she didn't need to go much farther than the droopy-eyed blond with a sharp chin and a star tattooed next to his right eye.

Holly pointed at the mug shot. "That's the man." She glanced up at the detective.

He nodded. "Thanks, Holly. We've already got him in custody. Now we can charge him with robbery at a minimum. It's a felony and if found guilty, he'll do time. We have a solid case."

"Will I have to go to court?"

He pulled a chair up and sat down. "It's quite possible.

Probably take many months before you'll be contacted, and that depends on the type of trial. Now that he's identified as the perpetrator, he might plead guilty. He might not. He's part of a criminal ring we want to locate. Det. Brooks worked on the guy all night and he extracted some useful information this morning."

She needed to go home and push Grayson out of her mind. "Is that all you need from me?"

"I'll have you sign some paperwork, and you can be on your way."

Forking her fingers together, she said, "Whatever I can do to help."

Part of her felt relieved she didn't have to face Grayson yet her heart shriveled with disappointment that she wouldn't see the handsome detective one last time.

After signing a few documents, Det. Sterling escorted her outside. She unlocked the Audi's trunk and removed the crutches. "Could you please return these to Det. Brooks?"

"Sure," he said, taking the crutches.

She closed the trunk and walked around to the driver's door.

Grayson's partner followed. "He really wanted to be here, Holly."

Why, she wondered. "I hope everything is all right with the detective's family."

"A year ago, his father had a heart attack. He had a triple bypass, but this morning he experienced some problems, and they took him to the hospital. Ivy, Grayson's sister, says the old man is in good condition and the family was waiting to see what the cardiologist had to say."

"That sounds positive. Oh, I almost forgot." She dug in the side pocket of her knapsack. "Can you give this to Det. Brooks? When I crossed the border, the officer said he went to school with Grayson and wants him to call."

He took the card and laughed. "Bob Sagle. That dickhead. He's US Border Patrol. Figures."

She couldn't help but smile. "Obviously, you know him too."

"Yeah, cocky little shit. Figured he should be QB instead of Gray. It was because of Grayson we won state finals."

She shrugged. "He didn't seem so bad. People change with time."

The detective slipped the card into his shirt pocket. "They do. Grayson certainly has. Are you staying at the resort?"

She'd received an open invitation from Neon Lights for all her future visits. "No. I'm going home and have no plans of returning."

The detective gnawed on his upper lip for a second. "Maybe you should stay one night, at least. Gray might want to...clarify a few things."

"Like what?"

The detective seemed hesitant to answer. "It's a long weekend for Canadians, right?"

Holly wished the heavy knot in her belly would dissolve. Not even the resort that had always cheered her up could make it budge.

"It is. If there's something else, he has my email and phone number." She nearly asked if Grayson received her *thank you* card, but the last thing she wanted to hear was that he'd taken his wife or girlfriend out to dinner. "Thank you again, Detective, and I hope his father makes a speedy recovery."

* * * *

Grayson, Ivy, and Jackson sat in the sterile waiting room on the second floor of the hospital. Their father had been moved from Emergency for tests. It had been nearly four hours and Grayson was climbing the walls. Ivy had her arm around Jackson's shoulders and whispered to him every once in a while, reassuring her son that Grandpa was a tough old man. He was going to be fine.

Every doctor who strode into the waiting area grabbed the attention of families anticipating word of their loved ones. The *word* sucked for three other families. The professional platitude of *we did all we could* from the physicians left the families in tears.

"That's Dad's cardiologist," Ivy whispered as a man in his early fifties with salt and pepper hair strode into the room and looked around.

He recognized Ivy and headed their way. Gray stilled his nerves when he stood. No doubt Ivy was holding her breath.

"You're the Brooks family?" the doc asked to be sure.

"How's our father?" Grayson asked.

The doc raised his brows. "Well, it turns out that your father hasn't been following the dietary plan I specifically wanted him to follow. He fessed up that he has a stash of contraband in his room."

"Contraband?" Ivy repeated.

The doc grinned. "Yep. Pork rinds, for one. Not to mention a bottle of whiskey. But he OD'd on the pork rinds last night. The older we get, the less we can handle, especially with a heart condition. Acid reflux can feel a lot like a heart attack."

"Pork rinds!" Grayson growled. "I'm gonna kill the old bastard myself. "You're telling me we sat here climbing the walls for hours because he's got indigestion?"

The doc lifted a hand in resignation. "Fortunately, that's all it is. Aside from that, we did several tests just to be sure. He's actually in pretty good shape. He just has to lay off the junk food and restrict his alcohol consumption."

It was close to twelve-thirty. He'd missed Holly because his old man wanted to shove shit in his pie hole. That was *fucking* great!

"Ivy, can you drive Dad home? I've got somewhere to be."

He turned before she answered and sprinted down the hallway, causing nurses and patients to pin themselves against the walls and get the hell out of his way. He reached the parking lot and jumped into the cruiser, calling Cole as he started the engine.

"Is she still there?" he asked without introduction when his buddy answered.

"No, she left five minutes ago. I think you're right about her assuming you're married. She was cordial, helpful, but definitely going home. How's your dad?"

Gray left rubber when he tore out of the hospital parking lot. "He'll fucking live if he stops eating pork rinds. What was Holly driving? Or did she arrive in a cab?"

"Pork rinds?"

"What the hell was she driving, Cole?"

"Umm, the red Audi."

"Plate number?"

"I wasn't pulling her over, bro. Listen, maybe you should abort the mission. Holly said she has no plans of coming back. This makes things easy, right?"

"Shit." He hung up and concentrated on the traffic.

Grayson's office was located only minutes from the hospital. He raced down the I-5 to catch up to her.

Zigzagging through Sunday traffic, he made a beeline for the border. Where the fuck was she?

Reaching the southern outskirts of Bellingham, he passed a rig in the right lane. Up ahead, he spotted a red Audi. Gray moved into the slow lane and closed in.

BC plates.

Had to be her.

He flipped on his lights and traffic behind him slowed. The Audi's right blinker came on and she exited at the next off-ramp. He followed as she came to the crossroad, turned right, and then right again into a strip mall parking lot.

He slid into the parking spot beside her and exited the cruiser with his heart in his throat.

CHAPTER SIXTEEN

Holly remained in her vehicle but rolled down her window. "I wasn't speeding."

With his gut embroiled in a scuffle between letting Holly go versus feeding his need to get closer to her, Grayson approached the driver's side.

"My partner told me you're going home."

Hanging onto the steering wheel with both hands, she looked up at him. "I am. How's your father?"

Her ability to shift gears and redirect a question impressed the hell out of him. "He'll live if he stops eating junk food."

The comment made her smile. Jesus, he'd missed the sweet upturn of her lips.

Holly's bangs always covered a little of her eyes, and he'd become addicted to those grey peepers. He saw them in his sleep or when his mind wandered.

"Good to hear. Why did you pull me over? I identified the guy who attacked me. Do I need to do something else?"

"Ma'am, please step out of the car."

He must have been too convincing, because the color drained from her cheeks. "O-okay."

Grayson opened the door, and she placed her feet on the ground, the brace secured around her left leg. After getting out, she stepped aside, and he closed the door.

A neon sign from a family restaurant chain caught his eye across the road. "Are you hungry?"

"No."

Damn it. He knew better than to ask a question like that and deserved the answer he got.

With her hands clutched together, she said, "I gave your partner the crutches. Thank you again for all your help, but I really need to go."

Cole had accused him of worrying about details that didn't matter. Some mattered. Holly mattered, and he wasn't that much of an idiot not to recognize she twisted him in knots.

"Listen, you phoned me and—"

"Sorry, you said to call if I remembered anything else. You weren't available but I did send an email."

Why was she sorry? "I got the email. I also received your card."

"Good." She offered him a sedate smile. "Nice seeing you again. Take care."

His muscles twitched with the need to hold her in his arms. Not like the day he'd carried her to the presidential suite, but curled in his embrace, staring at a fire or watching a movie. He wanted to make her smile, like he'd done when he'd found her romance novel or brought her the milkshake. Something so mundane, but the reward literally warmed his heart.

Maybe it was because she was so different from the type of women he'd hooked up with. Especially, Erika, who'd dropped hints like breadcrumbs. Sex was her currency. No work on his part except a good fuck and a shower to wash off the sweat. Erika's addiction and helplessness had kept him running to her rescue because that's what he'd been trained to do. Help people. No matter who, when or where.

Holly represented something else: a woman he respected. He couldn't let her leave without clearing the slate.

"The boy on the phone, that was my nephew," he blurted.

She paused, her expression confused.

"His mom is my sister, Ivy. You met her at the farmstead store, remember?" He cleared his throat. "Other than my father, that's my family."

"I remember your sister." Holly glanced around

nervously. "Brooks Farmstead is a real treasure. Maybe I'll come back and visit one day."

If Gray wasn't mistaken, Holly quickly blinked a sheen of tears from her eyes.

Although the weatherman had promised sunshine, dark-bottomed clouds opened, and light rain dotted the ground.

"Holly?" He didn't second guess himself and slid his hands around her slender waist. "Why the tears? Talk to me."

She quickly swept the back of her hand against her cheek. "Just relief, I guess. You caught the bad guy."

He fingered a stray, silky curl of hair from her cheek. "Don't lie to a sheriff."

"You're not a sheriff, you're a detective, and I'm not lying." She swept away another unrestrained tear. "I'm relieved."

Relieved that her attacker had been caught, or sad to learn that Gray wasn't married but never kissed her when he had so many chances?

He'd seen plenty of crocodile tears from Erika, and other women, for that matter. Some, he'd arrested. Some were from women he wasn't interested in getting to know better. But Holly's tears definitely gutted him.

From the moment he'd seen her, he'd been drawn by some invisible force. She'd always visited the resort alone. Maybe she was running away from something or trying to fill an empty hole. He barely knew anything about her because she'd always deferred to him. Asked *him* questions.

The time he'd spent in her company was irreplaceable. Their conversations ebbed and flowed with ease. Teasing each other always led to laughter. He couldn't remember a single time when he'd wanted to leave her.

"I haven't been totally honest with you," he said.

Her pretty gaze rose to connect with his eyes. Grayson's pulse increased ten-fold. Inhaling extra oxygen, knowing full well that courage wasn't in the air—it was in him—he considered how many ways he could fuck this up. The chance of him ruining the friendship they shared was infinite.

"Almost every time I've seen you, I've been wearing this uniform. Performing a duty."

Holly's brow rippled. "I don't think many officers spend the day with a stranded woman or jump out of bed to help her pee at four in the morning."

"No, and I've never done that before, either. Until you. I'm almost one-hundred percent certain that if you cross that damn border today, I'm never going to see you again, am I?"

She continued to stare at him, neither agreeing nor disagreeing.

Are you willing to let her go? Just tell her the fucking truth.

"I chased you down the highway because I didn't want you to leave with the assumption that I'm...I'm married or committed to someone. But more importantly, I never got the chance to tell you that without a doubt, you're the most beautiful woman I've ever met."

Holly's head tilted a little. "I'm not beautiful. Think you and I both know that."

She tried to escape his grasp, but he held on. "You're an attractive woman but I'm not defining your looks, I'm talking about...you. All of you."

Man, he was traversing virgin territory and shaky as hell.

After processing his words, her bewildered expression eased. "Det. Brooks, no one has ever told me that before."

Uniform or not, weeks of anticipation, her image always on his mind, he folded like a deck of fucking cards.

"Has anyone ever kissed you like this before?"

He barely brushed her sweet lips on the first pass. But on the second, he was all in. The knot in his chest liquefied, replaced by a familiar impulse—desire. But it wasn't raw or empty, nor impatient.

Their kiss deepened—bloomed—and he crushed her in his arms. Gray shed the brittle, useless skin of excuses from his past. He didn't need them anymore. Holly McNeela made him happy. Truly and completely happy.

* * * *

Holly's head swam and she floated with Grayson's incredible kiss. Euphoria raced through her blood. It wasn't the sensual touch of his lips, but the man. Confident. Strong. Ruggedly handsome.

Dizzy but warm all over, she opened her eyes when the kiss ended.

"No," she said, amazed she could even speak. "No one has ever kissed me like that before, either."

"Have lunch with me," he said, his arms refusing to loosen. "We can stay here or, better yet, let me take you to a place on the waterfront. Just don't get in that car and leave."

"I'm confused."

Wasn't that an understatement! Her pulse thumped with excitement and her brain couldn't string two cognitive thoughts together. A quirk of reality had plucked a few pages from her fantasies, but this wasn't supposed to happen. Not with a man like Grayson.

"That's my fault," he said, releasing his embrace. "Follow me. I want to drop off the cruiser and pick up my truck."

He was a detective and retired SEAL. The last man she trusted had kicked her to the curb. She'd analyzed her failed marriage to death. Men like Grayson with extreme careers needed exhilarating women. She was a scientist. A researcher. Holly saw herself as the farthest thing from sexually charged as a woman could be.

"I don't—"

"Please, Holly. I'll explain, just don't leave yet."

She had promised to buy him lunch for all that he'd done for her. Curiosity had always been her undoing. It was just a meal. No big deal.

"Lead the way."

Those three little words carved an enormous smile onto his defined jaw.

Thirty minutes later, she parked next to Grayson's truck, facing the waterfront.

With his hand at the sway of her back, he opened the oak-stained door to a restaurant called Lighthouse Bar and Grill. The place looked upscale with wood accents and a brick fireplace. Well past lunch, the tables weren't overloaded with guests.

The young hostess collected two menus without breaking her gaze on Grayson. Holly had to admit, he was a walking, talking fantasy in a uniform.

"Table by the window?" he asked the hostess.

The young woman smiled and led the way to a four-person table with a view of the ocean. Would have been nice to sit outside, but the rain continued to fall, removing that option.

"Can I get you some drinks?" the woman asked, handing them the menus.

Grayson removed the green sheriff's jacket he wore and dropped it in the extra chair. "I'll have whatever is on tap. Darker the better."

"Ice water," Holly said. The server turned and with the body-hugging black dress she wore, put a lot of hip action into her retreat.

"Swinging for the other team?" he teased.

"What? Get real." She laughed. "I've never had a body like that. Just jealous."

He sat back in his chair, removed his ball cap and ran a hand through his dirty-blond hair.

"You didn't have to arrest me to buy you lunch. I told you I owed you one." As if he was absolutely, completely content gazing at her, she squirmed a little in her seat. "Det. Sterling said you questioned the guy all night who attacked me."

"Nope."

Huh? That's what his partner had said. "Nope?"

"Not talking about the case."

The server returned with their drinks. "Would you like to order?"

Grayson didn't even look at the woman. "Holly, are you allergic to seafood?"

"No," she said. "I love seafood."

"We'll have the seafood appetizers. Clams, mussels, prawns, calamari and bread."

The server shifted closer to Holly, as if hoping the detective would look at her. "Yes, sir. Anything else?"

"That'll do for now."

When the server trotted off to submit their order, Holly said, "That's a lot of food, Detective."

"From this second forward, you're going to dump the *detective* bullshit. I carried your sweet, nearly naked butt in my arms to the bathroom in the middle of the night." He pointed at himself. "Grayson did that, not a detective. As for a lot of food, I don't want her interrupting you every five minutes."

"Me? You look like you're on a mission or an interrogation."

He cleared his throat and rested his forearms on the table. "You should feel guilty."

She had a few ideas why he might say that. "Because I left your office when you told me to stay? You went off chasing bad guys. I went home."

"You went home because you'd convinced yourself that I had someone in my life. And you never called me when you came back to the resort for the same reason."

Her gaze roamed toward the fireplace. "This is a really nice place. Have you been here before?"

He didn't answer until she returned her attention to him, and his lips lifted into a sexy smile.

"You're very good at redirecting questions and so far, I've let you get away with it, but not anymore. Answer the question."

"Maybe."

Grayson kept the spotlight on her as their appetizers were deposited on the table. Holly told him about her entire family in Nova Scotia. He asked about her job and seemed content to listen to everything she said.

"What about your family?"

"Nope." He slid the last calamari on the plate toward her with his index finger. "You're not finished. Nowhere near finished."

She popped the squid in her mouth. "Can't talk wid a foo mouf." She munched slowly on the lightly battered tender ring.

He chuckled, resting against the back of his chair and downed a deep swallow of beer. "Tell me why you were crying."

"I did tell you. Relief."

He sighed. "Okay, we'll do it the hard way." His gaze swayed toward the window. "You're a regular at the resort but it's not about the gambling, is it?"

As much as she enjoyed spending time in his company, she didn't want to bare the uglies of her life. "No."

"You always come alone."

She shrugged. "I'm comfortable there. The accommodations are perfect. I can step out on the balcony, and I'm surrounded by tall trees and flowering gardens. There's a swimming pool. Every morning, I use the workout facility and run off a few calories from the amazing food in the restaurants. The staff knows me, and the people are always friendly. In the summer, when the sun rises and I look out over the fields toward the Cascade Mountain range, I'm filled with a sense of peace."

He listened patiently then asked, "Who stole your peace, Holly?"

His intense stare had a way of drawing the truth from her. "I don't mean to make myself sound insecure, but I don't understand why you kissed me."

Grayson reached across the table and collected both her

hands. "Because I needed to." He paused and eyed her. "I'm getting close to the truth, and it makes you nervous."

"Have you ever been married?"

"No. But you have, haven't you?"

She wanted to navigate this subject without sounding like a complete failure. "Yes."

"But now you're not."

"Divorced. We were married for eight years. I didn't know he was seeing other women during most of them. He dropped the charade two years ago. One day, out of the blue, he came home after a shift and said he loved someone else. He packed a bag and left."

Grayson's blue gaze never wavered. "What did he do for a living?"

She withdrew her hands, placing them in her lap. Holly reminded herself that her ex had never kissed her like Grayson. When she reflected on their relationship, she realized she'd always come second place to Kevin's job, to his hobbies, and to his buddies. She was an afterthought, and no woman should be an afterthought to the man she marries.

"Holly?"

She licked her dry lips and collected the empty appetizer plates, piling them one on top of the other at the edge of their table.

"Does it matter?" She turned in her chair, looking for the server. "They should do a better job of clearing the plates."

"Miss McNeela, between the moments when you smile and literally affect me in a way I've never felt before, I've also seen wariness in your eyes."

Did she do that? If so, it was unintentional. "I think gawking like a crazy stalker chick would be more appropriate."

He crossed his arms over an obscenely firm chest. She'd know, since he'd carried her in his arms more than once.

"You said he came home after a shift. What did your ex do for a living?"

She sighed. Well, this was nice while it lasted. "Um."

"Um?" he repeated, raising one eyebrow. "Not the answer I'd expect from a linguistics expert."

She smiled. "You know, even after all that food, dessert would be good. How about you?"

The strap of his brow flattened as did his mouth.

Holly actually considered telling him that Kevin was an architect and put the entire business to bed, but she couldn't do it.

She tsked and tapped the table with her fingernails. "He's a police officer. RCMP."

Grayson leaned back in his seat and a slip of a smile tilted his lips as if he'd already figured it out. "I see. And by any chance, did he slide into the old trope of screwing his partner?"

Holly closed her eyes, embarrassed. Not because Grayson was correct, but because when your husband dumps you for another woman, or man for that matter, you can't help but feel inferior. "Yes, he did."

Unexpectedly, he rested his large, callused hands palms up on the table. Without him asking, she clasped his strong hands.

"Listen, not all cops are dicks. I've known plenty that are tried and true family men. You married an asshole. He burned you, but that doesn't mean we're all the same."

Here she was, sitting with a man who was more handsome than ninety-nine percent of the male population, but he was single. It didn't add up. His heart-throbbing masculine features never failed to make her heart race.

"I find it hard to believe you're not married."

Grayson's smile evaporated. "Because I'm not an asshole."

"No, but you're incredibly attractive."

"Glad you think so."

"Don't be a smartass. You're very familiar with the power of attraction, especially your own." After her bad luck in relationships, she needed to protect her heart and he was being evasive. "You know what I'm asking."

Grayson's thumb gently caressed her wrist, causing a storm of goosebumps. "Yes, I know what you're asking. Romance as a Special Operator isn't exactly like the books you read."

Her cheeks heated. "You sure about that? One of the main themes is most guys are the love 'em and leave 'em types. They can't commit."

"Okay, so maybe some parts are based in reality," he admitted and rolled his shoulders as if to loosen them.

Holly begrudgingly let go of his hands and relaxed against her backrest. "You don't expect me to believe you couldn't have married ten times over by now."

"Sure. And divorced ten times too." He scraped his palm across his defined jaw. "In my case, it's about bad choices."

"Bad choices." Weren't they all guilty of that at some point? Including her. "When it comes to women, I'm sure you have frequent flyer miles."

"I didn't spend more than two months at home when I was a SEAL. Either I was training or I was deployed. Doesn't leave a lot of time for a relationship. When I joined the San Diego Sheriff's Department, I treated the job like I did when I was in the teams. Threw myself into catching criminals while I transitioned back into civilian life."

A virile man like Grayson had more than his fair share of sex, but it wasn't her place to go picking through the debris of his life. Yet, the scarred part of her soul looked for warning signs.

"None of that sounds like bad choices. Sounds honorable to me."

"My profession, maybe."

Grayson picked up his lightweight jacket and withdrew a book from the inside pocket. When he laid it on the table and slowly pushed it with one finger in her direction, she laughed.

She picked up the paperback and said, "Aww, you

shouldn't have."

The novel was a non-fiction written by a real Navy SEAL.

"Thought you might appreciate a few pages of reality from the horse's mouth."

She flipped open the front cover and gasped.

Holly, hope you enjoy my book. Bone asked me to sign a copy for you. Be good to that frogman, he deserves it.

She gaped with surprise. "You know the author!"

Grayson nodded. "We were in the same platoon during my last three years of service."

"This is amazing. Thank you so much." She closed the book. "Your team name was Bone?"

"Yep. And believe me, it's not a story I like telling."

She laughed. "Oh, but you will."

They both grinned, looking into each other's eyes.

"Yeah," he said. "I will." He gently covered her hand. "Just like you're going to toss those romance novels in the fire once I've made love to you."

Her breath lodged in her throat and every degree of heat in Grayson's eyes was absorbed by the sharp ache between her thighs.

"Oh," dribbled from her lips.

"We're on your timeline, sweetheart. There's no rush." He cleared his throat. "I'll admit, saying that is a first for me, but I mean it."

Her nipples tightened and her breathing shallowed. "I'm not sure how to respond to that."

Grayson tipped his head to the side, his blue eyes simmering with meaning. "You already are, Holly." A subtle but satisfied smile touched his mouth as his gaze dipped to her breasts.

She hadn't given this man enough credit. His ability to notice little things was far sharper than she'd suspected. Holly crossed her arms over her chest because her tight tank top revealed how his words affected her.

A confident, sexy smile carved his jaw. "Far too late for

that, sweetheart. I can't stop thinking about you in that black negligee. But I guarantee the next time you wear it, I'm going to leave it in shreds."

It took all her willpower not to call for the bill and yank him to the nearest hotel room. She had no idea when this fairytale would end, but before it did, she was going to sleep with this enigmatic, sensual man.

They talked and talked some more over dessert and coffee.

"We're closing in fifteen minutes," the server said, and slid the bill onto their table.

Holly glanced at her watch, more than surprised to see it was ten o'clock. When she dug for her wallet, Grayson added a tip to the bill and handed the server his credit card.

"Hey, that's not what we agreed on," she said.

"Maybe tomorrow."

When the server returned, he put the card back in his wallet. She held the paperback to her chest, and they left the restaurant. The rain had stopped, and the air smelled fresh but salty. They walked to where they'd parked their cars. Saying goodbye wouldn't be easy.

"I'm sure the border isn't too busy this time of night. I better get on the road."

His hands slid around her waist. "Running away again."

Grayson was at least a foot taller than her, but she loved looking into his eyes and tipped her chin upward. When he touched her, tingles sparked all over her body. "I'm not running. I'm going home."

"Call the resort."

"I'm sure they're full. It's the long weekend."

"Not in the US. Not yet." The detective reached into his pocket and pulled his cell, dialed a number and put it on speaker.

"Neon Lights Resort."

Clark regularly worked the night shift, and she recognized his voice.

"Yes, this is Det. Brooks from the Skagit County Sheriff's Office. Holly McNeela has an open invite from management for an executive suite at the hotel. Any rooms available for tonight and tomorrow? In fact, we have a suspect in custody in regard to the incident at the resort. I'd like her to stay until the fifth."

Her mouth gaped. "What? The fifth?" she mouthed.

"Aaaah, yes, of course." The sound of quick fingers on a keyboard came through the line. "I'll make the arrangements," Clark said.

"Good. She'll be there in twenty minutes." Grayson disconnected.

"I can't stay until the fifth."

"Why not? It's summer. Don't you get vacation leave?"

"Yyyyes, but, but—"

"But what?"

He brushed his carved jaw against her cheek, causing ripples of excitement. Even the faint scent of his aftershave thrilled her.

"Why until the fifth? I brought one change of clothes. I can't stay."

"Yes, you can," he said in a seductive timbre.

Tilting his head down, Grayson's mouth eased over her lips and her body flushed with heat. He kissed her with a confidence that obliterated any argument and ignited her nerve endings. She couldn't help but slide her arms around his neck and paste herself against his firm body. Grayson's thick arms circled her waist with a possessive hold and Holly's heart thumped wildly.

"I'll work," he said, barely moving away from her mouth. "You shop. Relax. Swim. Research. But when four o'clock comes, you're mine. If...I can stay away that long."

His firm lips pressed against hers with such heat, she finally understood the term boneless that she'd read so often. She'd be crazy to refuse his offer, and she did have a stack of vacation she hadn't used.

"All right, I'll stay," she said when he gave her a moment to breathe.

"It's late. I'll follow you back to the resort."

She smiled at his concern. "You don't have to do that."

But that's exactly what he did.

Standing at the door to the suite, he drew her against his firm chest and laid a penetrating kiss goodnight on her lips.

"I'll be back tomorrow afternoon," he said drawing away, then stopped short. "There it is. That look of fear. I swear to God, if you cross that border, I'm coming after you this time," he warned.

"You didn't before."

"A mistake I paid for dearly since I took out my foul mood on my family. Luckily, they're the forgiving type."

She straightened her shoulders. "You might be able to sniff fear but really, it's self-preservation. I have an impending broken heart to consider."

He pinned her against the closed door. "I know exactly what you're afraid of, Holly, because I might have a mild case of it myself, but that's not stopping me. Not with you."

She snorted. "I doubt that, Dr. Brooks," she teased. "Seriously, what's happening here? You said you'd explain but instead, I did most of the talking."

His blue gaze coursed across her face. "Fair enough. I'll keep it short. The man I used to be would already have you in that room with your legs draped over his shoulders and his face between your thighs." Grayson paused to steal a kiss. "That's still going to happen, sweetheart, but the old me would take his sweet time fucking you, then leave and never come back."

She licked her lips and swallowed thickly. "And the new you?"

"He's patient and on his best behavior until you tell him to stop...and he is *most definitely* coming back."

Holly had never experienced desire like this before. It

burned with impatience. "Is there a good reason you're changing your ethos?

A beguiling grin slid across his mouth. "You're the reason. I'm more certain of that now than I was before."

God help her, because she was in no position to save herself.

"Here." She offered him the second key card to her suite. "Just in case I'm out or napping when you get here."

He slid the card in his shirt pocket and backed away. "Night, Miss McNeela."

Grayson swiftly disappeared around the corner. She waited until she couldn't hear his footsteps any longer before she forced her trembling legs to move.

CHAPTER SEVENTEEN

G rayson followed his partner into the interrogation room. Poor old Rory wasn't looking too good now that he didn't have another high to look forward to.

Cole took a seat at the table while Grayson leaned against the wall in the claustrophobic-sized white space.

Last night, they'd read him his rights and formally charged Rory on numerous counts. He got his one phone call and a visit by a lawyer this morning, who walked in wearing an ill-fitting suit and two days' worth of beard. To Grayson, the guy looked hungover and disinterested.

Cole opened a folder with Rory's paperwork. "Mr. Hannigen, you're being transferred to the county jail to await your initial court hearing. Your victim is willing to testify in this case, and I'm sure you'll be spending a few years in prison as a consolation prize."

Rory's leg pistoned up and down as he sat slumped in the chair and tapped a finger on the white table, glancing at Cole. "I tol' you where we store the shit."

"Yes, you did. But not the name of who's in charge."

"I'm no fucking snitch."

"Cooperating with law enforcement is a sign that you're willing to turn over a new leaf, especially to a judge," Cole stated.

The grimace on the guy's face told Grayson he didn't give a rat's ass about going straight. There wasn't a lot you could say to a criminal except offer a loose promise for less time behind bars. That's all they really cared about.

"I done time before," Rory scoffed.

Cole kept an even tone, doling out the details in a matter-of-fact manner. "You've been charged with Assault in the Second Degree and Burglary. You'll be spending at least ten years in prison, my friend."

The punk's brow cinched tight, and he bolted up in his chair. "Bullshit."

"Sorry, kid. Your victim ended up with a fractured knee. Not much your pro-bono lawyer can do. Proof is in the x-rays."

Cole closed the file and stood up.

"What if I tell you who's running the operation?"

The detective strayed a look in Grayson's direction, and he took over. "Look, we know you have more than one stash house. By now, the address you gave us is empty. You want to share who's running the show and all the other places you're using to hide the merchandise, there may be an option for lowering your sentence."

Twenty minutes later, Rory was shuffled to a holding cell to await a transport to county jail. The kid had done a bang-up job of spilling his guts.

Grayson joined his partner at Cole's desk. "We're dealing with a big operation here. Far bigger than we suspected."

Rory supplied the location of four other stash houses in Clayton and a warehouse on the waterfront. The ring had expanded to dealing drugs and running a prostitution operation. Rory said he'd heard a guy named Cage Martin was pulling the strings.

Cole entered Cage's name in CJIS, the information system, and searched for a criminal history.

"That's what I suspected," Cole said, reading the guy's record.

Gray leaned closer to see the monitor. Cage belonged to a one-percenter gang. He'd done time for numerous felonies, from sex to narcotics trafficking. Biker gangs were usually behind the bigger operations. This was no surprise.

"We need to scope this out before we put out a call to assemble a team. Rory can't risk tipping off his buddies or they'll find a way to punish him in prison. As long as word doesn't get out that we've got him in custody, the operation won't get nervous."

Cole printed the rap sheets and added them to the main file. "Neighbors in Clayton will be happy we take down the safe houses, but the big target is that warehouse."

Grayson looked over the desks toward Kline's office. "Lieutenant's not on the phone. Let's give him a SITREP and see what he thinks."

Forty-five minutes later, Gray and Cole left Kline's office. The lieutenant had some calls to put wheels in motion with other departments. Unlike the movies, SWAT wouldn't swoop in until there was some recon and a plan in place. More than likely, it would be a multi-location takedown that occurred simultaneously, hopefully catching as many bad guys as they could in one fell swoop.

Grayson headed for his desk to collect his ball cap and close his laptop.

"You headed home?" Cole asked.

He couldn't help but grin. "Nope. I got a date."

Cole blinked. "You're kidding! You caught up to her."

"Sure did. Gotta tell ya, I've never spent ten hours at a restaurant talking with one woman before."

"Ho, man. Sounds like you covered life from diapers to death."

Gray chuckled as he checked his phone. No messages. "I convinced her to stay until the fifth."

"You spent all that time with her, and she still wants to see you again. Damn. Aren't you a hot ticket item," he joked. "What about all the set-up for the Fourth of July celebration?"

"I wake up early and get things done before I come to work. Besides, Ivy's got you to order around now." He clapped his friend on the back. "Take care of things while I woo the pants off a very intelligent woman."

Cole walked with him to the parking lot. "What the hell's

gotten into you?"

He grinned. "I kissed her."

His buddy laughed. "Yeah, and what? Does that mean she reset all your factory settings?" He laughed again. "Pretty sure you've kissed plenty of women."

True, he had, but none like Holly. When he'd palmed her back and pressed her warm body to his chest, it was like switching the main breaker and powering his entire soul. Her energy and his ignited into something explosive. Something real. Something he had to pursue.

"That's the difference. She's sexy but intelligent too."

"So, are you taking this intriguing woman who's captured your heart to the library?"

Grayson plucked the sunglasses from his chest pocket and shoved them over the bridge of his nose. "I don't give a damn, long as I can look in those grey eyes of hers. Let Ivy know I won't be back for dinner."

He hopped into his truck and gunned the engine, feeling good all over.

* * * *

Holly swept the bedsheets aside and wandered to the window. Pulling back the heavy drapes, the morning sun streamed over the open fields with the Cascade Mountains standing like sentinels in the background. She'd never tire of the sight. Whenever she looked out her townhouse window, all she saw were other townhouses. She hated that. Maybe she should sell her place. Find a new space and make new memories without Kevin's shadows lurking in the corners.

After a quick shower, she walked to the coffee hut to get twenty-one ounces of dark roast java and sat at the wrought iron table, enjoying the summer warmth on her cheeks. Content wasn't just a word, it was a road to peace, and she was currently driving with the window down and the wind blowing through her hair. Last night, spending all that time with Grayson and his undivided attention was by far the best date she'd ever had.

Energized, she plotted her day after calling the university and shocking the hell out of her department head when she said she'd like to use some of her vacation time. Arthur Carlson had wholeheartedly agreed and approved the leave. They spoke for a while about the tablets from Jerusalem and she gave him her initial thoughts. They could have easily slid down the rabbit hole debating the subject, but he thoughtfully said they'd speak when she returned from vacation and wished her a good holiday.

After finishing her coffee, she dumped the cup in the recycling bin and walked back toward the resort. She'd spend a couple hours in the casino, go shopping, and if time permitted, a swim then maybe a nap before Grayson arrived. About to enter the casino, her phone alerted with an incoming text.

Run away yet?

She grinned.

Nope. I got your six.

Two eye-rolling emoji showed up, followed by *Stop reading those books.*

Gnawing on her bottom lip, she typed, *Make me.*

Say that again when I see you this afternoon.

She sent him two little sailors saluting.

You're making it hard to concentrate on the case.

Say again. What am I making hard???

He sent two laughing emoji with tears running down their faces. *Have a good day, sweetheart.*

She planned to do just that.

Holly slid her phone into the outer pocket of her purse. Entering the casino, the sound of machines, bright lights, and the ambiance made her grin. Wandering the colorful carpet, she spied a favorite slot. The bank was at full capacity. She eyed the progressive jackpot. Nearly four-hundred and fifty grand. This particular set of machines rarely got that high, that's why there was no room left. Standing at a respectable distance behind the players, the elderly gentleman seated right in front of her got up.

"I've donated enough. Want to play?" he asked

"Sure." She eased into the chair after he moved aside. "Thank you."

The man was somewhere in his seventies and winked. "Good luck. I gotta feeling that jackpot is going to pop today."

To her, slots were a mindless type of therapy. She was never a frenzied player, chasing jackpots like some people. She just got a kick out of the bonus rounds and the odd streak of luck if you happened to be on the right machine at the right time.

"Something to drink?" a woman said, passing behind Holly.

The seats swiveled, and she turned one hundred and eighty degrees.

"Hey, Sheila," she greeted, knowing the attractive brunette who'd worked the floor for many years.

"Holly. Hi! Hey, I heard what happened to you. Are you okay?"

She continued to leisurely hit the play button at the same time talking with Sheila. "For sure. My knee's fractured, but it'll heal. How've you been?"

"Really good. Looking forward to a week off. We're taking the kids to Lake Chelan."

"Camping?"

"You bet. Ever been?" Sheila asked, balancing the brown bar tray on one hand.

"Never, but I hear it's beautiful."

Sheila's eyes suddenly rounded. "Holy cow!" She looked past Holly at the machines.

People around her erupted with excited comments and pointed.

"What?" Holly asked, swiveling to look at the other machines around her. But the people were smiling and looking her way. It took a second before her eyes returned to her own machine.

"Congratulations," said the elderly woman to her right.

"Oh my God!" She couldn't believe it. The machine locked up and a large blue square appeared over the top of the monitor. *Jackpot. Call attendant. Hand Pay $449,997.* Music from the slot indicating a jackpot played loudly as Holly's mouth gaped. "I—I won!"

Before long, a huge crowd formed behind her. Two casino attendants slid through the lookie-loos and congratulated her. While one of the attendants accepted Holly's player card and driver's license to write the information on the tax forms used to pay out winners, Holly stepped away from the machine as a female slot attendant inserted a card and entered a code, which put her into the background settings of the machine. She checked a few things, spoke into her communications radio that all the attendants wore, and then reset the machine.

"Don't forget you've still got two hundred dollars in the machine," she said.

"Thank you."

The other attendant called for a supervisor. A few seconds later, the senior staff member, wearing a dark, pinstriped suit, eased through the crowd to join them.

"Congratulations," she piped as she reviewed the form. "How would you like the payout, Holly?"

With shopping on the horizon, she asked for a specific amount in cash and the rest in a check, which she'd deposit in her US bank account.

Today was going to be a great day.

By three o'clock, Holly's bedroom was filled with shopping bags. New shoes. New clothes—from jeans to a slinky black dress. And, yes, new lingerie.

Uncertain exactly when Grayson would get off work, she eyed the deep Jacuzzi tub in her room. She had time. After turning the taps on, she stripped then pinned her hair on top of her head.

The jets stirred the tub into a cauldron of bubbling goodness, and she eased into the sublime warmth, stretching her legs out and tipping her head back.

Heaven.

* * * *

Grayson clocked out an hour early. Instead of driving home to ditch the uniform, he headed straight for the resort. Striding past hotel registration, he nodded at the woman behind the counter. Not wanting to wait for the slow elevator, he took the stairs, two at a time. Holly's suite was situated at the end of the hallway and each step closer elevated his pulse.

Walking away from her last night had been damn hard. Back at the farmstead, he'd taken a shower to literally put out the fire Holly caused in his veins. Getting himself off wasn't something he'd done since high school, but the cold water didn't provide any relief.

With one palm against the shower tiles, he'd gripped his heavy cock and closed his eyes. He invited their first kiss into his mind. Lust took the helm, and he imagined her beautiful lips sliding over his shaft. The vision of her pretty cheeks hollowing and her brilliant eyes staring into his shoved him straight over the edge. His knees had weakened, tension coiled at the base of his spine, and his body shuddered with a wicked release.

Gray had taken the edge off, but his desire barked and lunged at the end of its chain like a rabid dog. The texts they'd exchanged earlier kept him in a heightened state of anticipation the whole damn day.

He paused in front of her suite. Should he knock? Yeah, he should knock.

No answer.

Grayson slid the key card through the lock and opened the light-stained wood door. Stepping into the comfortably appointed suite with a living room, large bathroom, and separate bedroom, he heard a low rumble. He couldn't see the bedroom from his position and ventured toward the living room. Flames licked the logs in the two-way gas fireplace, visible from the living room and bedroom.

"Holly?"

"In here."

He stopped in the bedroom doorway, resting his hungry gaze on Holly in the burbling tub. Raven-colored wisps of moist hair curled around her cheeks and the smile on the woman's face turned him inside out.

"You're early."

Not early, right on time. The slow burn in his belly threatening a jump to a four-alarm fire. He surveyed the room. She'd been busy, the green, fabric-covered bench next to the tub piled with shopping bags. Two shiny helium balloons, attached to a weight, floated above the bedside table, *Congratulations* written on one of them.

"I see you've had a good day," he said, not daring to step any closer.

The sweetest smile lifted her expression and made her eyes twinkle. "You could say that."

Trying to pace the mounting impatience to cross the room, he asked, "Balloons?"

She chuckled. "I got lucky."

He nodded slowly and raked his teeth over his upper lip. "Really."

"Mm-hmm." Her gaze swerved to the dresser where the TV monitor sat to his left. "Open it," she said, referring to a scroll of paper tied with a bright red ribbon.

He loosened the ribbon and fingered open the paper. "You're kidding!"

A note of congratulations on winning a few bucks shy of four hundred and fifty grand.

"I'm also officially on vacation, approved by my department head."

"Now it's *my* lucky day."

Her leave was far more exciting than her jackpot. Seeing her in the tub, the bubbles concealing her body, added to the sensual tension. He set the scroll aside, crossed his arms, and leaned against the doorway.

"Did you catch any bad guys?" she asked.

"We charged the guy who assaulted you, plus got some viable leads that could bring down a large criminal ring."

"Huh. That's impressive, and instead of kicking down doors and arresting more bad guys, you're here."

He recognized the standoff happening between them, and enjoyed the hell out of it. Gray's mind took snapshots of her in the tub while reality poked him in the ribs, reminding him that she'd have to go home and lived in another country.

"I'd work every day of the week if this was the sight I'd get when I clocked out."

Holly's dark lashes fluttered. "Are you going to come closer?"

"Are you asking?"

Her slender shoulder shrugged, and she raised her right leg out of the water, flexing her toes. "Up to you, of course."

He unlatched the leather guard on his holster, slowly removed his sidearm, and set it on top of the dresser.

She watched him with interest. "Disarming yourself. Is that wise?"

Things were getting increasingly uncomfortable behind his zipper. When it came to chemistry, he knew the intensity of raw lust. His past was littered with women he'd fucked and forgotten. That's not what was happening here. He wasn't only removing his weapon, he was disarming all the walls he'd erected over the years and leaving the door open for her to come and go as she pleased.

"You make me vulnerable," he said, playing along with her joke, but it was the truth.

She shook her head. "I'm pretty sure it's the other way around." Holly sidelined her playful tone, and her smile withered as if struck with a notion that pulled the plug on her confidence. "A guy with your extraordinary good looks, once a quarterback, a successful Navy SEAL, and now law enforcement, has a long list of gorgeous women in his past."

No way was he going to let her back down. "Yes, I have a past, but those women and my actions bear no resemblance to what's happening between us."

Her expression tightened with a concerned smile. "You know what I think?"

Worried the scars her ex inflicted kept her from trusting him, he said, "I'm listening."

"I'm attracted to a man I shouldn't be. I should know better. I *do* know better. Before I toss all my common sense out the window, should we stop at friendship?"

"If that's what you want."

Normally, he appreciated Holly's pragmatic character, but there was no way he'd let her fear veil itself as a reason and poison their relationship. He had a shitload to be worried about himself. Gray had no idea if he'd shut down emotionally after they got physical. It had happened so fast, and he had no control over the response. But he had to try.

"Don't you think it would be wise?" she asked.

"Before we make a decision, shouldn't we analyze the evidence?"

Her brow knit together. "Evidence?"

"Uh-huh. For example, you must assume that I chased you down the highway and asked you to stay because all I want is your friendship." One dark eyebrow lifted, but she didn't respond. "Guess I nearly tripped over my own feet when I first saw you because I'm a klutz and it had nothing to do with how truly attractive you are to me. I suppose when I spotted you at the farmstead and my pulse tripled, it was really angina. And the only reason I think about you every single day is because I've got nothing better to do."

Her moist, pink tongue slid over her bottom lip. "Um."

"Um," he repeated while grinning. That was twice she'd done that. A definite *tell* and one he'd store for future reference. "If you'd like to refute the evidence, I'm waiting."

"Grayson, it's one thing to be a hot superhero, but being a hot superhero with intelligence and integrity is disconcerting to me."

"Holly, I guarantee I'm no hero and at this moment, my integrity is stretched pretty thin." She certainly knew how to make a man feel good about himself. "I'm going to allay your confusion." His heart thumped like a war drum. "Integrity is the last word you'd use if you knew how fucking hot you look right now and what I want."

"I see."

"I don't think you do."

She cleared her throat. "You're telling me to stop being a chicken shit and grab the situation by both balls."

Her analogy made him laugh. "That's one way to sum it up," he said, still chuckling.

Holly's delicate hand rose from the tub, tipping a stream of water from her palm. "If I'm to foolishly assume that you like me as much as I like you, then what's the plan?"

He'd planned on taking her for a leisurely walk at a nearby park. The sun was out. Warm afternoon. "Think my plans have changed," he admitted.

"Have they."

Grayson crossed the bedroom and sat on the wide tile surround of the tub. Her brilliant grey gaze followed and threw him into complete and utter chaos. Except for one thought.

Holly's wet hand slid over his thigh, lighting a fire he wanted to extinguish on her. But he'd promised he'd be on his best behavior. If he was reading her sweet but sexy signals right, she wanted him but at this stage of their relationship, she would never make the first move. At least not without a little nudge.

The fireplace, located a few feet from the end of the tub, infused the room with heat. The heavy drapes were open, and the white sheers allowed filtered light but maintained privacy.

Communicating his feelings to a woman had never been his thing but with Holly, he'd cross every "T" and dot her lips with "I" really want you.

"I love kissing you, Holly."

He leaned over and pressed his mouth to her soft lips. With her response as heated as his own, he eased his tongue inside to explore, to penetrate, each motion like rocking on a gentle sea. Before retreating, he gently sucked on her bottom lip because he'd dreamed of doing it so many times.

She was taking a chance on him. He knew that. After ending a marriage of mistrust, she had a right to be skittish.

"Two things could happen here," he said, not moving far from the lips he wanted to kiss again. "I can wait in the living room while you dry off, get dressed, and we head out for a leisurely walk."

"Or?" she asked in a husky voice.

Only the tops of her full breasts showed above the bubbling waterline, and he traced his thumb where water and skin met. She rested her head against the tub's sloped edge, and he kissed her blush lips at the same time dipping his fingers beneath the warm water and teasing one very taut nipple.

"Or—we can stay here and burn those damn books."

"Option number two, please," she whispered against his mouth. "But...I have a confession to make."

Although he wanted to spend more time on her tight bud, he thumbed her delicate jaw and nodded for her to go on.

"I got into this tub an hour ago, but I couldn't get out." Her bottom lip shifted into a playful pout.

Gray turned his head away, his shoulders shaking as he laughed. And here he'd thought she was trying to seduce him the second he stepped in the door. Instead, she was stuck because of her fractured knee. He shook his head, unable to wipe the smile from his face. Fuck, he really liked this woman.

Gazing into her eyes, his heart swelled. "I'm more than willing to rescue you, sweetheart."

Lifting a very warm and wet Holly from the water, he set her feet on the top of the tile surround, putting her incredible breasts at his eye level.

"Ummm, Grayson, are you going to help me down?"

"Not until I'm ready, sweetheart." *Damn!* "And I'm a long way from ready."

He picked up the fresh towel that lay rolled next to her feet and dabbed her soft skin, following each motion with a kiss, until his lips brushed over one delicious, tight nipple.

Holly's fingertips sunk into his shoulders.

Teasing the full bud into his mouth, he rolled his tongue over the firm peak.

"Grayson." She gasped. "That feels so...."

He wanted to caress all her curves. His hand swam around her hip and palmed her ass, while his other hand grazed her flat stomach until he reached her clit, stroking the delicate, slick nub.

"God, I never thought I'd get to touch you like this."

Moisture coated her sex, and he eased his middle finger into her hot core. Holly gasped and her head tipped back when he increased the tempo and squeezed her nipple between his lips, laving the tip with his tongue.

Pleasuring her felt so goddamn good.

"My legs are going to give out," she warned.

Wrapping his arms around her waist, he picked her up and laid her on the king bed. Gently trapping her wrists, he slid them above her head then grinned. "Earlier, I detected a challenge when it came to those crazy books."

She smiled. "Every woman needs a little romance in her life."

"You need more than that." His gaze strayed across the soft angles of her face. "I want you to need *me,* not some fictional character from a book. I'm not a hero. I have flaws, Holly."

"I'm laying naked in front of you, and you think you have flaws."

He traced her bottom lip with his tongue. "I've wanted this since the second I saw you. You're my kind of perfect."

"Far from it, Grayson, but you make me feel good about myself. Is your uniform staying or going?" she asked.

He hadn't expected this to happen today and he sure as hell didn't carry condoms while in uniform. Pressing a kiss to her shoulder blade, then the fullness of her right breast, he acquired his target and nursed one firm nipple.

"Oh," gusted from her mouth before he found his way back to her lips.

As much as he wanted to bury himself in her heat, he could wait. But he couldn't wait to explore. Discover what turned her on and watch her come.

"I told you..." he whispered next to her ear, then kissed her slender throat. "I'm on my best behavior."

Her eyes opened, a wrinkle of doubt resting on her expression.

Shifting to her right side, he traced the contour of her sweet body with his hand and came to rest on her mons. With his middle finger, he made a whisper pass over her slick nub and a satisfying sound of pleasure escaped her throat.

"It's been so long, Grayson. I'm nervous."

His gaze strayed over her gorgeous breasts, no longer hidden behind that tempting black silk she'd worn the night of the attack.

He placed a kiss just below her navel. "You're beautiful to me, Holly. I want to make you feel the same way."

With her legs pinned together, he could tell she wasn't confident or comfortable with her body. Holly's modesty was commendable but not what he wanted. As he gently spread her gorgeous thighs, revealing her bare pussy, his heart thundered.

"Gray, what are you doing?"

"I promised you'd turf those books, now I'm going to show you why, sweetheart."

Shifting his position to kneel between her legs, he leaned forward and pressed a soft kiss on her clit. With her little ass in his palms, he went down on her with no mercy.

He'd been wrong about how enticing she'd looked sipping on a milkshake. From his angle, with her hips raised, her nipples peaked with desire and pleasure making her moan, she was gorgeous. He lost himself, taking her on a sensual ride to ecstasy.

But he only got partway there before Holly demanded he ditch his clothes. He didn't need to go into a long diatribe about not having protection. She'd figured it out. If she wanted him naked, that's what she'd get. This was the first time in his life when his thoughts remained solely on making a woman happy.

As he undressed, Holly sat on the edge of the bed and watched with a sexy little smile on her lips. He had no clue how she did it, but when he looked into her eyes, every woman he'd known was swept from existence.

His pulse drummed with anticipation when her fingertips trailed up his bare abs and she placed a gentle kiss on his right hip, then one above his navel and one on his left hip. His cock ached, but he watched, enraptured at how she touched him. Her index finger slid up his dick from root to tip as if making a new discovery like he imagined she read one of her ancient scripts. Holly tipped her chin and looked into his eyes.

"I want to taste you, Gray."

Already panting and certain he'd been waiting his entire life for her, he palmed her cheeks. "God, you are an amazing woman."

Holly's warm tongue licked his crown, and he shook all

over. But when her lips slid over his shaft, his imagination didn't come close. The hot walls of her mouth like velvet on his erection.

"Aw, sweet Holly."

He tangled his fingers in her soft curls. His body flooded with heat from the way her mouth glided up and down his cock. Her pace was perfect. With her dainty hands gripping his ass and all that practice sucking on a straw, the first ripple of release warned he was going to come faster than his first blowjob at sixteen.

Gray retreated from her sensual lips, then kissed her till her back lay against the bed. He kneeled between her open thighs, and she gripped his cock. He tightened his hand over hers and pumped.

"Oh shit, baby." Passion nearly blinded his vision. When she swept his crown through her silky moisture, he lost it. His cum coated her clit in thready streams and his body unraveled in a way it never had before.

Fuck, the little minx had done it again. Instead of deferring the conversation to him, this time she'd made him come before her.

"That was hotter than any book I've ever read," she said, grinning at him and propped on her forearms.

He wasn't angry, he was determined. He leaned over her, palmed the mattress by her left shoulder and used the bed sheet to dab her clean before he eased two fingers into her hot core. "No, Holly. Don't close your eyes. Look at me."

Her amazing silver gaze centered on him. "Why?"

Holly's hips began to shift, matching the tempo of his fingers.

"Because I want you to see how much I love touching you."

When he strummed her clit, Holly's brow crushed into tight lines and her teeth raked her bottom lip. "Gray!"

Shit, his cock was thickening again. "Jesus, you're so fucking hot." Her head rocked back, and her shapely thighs draped open. "That's it, baby."

He took his time, reading her body, and when she was almost at the point of no return, that's when he suckled her firm clit. Her back arched and she cried out in a shuddering release.

Holly napped in his arms while his palm gently caressed her back. He closed his eyes and must have fallen asleep. When he woke, it was near sunset. In no hurry to roll out of bed, he threaded his fingers in her hair because he loved the feel of her soft curls. As she came to, her slender arm squeezed his waist, and her warm breath caressed his chest.

He had no desire to untangle himself. None. There was no logical reason why he'd changed, but he needed to stop worrying about the past.

"Hey, sweetheart. You must be hungry."

"A little," she muttered, but snuggled closer, then blinked her eyes open and tilted her head back to look at him. "What time is it?"

He glanced at his watch. "Close to nine-thirty." He kissed her shoulder, then her lips. "I know a place with great food, and they're open late."

He had no complaints as her hand journeyed down his abs and curled around his erection.

"I don't want to keep you up past your bedtime," she said, teasing her thumb over the bulb of moisture that seeped from his crown.

Excitement fired through his blood. Rolling onto his side, he cupped her breast in his hand, circling the peak. "I have a better idea. I'm going to take my time eating you, and we'll order in later."

Holly's cheeks blushed. "I think I might like you a lot, Detective."

He grinned and rolled her warm, tempting body on top of his. "That's good, because I like you too, Miss McNeela." Then he kissed her, because he couldn't stop.

CHAPTER EIGHTEEN

Around four-thirty in the morning, Grayson woke to the subtle scent of Holly's perfume instead of the familiar aroma of breakfast in the farmhouse. Consciousness solidified his surroundings, and he opened his eyes. The silky skin of her back warmed his chest. Carefully, he eased his arm from around her waist and slid from bed without disturbing her. He collected his clothes from the bench and closed the bathroom door to wash up and change back into his uniform.

A huge part of him had feared that once they'd been intimate, his interest would flicker and die. That hadn't happened.

Last night, they'd ordered room service, talked, and then desire gripped them again. He was ten times more addicted to Holly now than a day ago. Hot didn't come anywhere near describing what she did to him or the level of contentment he'd felt with her cuddled in his arms as they drifted off to sleep.

Grayson had told her he'd leave early to get some work done at the farmstead, and then head to the office. Before leaving the suite, he wrote a note and left it on her bedside table.

Text me when you wake up, sweetheart. See you tonight.

When he strode into the old Victorian's kitchen, Ivy was setting the cast iron pan on the stove for breakfast.

"Good morning," she greeted.

"That it is. I'm going to change and head outside. Keep a plate warm for me, I'll eat before I leave for headquarters."

"Wait one second, brother," she said as his foot landed on

the first step leading upstairs to his bedroom.

He turned. "Problem?"

She tipped her head in question. "That smile on your face looks oddly out of character. You missed dinner last night. Didn't sleep in your bed. But I'm not getting the one-night stand vibe from you."

He winked at his sister. "Shoulda been a cop, Ivy. You've got good instincts. I'll move the folding tables and canopies to the driveway before I leave for work. What I don't finish, I'll get done this afternoon."

He took the stairs two at a time, changed into his Wranglers and a t-shirt, then hustled out the front door before his nosy sister could pin him down for more questioning.

By eight o'clock, he was at the office, scoping the geography around all four stash houses in the Clayton district, using Google Street View. The homes were contained within a five-block envelope. A circa 1960s neighborhood, mostly rundown rentals and a few derelict homes with boards nailed over the windows and graffiti on the exterior walls. The lawns had gone to seed, and the fences sagged. But even in low-income areas, people didn't appreciate a criminal element next door.

Cole strolled into headquarters and aimed for Grayson's desk. "Well, don't you look freshly fucked," his buddy said, pulling up a chair.

Technically, that didn't happen last night. "Sorry to disappoint," he fired back. "According to the calendar, it's July third. That means you're literally hours away from popping the question. You going to make my sister an honest woman?"

Instead of grinning, Cole's expression darkened. "I'm ready, but Ivy isn't."

If something was wrong in paradise, it didn't show on Ivy this morning.

"Case of cold feet. Over what?" he asked, after sipping

from his lukewarm coffee.

"My past. At least that's the excuse she used last night when I took her out to Roosters after dinner. I wanted her to come over to my place. She refused, and we got into a fight." He gnawed on his lip for a second then said, "I know you and I agreed not to talk about this, but aside from first base, Ivy and I have never—"

Grayson raised his hand. "I get it. Listen, she's busy with the prep for the Fourth of July celebration. Add Dad's false alarm and trip to the hospital, she's stressed. That's all."

"I don't think that's it." Cole removed his ball cap and rolled the brim in his hands. "Ivy looked me straight in the eyes and said she didn't think I could be faithful." He shook his head, his brows knitted together. "How am I supposed to prove she's wrong?"

The rest of the detectives had arrived, greeting each other with good mornings and heading to the lunchroom to refill their coffee mugs. Cole's scowl and clenched jaw signaled he was seriously pissed. Grayson certainly wasn't the go-to guy when it came to relationships, but he had a couple of educated guesses about why Ivy might push Cole away.

"Partner, I think you need to take a personal day. Sit Ivy down and dig for the truth. You're good at that."

"Like you said, she's busy. Even if I could convince her to take an hour off, I have nothing to say. It's not like I can prove she's wrong." He shrugged. "Maybe she isn't."

Wow. Yup, Cole was definitely pissed off. "Has she talked about Jackson's biological father?"

Cole scrubbed his jaw. "Not really. I know he was a Marine and died overseas."

"Unless you want that engagement ring sitting on your dresser for the next ten years, you might want to coax her into discussing the subject."

His friend leaned forward. "I'm not following. Are you saying she still loves him?"

"No. Not at all. I knew a lot of military wives who lost

their husbands. Some wanted to fill the void and married the first guy that came along. Others were so gun shy from grief, they didn't want to ever walk in those shoes again. Law enforcement isn't as deadly as combat, but there's a certain amount of risk. I may be way off course, but it's possible she has concerns that history will repeat itself."

Cole's gaze darted from side to side as if evaluating the possibilities. "You think it's my job that's scaring her?"

If it wasn't the job, Grayson had another guess as to why Ivy shied away suddenly, and it had nothing to do with law enforcement and everything to do with the fact she hadn't been with a man since her husband died. Cole had to start the conversation somewhere, and it would eventually lead to the truth.

"I think women consider probabilities a lot more than guys like us. Some gals turn themselves inside out with *what ifs*. If you want to allay Ivy's worries, then replace her *what ifs* with *more than likely* scenarios. Convince her to see the future with optimism instead of fear."

Kline exited his office and strode toward the security coded door that kept Joe Public out. Three men and one woman entered. First guy through the door wore a jacket with SWAT stitched on the back. The other two men wore suits, and the blonde female brought up the rear wearing street clothes. Probably from the Drug Task Force. They all shook hands with the lieutenant, then followed him into Kline's office.

Cole watched the newcomers as well. "Think it's about our case?"

"We'll know shortly." Gray turned his attention back to his friend. "Go home and deal with Ivy. I've got it covered here."

"No, I'll talk to her tonight. For now, I'm gonna grab a coffee while there's still some left."

Kline exited his office and headed for Grayson and Cole. "Like you to meet the unit heads that'll be working with you on the Clayton case."

After Cole made a side trip to the breakroom, Grayson and his partner joined the others in the lieutenant's office.

Kline introduced Cole as he closed the door for privacy, and then said, "This is his partner, Grayson Brooks. He spent five years with the San Diego Narcotics division after his ten-year service in the Navy SEALs."

The blonde smiled at Grayson. "You must have joined vice just after I left San Diego."

Grayson took a seat. "Guess we know some of the same people."

She tilted her head a little to the right, her blue eyes giving him the once over. "Probably. I'm Lt. Kate Billings, Drug Task Force. My brother's still serving, he's a physician with the Navy."

Just about everyone had someone in their family tree who served or had served.

The two men in suits were both State Police. With introductions out of the way, they got down to business. It turned out Kate's unit had been alerted to the stash houses in Clayton last week and were monitoring. The waterfront warehouse that Rory Hannigen revealed to Grayson under interrogation was news to everyone.

He was used to lengthy meetings and work-ups to an operation. Both the SEALs and law enforcement used intelligence to their advantage. Cage Martin was well known to State Police and associated with a bike gang called the Werewolves. They weren't the largest gang in Washington, but they were responsible for a hefty share of criminal activity.

After three hours, Grayson's ass ached from the solid wood chair. In the short term, the team agreed they needed more intelligence on the warehouse. They had consensus that a takedown should happen simultaneously at the stash houses and the warehouse. Kate Billings wanted to know if there were other key players before the bust. She'd send undercover officers to scope the neighborhood and speak with some CIs, *confidential informants,* she worked with. SWAT would familiarize themselves with the landscape and be ready to go when given the green light.

Lt. Kline stood, as did their guests. "Think we've covered a lot of ground today."

The officers all nodded and shook hands.

As their guests filed out, Kate was the last to leave. Kline put his attention on Grayson and Cole. "Guess you two need a few hours off to help the family out at the farmstead."

Grayson had already spoken with Kline about taking the afternoon off and thrown in a word for Cole.

"Appreciate that, Lieutenant," Grayson said. "You bringing the family to the farmstead celebration?"

"Wouldn't miss it. Kids look forward to it every year."

Kate stopped in the doorway. "Are you talking about Brooks Farmstead?" She blinked her blues at Grayson. "That place belong to your family?"

"It does."

"I shop there quite a bit. Love the fresh produce. Think I saw a sign about the July Fourth festivities last week."

Gray nodded. "Popular event. My sister is the brains behind the operation."

He skirted Kate and headed for his desk. Cole didn't waste time and aimed for the exit. Grayson wouldn't be far behind his partner. While shutting down his laptop and locking his file drawer, Kate strolled up to his desk.

"Got time for a beer?" she asked.

He paused and gazed at the blonde. Law enforcement had a healthy mix of genders in the county. Kate's soft, attractive features probably helped in her undercover role. At five-nine and physically fit, somewhere in her thirties, she obviously was dedicated to her career and earned a lead position on the task force.

"Miss something in the debrief?" he asked.

She did a quick survey of the other officers in the room.

Everyone had their head down, engaged in their work. "No, just could use a cold drink and company never hurts. Why don't I buy you lunch?"

"I have a long list of chores waiting for me at the farmstead."

"Some other time, then. Maybe I'll drop by the farmstead. Sounds like fun."

"Everyone is welcome to the celebration," he said, then walked past her like she didn't exist. He'd been around the block a few hundred times. Some women were pros at subtlety, and guys like him could sniff an offer that led straight to the bedroom.

If Kate hadn't mentioned she shopped at the farmstead store, his approach would have been a little more direct, as in not interested in fucking a co-worker. But if the woman showed up at the celebration, she'd see Holly by his side. End of problem.

* * * *

Holly waited at the hotel entrance. She'd made a dinner reservation at a five-star restaurant in Bellingham and texted Grayson to meet her outside the resort.

She knew better than to let him come up to the suite. If he did, they wouldn't leave the room. Not that she wasn't jonesing for a passionate repeat of last night with the big, handsome detective, but Holly didn't want their relationship to hinge on sex alone. But Holy Mother of God, he was good at it.

When he took his time undressing last night, it was like experiencing her very own *Thunder Down Under*. Grayson's broad shoulders and firm pecs didn't disappoint. The man's body was all rolling muscle and taut ligaments. When Grayson tossed his pants, what he packed below the belt didn't disappoint.

A few minutes past five, Grayson arrived in his black

Ford pickup while she was still daydreaming over her pornographic perfect detective. She opened the passenger door, but he hopped out, strode around the truck, swept her into his arms and kissed her like a woman dreams of being kissed.

"Hey, sweetheart," he said, his thumb grazing her cheek. "Do I need to mention that I missed you, or can you tell?"

She chuckled and shook her head. "Think I can read between the lines."

His firm lips made another pass over her mouth while his hands slid down her back and squeezed her ass.

"I like the hair." His gaze skated over her dark locks.

"Do you notice everything?" She'd gone to a local hair salon after spending the morning poolside with her laptop.

"Are we talking generalities or about the fact you're waiting out here instead of in your room?" He popped his eyebrows and his carved jaw tightened with a grin.

"Stop that," she said, easing out of his grasp. "We're going to be late for dinner."

Holly hitched the hem of her snug dress a little higher and stepped onto the running board. Once seated, Grayson closed the door.

On their way to the restaurant, he said, "Looks like you spent time in the sun today."

"A little relaxation and a lot of work." She shrugged. "I can't resist the images of those two tablets my department received. I threw on a bathing suit, grabbed my laptop and dove into research by the pool."

Grayson steered the truck with one hand and glanced across his broad shoulder at her. "I can hear the excitement in your voice. What are these tablets?"

In a very short time, Holly came to love how he seemed interested in her career. He asked questions and she didn't get the feeling he was doing it out of sheer politeness.

"They were found outside of Jerusalem. The script isn't one we've seen before. They pose a mystery."

"How so?"

"The tablets were found in a dig outside of the city but if I'm right about the origins of the script, they're about four thousand miles from where they should be."

Grayson tossed another glance her way, then smiled. "I love that look in your eyes right now."

"What look?"

"It's a cross between Nancy Drew and a fox in a hen house. You love your work, don't you?"

"Yeah, I guess I do. Unraveling humanity's history by the words our ancestors left behind is awe-inspiring. I've held ancient scripts in my hands that are thousands of years old. It's amazing," she said, looking out the front windshield as Grayson whistled down the I-5.

"Yeah, sounds amazing."

She heard a hesitancy in his tone. Holly had probably considered the same things as Grayson regarding their relationship. They were on a journey where their roads would never cross. Where and when would they be forced to face the facts?

"Is it too early to state the obvious without raining on this...beautiful evening?"

As if he could read her mind, she watched his carved jaw flex. "I know what you're gonna say. I'm sure you've already considered the same issues I have."

If anything, she loved that he wasn't trying to blow off her concerns. "They're issues we can't ig—"

"They're issues, not roadblocks." His fingers squeezed the steering wheel. "Not if we don't want them to be."

"SEALs put in a lot of planning before engaging in a mission," she said. "Did you ever abort a mission that you knew wouldn't succeed?"

After a few seconds, he said, "I get the metaphor you're posing. The answer's no. We always found another way."

"Never quit," she said wistfully.

He chuckled and swayed his head. "Okay, guess I'm gonna

have to actually read one of those crazy books you buy."

"I did drop by a bookstore today and purchased a new novel." She smiled without looking at him. "A murder mystery by a debut author. Seems my romance book got lost."

She glanced over at him and the smile on the man's face stretched from ear to ear. Holly tugged the hem of her dress closer to her knees. A second later, Grayson's large palm reached across the truck's center console and slid the fabric up her thigh.

"I appreciate that you're the type of woman who wears dresses with a modest length, but sweetheart, you shouldn't when you're around me because your legs are gorgeous." He winked at her. "And I want to see them."

"Sure. Me and my sexy support brace," she teased.

They'd veered off topic and Holly realized he'd done it on purpose. The real test was the day after tomorrow when she'd have to point her car north and head home. She pushed the thought from her mind. "Tomorrow is July Fourth. Are you working?"

Grayson took the off-ramp and turned left at the intersection to take them down to the waterfront. "Just so happens Brooks Farmstead puts on an all-day celebration. Local farmers bring their produce to our place. Pretty much like a huge, open-air market. We have a barbeque dinner for our clients and friends in the evening. Once the sun goes down, there's fireworks."

"That's so American."

"Independence Day, sweetheart. We have good reason to celebrate."

"You do," she agreed. "As close as America and Canada are, there's a distinct difference. I feel it, I just can't express it in words."

He came to a stop at a red light. Traffic flowed by, bumper to bumper, on the crossroad. People wearing shorts and summer clothes strolled the sidewalks.

"For my family, it's not only about tossing back a few

beers with a side of patriotism, it's about community."

"You've got your hands full," she said. "Sounds like a lot of work for you and your family."

The light turned green, and Grayson rolled through the intersection as a straggler ran the crosswalk ahead of them.

"I've been getting up early all week, setting up the equipment for Ivy. Tomorrow, it's a matter of keeping the op going smoothly." He nibbled on his lip. "I was hoping when we get up in the morning, we can head over to the farm together."

Her pulse thudded. Grayson wanted to stay another night with her. She'd bet a million bucks he was armed with a whole package of condoms.

Instead of teasing him about it, which was her first thought, she said, "Well, I have two very capable hands. If you need help, I'd love to be part of the celebration."

Grayson found an empty spot in a metered parking lot and turned off the engine. After releasing the seatbelt, he shifted onto his right hip.

"You don't have to help, I just want to make sure I can kiss you every chance I get." He leaned over and gently placed his hand at the back of her neck, drawing her closer.

"You mean like now?" she asked smiling at him, her heart expanding.

"Like now." He pressed a deep, passionate kiss on her mouth.

They held hands walking into the restaurant and Holly had to admit she felt more than special as she watched women stop their conversations or hover their forks mid-air and glue their eyes to Grayson as the hostess led the way to their table on the patio. He definitely caught a woman's eye, but Holly still had a bit of a problem as to why he'd never married. Or why he'd chased her down the highway.

* * * *

Pleasure boats motored past the patio on their way out to Bellingham Bay for an evening cruise, the summer breeze sultry and warm. For the first time in a very long time, Grayson looked forward to every day, especially spending time with Holly.

"You sure you don't want to share a bottle of wine?" he asked. Holly had ordered water with a twist of lime. He'd ordered a whiskey on ice.

"Positive." She moved the cloth napkin aside. "I don't mind a drink in the right environment, but I prefer water."

"What's the right environment?" he asked, curious what she considered an occasion to imbibe.

"Hmm." She grinned at him. "Independence Day?"

The server arrived, and they ordered appetizers and their main courses.

"So, you're more a weed girl, huh."

Holly wrinkled her nose. "Definitely not. Are you looking for my vices? You know one of them already."

Why was he asking? Holly was nothing like the women from his past. He couldn't even use the word *dated* because he hadn't done that since he was a teenager. Even back then, he got bored quickly and had worked his way through the entire cheerleading squad.

"I think I know more than one," he said.

"Really?" She settled back in her chair. "Go on, Detective. Let's see those deductive powers in action."

"Maybe not vices, but you enjoy staying at the resort. Which means home isn't where you're happiest. Instead of remaining in Canada, you cross the border and that translates into a fondness for America. You love to lose yourself in a book and your job. One is an escape, the other is a challenge." Grayson paused. "How am I doing so far?"

Holly crossed her arms over her gorgeous breasts. He chuckled at her non-verbal cue. On target. The snug-fitting black dress she wore amplified the woman's cleavage which, in his opinion, ranked in the top one percentile. The night he'd carried her to the bathroom wearing the see-through negligee had definitely fired him up.

But last night. *Epic.* When he'd turfed the pants and Holly had sandwiched his erection between those breasts and traced the tip of his cock with her moist tongue... Fuck, he'd nearly lost it. For him, their intimacy far surpassed the physical. Making love to her wasn't about his gratification, it was about hers.

She raised one eyebrow. "Anything else?"

"Mm-hmm." There *was* a concern, and he was going to deal with it right fucking now. He leaned a little closer and glanced at the tables closest to them to make sure the other couples weren't listening. "As much as I enjoyed last night, and I did, I could tell you were holding back. Modesty has no place in our bed, Holly." The color in her face drained and she swallowed as if he'd caught her in some heinous act. *Oh, damn.* "Listen, I want the real you, not some other man's version, especially if your ex is responsible."

Holly's gaze slid to the window. "I didn't realize I—" Her brow pinched in thought. "Wow, are you sure you don't have x-ray vision too?"

He waited instead of letting her redirect the conversation.

Holly toyed with her fork, flipping it over in her dainty fingers. "It's stupid, and to be honest, I cringe thinking about it, but you're right. Two words. Two silly words. It happened the first time Kevin and I made out. Young and inexperienced, obviously I showed too much enthusiasm because he gently pushed me back and said, '*Easy now.*' The way he said it made me feel overzealous. Improper. I'm not sure what word to use. I just know from that point onward, I restrained myself." Seemingly too embarrassed to look at him, Holly reached for her water and took a long swallow. She set the glass down, keeping her gaze on the table. "Like I said, stupid."

Grayson slid his palm over her hand to stop her from fiddling with the cutlery. "Is it too late to drop your guard? I want the original Holly. The one no other man has seen, because you're seeing a side of me that I didn't know existed."

She glanced at him with a distinct look of concern. "I guess that's what you're used to, eh."

She'd said "eh." He curbed himself from kidding her about the prompt. Grayson had a feeling the common Canadian term would tack itself to the end of some of his sentences the more time he spent with her.

"If I told you what I'm used to, you'd probably dump my ass." Talking with Holly, the truth poured from his mouth. "The guy I used to be isn't who I am now. I'm a little concerned because if I had my way, I'd lock us in a bedroom for a week until I made love to you so often you couldn't walk. And believe me, I've never wanted that with anyone but you."

"Have you always talked so...openly with your girlfriends?"

The dry ribs and steamed mussels arrived, and they both sat back while the server set the plate between them. "I'll be back to refill your water, ma'am."

"Thank you." She lifted the cloth napkin, gave her wrist a flick and placed it on her lap. "You were saying."

Grayson used the serving spoon and shifted a few appetizers onto her plate. "*Girlfriend* would infer someone I spent more than one night with." Erika had been the only repeat offender in his bed, but she didn't fit the description of a girlfriend.

Holly picked up her fork. "Yes, that's a satisfactory definition. So...?"

He considered skirting this subject for now. The food smelled great, and his stomach grumbled. *Shit*. Sidelining Holly, even to save himself grief, wasn't a habit he would allow.

"The answer is no. No, to talking openly, because pillow

talk wasn't my thing, and no to the definition of a girlfriend."
He downed his whiskey and Holly raised both eyebrows at
his response.

"I've always hated the term *girlfriend*. It's attached to a
thirteen-year-old the same as it's stuck to a thirty-two-year-
old woman and sounds juvenile to me."

Okay, what just happened? He was expecting a full-scale
investigation into why he didn't have a so-called girlfriend
in his past but instead, Holly laid down an opinion on
terminology.

She slid the dark-blue shell from a steamed mussel to the
side of her dish. "And before you suggest f-buddy or friends
with benefits, I'll pass on those too."

Bam! Out of left field, she voiced the unexpected and
cracked him up. "I'm on side with that."

"I do have one question," she said. "We spent an entire
day together at the farmstead, but you never mentioned
your service time. I thought you'd always been in law
enforcement."

The restaurant hummed with conversation, and Grayson
attempted to come up with a suitable response. As much as
he didn't like the answer, he offered the truth. "I guess there
were a few times I could have mentioned it."

Holly placed her fork on her plate and dabbed the cloth
napkin against her mouth. "But you didn't and there's a
reason."

His *girlfriend* had a natural curious streak. She wouldn't
be a researcher if she wasn't. "Yeah, I suppose there is, and it
was intentional in a way."

Holly's gorgeous grey gaze landed on him. "You didn't
want me to know."

"No, I didn't. Team guys are aware of their reputation in
the public's eye. Those books I tease you about are a prime
example. They're a conflation of truth and exaggeration.
Some guys who are interested in a woman won't mention the
trade at all. They don't want her opinions clouded by hype.

Others"—he cleared his throat—"use their career as bait."

Holly bobbed her head. "As in, to attract a woman for sex."

"Yup."

"But," she drawled. "You don't need to impress a woman with your profession. You're extremely handsome. Women stare when you walk by. I'm sure you're aware of that."

Grayson smiled. She'd missed the point, or he hadn't explained himself correctly. "Personally, I mentioned my job to make it clear that when morning came, I'd be gone. I never wanted anything permanent."

"So, it was your justification for *avoiding* a relationship."

Holly nibbled on her bottom lip, which was something she did while thinking. "Exactly. In a roundabout way, I'm trying to say that I didn't bring it up because my old habits don't apply to you."

About to wave at their server to order another drink, his cell rang. He should have turned the damn thing off. He pulled it from his shirt pocket. Not a number he recognized.

"Hello?"

"Detective Brooks, this is Kate Billings."

"What can I do for you, Lieutenant?" That was her rank, and he wasn't interested in using her first name.

"Sorry if I'm interrupting, I'm sure you're busy preparing for the festivities tomorrow. But there's something you need to see. I'd like you to meet me at the Purple Orchid on Fifth Street."

"Det. Sterling and I already scoped that place out. It's where Rory Hannigen and his boys from the stash house hang out."

"I told you, we were monitoring the houses in Clayton and the men involved in the ring."

Get to the point, lady. "And?"

"And I'm here with homicide. It looks like the boys decided to go for a drink tonight. Except four of them are lined up against the bathroom wall with bullets in their heads."

"A hit is homicide's responsibility. Lt. Kline is the Proactive Unit's lead, call him to attend."

"Responsibilities have changed, Grayson."

What the hell was she talking about? "Not to my knowledge. I appreciate the update, Lieutenant, but call Kline."

"It's yours now too," she said quickly. "I'm understaffed. With your background and experience, you're being underutilized in the Proactive Unit. Kline has approved a temporary transfer to my task force until this case is resolved. It's a major multi-agency operation with these murders. It's going to involve long hours, but I know you're used to that."

What the ever lovin' fuck was going on? Not even a call from Kline to give him a head's up? What kind of pull did this chick have?

"You still there, Grayson?"

"Yeah. I'm here." The reason he'd taken the job with the Proactive Unit was for the regular hours. The narco and homicide divisions meant twenty-four/seven callouts. "That's not going to work for me, Lieutenant. I returned to the Pacific Northwest because the family needed my help."

"I need your experience. It's temporary, Grayson. You and I are going to make a great team and bring these guys down."

Bullshit! "When does this transfer take effect?"

"Immediately. See you in twenty minutes. It's going to be a late night, but I promise your plans for tomorrow won't be interrupted." She hung up.

"Fuck." He slid the cell back into his shirt pocket.

Grayson glanced across the table at Holly, who shifted the napkin from her lap to beside the plate. As the server walked by, she waved him over. "Is it too late to cancel our meals?"

"They'll be up shortly, ma'am."

"Can we have them to go, please?"

"Yes, ma'am."

Holly turned her attention back to him and shrugged. "Police work. It's the nature of the beast."

Maybe for some departments, but Grayson had a bad feeling. Kate was more than a dedicated cop, she was one of those women who didn't take no for an answer and when she wanted something, she manipulated the chess pieces to get it.

"Holly, I'm—"

"Please don't say you're sorry. It's your job."

They waited for the server to bring the take-out and Grayson paid the bill. On their way back to the resort, he got a call and he answered using the Bluetooth in the truck.

"Brooks," Lt. Kline said when Grayson activated the call.

"Lieutenant. What the hell is going on?"

"To be honest, I don't know. I got a call from Capt. Baker telling me you've been transferred. Kate obviously wants you working on the drug task force with her and has pull somewhere up the food chain. I wasn't given an option. But Baker assured me this was a temporary move."

Damnit. It was too late to switch the call from the truck's speaker to his phone. Holly sat quietly in the passenger seat with her hands folded in her lap. If she could unravel the mysteries of a four-thousand-year-old language, hearing a woman was involved in his rapid transfer wouldn't be hard for her to decipher.

"Lieutenant, I'm heading to Fifth Street to check out the scene. Murders sound like a hit to me. For the record, I don't want the transfer."

"I know you don't. Listen, I'm bringing the wife and kids to the farmstead tomorrow. We'll talk more then."

Grayson disconnected the call as they rolled up to the front of the hotel entrance. Holly immediately opened the passenger door before he'd come to a full stop.

"Be safe," she said and quickly slid out.

He threw the truck into park and leaped out, stopping her before she could disappear inside the hotel. Grayson wrapped his arms around her tense body. "I know what's running through your mind. Don't go there. I'll be back as soon as I can."

She tilted her head to look into his eyes. "You and I both know these investigations drag on. You've got a busy day tomorrow. You don't have to come back here. Go home. Get some sleep."

"Holly, I'm coming back here tonight. I don't give a shit if I only get an hour of sleep, as long as it's next to you." He raised one of her hands to his lips. "Do you hear me?" He placed a kiss on her knuckle.

"I do," she said quietly, but wouldn't look at him.

Holly stepped back and eyed the entrance to the hotel then shifted her gaze toward the casino's glass doors. As if neither were acceptable, her gaze strayed toward the Cascade Mountains in the distance, and she smiled.

He didn't need to involve her in office politics. He'd set things straight with Billings and more than likely be reassigned to the Proactive Unit. "This isn't how I envisioned our evening going, but it's not a write-off."

She nodded. "You better get moving."

Kate's motivation had better be job-related or so help him God, he'd set her fucking straight.

CHAPTER NINETEEN

Cole parked the John Deere tractor in the equipment shed, a ninety-foot-long metal building with high ceilings. Ten past eight p.m. and the area surrounding Brooks Farmstead Store was ready for the Fourth of July festivities. Tomorrow, local farmers would set up at the tables and bring their produce and signage. A veritable public market with plenty of freebies to lure new customers and thank existing ones. Numerous barbeques were lined up, ready to start smoking and cooking organic meats. Some would sell during the day for hungry guests. The dinner planned later in the evening was supplied by the Brooks family as a thank you to special clients and farmers.

He shut the machine off, and it rumbled to a stop. Cole stepped down from the tractor, appreciating the quiet. Plenty of neighbors had showed up to help out. Grayson had pitched in, then left a little before five p.m. to take Holly out on a date.

Cole hadn't bothered trying to talk with Ivy. There was no point discussing her opinion of his ability to commit.

As he headed for the exit, Ivy walked into the shed.

"Hey." She stopped and shoved her hands into her back pockets.

Even wearing a t-shirt and jeans with dirt smudges, the woman tripled his heart rate, but it didn't make a difference. She'd put the brakes on their future.

"Everything's ready for the celebration," he stated as he approached her.

"I threw a casserole in the oven. Come inside and eat."

"No, thanks." He veered right, not intending to stop. "I'll grab a bite at home."

All afternoon he'd avoided the beautiful woman. She'd

made her decision. Taking another kick in the nuts wouldn't happen.

"Why are you angry?" she asked, stepping into his path.

He stopped and looked her in the eyes like she had done to him last night. "I'm taking my tired, unfaithful ass home. Good luck tomorrow."

She dropped her arms to her sides and tears welled in her eyes.

Cole hated drama, especially when it came to women. As soon as the gals he'd dated started playing head games, he was gone. Maybe Grayson was right, and Ivy was overworked. Stretched to the max. She did that to herself all the time. Cole wasn't a mind reader, he had to take Ivy at her word. She didn't trust him.

Tears slid down her sun-kissed cheeks. "You're not coming back, are you?"

He planted his hands on his hips and eyed her. "There's no way for me to disprove your accusation. I'm sorry, but I'm not the kind of guy who jumps through hoops." He stared at the entrance, the sun falling on the horizon. "If you don't think I can be faithful, then no, there's no reason for me to come back."

Cole put his feet into gear. He needed a cold beer and time to come to terms with a future that didn't include Ivy.

Jackson ran across the yard toward the equipment shed at full tilt. "Cole!"

"Hey, buddy. What's up?"

Grinning and out of breath, Ivy's son gripped two baseball mitts. "I finished my homework. Ya wanna play catch?"

Cole's heart ached with regret. It wasn't only Ivy that he'd miss. Jackson had become an important part of his life. He loved the kid.

"Honey." Ivy stepped up to Cole's side. "Cole's tired. He worked all day. He needs some rest and dinner's almost ready. Go wash up."

Jackson made a face only a disappointed eight-year-old can make. "Please, Mom. I wanna show Cole my new pitch."

Ivy might have clipped their relationship like a toenail into a waste bucket, but he didn't want the kid to pay the price. Spending fifteen minutes with the boy wouldn't hurt. "Okay, let's see what you got."

Jackson thrust one of the mitts into the air. "I've been practicing what you showed me. Watch!"

Cole accepted the mitt and slid his hand into the stiff leather as Jackson turned and ran to put distance between them. Ivy palmed Cole's arm.

"Better back up," he said without looking at her. "The kid's aim isn't that great yet."

"I love you," she said softly.

She might love him, but she didn't trust him. "Listen, I'm not going to abandon ship, especially not Jackson. Gray is home to do the heavy lifting around the farm. You don't need me anymore. I won't be around as much and eventually not at all. The kid will hardly notice."

A sharp inhale made him turn his attention toward her. Ivy stepped away, tears raining down her cheeks. Unexpectedly, the kid's aim had improved, and the ball nailed Cole on the left shoulder. He winced and retrieved the ball. By the time he looked up, Ivy was striding quickly toward the house.

I'm sorry, sweetheart, but my heart is breaking too.

Jackson leaned forward, hands propped on his thighs. "I'm ready, Cole!"

He pitched a ball in Jackson's direction. It strayed to the left. With spring-loaded legs powered by youth, the boy lunged for the ball, catching it in his glove and rolling on the ground.

"You're gonna be a star player one day, Jackson!"

The boy jumped to his feet and lobbed the ball at Cole. With little effort, Cole caught the ball in his glove. He'd miss this place, but most of all he'd miss the chance at happiness that Ivy didn't want to take with him.

* * * *

Red and blue flashing lights from more than a dozen police cruisers parked on Fifth Street garnered a thick crowd of bystanders.

Grayson parked his truck outside the circle of law enforcement vehicles and strode through the people loitering to catch a glimpse. With the coroner's vehicle on-scene, folks automatically knew there was a dead body. When he reached the police block around Purple Orchid's entrance, he showed his ID.

"Where's Lt. Billings?"

The patrol officer from the sheriff's department pointed toward the bar. "Inside."

Grayson ducked under the yellow-taped perimeter and headed into the grungy drinking establishment. Suits and uniforms filled the place, the air rank with rancid beer and hourly hook-ups. When he and Cole had surveilled the place, hookers used the bar to find their next John.

Kate stood with two other men in State Police uniforms near the men's restroom sign attached to the wall.

He didn't bother stopping to talk and headed for the crime scene. The dark-stained, scuffed door was wedged open, and he peered inside. Against the back wall adjacent to the urinals, four men in their twenties sat on the dirty tile floor, a bullet in each of their foreheads. A guy with *Forensics* stitched on his jacket took photographs of the scene.

"We've identified all four," Kate said from behind him.

He scanned the room. Nothing out of place. No signs of struggle. Just four dead guys. "What's the purpose of me being here?"

Forensics would collect all the evidence. Homicide detectives would assess the area and take witness statements. Unless there was a metric ton of coke he wasn't seeing, there was no reason for his presence.

"Let's talk out there," she said.

He followed as she aimed for an alcove void of other cops, where four pool tables sat. The place reeked of stale cigarette smoke. Billings turned to face him.

Grayson eyed the blonde wearing tight jeans and a low-cut tank. "Looks like a hit. Again, we'll start with why am I here?"

Her blue eyes traced over his face, then slithered down his body. "From the tone of your voice and the suit jacket you're wearing, I did interrupt something."

He glared at her, waiting for an answer.

Kate's expression tipped from a suggestive smile to apologetic. "Sorry, but as I mentioned on the phone, I'm understaffed and I need an officer with your skills."

"That may be, but let's get this straight. I don't appreciate being blind-sided and transferred without my knowledge. There's a reason I left narco. For the third and final time before I extract, why am I here?"

"Because I want you on this case at the grass-roots level. The murders are linked to our case. Now that you're in my unit, we have things to discuss. I'm starving. Let's grab a bite and I'll bring you up to speed."

Time for a reality check. "I have no issues with a debrief. We'll talk during business hours. At the DTF office." She blinked and swallowed deeply. "This is the second time you've asked me out. First for a drink. Now for dinner. The answer is no. When I break bread, it's with the gorgeous woman I'm in love with. You want me on this case as a temporary assignment, no problem. Are we crystal clear on my priorities, Lieutenant?"

Kate leaned her ass against the pool table, palming the green felt edge near her hips. "I think we got off on the wrong foot here. I run my team with open dialogue and respect—"

"Not much respect using whatever pull you have in the upper ranks to yank my ass onto your task force without talking to me first. So, stifle the bullshit, lady."

Instead of backing off, the heat in her eyes seemed to flash with intensity. "You're right, I should have approached you differently. I jumped the gun. But I need you. My instincts tell me that the warehouse is a major hub used to move drugs through the county. I need experience like yours to bring them down."

Kate had jumped to a lot of conclusions, the worst one thinking she was gonna ride his dick. He needed her and this transfer like a hole in the head, but he also wanted to clean up the streets and stop these assholes from putting drugs in kids' hands.

"If that's the case, then we're on the same page. I'll be at the DTF office Monday morning. Look forward to meeting and working with the rest of the team."

She nodded, crossed her arms over her chest and put her attention on the wall where the pool cues were stored. "Have a good evening."

After weaving his way through the cluster of law enforcement officers, Grayson jumped in his truck and dug his cell out of his shirt pocket. He replayed some of the conversation with Kate he'd recorded, then shut it off. Never hurt to cover his ass. Smart woman. She hadn't copped to having an alternate reason for his transfer. There had to be at least ten other members on the drug task force. It would be a cold fucking day in Hell when he'd agree to any duo surveillance with her.

Grayson spun through his contacts until he found Orson's number, then dialed.

"Shit, man. About time you called," his old partner said over the truck's speaker.

"How's sunny San Diego?" He grinned, hearing his friend's voice.

"Not the same without my wingman around. How's the farmstead? You sick of the smell of cow shit and ready to come back?"

Orson was a few years older than him. He'd been with vice for several years. They'd clicked from the start and remained partners until Grayson left San Diego.

He laughed. "Sorry to break your heart, buddy. Anytime you want some fresh air, get your ass to the Pacific Northwest. I got piles of dung you can pitch."

"Asshole. I'll troll the bars with ya, but I'm not putting on rubber boots. Then again, you got sheep, right?"

"Jesus!" Grayson laughed. He missed Orson's off-color humor. "No more trolling for me, I met someone."

Orson groaned. "And another good man bites the dust. By that tone in your voice, it sounds like she's more than *someone*. Well, you better give me lots of lead time if you're gonna put a ring on her finger. No one's getting vacation time these days. We're up to our eyeballs in assholes."

"I'll do that."

When he'd told Kate he only ate with the woman he loved, there'd been zero hesitation. He sincerely loved Holly's intelligence, her wit, and her sweet smile. Yeah, they had technicalities to work through, but nothing he wouldn't bulldoze over to keep her in his life.

"So what's up, Grayson? You just call to make me jealous?"

"Need to know if you recognize a name."

"Okaaay, shoot."

"Kate Billings. Apparently, she left narco a year before I got there."

The sound of a can snapping open in the background was probably a beer, since Orson was known to put back a few after work.

"How the hell did you get that name? Oh, man. Did she end up in Washington?"

"Yup. She's a lieutenant at the drug task force."

"Phew, steer clear of that bitch at all costs."

Grayson wasn't surprised by the advice. "Why do you say that?"

"Remember that movie *Fatal Attraction*? She might not

be whacked as Glenn Close, but she's poison. She's the reason Captain Gordon's marriage tanked."

Gordon was their division's ranking officer. "What happened?"

"Don't know all the details, but rumor was Kate offered her wet pussy and before ya knew it, the captain cheated on his wife. Once Mrs. Gordon kicked his ass out, Kate left San Diego."

"She certainly climbed the ladder fast, she's already a lieutenant."

"By the sounds of it, you've met her in person," Orson said.

"Unfortunately. Met her today. She's part of a multi-agency case we're working on. By five o'clock, I'd been transferred from the Proactive Unit to her team on the DTF."

"Oh, shit. Listen, man, tread carefully. You know how much I love women, but that chick always scared me."

That was saying a lot, considering Orson's fondness for women. He'd never played favorites. He liked them tall, short, thin, curvy, sharp-tongued or shy. Never mattered to his former partner, long as the chemistry led to the bedroom and a few laughs. But he was a die-hard cop and no woman he'd met replaced his dedication to police work.

"We just finished clearing the air. I think I made my point."

"Yeah, well, if I were you, I'd still watch your step. As I understand it, Capt. Gordon was a happily married man before this all went down."

"Appreciate the info. She asked me out twice, using the premise of work. I get the feeling she's trouble. I just want to know how much."

"No problem. I'll do a little poking around and see if I can't get more details. And, hey, is that invite to Washington the real deal?"

"Damn straight. Any time, partner."

"Good to hear from ya, Gray. We'll talk soon."

Twenty-five minutes later, he parked at the Neon Lights resort. Something told him Holly wouldn't be in her room and he aimed for the casino. Took a while trolling the aisles, but he found her at the same machine where he'd seen her the first time he'd been on patrol with Cole. He stood back and observed. The casino floor waitress stopped and handed Holly a glass of red wine.

As the waitress whisked toward him with a tray full of drinks, he stopped her.

"Hey," she said, "I've never seen you in here without your uniform."

Sheila was written on her name tag. "You mind telling me how many of those she's had?"

She grinned. "Holly? Heck, this is the first time I've ever served her. Normally, she orders water or a soda. That's only her second one, but she's legal."

He chuckled. "Yeah, I know she is. Just curious."

The waitress tipped her head. "She's not in any trouble, is she?"

"None whatsoever."

As a server, Sheila interacted with customers all the time. Reading people came naturally. "Ah, are you two by chance... an item?"

He nodded, watching Holly play the machine. "We're definitely something. Bring her another glass, and I'll have a whiskey on ice."

Sheila winked. "Getting the party started, huh?" She nodded to someone behind them, probably getting the high sign for service. "I don't know her all that well, but she's always been polite. Folks come in here for all sorts of reasons. Some have problems. Some just for a little fun, but I always got the feeling she was lonely and wanted to be around people."

Grayson pulled a twenty from his wallet and placed it on Sheila's tray. "She's not going to be lonely anymore. Keep the change."

"Thanks, I'll be right back with your drinks."

He watched Holly down her wine in three gulps, then closed in on his target and slid his arms around her body, stopping her from reaching the play button.

"You winning, sweetheart?"

She gasped with surprise. He let go and sat in the empty chair next to her. "What are you doing here? I thought you'd be working...all night."

His heart ached for Holly. He wondered if that's the excuse her ex used to give when he was fucking some woman behind her back. Gray palmed her neck, leaned forward and traced her bottom lip with his tongue, then followed with a kiss he hoped would dispel her fears.

"I'm here to spend the evening with the only woman I want." He picked up the empty wine glass. "Is this a special occasion?"

Her cheeks bloomed with color. "Not really."

Grayson set the glass down, then squeezed her hand. "Holly, your ex betrayed you, but believe me, if I make a promise to you, I'll keep it. I have a past littered with women, but I was always straight with them from the start."

She pressed their joined hands between her breasts. "You didn't keep any of them, Grayson."

He swept a curl from her cheek. "No, I didn't, because they weren't Holly McNeela. You know, you're sitting at the exact machine where I first saw you."

Holly shrugged. "I'm a repeat offender."

He chuckled. "When I first laid eyes on you, I wanted a life sentence with no possibility of parole."

Her brows shot up with surprise. "Hey, that's a pretty good comeback!"

Sheila returned and handed them the drinks. "Enjoy, you crazy kids."

"What's this?" Holly asked, taking the wine.

He swallowed a sip of whiskey. Not exactly top shelf as the liquor burned its way down his throat. "I'm gonna watch you waste your money and when you're tipsy enough, I'm taking you upstairs." He paused and placed his mouth next to her ear. "I'm gonna make love to you, but I'm going to edge you to the brink of insanity first."

She quickly glanced around, but they were alone on the bank of machines. "I'm sorry but, um, what's edge mean?"

Man, her ex must have been a moron. Gray looked forward to satisfying her natural curiosity and taking his sweet fucking time doing it.

He tilted his head, swept her hair aside and kissed the pulse on her neck. "Guess you're just going to have to wait to find out."

"And you expect me to keep playing with that offer on the table?"

He placed a finger on the play button and pushed. The wheels of chance spun the colorful images until they landed, adding a few bucks to her total.

"The anticipation makes it that much better."

Holly straightened her shoulders. "You're quite naughty, Det. Brooks."

Raising his glass, he grinned. "Pleasuring you a hundred different ways is at the top of my list, sweetheart."

He tipped his glass to hers.

Holly didn't seem interested in drinking. Instead, she slid an arm around his neck and kissed him like he wanted to be kissed by her. Confident. Passionate. He was crazy about her, and if she kept this up, he'd have a seriously hard time watching her leave the day after tomorrow.

Leaning back in his chair, he nodded toward the slot. "You better play, babe, or else casino security is gonna get one hell of a peepshow."

While she played the game, he played a different type by whispering in her ear what he was going to do once they got upstairs.

They lasted a sum total of fifteen minutes until she leaned over and said, "Honestly, Grayson, how do you expect me to sit here when my panties are soaking wet?"

Her innocent admission sent shockwaves of need rocketing through his cock. He cashed out her ticket, held her hand, and headed for the exit with her laughing at his loss of control.

Nicely played, Holly.

In the elevator, he pinned her to the wall and kissed her all the way to the third floor, but wished there were thirty. When she unlocked the door to the suite, they tumbled inside. A trail of clothes and breathless kisses marked their path to the king-sized bed.

They touched, teased, and caressed with frenzy, but it wasn't until he eased his heavy shaft into her hot core and gazed into her eyes that his heart had something to say.

"I'm falling fast for you, Holly." He clamped his jaw against a fierce wave of pleasure. Craving sex was one thing, but he'd never experienced a depth of emotion like this with anyone.

Holly palmed his ass when he rotated his hips, stroking her wet channel with slow, deliberate thrusts. She gasped and her head rocked back into the pillow. He wasn't separated from her arousal, he felt fucking amazing being the reason for her pleasure.

"You forgot to mention your rules of engagement," she said.

Pausing, his erection buried to the hilt, he stared into her grey gaze. "Sweetheart, there's just you and me. Full stop."

A little sigh rose from her throat. "I'm trying to stop myself from falling for you."

"Don't do that." He teased her peaked nipple with his tongue. "I'm not fucking you, baby, I'm making love to you, and it feels damn good."

Her eyes closed and her head pressed into the soft pillow as he rocked into her heat, filling her silky channel. The friction built. The ecstasy unraveled. Buried deep inside her, his fingers nearly tore through the bedsheets.

Watching her orgasm, Holly's inner muscles clenched his cock and her cries set him off. He couldn't hold back; the powerful release rolled through him like an enormous wave.

It took more than a few minutes for him to settle back to Earth. He disposed of the condom in the bathroom and returned with a warm, wet hand towel and gently washed her clean. Grayson slid into bed, and they laid on their sides, facing each other.

Toying with a strand of her hair, he said, "Not sure how I'm going to let you go the day after tomorrow."

Her warm palm rested on his hip. "At least you won't cry," she said, smiling.

He grinned. "Maybe not, but it doesn't mean I won't miss you."

Holly placed her index finger on his lips. "I'm trying very hard not to think about it. I'm glad I never met you when you were a SEAL. I'd be a hot mess if you left for seven months. I'd worry about you every single minute. How do the wives and girlfriends do it?"

"Some can't. Divorce is pretty common. Takes real commitment on both sides."

She nibbled on her bottom lip for a second. "Are Frog Hogs a real thing?"

"Now what made you think of that?"

"Just wondering."

He hadn't been kidding when he admitted his past was littered with women. The wrong kind of women. Pillow talk other than *thanks, I gotta go*, wasn't something he'd engaged in. Erika popped into his head. She'd been a groupie, but the same rules applied to her as everyone else. He didn't linger.

"Yeah, it's a real thing."

Holly narrowed an eye at him. "Guess you tapped into that a few times."

He groaned. "I told you already, I've made bad choices in the past."

She flopped onto her back and stared at the ceiling. "I

won't hold it against you."

Grayson leaned over and kissed her shoulder. "Sweetheart, I definitely want you to hold it against me."

Holly laughed and rolled her head to look at him. "You're not talking about bad decisions, are you?"

"Nope," he said and kissed her swollen lips. "You're my best decision."

When his stomach rumbled, she sat up. "Did you eat dinner?"

"No. It's still in the pickup."

"The suite has a microwave," she said. "I'm kinda hungry too."

"Then I'll get our take-out."

Grayson dressed and headed out to the parking lot. Unlocking his truck, a sheriff's vehicle caught his eye. The car drove down the main road that split the hotel guest parking from the rest of the casino parking. There could be any number of reasons why a unit was on the premises.

He squinted to see the driver.

What the fuck!

Kate Billings was behind the wheel. What the hell was she doing here? Grayson collected the take-out and locked the door. The lieutenant drove up and down the lanes between the parked cars. The sun sat near the horizon, but he had plenty of light to observe her movements. The cruiser disappeared into a lot on the other side of the casino, and he strode toward the hotel, keeping an eye out. Wasn't long before the vehicle returned, and he took cover behind a black SUV.

When the patrol car rolled past his truck, Kate stopped the vehicle and got out. Grayson had his phone out and started video recording. He watched her kneel at the left rear tire and stick her hand inside the wheel well. She got up, looked around, and then got back in the cruiser and left the parking lot.

He stashed the phone and retraced his steps to the truck.

Sitting on his ass and going mostly by feel, it didn't take long to find the device. Turning it over in his fingers, he recognized the piece. Until he figured out what her play was, he returned the GPS unit. Was she psycho or was something else going on here?

Timing was everything and he'd lucked out, but he'd be watching every move the bitch made from here on in.

Holly was dressed in jeans and a turquoise blouse by the time he got back to the room.

"What was that about?" she asked the second he came through the door.

The suite's windows looked out over the parking lot. "You saw that, huh?"

"I saw a sheriff's patrol car stop behind your truck and you taking a video. The officer knelt by the back wheel and then left. What did I see?"

He set the two take-out cartons on the small pine dining table. "Nothing for you to worry about."

Her brow creased with tight lines. "Are you trying to ease my concerns? Because that looked weird."

Figured he'd fall for a woman with a high IQ. "Come here."

Holly strode across the room and into his arms. "If there's something to be concerned about, you're the first person I'll tell."

She shook her head at him like a mom catching a kid stuffing his face with junk food before dinner. "Liar."

CHAPTER TWENTY

I vy sat on the porch swing, serenaded by crickets. Long shadows crept across the lawn as the sun slid behind the majestic mountain range. Rocket, the family's German Shepherd with a belly full of dinner, snoozed a few feet away. Dad had retired to his room and Jackson was in the bath.

Normally, moments like these gave her time to breathe, but not tonight. Ivy sat in silence, her heart heavy. Her thoughts centered on Cole instead of the busy Fourth of July celebration tomorrow.

Didn't she have a right to be nervous? Last night, Cole had suggested they go to his place. She'd lashed out to hide her insecurities and used a cheap reason to protect herself instead of admitting the truth.

Cole's elusive mannerisms screamed raw sex appeal. Women loved the chase and he'd let plenty catch him for one night. But she knew him better than any of those women. His values never wavered. Straightforward. Always honest.

For the last seven years when he'd work at the farm, she'd hidden her attraction to him. Whenever she'd caught wind that he'd hooked up with a woman, she'd bury her jealousy. Cole had never flirted with her, and she'd believed her crush was one-sided, until last month.

After telling him last night that she didn't think he could be faithful, he'd tossed in the towel. Cole accepted her words as gospel and walked away.

Tears swarmed in her eyes. She'd hurt him. Rehashing what she'd said, Ivy realized her accusation was a death blow. A statement of his character. Cole prided himself on his integrity. The type of man who never broke his promises.

Soon, she'd hear gossip from friends about a new woman in his life and her heart wouldn't recover this time. She buried her face in her hands and tucked her knees to her chest.

"Mom?"

She sniffed and quickly swiped her tears away. Jackson, her beautiful blond-headed boy, smelled like shampoo and stood barefoot next to the porch swing in his Batman pajamas.

"What is it, honey?"

Jackson crawled onto the swing and leaned into her side. "Why are you crying? Did Grandpa yell at you?"

She choked on a laugh. "No, Grandpa didn't yell at me. I said something and hurt someone's feelings that I care about."

His big blue eyes gazed at her. "Was it Cole? He was really sad when he left."

She gulped in air between her tears and nodded sharply.

"Don't you want him to be my dad?"

Ivy's heart shattered into a million pieces, and she wrapped her arms around her boy and pulled him onto her lap. Why hadn't she just been honest with Cole? Told him she was insecure because she hadn't been with man in so long. Admitted that she compared herself to those loose but gorgeous women he'd taken to his bed and found herself lacking. Instead, she'd attacked him. Blamed him for something he hadn't done and trashed his character.

She swept her son's moist bangs from his eyes. "He'd be a great dad, and he loves you."

Jackson nodded his head in agreement. "I love Cole too. He always plays with me and shows me stuff. You told me that I should apologize when I do something wrong. Did you tell Cole you were sorry?"

Hugging her son, she rested her chin on his head. "No, I didn't."

He wiggled and Ivy loosened her grip. Jackson slipped

from her lap and faced her. "I can put myself to bed, Mom. I'm old enough now."

"Are you?" She smiled at her little man. God, she hated that he was growing up so fast.

"Uh-huh, and you can go see Cole and tell him you're sorry."

Ivy had torpedoed their future. She'd live with the consequences, but her son was right. She owed Cole an apology.

* * * *

After showering the day's sweat from his body, Cole nursed a cold beer. The one-story rambler he'd bought three years ago sat on a couple acres of land, mostly treed. The summer heatwave raised the interior temperature of the house to sweltering. Barefoot, wearing a fresh pair of Wranglers and no shirt, he sat by the open kitchen window to catch a breeze.

He tipped the beer back and emptied the bottle, quenching his thirst but not doing much to heal the emptiness in his chest. He could do the *dick* thing and head to Roosters, pick up some woman and pretend Ivy's comment didn't burn like a sonofabitch. But self-medicating with meaningless sex wouldn't help.

It was time for a change. Leave Washington behind. The laptop on the kitchen table showed his earlier search results. With his Criminal Justice Degree and experience, he could move anywhere in the US and find a job in law enforcement.

A light knock landed on the front door. He eased the kitchen blind aside and saw a white Acura in the driveway. Running a hand through his wet hair, he considered not answering.

He wasn't surprised when the front door cracked open. "Cole?"

"In the kitchen," he said loud enough for her to hear.

Ivy stopped in the archway between the living room and kitchen. Her gorgeous blonde hair flowed past her shoulders. She hardly ever wore it loose. No matter how angry he was, his pulse increased as his gaze slid from her cowboy boots, up her firm bare legs, over snug, white jean shorts and a sky-blue tank top. She must have shed a lot of tears with the puffy skin around her eyes, but it didn't mar her beauty.

Instead of asking what she wanted, he waited. Ivy's gaze swept across his bare shoulders, down his abs, and then fell to the floor.

She opened her mouth then closed it again. He didn't mean to torment her by staying silent, but he just stared, his jaw clenched, his heart a fucking wreck.

Ivy swallowed and tried again. "Jackson reminded me tonight, that when you hurt someone," —she licked her pretty lips and inhaled a deep breath— "you should apologize. What I said last night wasn't true, and I'm truly sorry, Cole."

She cleared her throat, nodded sharply, and backed up as if to leave.

"Then why did you?"

She winced as tears flooded her eyes. "I can't stop crying, and I know you're not the kind of man who wants to hear a woman blubbering about her feelings. I hurt you and needed to apologize."

Cole rested his right forearm on the kitchen table. "So, I'm not an unfaithful jerk anymore but instead an insensitive prick who doesn't give a shit about the woman he loves?"

She blinked and her shoulders trembled with a shaky inhale. "I didn't say that."

He tipped his head to the side. "Maybe if you'd stop assuming what I think and just be honest about why you got scared last night, there'd be no reason to cry."

He leaned forward, pulled the other chair out from the table and then propped his elbows on his thighs.

She'd either run or stay. His heart wanted her to stay

while he pretended not to care.

Ivy hesitated, swept her blonde locks over her right shoulder, crossed the kitchen, and eased into the chair.

Sitting knee to knee, he brushed a thumb across her blotchy cheek. "I know you're under a lot of stress, but that's not the reason you pushed me away."

She shook her head.

"Are you scared that I'm going get hurt on the job?"

Her watery blues shifted from his chest to his face. "Always, but not the reason."

After wiping her tears, he cupped her neck, resting his thumb on her smooth jaw. "Ivy, when it comes to running the farmstead and the store, you're confident, a little bossy, and capable, but I've never seen this side of you." He narrowed his eyes, trying to figure it out. "When I suggested we come back here last night, you knew I wanted to make love."

Her eyes rounded and Cole caught a flicker of fear. *Ding. Ding. Ding. You idiot.* "Please tell me you're not insecure about your body or you think you won't live up to my expectations in the bedroom."

Ivy clenched her teeth and her eyes snapped shut. "You have to understand, you have a reputation. I—I used to die inside when my friends told me, with far too much detail, how good you were in bed. How rockin' hot your body was and how you made them come. Mark took my virginity, but I haven't been with anyone since."

Ivy glanced at the kitchen tap, but he went to the fridge and collected two beers. Placing one in her hand, he said, "And when he died, you were crushed."

"No. I—Mark and I dated in college. A few days after I graduated, I found out I was pregnant. He'd joined the Marine Corps, which is what he'd always wanted. Before he left on his first deployment, we got married, mainly so I'd have healthcare and his benefits from the military." She took a long gulp from the beer, then fiddled with the label. "He did the honorable thing, but we weren't crazy in love. We were just young, carefree, crazy college students." She sniffed and tucked her hair behind her ears. "I moved back to the farm, and Mark never made it home."

At eighteen, Cole had attended college in Arizona with an eye on law enforcement. Ivy had gone to Washington State for a Biology degree. By the time he'd returned from Arizona with his head screwed on right, she was a widow.

He took a quick sip and set the bottle down. "As a teenager, I did some crazy shit."

A small grin lifted Ivy's lips. "I remember when you tied that red shirt around your waist, and we hopped into the field where Bruno was grazing."

He'd been a badass bull with a cranky attitude. Chased Cole all over the place, but he survived to tell the tale.

"I was seventeen and an idiot. The truth is, I was showing off for you."

Halfway through a pull from her beer, she paused. "For me? You were always talking to the older girls. You hardly said two words to me."

"That's because you were Gray's little sister, and he was always protective over you. If I'd admitted I had a crush on you, he'd have knocked me into next week." Cole chuckled. "Besides, you made me nervous.

"Pretty sure you have no problem talking with women now. I barely recognized you when you came home." She kept looking at everything but him. "You were, you know—a man. A very handsome man."

During his last year of college, he'd gone from a leaner build, working with weights and dedicated to a strict fitness regime, to a much heavier frame. As he'd changed, the co-eds paid more attention. There was no end to the pretty, young women. With the completion of his degree in sight, he'd gained confidence and took a serious look at his future. A career in law enforcement seemed obvious. When he'd heard Ivy was pregnant and married the guy, Cole decided to stay in Arizona and joined the Tucson Sheriff's Office.

He and Grayson had always kept in touch over the years. One phone call changed Cole's future. Gray told him that Ivy's husband had been killed in action, and that's the real reason he came home.

"You put on a brave face after losing your husband and raised your son. I stood back and watched, never daring to get too close." Ivy's hand rested on her thigh, and he slid his palm over her slender fingers. "Did you really think I was always helping out at the farm because I loved walking in ankle-deep shit?"

Gazing into her lap, she shrugged. "I thought you were doing it for Grayson."

"Ivy, you thought wrong. And you're wrong to assume that I could ever see you as anything but irresistible."

She turned her head and glanced at the laptop. Her brow creased and she pivoted the computer to read the employment page that listed openings in law enforcement by state.

Staring at the screen, she palmed her heart. "When are you leaving?"

Tears drizzled down her cheeks but her tone hardened. He recognized the first flickering sign of her temper.

He reached over and closed the cover. Grayson had warned him to use the head on his shoulders to connect with Ivy before using the one below his belt. Without giving away his sister's secrets, this is what he'd meant. Cole had gone about intimacy with Ivy all wrong.

"Nothing is carved in stone," he said.

"Only my mistakes." Her pretty blue eyes flashed like afterburners on a rocket. "Definitely can't accuse you of waffling with indecision."

She started to get up and Cole clasped her shoulder then gently restrained her. "I made assumptions too. I just didn't voice them. I never considered your experiences or reservations."

"I don't have experience, Cole. I think you know that." She

pointed at the laptop. "You should match your career search with highest single sluts per capita."

"Are we going to talk about what happened last night or let your temper stir itself into a storm?"

"I'll give you the summarized version before you leave." She guzzled the rest of the beer, then slammed the empty on the table. "Mark and I had sex a total of three times. It was a fumbling, ridiculous joke. I saw a train wreck ahead if you found out how little experience I had, compared to all the other women you've screwed. I was embarrassed and I panicked."

"But you're not like those women, and I know that."

"It doesn't matter," she said, her voice rising. "I blurted out the first thing that came into my head. I do that when I'm scared, Cole." She waved her hand as if to ward off other thoughts. "Anyway, I've aired my dirty laundry and apologized." She swiftly got up and stepped away, her gaze landing on the laptop. "You're an idiot for leaving just because I screwed up. This is your home." Her bottom lip quivered, but her eyes snapped with anger. "Don't you dare leave without saying goodbye to Jackson. He loves you."

Ivy believed her apology and explanation wouldn't make a difference. She'd accepted his decision as irreversible.

Was that the image he showed the world? Worse, was that how she saw him? But it all tracked, didn't it? For the last seven years, she'd had no clue how much he loved her.

She was already halfway through the living room when he launched himself from the chair. He caught her at the front door and wrapped his arms around her from behind. Ivy stilled and her hand released the knob.

"I would never hurt Jackson. I love both of you."

"Have a good life, Cole."

He pressed his palm against the door. "Why are you so willing to accept this?"

Ivy took a shuddering breath. "As much as all those women know what you're like in bed, I know you better.

When you make a decision, it's final."

"And that's the problem, isn't it?" She turned to face him. "Love isn't a decision. It's an emotion. A commitment. Trust."

"And intimacy," she added. "But you've had plenty of that."

Was she actually scared she wouldn't meet his expectations, or was this about old wounds? Through gossip, she knew a lot of the women he'd screwed, each one adding a layer of resentment. He'd chosen *them* over *her*.

At the height of their argument last night, Ivy had slaughtered his character for something he hadn't done. Angry, he'd made a rash decision to sever their future. But until this second, he'd never considered that he'd hurt her over and over again, for literally years, with every woman he'd slept with. It didn't matter that he'd been single. At least, not in her heart.

"I've told you this before, Ivy. But I'll say it again, and maybe this time you'll hear me. I'm sorry I hurt you, sweetheart. If I'd known how you felt about me, I would have never slept with those women. It would have been *you* in my arms. And the only reason I'm looking for another job is because eventually you'll meet someone, and I can't handle seeing that."

"Better to end this now than later, Cole. The next time we have a fight, you'll pack your bags then too. You decide, then execute. You've always been that way. You might love me but the next time I say something you don't agree with, you'll react the same way. A marriage can't last if you treat it like the criminal code."

He slammed his eyes closed. "I certainly cuffed my feelings for you and tossed them in solitary confinement for years."

"Face it, Cole. You want sex, not marriage."

"That's not true. Somewhere in the back of my mind, I know I'm going to fuck this up, just like my parents screwed up their marriage. Your brother called me a gutless bastard, and he's right. I love you so deeply, so completely, I'd rather bolt than hurt you, Ivy."

Her gaze rounded with surprise. "You're nothing like your parents, Cole. Nothing. No matter who you're with, you're going to hurt her. That's life. You're going to fight. That's marriage."

"I know that."

"No, you don't. You're the one who wants to walk away after one argument. So, keep walking. Blame me if you want. I don't care."

She pivoted and yanked the door open, but he slammed it shut before she took a step.

"I'm not blaming you, Ivy, I love you. But there's no way for me to prove that I don't want anyone else."

"Cole, every time I run into one of my friends who you screwed, I have to suck it up. I see the smirks on their faces. They jumped into your bed because you're the type of rare man whose aura screams sex appeal and integrity. Strength and virtue. Possessive but sensitive. You're wickedly handsome, and those women had you first. They know what making love to you is like."

"But you don't, and you're the only person who's ever mattered. I want the truth. Last night, did you say that because you were intimidated or because you're still angry and hurt that I slept with women I didn't care about?"

Her forehead creased. "It doesn't matter."

"It does." He grazed her cheek with his curled fingers. "Do you have any idea how many times I've undressed you in my mind?"

"No," she said, gazing up at the ceiling. "It can't be near as many as I've undressed you, but they're just fantasies. Believe me, you'll be underwhelmed with the real thing." She paused then cleared her throat. "And yes! I'm still angry and it hurts."

He drew her to his chest, his chin grazing her silky, blonde hair. "I should have told you how much I loved you a long time ago."

She sniffed and tilted her chin upward. "So instead, you gave me a speeding ticket."

He chomped down on his bottom lip in order not to make light of her comment. He fingered a few strands of hair from her cheek. "I've attended a lot of accidents where the cause was excessive speed. I wanted you to slow down because the last thing I could live with, even if I didn't have you, was losing you." Holding her by the waist, he backed them into the living room.

"Then you should have kissed me instead."

He chuckled. "You're right. I should have." Cole guided her hand to the bulge in his jeans and flattened her palm over his erection. "You're more than a fantasy to me."

Ivy shook her head, refusing to listen or afraid to hear the truth.

"I know what scares you." He waited until she gazed into his eyes. "You've controlled everything in your life. But making love means letting go, losing complete control, and you've forgotten what that's like."

"Cole, I've never known what that's like," she said, as if exasperated he didn't know that already.

"I don't even think it's fear." He released the button on his jeans and eased his zipper down. His erection throbbed, stiff with need. "It's because you're trying to rein in the passion, and it wants to be free. If anyone is going to show you what ecstasy is really like, I want it to be me."

Under her tank, Ivy's nipples hardened, pressing against the fine fabric of her blue shirt. Gazing into her eyes, he barely brushed his thumb across one perfect bud, and she sucked in a sharp breath.

"I want to ease that ache between your thighs, Ivy. Touch you in ways you've never been touched. I won't hurt you, honey, but it's going to feel like sweet torture." Acutely aware of her body's signals, Ivy's breathing shallowed. "Do you want that?"

She licked her bottom lip. "I want what *they* experienced."

"No, sweetheart. You have all of me. I won't share that with anyone but you. So, undress me."

"Unnn...Undress you."

She was totally out of her comfort zone, her body willing even if her mind needed reassurance.

"I want you to see what you do to me."

He exhaled impatience and inhaled willpower as Ivy slid her thumbs inside the waistband of his jeans and eased them off his hips. Kneeling, she rolled the pants down his legs to the floor, and he pushed them aside with one foot. Her lashes fluttered and her chest rose and fell as Ivy's index finger traced the length of his erection.

A wave of raw heat weakened his legs, and he inhaled sharply as her sweet, hot mouth slid over the crown of his cock.

"Oh, fuuuck."

Her wet tongue teased the tip, sending him into a tailspin. When her lips slid down his rigid length, every muscle in his body constricted. If she were anyone else, he'd tangle his hand in her hair and encourage her to keep going, but this was Ivy, and he eased himself from her mouth.

Cole gripped the hem of her tank and pulled it over her head, wrapped his arms around her waist and stood her up, then powered a kiss on her lips with an intensity that even scared him. Her full breasts pressed against his bare chest, pushing his desire into overdrive.

With their lips still touching, he said, "I want you, Ivy. Always you. Only you."

He cupped her breasts and she sighed into his mouth. Cole loosened the button on her shorts and without hesitation, got rid of the barricade between them.

She palmed his jaw when he gripped her ass and hoisted her lean body against his chest, her thighs clenching his hips.

"I'm shaking all over, Cole."

His heart thumped a thundering beat as he carried her toward his bedroom.

"Do you trust me, Ives?" He laid her on the taupe comforter draped over his bed.

"It's more than trust, I want you to be satisfied too." She parted her gorgeous legs, causing his cock to flex at the sight of her bare, wet pussy. Jesus, he'd dreamed of this moment so many times.

Cole leaned over and kissed her soft mouth. There was no doubt she'd always satisfy his hunger.

"Sweetheart, we've known each other nearly all our lives but I don't think you really understand me, and that's my fault."

Tears leached from the edges of her eyes but at the same time, she smiled. "Before you leave, I know you want this, and so do I."

Cole bowed his head. His message wasn't getting through to this sweet, stubborn, strong-willed woman.

He didn't want to wait. Didn't need an audience. Cole opened the bedside table's drawer and retrieved a small box.

"My life is here with you."

"Does that mean you're staying?"

"Only if you'll be my wife."

He flipped open the lid and took the engagement ring from its satin-lined bed.

She palmed the mattress and sat up, shock rounding her eyes. "Cole, it's beautiful."

When Ivy lifted her left hand, he slid the white gold band with sparkling diamonds onto her ring finger. The anxious energy he'd carried around in his gut finally stifled by hope. Cole's parents' failed marriage had a lasting effect on his relationships. Shuffling through women had been easy. If he didn't commit, he couldn't fail, but his love for Ivy refused to die.

"You, me and Jackson. You're the family I want."

"Jackson wants a little sister."

Cole grinned. "Then let's give him one."

She slid her arms around his neck and drew him down as

she laid her head on the pillow. "I love you, Cole. When you look at me like that, the answer is always going to be yes."

CHAPTER TWENTY-ONE

By six-thirty in the morning, the sun had climbed past the mountain range and lit the white fence that lined Brooks Farmstead's gravel driveway. Holly followed Grayson's truck in her car. White canopy tents lined either side of the drive and covered the mowed lawns. Before they left the resort, he'd told her to park in front of the family's old Victorian home.

Holly smelled the glorious aroma of bacon when she opened the driver's door. Grayson held her hand as they ascended the eight steps to the wide, covered veranda. She was still plagued with a small limp, though her knee was definitely improving. The front door stood open, but a screen kept the bugs out.

He led the way into a huge country kitchen.

"Morning, family," he said, stepping inside. "Hope you don't mind one more for breakfast, Ivy."

Holly recognized his partner, Cole, and his sister, Ivy, who stood next to the stove. All eyes turned their way, including a young boy with blond hair sitting at the kitchen table next to an older man sporting a prominent silver moustache with tapered wings.

The older fellow set down the newspaper and got to his feet. Tall and lean but sturdy on his feet, he strode around the massive kitchen island.

"About time my boy made some introductions."

"Dad, I'd like you to meet Holly McNeela. Holly, this is my father, Samuel."

She shook his callused paw. "It's nice to meet you, Samuel."

The glint in the old man's blue eyes reminded her of

Grayson.

Grayson tipped his head toward the kitchen table. "That's my nephew, Jackson."

She waved at the boy.

Ivy strode over to say hello.

"And this is my sister, Ivy, you've—what the hell is that on your finger?"

Holly blinked with surprise as Ivy grinned from ear to ear, raising her hand and wiggling her fingers to show off the engagement band. Cole looked like he'd swallowed a herd of buffalo and they were all stacked in his puffed chest.

Jackson piped up. "Cole wants to be my dad, so he's marrying Mom." The boy got up from the table and ran to Cole, wrapping an arm around his soon-to-be stepfather's hip.

Grayson's partner ruffled the kid's hair, smiling proudly, but it was the look Cole and Grayson shared that warmed Holly's heart. He'd told her they'd been best friends since they were very young. She could see by the smiles on everyone's faces that the news was welcome.

"Congratulations," Holly said. "May I see?" The engagement ring was a white gold band covered with low-set diamonds. A ring meant for a woman who worked with her hands. "Beautiful."

"Thanks," Ivy said, turning a smile toward her fiancé, who winked at her.

"Grayson invited me to your celebration today, but I'd like to help, so put me to work."

Ivy nodded. "If that's the case." She left the kitchen and disappeared into a side room, then returned a few seconds later holding two folded shirts. "Then you're part of the Brooks team."

Holly accepted the shirts and unfolded one. The rest of the family were already wearing theirs. The same Brooks Farmstead logo she'd seen stamped on the grocery bag from the store was on the chestnut-brown t-shirt.

"Thank you." She didn't hesitate and wrestled it over her head and flattened the fabric over her tank top.

Grayson tipped his head in approval. "Suits you," he said as an easy smile slipped across his lips.

Ivy returned to the stove. "Have a seat. Grayson, pour her a coffee. Breakfast is almost ready."

Samuel sat at the head of the table and Holly was seated at his right elbow. He nodded his thanks when Grayson refilled the coffee mugs.

The old man dropped his newspaper on the turn-of-the-century china hutch and put his attention on her. "I'm just an old farmer, but I'm gonna take a guess and say you're not from around here. In fact, I bet you're Canadian."

Shocked, she sat back in surprise. "How did you know?"

Grayson settled the pot back in the coffeemaker. "Yeah, how the heck did you know that?"

The old boy shrugged his lean but broad shoulders. "Recognized the accent."

Holly chuckled. "I don't have an accent anymore."

"Ooooh, you do. Same one as Ivy and Grayson's momma had when I first met her. God rest that beautiful woman's soul."

Grayson's eyes widened. "Whaaat?"

The old man chuckled as he added some cream to his coffee.

Ivy set a plate piled high with pancakes on the table. "Mom was born in Canada, Gray. Didn't you know that?"

Samuel grinned. "She surely was."

Grayson looked astounded as he sat next to Holly. "You're kidding. Why didn't I know this?"

Samuel sipped on his coffee then leaned back in his chair. "Back in the day, if you wanted to immigrate, ya had to give up your citizenship. The year after I married your mother, they changed the rules, but she never bothered to fill out the paperwork."

"Holy shit," Grayson muttered. "I remember Mom's parents coming for a visit when I was very young."

Samuel picked up his fork and pierced a couple pancakes, shifting them to his plate. "They used to visit at least once a year. But they both died relatively young, and your mom didn't have any siblings. Your grandparents on her side had emigrated from Ireland. She didn't have any contact with those kin, but she was born and raised in the Maritimes."

Ivy returned to the table and set down a plate loaded with bacon and sausages before she took a seat.

"Where's your family, young lady?" Samuel asked.

Holly plucked a few pieces of bacon from the plate Grayson offered. "Cape Breton, Nova Scotia. My grandparents emigrated from Ireland too. Back in the sixties."

Grinning, the old man said, "Yep, history does have a way of repeatin' itself."

Holly's cheeks burned hot with Samuel's meaning, especially when Grayson leaned closer and rumbled in a low voice, "Falling for a Canadian must run in the family."

* * * *

Holly manned the Brooks Farmstead booth to allow Arlene an early lunch. The woman's due date was this week, yet here she was helping out. Grayson had told Holly the celebration was popular. She didn't expect the hundreds of people who swarmed the farm, enjoying the warm Fourth of July weather, stopping at the booths that sold an endless variety of fresh produce, baked and canned goods.

The delicious scent of meat grilling on the barbeques wafted through the air, stirring hunger in Holly's belly. The Brooks booth sold mainly fruits and vegetables. If folks wanted fresh meat, she'd been told to direct them to the farmstead store.

Holly had never worked a cash register before, but Arlene gave her a crash course and said if she ran into trouble to text her.

Grayson and his father, Samuel, were giving the owner of a restaurant chain a tour of the beef operation. Her handsome lover had promised he'd be back to collect her for lunch. In a few short days, her social life had gone from lone wolf to part of a pack. So far, she'd been introduced to several friends and neighbors.

"Wow, this is some turnout."

She shifted her gaze from the stream of people using the gravel driveway as a main artery to find a woman in her thirties on the other side of the makeshift checkout table. The gal certainly took her physical fitness serious by the defined muscles on either side of her stomach. Obviously, she was proud of her body, wearing low slung jeans showing her navel and a sports bra to reveal all her hard work.

"Hi, there. Yes, it's incredible." A recyclable bag filled with ripe red tomatoes and a bag of fresh beans sat next to the scale and register. "Can I ring this up for you, or would you like to look around some more?"

The customer grinned. "Tempting, but I think I found what I was looking for."

Holly weighed the vegetables and punched the items into the till.

"You must be one of the Brooks family members," the woman said.

"No. I offered to help Grayson today. He's a Brooks."

The woman eyed her. "I'm not familiar with him. Is he around?"

She seemed friendly enough, but her sharp, steel-blue eyes didn't hold a speck of warmth. "He's around here somewhere. Is this your first time at the farmstead?"

"No, I shop here once a week. I live about twenty minutes away."

"That'll be eight dollars," Holly said.

The blonde dug in her front pocket and pulled out some bills then dropped a ten on the table. Holly gave her two dollars change and closed the cash drawer.

Instead of leaving, the woman said, "You must be local if you know the family."

For ease, Holly had tied her hair in a bun, but the breeze whisked a strand across her cheek. Tucking the stray behind her ear, she said, "Just visiting."

"Holly!" Grayson's tone was sharp when he approached at a fast clip between the bins of vegetables.

The blonde grabbed her veggies and turned to leave but Grayson stepped right into her path. Deadly didn't begin to describe the fierceness in his eyes.

"Lt. Billings, I see you dropped by to enjoy the celebration."

He knew her?

The woman's body tensed for a second, then her lean shoulders relaxed. "Wouldn't want to miss the excitement. Just checking things out."

Grayson's gaze shifted to Holly. "Sweetheart, this is Lt. Billings with the Skagit Drug Task Force. The person I told you who's responsible for my temporary transfer."

When the lieutenant turned to face her, a subtle but obvious contempt coated her expression.

"I don't understand." Holly narrowed her eyes. "You said you weren't familiar with Grayson."

One side of the woman's lip tilted upward. "You must have misunderstood."

That was a lie! Holly didn't dare break eye contact. "No, don't think I did."

Gray rounded the table and slipped his arm around Holly's shoulders. "Well, Lieutenant, now that you've met my better half, thanks for dropping by."

If Holly didn't know better, his friendly greeting sounded more like a warning to take her purchase and get lost.

"My pleasure." Her attention shifted to Holly. "I always like to know the men on my team. Long hours and close quarters. We spend more time together than with our significant others. Hope you're not the jealous type." A stiff smile plated her mouth. "It's the nature of the job." Kate slithered a head-to-toe look over Holly's lover. "See you on Monday, Grayson."

She slipped into the crowd and disappeared from view.

"I didn't misunderstand." Holly turned to face Gray. "Was that the same woman who stopped behind your truck at the resort?"

He eyed the booth and the customers moseying about. "That's her."

"Are you going to tell me what's going on?"

He sighed. "I just got off the phone with my old partner from San Diego. I called him yesterday for some background."

Holly shrugged. "About?"

A woman with two kids in tow strolled up to the register. She set the handbasket on the table, then glanced up. "Grayson! Hey, I heard you were back."

He grinned. "Kay. Long time. How ya doing?"

She chuckled. "Busy." She nudged her head toward the youngster on her left. "Ivy tells me you moved home." Kay finished emptying the basket and set it on the ground. "And this is?"

"Holly, this is Kay Darwin. We went to school together."

"Nice to meet you," Holly said.

"You too, Holly." Kay's daughter sniped the bag of carrots from the table. "We need to buy and wash those before we eat them, honey." The little redhead stuck her bottom lip out and put the bag back on the portable table. "I take it from that shit-eating grin on Gray's face, you two are a couple. You live in the area?"

"Not really. Can I ring this up for you?"

"Yes, please."

The woman's son, with dusty red hair, gripped the edge of the table with the tips of all ten fingers and watched as Holly weighed the veggies.

"Gray, I bumped into Ivy a few minutes ago. Couldn't help but notice that beautiful ring on her finger. Is it true about her and Cole getting married?"

"Sure is. We just found out this morning," he said, his gaze surveying the crowd. "Guess we can look forward to a wedding."

Kay winked at him. "Your best friend marrying your sister, that's kinda cool." She handed a twenty-dollar bill to Holly.

"Mommy, I want to ride the horses!" her redheaded daughter exclaimed.

"We'll put the groceries in the car first, then go for a ride."

Grayson put the produce in the tote bag Kay laid on the table. "Follow the driveway to the end. You'll see it. Neighbor brought over some of his ponies. Kids are having a great time."

"Thanks," she said, heaving the bag off the table. "Hope to see you again, Holly."

"You, too." She watched as Kay guided her children away. The other customers in the Brooks booth were still looking over the fresh produce. "Nice woman."

Grayson chuckled. "Yep. She was Cole's high school date for prom. They were an item once upon a time."

"Oh, the drama," Holly teased. "Looks like she has her hands full now." She crossed her arms and gazed up at her boyfriend, if that's what he was. Last night in the heat of passion, they'd shared a few meaningful words. She questioned whether it was the sex talking on his part. But of more concern was that blonde cop. "I get a bad feeling from Lt. Billings. Did you know her before being transferred to the DTF unit?"

Grayson shook his head. "Not at all, but she worked in San Diego on the narco squad before I joined."

"You didn't look pleased that she was here. Maybe it's completely innocent."

"I could accept that, except my old partner called me back. That woman's trouble, and I don't want you involved."

"What kind of trouble, Grayson? You looked like you wanted to rip her head off."

"Not a topic you need to hear."

His authoritarian tone made her blink, unsure whether that was the SEAL or the detective flexing his muscles.

"Thank you, Det. Brooks," she replied sharply. "But I'll be the judge of that!"

"Ah, okaaay." His eyebrows rose with surprise. "When, um, you call me detective in that tone and all of a sudden, I hear a hint of an Irish accent, that's a sign I'm being a dick, right?"

"Imagine dat. Ye heard an accent, *didja*. It's Cape Breton, ye *knowittall*."

Grayson cleared his throat and Holly tilted her chin upward as an exclamation point.

He offered a churlish grin. "Well, least I'll know when I'm in the shithouse."

"Stop stalling."

"It's a sensitive topic that you're familiar with, but I don't want you drawing the wrong conclusion, all right?"

A fair request. She nodded.

"Billings had an affair with the captain of the San Diego narco division. Destroyed the man's marriage. While Kate was screwing the captain, my old partner said she'd befriended the captain's wife, looking for weaknesses in the marriage. Then she sent his wife a video of the captain cheating without giving away her own identity. When the marriage ended, Billings put in her resignation as if that's all she'd wanted to accomplish."

Holly grazed her upper teeth over her top lip. "It's one thing to lure a man into adultery, but she sounds more like a femme fatale. Why did she stop behind your truck last night?"

Grayson slid his arms around her waist. "She put a tracking device on the vehicle."

Holly blinked. "Did you get rid of it?"

"Not yet. I want to know what her deal is first. When I spoke with my partner from San Diego and he told me she'd befriended the captain's wife, I got a bad feeling. Sure enough, Billings had already found you. I cut her off at the pass. Now you know who she is, so that avenue is blocked."

"But if she was at the resort yesterday, that means she'd already seen us together and knows who I am."

He smiled sedately. "Sweetheart, you don't miss a beat, do ya? She must have followed me earlier when I picked you up for dinner. Depending on her motivation, all I can do is monitor the situation."

"Sounds like her motivation is you. She practically licked you with her eyes."

Grayson slid his hand behind her neck and kissed her gently. "Too bad, I'm devoted to one woman."

She let him kiss her again before she said, "Grayson, you have a way of making me feel all warm and squishy inside."

His hand slid down her side and paused at her waist. "What we have is new, but we're solid, Holly." Grayson squeezed her gently. "Listen, I don't want you to worry about Billings. You're probably right about her reason for being here. But until I figure out if she's up to something, keep your eyes open."

"Hey, you two, none of that!" Arlene said, interrupting as she returned from her lunch break, followed by a man wearing a cowboy hat, Levi's and a grey shirt.

"Hugh." Grayson shook the guy's hand.

"Great turnout," he said.

"Holly, this is Arlene's husband."

"Hello and congratulations. Looks like you'll have a new family member very soon."

"Ugh." Arlene palmed her huge belly. "Not soon enough. This kid better be on time. I'm ready."

"I bet." Holly always wanted a family of her own. She was an aunt five times over, thanks to her sisters.

Arlene strode around the table to take over the till. "Do you have children, Holly?"

"No."

Arlene winked at Grayson. "The correct answer is, not yet."

Holly's cheeks heated. It was a little early to consider anything other than getting to know Grayson better.

"Well, you're relieved of duty," Arlene said. "Enjoy the celebration."

Holly lifted her cell. "If you need me for another break, send me a text."

"You can count on it."

Grayson held her hand and led her into the sunlight to stroll among the crowd. "Any particular reason you didn't have kids?"

"Besides an unfaithful husband?" she countered. "In the early days, I concentrated on my research at the university. It was a dream job for me. Kevin worked twelve-hour shifts. Even at the beginning of our marriage, our time together was disjointed. We were both busy and dedicated to our professions. In retrospect, I blindly believed our marriage was solid. His wandering eye was my fault. I should have focused more attention on him."

"Whoa, now." He palmed her shoulder and stopped, causing a stream of people to wash around them. "That's bullshit. Don't give him an excuse for his adultery. His attention should have never wavered from you. That's on him."

"We're blocking traffic, come on."

They cleared the crowds and Grayson steered them toward the old Victorian. Holly paused at the foot of the front steps.

"I wanted a family but not before I'd made my mark at the university." She paused, afraid to ask. "I suppose you have the same reasons."

Grayson headed to the top of the stairs, then turned and curled his finger for her to follow. "Not exactly."

The glint in his eyes reminded her of a teenage boy. "Okay, let me rephrase. You're a manwhore with no intention of having children."

His rugged features split into a handsome grin. "Got something against manwhores?"

Holly perched her hands on her hips. "Are you up to no good?"

Her gorgeous lover shrugged. "House is empty. Thought I'd give you a tour."

She narrowed an eye at him. "Any room in particular?"

He flattened a palm over his heart. "Miss McNeela, are you accusing me of luring you into my lair under false pretext?"

Her fractured knee rebelled a little as she hobbled up the stairs to join him. "You better be."

Grayson laughed and opened the front door. "I'm making you lunch, sweetheart.

A few minutes later, they sat at the kitchen table enjoying a cold drink and a sandwich.

Grayson sat back after finishing his meal. "I have an idea for next weekend."

"Does it involve a locked room and forty-eight hours of lust and debauchery?"

His large palm slid across the tabletop onto her hand. "If you insist, we can squeeze in a few meals."

She looked into his amazing eyes, her body heating

with his idea. "I get the feeling you're trying to seduce me, Detective."

"Oh, baby, when that knee of yours is all healed up, I'm going to turn up the heat."

She grinned at his promise. "Think you already have, Grayson. In so many ways."

His gaze became thoughtful. "Nothing makes me want to question how addicted I am to you. You live on the other side of the border, but I still want...us."

Insanely attracted to a man who lived in another country didn't bode well for a long-term relationship. "If I was an optimist I'd say, at least you're not a SEAL anymore and deploy for months at a time."

"And if you were a pessimist?"

"I'd say, eventually one of us has to make a sacrifice. Give up something we love. Or someone we love. Only a couple days ago, I swore I'd keep my head when it came to you." Holly thread her fingers through his. "But the truth is, even your creepy admirer has better odds."

Grayson shoved her plate aside and cupped her hand. "I don't have all the answers—yet. I've always relied on my instincts. They're telling me, no one's giving up anything." His gaze locked on her. "Sweetheart, you have no idea how special you are, but I see it."

She'd been born with a healthy dose of pessimism but the way he made her feel so alive and anxious with hope, her doubts slithered back into their dark corners.

"Guess this means I'll have to keep my passport current."

He leaned across the table and pressed a knee-melting kiss on her mouth. "Babe, I can make love to you in any country. No border will stop me from doing that."

CHAPTER TWENTY-TWO

After their early lunch, Grayson was needed at the grilling station. Holly perused the farmers' stalls and returned to her vehicle to unload two grocery bags of goodies she'd purchased. Luckily, she'd parked under a beautiful, large oak with sprawling branches that provided some shade.

"British Columbia. Guess you are just visiting."

The sound of Lt. Billings' voice slithered up Holly's spine. She closed the trunk and faced Grayson's stalker.

"You're still here, Lieutenant."

"Please, call me Kate."

A barricade, although not more than a few posts and strung tape, diverted the crowds toward the barns, but the house was off-limits.

"Looking for something?" Holly asked.

Kate smiled. "The line-up at the portable toilets is pretty long. Thought I'd use the bathroom in the house."

Holly knew of another row of portable facilities close to the barn and corral where the pony rides took place.

"Let me take you to the barn. Line isn't long there."

The smile dipped and a snide expression slid onto Billings' pretty face. "I'm sure Grayson wouldn't mind me using the bathroom."

"Sorry. No one's allowed in the house but the family."

Billings made a tsking sound and headed up the stairs. Little did she know that Holly had closed and locked the door. She stood at the bottom of the steps and waited for the inevitable. Billings opened the screen and tried to turn the handle. The officer bristled and retraced her steps but didn't descend the stairs.

"I'm guessing you have a key. You mind? The bladder's getting full."

Holly crossed her arms. "I'm sorry, Lieutenant, but you're not welcome to the family's bathroom." She shrugged. "Or anything else in the house that you're looking for."

Kate trotted down the steps and walked to within three feet of Holly. "I get the feeling you don't trust me."

"Why would you think that?" She paused and slapped on a syrupy smile. "I mean it couldn't have anything to do with lying an hour ago, or that you asked Grayson out for a drink after you first laid eyes on him, and then interrupted our dinner last night with a bogus call and another attempt at a drink." She shook her head at the woman. "Listen, I get it. He's extremely handsome, but he's been around the block a few dozen times. If he was interested in you, you'd know it."

The DTF officer took an intimidating step closer. "I like a challenge." Her expression pinched with apparent malice. "If I were you, I'd pack my shit up and go home. You don't want to test me or the badge I carry."

Instead of backing up, Holly got in her face, the Irish in her blood ignoring the dangers of pissing off a cop.

"If I were *you*, I wouldn't forget that Grayson isn't some rookie cop with a hard-on, and I bear no *fucking* resemblance to Mrs. Gordon. If a bag of narcotics ends up in my vehicle, you can be damn sure there'll be an internal investigation and your little game in San Diego will play a big part." At the mention of Mrs. Gordon, the smug expression on Kate's face dissolved. "You want a challenge? How about a goddamned nightmare?"

The sound of someone walking on gravel attracted Kate and made Holly take a step back.

Ivy approached with a quizzical brow. "Problems?"

Holly shook her head. "This lady was looking for a bathroom. I told her she could use the ones by the barn.

Shorter line."

Kate plastered a disarming smile on her face. "You're Ivy, right? I'm Lt. Kate Billings. Grayson's OIC at the Drug Task Force. Thought I could use the bathroom in the house. His friend here is being inhospitable."

Ivy slung a look at Holly and back to Kate. "Yeah, I know who you are. Portable toilets are on the right side of the barn."

Kate blinked with surprise but didn't question Ivy's blunt response and strode quickly toward the barrier tape.

Kinda shocked, Holly asked, "How?"

Ivy kept her gaze on the retreating lieutenant. "Grayson gave me a summarized version this morning and asked me to keep an eye out." Seemingly satisfied the lieutenant wasn't coming back, Ivy smiled. "We Brooks take care of each other."

"I hope for Grayson's sake she gets the hint and moves on, but I have a feeling that woman isn't a quitter."

Ivy wrinkled her nose. "Probably not, that's why Gray's worried about you."

"I can take care of myself."

"From what I heard, I think you just did. Anyway, I'm taking a quick break. Can I interest you in a cold glass of lemonade?"

Parched and still in fight mode, she agreed to a time-out.

* * * *

Holly found Grayson at the barbeque station. Three o'clock and a crowd still swarmed the market.

"Think she's gone?" Holly asked as Grayson flipped several racks of ribs then lowered the lid on a massive smoker.

"Haven't seen her in hours. She probably packed it in."

Holly hated that the day had been disturbed by his

stalker, but it hadn't been ruined.

"Hey-hey, Brooksy. Been a long time," a man said, approaching the grilling station.

The guard who had given Holly his card when she'd crossed the border swaggered up in a tight-fitting t-shirt and cycling shorts that showed off his muscular legs. He reminded her of a bodybuilder on steroids. A brunette hung on his arm, the woman's overly swollen lips resembling a puffer fish. Extremely long eyelashes swayed in the breeze, but her mussed hairstyle didn't move an inch. Rounding out her fashion statement were double Ds under a paper-thin, tight t-shirt with two predominant nipples in full frontal attack, as if trying to escape their confines.

"Bob Sagle," Grayson greeted. "Thanks for coming to the celebration."

Sagle, a nice-looking man no taller than five-ten, turned his attention to Holly. "You look familiar."

"I spoke to you when I crossed the border."

"Yeah, right. Well, I see a lot of faces every day."

Since meeting Grayson, Holly had noted the way his eyes spoke volumes without his mouth uttering a word. Today, she'd seen utter intimidation when he'd stared down Kate Billings. His current expression was one she'd never seen yet. Rife with dominance, a look no man or beast would dare cross.

"This is Holly McNeela." Grayson's stare literally pierced Bob through the heart with a look that demanded he try again.

Bob darted a glance her way. "Nice to meet you, Holly," he said with a nod.

Grayson set the barbeque fork on a mobile cart. "Heard you're working the border."

"Been there for two years now. So, I, uh, ran into a few old faces here today. Thought we'd put together an ad-hoc backyard game for fun. What d'ya say? That lawn behind the barbeques looks like a good place."

"I'm in," Cole said, strolling up with Ivy beside him.

"Bob Sagle?" Ivy greeted. "Didn't know you still lived around here."

"Moved away after high school. Spent a few years in L.A. This is my girlfriend, Sandra."

"Hey," Sandra greeted, but her brown eyes were hooked on Grayson instead of Ivy.

"So, what d'ya say, Brooksy?" Bob urged. "Still got what it takes to score a couple downs?"

Grayson flicked a look in Cole's direction. Holly'd give her eye teeth to know what he was thinking, but according to Cole, good old Bob still carried a chip on his shoulder from their high school days. Grayson, on the other hand, had killed men in combat and probably wasn't interested in bumping chests with Bob's adolescent hang-ups.

More men in their early thirties wandered up, greeting Cole and Grayson. Some were in good shape, but others packed a few extra inches around the middle.

A guy named Mark, wearing a Mariners t-shirt and faded jeans said, "If Grayson's in and Cole's taking running back, I'm on their team."

Bob shook his head and in a condescending tone said, "Let's not get all serious here. This game is for fun. We don't want anyone getting hurt."

The men jeered and made a ruckus.

Grayson still hadn't agreed to play. Holly slid her arm around her boyfriend's waist, and he tilted his head in her direction, flexed his eyebrow then curled his thick arms around her.

He put his lips to her ear and whispered, "I'm gonna mow the lawn with Bobby's fucking teeth."

She laughed and leaned back enough to look into his eyes. "I'd say that's an appropriate penalty for a cocky attitude."

"You know what's really important?" Grayson asked in

a lighthearted tone.

"No, what?" she replied, emulating his playful tone.

"Not only did I wipe the floor with his ass when we were seventeen, but as men, my intelligent, classy girlfriend makes his tramp look like a pole dancer from a skid row strip club."

Holly's knees weakened a little. "Grayson Brooks, I want you."

His answer was to palm the back of her head and ease a blistering-hot kiss on her lips.

The crowd didn't pay any mind to their intimacy, still squabbling good-naturedly over who would play on whose team.

Nose to nose, Grayson smiled at first, then his expression mellowed. "You fill all the empty space in my heart, Holly."

She kissed his nose. "Kick that egomaniac's ass, but don't kill him."

Grayson's cheeks lifted with a grin. "If you say so."

Something behind her caught his eye and he straightened. Unlike his unfazed attitude toward Bob, Grayson appeared wary, and his body stiffened.

Holly was almost afraid to turn around. Had Kate returned?

A man's strong but confident timbre said, "Petty Officer Brooks. How the heck are you?"

Grayson's eyes flashed between her and the man who'd said hello. "Chief. What are you doing in these parts?"

Holly pivoted to see a guy slightly leaner than Grayson, with dark brown hair and shocking green eyes.

The man's gaze shifted to her and a slip of a smile coated his lips. "Are you going to introduce me to this lovely woman?"

"Holly, this is Dirk Larkin. We served together."

Maybe it was her imagination, but Grayson seemed tense. She, on the other hand, didn't get any bad vibes from his teammate.

"Nice to meet you, Dirk."

"What brings you to Washington State?" Grayson asked.

"I live here now. Well, part-time, anyway. After I left the teams, I went back to college. Finished my Masters in archeology. My old man was happy I followed in his footsteps. I travel between Seattle and the Middle East."

"That's fascinating," she said. "At the moment, I'm researching the scripts of two tablets found outside Jerusalem."

Interest lit Dirk's eyes. "You're kidding. The West Wall tablets?"

This man certainly was tuned in. "Exactly."

He stepped closer. "You're an ancient text linguist?"

"I am. I work with the archaeology department at UBC."

His handsome features erupted with interest. "You're Holly McNeela, aren't you?"

She blinked with surprise. "How did you know that?"

With a fetching grin, he said, "I've read your work. Impressive. That's why we sent the tablets from our find to your university. Talk about fate. Unreal."

Grayson's hand squeezed her hip to the point of pain, and she pried his fingers from her skin.

"Your find? Seriously? I'd say this is fortuitous. The tablets are in incredible shape."

"They certainly are." Dirk flashed a look toward Grayson. "Makes me wonder what you're doing with this guy?"

Grayson grilled a wary look at his fellow retired SEAL. "She's..."

Bob's voice broke through the chaos. "All right. We doing this or what?"

"Dirk, why don't you join us?" Grayson suggested.

"Thanks, but I'll pass. Besides, I'd like to speak with Holly."

"Uh-huh. I bet you would, but she's busy."

Not that busy, she thought. "Dirk, I'd love to discuss the tablets."

"Great, can't wait to hear your initial thoughts. But unfortunately, today isn't a good day. How about if I contact you next week?"

"Absolutely."

Dirk stepped aside to let two children who'd been talking to their father escape from the clutch of people standing near the barbeques. "Gray, I can't stay long. I just wanted to stop by and say hello." He turned his gaze to her. "Certainly glad I did."

"Yeah," Grayson said. "Drop by again so we can talk."

Again, Holly heard something slightly threatening in Grayson's tone, but Dirk didn't seem offended.

"We definitely need to reconnect."

Cole intervened. "Time to toss a ball, Gray."

Her monster of a detective and his buddy, Cole, knocked fists and both of them gripped the hem of their t-shirts and tore them over their heads. Holly's breath stuttered a little at her boyfriend's four-by-four track of abs and a sleeve of tattoos covering his right arm, ending above his firm bicep near his shoulder.

People from the celebration had come to investigate, and a group of women in their thirties whistled and cheered. The other guys in the game followed Cole and Grayson's lead, removing their shirts. More wolf-whistles and clapping followed.

Good old Bob opened his mouth to say something, but Grayson's deep, commanding timbre attracted the crowd's attention.

"Okay, everyone who wants in for a Brooks' backyard game, line up over there." He pointed to the lawn behind the barbeques.

Holly stood next to Ivy and watched as Bob and Grayson picked their teams, eight guys on each. Bystanders lined the playing area, three bodies thick.

"I don't know the rules of football," Holly admitted.

Ivy grinned. "Well, I'll give ya a play-by-play, but I can tell you what's gonna happen. Cole and Gray are gonna give that dickhead, Sagle, a reminder why our team won the state championship."

The hot sun shone overhead and sweat glistened on the players' backs as they formed their huddles.

"They don't have any equipment. Are they going to play tackle?" she asked.

Ivy's pretty blue eyes, identical in color to Grayson's, turned on Holly. "I hope not. If they do, it'll get rough."

"Mom! Mom!" Jackson shoved his way through the crowd and wedged himself between Holly and his mother. "What's happening?"

Ivy tossed an arm around her son's shoulders. "Uncle Gray and Cole are gonna play some football."

Jackson's boyish good looks lit with a smile. Holly grinned, seeing the pure hero-worship in the kid's eyes.

"They're gonna kick butt," Jackson said.

The lush lawn looked thick enough that there wouldn't be too much damage if one of the players went down. A guy wearing a dark brown cowboy hat set neon road pylons on either side of the field.

"That's to mark the yard lines," Ivy said.

"Wooooo hoooo!" a woman cheered at the top of her lungs from behind Holly. Wendy muscled in next to Ivy's right side, looking country girl gorgeous with her straw cowboy hat and blonde hair. "Go, Blue Eagles!" she shouted. "Wooo hoooo!" A beautiful smile revealed her pearly white teeth. "Isn't it excitin' to see the boys playin' again?"

Ivy laughed. "I know who I'm cheering for."

Wendy, with her eyes glued to the field, hadn't seen Holly. "Oh, my Lord, your brother is one step from heaven, Ivy. I want that man so bad, I can taste it." She raised her arm in the air and cheered again.

Ivy glanced at Holly and gave an exaggerated shrug as if to say *sorry*.

The excitement had drawn a big crowd, but Holly got the feeling these were all locals, with people shouting at the players by name.

Someone in the crowd gave a loud whistle and a voice called out, "Wait one darn minute. You boys think you're playing a game without me?"

The players noticed and their heads started turning, looking at the crowd with surprise. A few feet to Holly's left, a man broke through the line of guests and walked onto the field. Wearing beige slacks and a red golf shirt, he strutted with a healthy senior's stride. A few strands of hair graced his mainly bald head, but when he stepped onto the field, the players clapped and whistled.

"Oh my, God," Ivy said. "Is that Coach Baldwin?"

"Who's that?" Holly asked, seeing the old guy grin as he raised his hand in the air and the people cheered.

"He coached the high school football teams for forty years. I thought he retired to Boca Raton."

When the coach reached the guys, he received plenty of pats on the back.

"Okay, now," he said in a booming voice. "We got ourselves some varsity state champions to cheer for today."

The crowd responded with a roar of applause as if this was a real game.

The coach raised his hand and the noise settled down. "I had the honor of watching some of these guys tear the field up in Oh-Seven to win the 4A State Championship. The quarterback that year was none other than Grayson Brooks and it's him and his family hosting this fine July Fourth celebration."

As Coach Baldwin spoke, birds tweeted in the trees surrounding the playing field. High overhead, a jet cut through the clear blue sky, leaving a contrail in its wake.

"I'm an old fart now, but I keep my ear to the ground and learned that Gray far exceeded my expectations to go on and serve this great country as a United States Navy SEAL. And when he hung up his flippers, he became a law enforcement officer and recently returned to Washington State.

"When it comes to football, no one man takes a team to victory, and Cole Sterling's feet had wings. When you put these two in a play, you've got magic. Just so happens Cole saw a future in law enforcement too. All you nice folks out there eyeing that bottle of pinot you bought today, keep it corked until you get home."

The crowd chuckled and some hooted.

Dirk stood behind Holly's right shoulder and put his mouth next to her ear at the same time Grayson turned his attention to her side of the field. The scowl on her detective's face extremely clear.

"Gray was one helluva warrior," Dirk said. "He broke as many heads as he did hearts. I was proud to serve with him."

"I had no idea he played football."

Dirk chuckled, his eyes on the field. "You'd be surprised at the man's talents. I certainly was."

The coach continued, naming a few guys on the field, and then said, "Today is Independence Day. We celebrate freedom and the struggle to ensure liberty and justice for all. For the last one hundred and fifty years, the Brooks family has given back to this community. Samuel, the patriarch of this fine family, where are ya, old man?"

Holly didn't realize it, but Samuel stood just behind her left shoulder.

"Thanks for coming, Coach," he said in a strong voice.

The coach pointed at the crowd. "And we all know the firecracker who organized this shindig and runs the farmstead store is Ivy Brooks, and that little fella standing beside her is the next generation, Ivy's son, Jackson."

They both smiled and waved.

"Now, I got some good news and some bad news."

On cue, the crowd started shouting, *"good news"* while others shouted, *"bad news."*

"I know you single ladies out there in the crowd are eyeing our all-star running back, Cole Sterling. Rumor is Cole has always had his eye on one little lady. Like any good love story, everyone had it figured out long before the hero and heroine, but last night Cole finally plucked up enough nerve to ask Ivy Brooks to marry him."

Ivy covered her face while the players on the team gave Cole *Atta boys.*

Coach turned to look at Gray's partner. "Um, she said yes, right?"

Cole broke into a laugh and gave a thumb's up, which received a round of applause.

Coach Baldwin shushed the crowd. "So that leaves our high school's highest-scoring quarterback of all time. I bet you ladies in the crowd are wondering if you got a hope in hell with this handsome, retired SEAL and law enforcement officer behind me," he teased.

Gals in the audience catcalled and whistled, but Wendy put a hand to her mouth and yelled, "He's mine, bitches."

Ivy slapped a hand over her face and groaned.

The coach chuckled. "To be honest, I don't know if Grayson here is the most eligible bachelor around. What of it, son?"

Grayson stood among the other players, his head bowed and hands on his hips. To Holly, he reminded her of an action movie hero. His broad shoulders straightened as he looked up, his carved jaw taut with a sexy smile.

He pointed straight at her. "That gorgeous woman over there burned my bachelor card. Didn't ya, Holly?"

She laughed and blew him a kiss. The beauty queen didn't always get the most popular guy, sometimes the high school nerd or the girl with her nose stuck in a science book won the heart of a hero. At least until he came to his senses.

"Lucky man," Dirk muttered. She turned to look at the archaeologist. "I'd love to stay but I should go. I'll head across the border next week. Can't wait to discuss your findings."

"Certainly. See you then."

Coach Baldwin gave an exaggerated sigh. "Sorry, ladies. Sounds like Grayson has his heart set on one lucky lady. But there's still good reason to gather as friends and neighbors on the farmstead and celebrate. So, let's give these good folks a round of applause."

As the crowd clapped and cheered, Wendy asked Ivy, "Ya think it'll last, because I can hang in there."

Ivy rolled her eyes. "Jesus, Wendy. Give it up."

When the coach stopped clapping, the crowd quieted. "Should we see if these boys still got their game? Touch or tackle?"

The crowd all shouted their preference, but tackle came out louder than touch.

"Tackle, it is!" Coach Baldwin shouted.

"Uh-oh," Ivy said. "I better get the EMT's number on standby."

Coach Baldwin announced they'd play to twenty-eight and rattled off a bunch of football jargon Holly didn't understand. During the speech, she noticed Bob Sagle stood with his arms crossed, looking less than pleased, as if someone had stolen his thunder. The coach had barely mentioned him.

"Let's play some football!" Coach shouted, and the guys got into position.

Holly didn't know much about the game, but she knew where the quarterback stood behind the offensive line. There was a kickoff and then she was lost. The lawn wasn't nearly the size of a real football field, but it had room to run.

Grayson caught the hiked ball and put it into high gear for the end zone. When a guy tried to take him down, Gray drew his arm back. With wicked accuracy, he sailed the ball through the air and Cole caught it, darting around the defense and scored a touchdown, just like that.

While the game progressed, Ivy gave her a play-by-play and kept score. "He's still got it."

"Grayson?" Holly asked.

"Yeah, him too. But no, I'm talking about Cole."

Jackson cheered and jumped up and down any time his uncle or soon-to-be stepfather scored points.

As the crowd watched, cheers intermingled with boos and the odd *oof* when someone went down hard, keeping the excitement at a fever pitch. Sagle, try as he might, couldn't bring Grayson down, and he tried whenever her boyfriend had the ball.

Grayson and Cole's team were winning by six points. The guys certainly were getting a workout under the hot sun.

"Fourth down," Ivy said. "If Gray's team scores a touchdown, they'll win."

Sagle, with his fingers on the ground and his brown gaze pinned to Grayson, waited. The center hiked the ball and Grayson snapped it out of the air. Instead of running, his arm powered back, and he sent the ball bulleting toward Cole. The football was halfway across the field, but Sagle bolted and launched himself at Gray for a cheap-shot tackle.

Two things happened simultaneously: Cole caught the ball and scored a touchdown at the same time Grayson reacted to Sagle's attack. He twisted, gripped old Bob by the neck and redirected his momentum, ramming Sagle's face into the ground.

Holly blinked and wished she had a replay of that move. Bob stood up, spitting grass out of his mouth, and

Holly burst into laughter.

Samuel was chuckling in a deep baritone. "You caught that, huh?" he asked Holly.

"Grayson said he was going to mow the lawn with Bob's teeth."

His father bent over laughing.

"Uh-oh," Holly said when Sagle's body language turned hostile, and he poked the air aggressively toward Gray.

Words were exchanged, but she couldn't hear because the crowd was cheering Cole's touchdown. Coach Baldwin must have seen what happened and put it into a trot. The other players noticed Sagle's mounting anger and turned to watch.

Gray looked calm and collected while the angry border guard mouthed off. The coach got between them, and whatever he said sent Bob marching across the field with a scowl on his face. But at least the testosterone evaporated, and it was over.

The winning team huddled for a second, then shouted, "Eagles rule!"

The rest of the players shook hands and congratulated each other.

Two men muscled through the crowd, each carrying a large cooler. They placed them on the grass in front of Holly. When the lid was flipped back it revealed water bottles in an icy bath.

Ivy yelled, "Waaaater!"

CHAPTER TWENTY-THREE

T he team's players lined up in front of the cooler, plucking large water bottles and getting out of the way for the next guy. Cole and Grayson were the last to arrive.

Like the other men, they snatched bottles from the icy bath and unscrewed the top, guzzled, then poured the remainder of the water over their heads.

Grayson's warrior-like features never failed to send shivers up Holly's spine, but when streams of water wet his dark-blond hair and drizzled down his sweaty, muscled chest, her lady bits went into a seizure.

Quenched, Grayson's eyes connected with hers, his pecs and abs still rising and falling from exertion. But it was the heat in his gaze that stirred Holly into a sensual storm.

"You won," she said.

There was plenty of activity around them, but it didn't penetrate the brain fog caused by his attention on her.

"Where is he?" Grayson asked in a gruff tone.

"Who?"

"Dirk."

"He had to leave."

Grayson tilted his head and kissed her as if he hadn't seen her in days, making Holly's toes tingle. As she slid her hands over his firm, moist shoulders, he deepened the kiss. How would she concentrate on her work at the university, or anything else for that matter, without getting her fix of him each day?

She leaned back and eyed him. "Did you kiss your favorite cheerleader that way after a game?"

"I don't remember," he said sharply, grasping her hand.

"I need a shower."

"Okay, I'll go see if Ivy needs help."

"I need a shower…with *you*."

With a steel grip on her hand, Grayson led the way through the crowd while people offered, *"Ya still got it, Gray."* And *"Nice tackle on the 4th and 3."*

He barely acknowledged the comments. With the crowd behind them, they walked in silence toward the tractor shed instead of the house.

"I thought you said you needed a shower."

Grayson steered her to the left side of the eighty-foot-long shed and entered through a rear door. She was surprised to see a tidy but small suite. Holly sensed something off about Grayson as she stood in the dime-sized living room.

Defined muscle rippled down his strong back as he locked the door. He turned and thrust his shirt at the couch. The fire in his eyes ignited butterflies in her belly. His high cheekbones and carved jaw liquefied her body. Without a word, he released the zipper on his jeans. Waves of sexual energy hit her square between the thighs. The man was unadulterated perfection.

She'd never had shower sex, but she was pretty sure that's what he wanted. Grayson removed his pants, then strode toward her.

"Grayson—"

His hands cupped her cheeks and his mouth slammed against her lips while urging her backward. She couldn't see where she was going but trusted he wouldn't let her trip.

Within a few steps, he steered her into a bathroom with rough, cedar plank walls that reminded her of a cabin in the woods. No luxuries, only a pedestal sink, small medicine cabinet with a mirror, and a toilet.

So far, he hadn't said a word, and didn't utter any as

he removed her brace and stripped her clothes. He reached behind her and turned on the shower.

"Grayson, is something wrong?"

Instead of answering, he spoke by touch, rolling her nipples between his thumbs and index fingers. She shivered with anticipation as his tongue probed her mouth. His rough hands and firm lips traveled across her skin as if desperate to touch her all at once. Grayson's intensity thrilled and scared her a little.

The spray of water splattered on the tiles of the large shower stall that was roomy enough for two people. He placed his hands on her shoulders, urging her backward.

"Turn around," he ordered.

Holly flattened her palms against the tiled wall and his large hand slid over her hip to her thigh, lifting her injured leg and settling her foot onto a built-in bench seat. The droplets of water practically sizzled on her heated skin.

"Does the knee hurt?" His tone steely.

His warm tongue licked the skin on the side of her neck. "No." She gulped in more air. Grayson had never flexed his sensual dominance like this before. It felt raw, almost savage, and it made her body tingle with excitement.

Standing behind her, he grazed her ribs with a slow crawl of his palms, then cupped her breasts. "I just want you to feel, baby."

The low timbre of his voice skittered through her veins as his erection slid between her parted legs against her wet crease. Instead of breaching her aching channel, the crown of his head rocked back and forth over her clit. Impatience twisted her into a needy coil.

His strong hand gripped one hip, and he laid his other on her back, leaning her forward.

"Oh God, Grayson. Please."

Her nipples hardened into firm nubs with his fingers tugging and teasing. His rough palm slid over her ass and between her thighs. He fingered her clit, and she trembled all over.

"You're so wet, babe. Do I do that to you?" he asked, leaving a trail of kisses down her spine.

"Yes," she whispered.

He touched to torment her but wouldn't give her release. When he eased two fingers into her core, it wasn't enough.

"No. I want you."

He retreated from her pussy to thumb her sensitive bud. "I don't have protection."

The needy ache became unbearable. "There's no one else but you." Reaching between her legs, she pressed his hard shaft against her crease as he surged back and forth.

He groaned. "Fuck, I want you."

Shaking with desire, she guided his crown to her entrance. "Don't stop."

Grayson eased his thick tip into her body, and they both moaned with relief.

"More," she gasped, desperate to feel his fullness inside her.

His hand slapped the wall beside hers as if trying to resist the temptation. "I won't be able to stop."

Panting, her body wound tight, she said, "I don't want you to stop."

He withdrew, then surged forward. "Ah, shit. So good."

With the empty ache satisfied, each powerful thrust drove her toward the edge. Ecstasy swarmed through every cell in her body.

Every sweet thrust made her gasp. "Faster."

To torment her, he slowed each blissful stroke. She whimpered each time his powerful hips drove his cock to the hilt.

Grayson groaned with pleasure. "Christ, you feel like silk."

Desire captured her heart, deepening the connection to

this man.

Gray plunged his erection, quickening the pace. "Shit!" he hissed. "I wanna feel you come."

His words shot a hot wave of pleasure to her core and sent her tumbling into a mind-blowing release. She couldn't hold back and cried out, gasping and shuddering, her inner muscles milking his shaft.

"Yes, sweetheart. Oh, fuck, yes."

Grayson growled and his forceful thrusts became frantic. He pinned his cock deep inside her body and warmth erupted in her channel. His throaty moans filled the confines of the shower stall and his massive body bucked.

After catching her breath, Holly straightened and eased her leg off the bench. The knee throbbed, but it was worth every uncomfortable pulse.

Grayson's thick arm instantly wrapped around her waist, and his chin rested on her wet hair. He cupped the water raining from the shower head in his palm and gently rinsed her sex.

She wasn't just falling in love with this man, she was addicted to him.

"Look at me, Holly." She turned in his muscled embrace. Grayson tilted his head and gently kissed her.

"What was that?" she asked, still lightheaded.

"I won't share you." He pressed his firm lips against hers again.

"Wait. What?" She blinked. "Share? With whom?"

He shook his head as if ridding himself of a thought. "I'm sorry."

"Sorry for what?"

"What I just did was irresponsible." Grayson's brilliant eyes centered on her. "I haven't been with anyone in months. I'm clean, but you're not on birth control, are you?"

She swallowed thickly, expecting anger or at least

irritation when she answered. "No. But I lost my head too. You're not the only one responsible."

Finally, the intensity in his eyes softened, and he fingered a wet strand of hair from her cheek. "I've never taken that chance before with anyone, but I'm willing to take a million with you."

"You don't want children, do you?"

He dropped his gaze. "If you would have asked me that before June, I'd have said never." He nodded as if talking to himself. "That isn't my answer anymore."

"You do realize that you're cavorting with the nerdy science girl, Mr. All-star Football Champion."

A flicker of concern creased his brow as his thumbs blazed a trail from her shoulder blades to her breasts. Grayson sat on the bench and pulled her between his muscular thighs. She loved their intimacy and how he didn't turn his back on her after sex, but instead, remained close.

"Would an archaeologist be a better fit?"

The grit in his voice disturbed her. Did Dirk's appearance cause all this?

"Of course not."

Grayson's tongue laved the tip of her nipple. He groaned deep in his throat and sucked the bud between his lips, causing darts of excitement to sweep through her belly.

"You're an intriguing woman," he said, raising his gaze to look in her eyes. "Made of innocence, sweetness, sensuality, and intelligence." He eased his middle finger into her pussy, his thumb slowly strumming her clit. "Every time we're together feels good. And I fucking love making you come."

As his long middle finger surged in and out of her wet channel in a delicious rhythm, her mouth parted, and the sensual rapture started all over again. Her nipples hardened with his possessive touch.

"Shit. The way you respond when I touch you is so

goddamn hot," he said.

She craved his confidence and the way he caressed her body. Holly's fingers dug into his shoulders.

"I love how you listen to me. How you look at me."

She inhaled deeply and closed her eyes. His mouth clasped one breast, nursing her nipple. Each delicious tug made her wetter.

Suddenly, he picked her up around the waist and carried her from the shower. They left the bathroom and turned the corner into a small bedroom where a brightly flowered quilt covered a queen bed.

He moved one of the pillows to the middle of the mattress and laid her down, then rolled her onto her stomach with her hips propped up by the overstuffed pillow.

When his fingers penetrated her wet core, the sensation was like nothing she'd experienced. Holly couldn't stop gasping and moaning. She clawed the sheets, climbing a spiral staircase to another orgasm. Then his mouth was on her sex, licking her sensitive nerves and darting his tongue in and out of her vagina.

As if he knew exactly when she was about to come, he paused long enough to let her catch her breath, then thrust his fingers in and out of her body with a tempo that made her float in waves of erotic bliss.

About to come again, he withdrew his fingers and smacked her ass.

She gasped with shock.

"Don't you ever walk alone in the dark again," he growled in a gravelly voice. "I'd lose my fucking mind if I lost you."

His punishment stung, but his reason made her heart swell.

"I'm sorry."

"I love you, Holly. Lord help me, I love you so hard."

He scooped his arm under her hips and lifted her ass,

then plunged his swollen shaft into her slick core with deep thrusts. She toppled into an earth-shattering orgasm, crying out his name.

His muscled arm squeezed the breath from her. "Oh God, babe. He groaned and hot cum jettisoned into her channel as Grayson's hips pressed against her ass.

When he loosened his grip, she collapsed and rolled onto her back, completely drained. Gray laid on his side with his head propped in one hand while the other caressed her moist crease with a flat palm, causing her to shudder with aftershocks.

She tilted her head toward her handsome lover and said, "My butt stings."

The lines around his blue eyes deepened with a subdued grin. "Good. Then you'll remember the warning."

"You're not into the BDSM stuff, are you?"

He arched a brow. "Been there, done a little of that, but no, I can't dominate you. Wouldn't want to. But when I warn you about something *that* important, don't ignore me."

She smiled. "I'm flattered you care about me."

Gray shifted his hand from her sex to the slim space of mattress between them. "That ship has sailed. I'm captivated and concerned."

"Concerned?" She rolled onto her side and leaned on one elbow. "About me or your feelings?"

Grayson threaded his fingers through her hair and brushed a swath of curls over her shoulder. "About you. Dirk is going to come after you."

"I could see you weren't comfortable with him. You obviously have history, but I didn't sense he was a threat. He seemed nice."

Grayson huffed out a deep breath. "He's a threat, but not the way you might assume."

"Do you want to share or is this a no-go topic?"

Grayson traced her bottom lip with his thumb. "I have

to talk about it and there's just no polite way of doing that."

"Okay," she said warily.

"Okay. But I want to make sure you understand that what happened in my past remains there. Nothing I did before has any bearing on what I want now. The only reason I'm going to tell you is because I know Dirk. He will make a play for you, and he's extremely good at it."

She gripped his fingers and smiled. "I think your assumption is completely wrong. What's happened between you and me goes against all the rules of attraction. Someone who looks like you isn't supposed to be lying in bed with someone like me. For some reason, you like me. But go on, I'm listening."

"Back in the teams, I never had a problem finding a willing woman to share my bed. Neither did Dirk. He made me look like a rookie, actually. He's a few years older than I am. When it comes to sex, he has no limitations. The guy's done it all. Women. Men. BDSM. Orgies. He thrives on variety, and I know when he's interested in a woman. As you mentioned, he is a nice guy. There's no issue there."

"So, he likes sex. Good for him."

Grayson leaned his head back, stretching his neck, then put his focus back on her. "Holly, he and I used to tag-team." When she shrugged, he said, "We used to find one woman and enjoy her together. We did that a lot."

"Oh," she said, understanding. "And did you and he..."

Grayson worried his bottom lip for a second, then said, "Did I let him suck me off—yeah, it happened. Did I let him fuck me while some blonde deep throated my cock— once. I was new to the teams. Experimenting. Flexing my freedom and high on hormones. Mostly, we'd please the woman at the same time or watch each other. What I'm trying to explain is, it was a phase for me. Enjoyable while it lasted, but I moved on. Dirk respected my decision, but I got the feeling he didn't want it to end."

"Do you think he loved you?"

Grayson sighed. "No, but we both used sex as a distraction. At times, it got pretty intense."

"He had nothing but praise when you were out on the field today."

"What did he say?"

"Something like, you were one heck of a warrior and broke as many heads as you did hearts."

Grayson sighed. "When it comes to coincidences, you and I have had more than our fair share. I can't believe you're connected to him through your work. This is an easy in for him."

Concerned just a little, she asked, "Do you think he'd use my work to coerce me into something I don't want to do?"

"No, nothing like that. But I know how good he is at convincing a woman into his bed. I'm only telling you my history so when you and he meet, and you will because of the tablet you're researching, that you've heard my side of the story first." Grayson leaned over and kissed her. "No matter what he tells you, no matter how he packages the offer—and he will offer—you're mine and I'm not sharing."

"I think you're wrong, but fair enough."

She certainly wouldn't share Grayson with another woman. But she did feel a titch guilty with the flash of heat she got imagining both attractive men in bed. She'd read plenty of M/M romances. They were hotter than hell. Even more so, envisioning Grayson's hard body torqued with pleasure and Dirk's mouth going down on his erect shaft.

"Now," he said, interrupting her thoughts. "Before one more minute passes, I want to hear you accept that what I said a few minutes ago is the truth."

She swallowed thickly, knowing exactly what he was talking about. "As in, you—"

"That I love you. I can stop saying it and wait for an acceptable amount of time to pass, but that's how I feel."

For how long, she wondered. "Eventually, you'll come

to your senses."

"I already had when I chased you down the highway. Up until that point, I'd tormented myself for no good reason. You're just gonna have to trust me because you're it, Holly."

"It's the mechanics. We're both logical people and we shouldn't ignore the obvious."

His mouth seamed with apparent disapproval. "We're also both problem solvers."

"Touché."

"Then let's tackle them one at a time," he suggested. "What's our biggest challenge?"

She shrugged. "You've got a stalker chick hovering in the background, and I'm pretty sure your friend, Wendy, wants me to get into a fatal car accident."

Grayson chuckled and cupped her hand. "Neither is an issue. And as much as Dirk just proved I do possess a jealous bone in my body, that isn't an issue, either."

Holly knew what her two biggest stumbling blocks were. "Time and trust."

"Okay, I understand where that comes from. Time, we have. Aside from border lineups, we live forty minutes apart. I'm gonna have a brother-in-law soon and he doesn't know it yet, but his free time just got shorter and mine got longer. As for trust, we're both going to travel that road together."

"Uh-huh. So, this is happening. I mean, you and me. We're an...item."

Grayson grinned and laid on his back, draping an arm over his forehead. "More than I ever could have hoped for or probably deserve."

"Whose room is this?"

"No ones. We keep it as a spare. Sometimes we need an extra ranch hand on a temporary basis. If they need a place, we let 'em stay here."

Holly gazed around the tidy but sparsely furnished bedroom with one pine dresser and an oval wall mirror.

"Shouldn't we get back to the celebration?" She checked her watch. "Ivy probably needs help."

Grayson slid one arm under her waist and rolled her on top of his firm body. "Shower first."

"For real this time."

"Mm, possibly," he said, but Holly felt something distinctly hard tease the entrance to her vagina.

"I think you're fibbing again." She planted a kiss on his lips.

Grayson's large hands palmed her ass. He lifted his hips and with slow thrusts, worked his semi-erect shaft inside her channel.

"I told you," he said in a low timbre. "I'm obsessed."

Keeping her legs straight, she palmed the mattress on either side of his shoulders and lifted her upper body. With the forward, backward gliding motion while pinned to his lower body, the pressure from his erotic thrusts massaged her clit, and she bit her bottom lip.

"My knee is never gonna heal."

"Then you'll just have to stay and I'll take care of you." He gripped her neck and drew her closer, probing her mouth with his moist tongue, rocking his stiffening cock into her core. "You have a very greedy pussy, Miss McNeela, and it makes me fucking hard."

Lightning coursed through her veins when he talked dirty to her. Kevin had never said things like that. Holly's nipples grazed over Gray's molded pecs as his shaft stroked all the right places.

"You wanted a Holly that no man had seen before."

Her retired SEAL rolled them so he was on top, then he kneeled, hooking his forearm under her right thigh, and raised her leg. He brushed the crown of his penis against her nub, taunting her lust.

"I'm keeping you, Holly. I love the way you taste when my tongue's on your clit and how beautiful you are when you ride me."

"Does it feel good?" she asked, her eyes traveling down his massive, hard torso covered in a sheen of sweat. Two bulging ligaments stretched from either side of his hips to his shaft. The light brown treasure trail connecting his navel to the root of his erection was so damn sexy.

"Too good."

His eyes reminded her of two shimmering gemstones. Gray poised his erection at the entrance of her channel.

"Babe, I can stop now if you want, or keep going. But if I do, I'm going to come inside you again." His brow creased and he exhaled a stuttered breath. "I'm not gonna lie and say I don't want the latter, because I do."

Holly bit her bottom lip when his crown penetrated her channel and a strong pulse of pleasure ripped through her belly. "I'm ready to be a mother, Grayson, if that happens."

She squeezed her inner muscles and his head rocked back, the sizzling hot image of a man gripped by desire burning itself into her memories.

"I'll be right there with you, Holly. Every step of the way."

Everything about Grayson Brooks turned her into a wanton woman. His hips gyrated in a delicious rhythm, their bodies in sync. She slid her arms upward, threading her fingers through her own hair, her hips rising to meet each blissful stroke. Each plunge was a catch and release of lust.

"You're so beautiful."

He wasn't just saying it to make her feel good. Holly saw the truth in his eyes. To him, she was beautiful.

"I'm different when I'm with you, Gray."

Holly tapped her bottom lip with her index finger and smiled. As if he could tell what she thought, he eased his erection from her body and leaned over to kiss her.

"I can't last with those beautiful lips on my cock, sweetheart."

They were in no hurry this time and she was ready for a

marathon of making love to the man who made her feel so desired.

She grinned and gripped his ass. "I'm an injured woman, you're going to have to slide a liiitle higher. Don't be shy," she teased.

Grayson's rugged features split into an earth-shattering smile. "You're wicked."

"Less talking, more shifting, Mr. Brooks."

"Tell ya what, babe." He pivoted into the sixty-nine position, then rolled his tongue across her clit.

His stiffening cock was too good to resist. "I want to do naughty things to you, Detective."

She teased the bulb of moisture from the tip of his head with her tongue, then sucked his thickness into her mouth.

His abs clenched. "Jesus, woman. That feels good."

But there was no more conversation, just the sweet sighs of pleasure.

CHAPTER TWENTY-FOUR

As the crowds thinned and the clock struck six p.m., Grayson kept his eye out for Lt. Billings. With no sign of the woman, he assumed she'd probably left. Ivy had dropped by the barbeque station before the football game and told him she'd found Holly and Billings toe to toe. She hadn't copped to all the words exchanged, but Ivy said Kate had tried to get into the house and told Holly to dump him.

On Monday, he'd get a read on the situation when he joined the DTF. Until then, he had a few precious hours left with Holly and wasn't going to waste time thinking about the crazy bitch.

After nearly a hundred guests enjoyed a buffet-style dinner, everyone pitched in to clean up. It had been a good day for the local farmers. A guy named William Humphrey, who owned a popular chain of steakhouses, had returned for dinner and sat next to Dad, enjoying a beer. Sounded to Grayson like the guy wanted to secure a contract with the farmstead to supply organic beef. If so, they'd have to expand the herd. The land they owned was at capacity for the number of cattle they currently ran, but they could lease, if necessary.

By nightfall, the stars shone in the clear night sky. Cole and some old friends manned the fireworks show. Grayson borrowed a blanket from the house for him and Holly to sit back and watch.

"Thank you. Best Fourth of July I've ever had," she said after he'd kissed her so many times, she had to be getting sick of him.

"Me, too." The first firework whistled into the night sky and exploded into a ball of red, glittering dots. "You must be tired. You worked your ass off today."

She smiled, her eyes following the next sparkling display. "Are you referring to our sexual marathon?"

He laughed. "I'm referring to work, not pleasure."

"It's a good kind of tired. I told Ivy I'd come back for a few hours tomorrow and help break things down."

"Maybe you should stay here tonight."

God, if he didn't put the brakes on soon, he'd be asking the woman to marry him next week. But that thought only proved to make his heart tick with excitement. He respected Holly's intelligence and level-headed characteristics. Most women were once, maybe twice, then done in the bedroom. He'd found a treasure because her sexual hunger matched his.

For a guy his size and a delicate woman her size that could be a problem, but every time they'd made love, her pussy was drenched with silky moisture. Watching her in the throes of passion made him fucking crazy.

Holly shifted onto her right hip. "Think staying here at this point would be a little too impertinent. Your family only met me today."

He grinned. "And they know that I slept with you last night and the night before. But you're right."

Holly's beautiful eyes settled on him. "I'm happy you chased me down the highway, Gray. For some reason, it feels like months ago versus only days."

He felt the same way. Instead of watching the fireworks, he gave her his full attention. "Scariest decision I ever made, but also the best."

"That's saying a lot from a man who served as a SEAL and now wears a badge." She grinned at the obvious paradox.

Aside from physical attraction, he found it easy to talk with her. Their conversations flowed effortlessly. "Before you, I had zero interest in relationships. My motivation was sex, nothing else."

Holly listened then said, "A real relationship carries benefits, but you also forfeit variety. If you thrive on diversity, eating the same salad every day gets boring."

She had a point. He never needed to know the women on a personal level before. Initially, most of them wanted a brief physical connection, but not all. Some of the gals had wanted more, like Erika, but he'd rejected her propositions like the rest.

Holly nudged him back into the conversation. "By coming home, you're not in the same environment as San Diego. You might find you miss it, and one day wake up and realize it suits you better and return. People change."

He appreciated her analysis but knew her failed marriage warned her to be careful. "You mean, like an addict."

"That's a harsh comparison. No, I mean some people don't need a deeper connection. Or they're looking for something in particular. I learned that lesson. Kevin was attentive at first, then slowly his job, his buddies, and other interests took precedence. Eventually, his eye wandered and he had his first affair."

First? "What do you mean his first affair?"

Her gaze quickly reverted to the fireworks. "He had three that I knew of."

"Three," Grayson repeated. "And you forgave him every time?"

She nodded. "Until he moved out. I'm not sure how long he was screwing his partner, Natalie. Months, probably. Before he left, I didn't see myself as pathetic or a doormat. I hope that's not how it sounds. Kevin apologized, and I had faith in our vows. But I learned my lesson. That'll never happen again."

He muted a grin. Warning noted. Like most experiences, good or bad, she'd become stronger. "You obviously liked him, but you didn't love him, Holly. That's why you let him get away with it, because on a deeper level, you didn't care."

"Are you saying if you love someone and they screw up, you should walk away for good?"

Hmm. He didn't want his words to come back and bite him in the ass, because he knew somewhere along the way he was going to piss her off.

"There's misdemeanors and unforgivable violations. What he did was unforgivable."

She eyed him. "Hindsight is twenty-twenty. After the first couple years of marriage, we slept in the same bed, but that was it. Well, at least I wasn't having sex." Holly shrugged. "That's when my little vice of reading romance began."

Grayson reached for her hand. He got the feeling that Holly didn't share her personal life with many people. "Did your family know?"

She glanced at him then smiled. "Not something I wanted to share. Once Kevin moved out, then I told them everything." She paused. "He came back, you know."

The way she said *came back* sent up a flare. "When?"

"Remember when I broke down in front of Roosters?"

"What?" That was only last month. Maybe her ex had come to his senses and realized what he'd lost.

"He showed up at my door. Natalie left him."

Grayson laughed. "Serves the fucker right."

"They broke up because he was charged. Driving while intoxicated. He had an accident and killed someone."

Grayson ignored the display, concerned by the empathy in her tone. "Everyone screws up, but he should have known better. Think I'm getting a pretty clear picture of his values and ethics. Why was he at your door?"

"When we divorced, our townhouse was paid off. I gave him half the equity in the divorce and applied for a mortgage. He invested the money in a new house for him and Natalie. She took him to court and won most of it. With all his legal fees, he said he didn't have any money and asked to stay during the hearing."

Holy shit. Erika was squatting at his place but for different circumstances. He felt a stab of guilt, but there was no way he would bring her up. He'd already spilled his guts about Dirk and surprisingly, Holly hadn't gotten in her car and left.

"Is he still at your place?"

"No. He's renting a suite about two hours from the city. The provincial hearing was the following Monday, and he couldn't afford a hotel. Kevin seemed shocked when I packed a bag and said I had somewhere else to go. He didn't want me to leave."

Grayson snorted. "He wanted more than that. You were smart to get out of there."

"It felt like Kevin's bad luck followed me when I broke down in front of Roosters. Then I saw Wendy come out of the bar and I assumed she was your wife."

"That's exactly why I clarified she wasn't."

Holly stared up at the sky. "I remember feeling so alone that day. I had to deal with Kevin, and my car broke down, then of course Dad's accident."

He threaded his fingers through her loose curls. "You weren't alone, sweetheart."

She smiled. "I know. You were there, even though I was sure you had someone in your life. But I could have sworn you wanted to kiss me in the gardens at the resort."

"Your instincts are bang on. I did." He laughed, remembering that moment. "Was Kevin there when you got home?"

"He was. Said he'd waited for me."

Gray sat up and rested an arm over one bent knee. Did he really want to hear this part? Stalling, he asked, "Was he found guilty?"

She nodded. "Sentencing isn't until next week."

"When?"

Holly gave him a humorous look. "You're using that

scary Navy SEAL tone again."

He rolled his eyes. "If he's staying at your place, I'll be there. Your ex can look me in the eyes, and I'll square him off."

Holly laughed and leaned over, kissing him on the cheek. "Kevin still has to face the internal investigation with the RCMP. He'll probably lose his job."

"I know if I ask what he said to you when you got home, it will only piss me off, won't it?"

"Depends."

"Sonofabitch wants you to forgive him and move back in, doesn't he?"

"He hinted at the possibility."

"What an *asshole*. You're not a pushover, but he thinks you are. He's either stupid or has balls the size of Texas. Did you tell him to leave and never come back?"

"No," she said quietly. "Well, I told him he couldn't move in, but he could stay for his sentencing date."

Grayson knew he was being a hypocrite. Now was the time to clean the slate and mention Erika, but it was different. Wasn't as if he'd ever see her again.

"When I talk with my sisters back home, they think I should move back east."

"What? To Nova Scotia?" That was on the other side of the damn country. His instincts told him to jump on that grenade. Instead, he pulled back the reins on controlling her decisions, which was his normal way of dealing with something he disagreed with. "Are you considering that?"

"It's an option."

If he wasn't sure about his feelings for Holly before, he had zero doubt now. It felt like a mirror shattering inside his chest. He certainly understood the yearning to be with family.

Tomorrow she'd leave, sucked back into her routine of work and coming home to an empty house. His job and responsibilities at the farm ate up his days, but not all of them. Not to mention Dirk would eventually pounce.

"Holly, we don't have to curtail seeing each other only to the weekends."

She shrugged. "Crossing that border will get old pretty quickly. And I usually work until eight p.m. at the university."

Man, he hated when she pointed out all the responsibilities that cuffed them both. "Yeah, and I usually work till sundown around here, but not on the weekends. Not anymore."

The fireworks continued to light the sky with multi-colored patterns, which pleased their guests. Children clapped and oohed at the display while the faint smell of sulphur lingered in the air. Watching the show with Holly lying next to him reminded Gray that he'd turned a new page in his life. One he hadn't expected. Like none before. He felt calmer. Whole.

Holly sat up and curled her arms around her knees. "You said you had a plan for next weekend—if that comes to pass. As of Monday, you're back on the drug task force. I know their hours are all over the map, so I won't pack until Thursday."

Unfortunately, she was right, but he'd been transferred to work on the Clayton file, not get caught up with a desk full of open cases. "First things first. What day is asshole showing up?"

"Grayson, name calling is beneath you."

"No, it isn't, actually. What day is your ex showing up?"

"Wednesday. Why?"

"I'll bring an overnight bag and be there by five. Make dinner reservations for six. I'm taking you out. I'll eat anything except MREs."

Holly barked with laughter. "I don't think many restaurants serve Meals Ready to Eat, military style."

Of course, she knew the terminology and got the joke. He leaned over. "But I do love eating you, and love it even more now that you're not afraid to vocalize your pleasure, so maybe we should stay at your place. Townhouses have thin walls, right? Your ex will certainly get the picture."

She shook her head in mock exasperation. "Det. Brooks, if I'm not mistaken, I smell a little jealousy."

"No, you smell a lot of jealousy. Holly, other than being an idiot and not chasing your ass the moment I saw you, I'm a pretty direct guy."

"Think I've figured that out."

"Good. Because come Wednesday, *Asshole,* is gonna be real clear on what's happening between us."

"I appreciate the chivalry, but I can handle Kevin. So you keep your butt south of the border on Wednesday."

"Yeah, sure. No problem." *Like hell he would.*

"So what's your plan for next weekend?"

"What?" he teased, and focused his attention back on the exploding fireworks their guests cheered at when another volley filled the sky.

She tackled him and he lay back on the blanket, holding his mystery woman in his arms. As each hour passed, she'd become less of a mystery and more a part of his life. The best part.

"Tell me," she pressed, then kissed the end of his nose.

"Shouldn't you two get a room," his best friend said.

Holly quickly sat up and grinned while he tucked his arms behind his head and stared up at his sister, Cole, and Jackson. The kid's head was turned, watching the show.

"Abandoning your post?" Gray asked.

"They got it all in hand. Thought we'd join you, but not if we're interrupting."

"Grab some blanket," Grayson said. "Where's Dad?"

"Right here, son. Just waiting for you two to stop necking." A foldable camp chair popped open to Gray's left and his old man sat down.

Ivy cracked up. "Yeah, we were kinda waiting too."

Jackson scrambled onto his grandfather's lap and laid

back against the old man's chest.

Grayson's gaze drifted higher than the bloom of colorful explosions in the sky. The scent of dewy grass and Mother Earth filled his nose. Holly's head rested on his shoulder. He had a thousand reasons to thank God, but tonight was about family and friends. He wouldn't trade his for anything. At least, that's what he thought last week before he'd kissed Holly.

* * * *

Sunday afternoon came far too quickly for Grayson's liking. Last night, he'd driven Holly back to the resort in his truck. She probably thought he was being a gentleman, but he had concerns about leaving her vehicle unattended in the resort lot until he figured out Lt. Billings' angle.

The next morning they'd slept in, made love and ate at the resort, then returned to the farm. With all hands on deck, the equipment was stored in the shed by four o'clock, ready for the next festival in August.

Holly said her goodbyes to the family, and he escorted her outside.

"Guess it's back to sloppy romance books," she said with a teasing tone and opened the driver's door.

He wanted her to leave smiling. Hopeful. "You're going to text me when you get home, right?"

Grayson closed the door before she got in, an unconscious action to keep her even a few seconds longer. Her impending departure was making him nuts. He was a control freak like many first responders and special operators. Restraining the urge wasn't easy.

"I will," she promised, her grey gaze centered on his chest.

Damn, he wanted to wrap his arms around her but if he did, he wouldn't let go. So instead, he palmed the car on either side of her shoulders.

"You know, the first time I deployed with my platoon, although I'd trained through the teeth and passed BUD/S and my Quals, I had doubts. Scared shitless."

"That you'd die?"

"No. That I'd let the team down. Do something stupid to put them in jeopardy. But I didn't let them see my fear. Every mission that followed, I gained confidence. I learned that I could rely on them, and they could rely on me."

A hint of a smile slipped across her pretty lips. "Are you trying to tell me that I can trust you?"

"I'm saying every hour without you will be torture, but I'm looking forward to Friday."

Her beautiful eyes welled with tears. "Told you I was going to cry."

Grayson palmed her soft cheeks and kissed his lover's lips with promise, but it wasn't enough. He eased his tongue into her mouth, tasting her and pinning his chest against her breasts. If he couldn't keep Holly with him, he wanted to make damn sure she knew how much he cared about her.

Stepping back, he reached into his pants pocket. "I have something for you that I think you'll understand. Of course, it's not quite as valid now, but the meaning still stands."

Grayson held up his clenched hand, pinched a couple links, and let gravity unravel the chain.

Holly gasped and her beautiful eyes rounded. "That's... that's your SEAL Trident."

Yeah, she understood.

He separated the chain and hung it around her delicate neck. "That's the one Cmdr. Austen pinned on my chest the day I graduated."

Holly passed her fingers over the Budweiser as if in reverie. "I know how hard you worked for this and the depth of its meaning."

"Then you probably understand why I want you to

wear it."

Holly's eyes glistened with tears. "I don't know what to say."

The Trident represented one of his greatest achievements. Commitment. Faith. Sacrifice. Each woman who captured a SEAL's heart was unique in her own way.

"I never thought I'd meet a woman like you. I'm excited to see what happens next. When we're apart, you'll have something of mine that rests next to your heart."

Holly stood on her toes and brushed the softest kiss against his mouth. "You were right, you know. I didn't really know what love felt like until I met you."

* * * *

A few minutes later, Grayson watched the Audi disappear around the curve in the driveway. His father walked up and crossed his arms, looking down the drive.

"I remember the first time I said goodbye to your mother. Wasn't easy. I knew I was head over heels in love with her. I had plenty of pretty girls to pick from, but there was just something about Kira I couldn't shake."

Grayson cleared his throat. "You met Mom at a rodeo, didn't you?"

"Yep. Trying my hand at saddle bronc riding. She'd come with a group of girlfriends. I was twenty-five and full of myself. Your mom caught my eye, and I couldn't look away."

"How'd you convince her to cross the border for good?"

His old man adjusted his worn leather cowboy hat. "Not the same way you'll convince Holly."

Grayson chuckled. "Written all over me, isn't it?"

Dad patted him on the shoulder. "Like a painted Easter egg, son. But if you survived the SEALs and five years as a detective, you've got the chops to prove to that little lady you're worth taking a chance on. She's smart, just like your mom."

"That's the problem," he muttered. "She has a career. One she loves. When you put a ring on Mom's finger, she didn't have to give up anything."

The cowboy hat tipped in agreement. "True, so you're dancing to a longer waltz. Eventually the song ends. Look at your sister and Cole. Didn't take me a minute to see your best friend loved Ivy but for some reason, he walked the long road."

A crow landed on the lawn a few feet away, ruffled his sleek feathers, then pecked at an unsuspecting bug.

"I should probably put on the brakes, but meeting Holly was like someone shining high beams in my face. It was strange." He balled his fist and tapped his abs. "I felt this odd sensation. If I hadn't been in uniform and on the job, I get the feeling she would have told me to get lost. And that would have been a first for me. I hid behind my badge. Kept things professional. Then we talked. Only a few words, but I couldn't forget her. Against a lot of odds, our paths kept crossing."

Dad's eyes creased at the edges. "Since ya didn't bring anyone with ya from San Diego, I'm guessing this is the first time Cupid shot an arrow in your ass."

"That's what worries me. What if what I'm feeling for Holly is because she's not American? What if I ask her to change her life for me and suddenly the challenge is gone and so are my feelings? I mean, this is the first time I've—"

Dad's long mustache curled upwards at the tips, the smile evident.

"What?" Grayson asked, seeing humor in his old man's eyes.

"Sounds like you're coming up with excuses on her behalf," he drawled. "You're putting Holly's welfare before your own. Even though I was part of the sixties, I'd drive a feminist crazy by saying a real man protects the woman he loves. But that's how I see it." Dad slid his palm across the stubble on his weathered cheek. "You're thirty-four, and I know people nowadays wait before starting a family, but son, time is tickin'. If your mother was still here, she'd say, '*Grayson Clint Brooks, don't be stupid. That woman is the mother of my grandbabies.*'"

Gray laughed at his father's impersonation. "Yeah, she probably would." Mom had a sharp tongue but even when they got bawled out, she did it with love. "You miss her, Dad?"

"Every day." His gaze swung toward the house. "I begged for more time, but God didn't agree." He sniffed and ran a finger under his nose. "Don't you waste that lovely woman's time. Tell her what's in your heart. Show her. Put a ring on her finger and remind her every day how much you cherish the ground she walks on because you just never know what's 'round the next bend in the road."

Ivy pushed open the screen door. "Dinner's ready."

Their father raised a hand to let her know he'd heard. "Cole's hanging onto his place but rentin' it out. He's moving here to the farm."

That was news to Grayson. "I didn't know that."

"I think before long, we're gonna have another little one running around."

Grayson didn't share his and Holly's afternoon adventure with the old man, but the way he'd come inside her—three times—they might have Ivy and Cole beat by a long shot. He'd told Holly he was ready to share the responsibility if she got pregnant, but it went far deeper than that.

Guilt nibbled at his belly. He would have stopped if Holly had asked, no question. But he also knew that he'd touched and teased her to the breaking point on purpose. He'd heard the term *insane with lust* before, but he'd never reached that point until yesterday. He needed to come inside her more than he needed air. The craving struck him on a primitive, undeniable level.

As far as Cole moving in and another baby, possibly two, there weren't any more empty bedrooms. "Um, are you kicking me out?"

As they walked toward the front stairs, Dad removed his hat. "Not yet. Ivy said you got your place up for sale in San Diego."

"Yeah, I do."

"Your mother always thought that natural clearing next to the creek would be a great place to build a house. It's within eyesight of the main house, but still private. Wouldn't take much to subdivide ten acres and put it into a separate title."

Grayson stopped with one foot on the first step. "Are you serious, Dad?"

"Yeah, well, you know women. They like to have a say in how many bedrooms there should be and what color to paint the house."

He couldn't believe it. "I don't know what to say, except Holly and I have literally known each other for, well, technically days. By next month, she might realize I'm an overbearing asshole and tell me to take a hike."

Dad climbed the stairs and looked down at him from the veranda. He chuckled with that lazy, low timbre they were all used to.

"Son, I'm willing to bet the farm that by the end of summer, she'll be wearing your ring. The one thing a farmer knows is the cycle of life. Holly's just one question away from taking a chance on you. All depends on when you're ready to stop shoveling cow shit. If a bull can figure out when it's time to mate, you sure as hell can too."

Grayson laughed all the way up the stairs. "Thanks for the clarity, Dad."

"Don't mention it. You can pay me in pork rinds and a bottle of whiskey."

"Forget it, old man," he said, opening the screen door and letting his father lead the way into the house.

CHAPTER TWENTY-FIVE

Let the games begin, Grayson thought, arriving a few minutes before seven a.m. The Drug Task Force office was located at the same location as the Proactive Unit. He entered the DTF office to see a room full of cubicles. A mix of male and female detectives worked their cases. No matter what county you joined, the DTF achieved their mandates of cleaning the streets through covert surveillance, undercover drug buys, and in-depth investigations based on intelligence gained from the community.

The environment felt familiar, but he wasn't looking forward to eating, sleeping, and breathing life through this department's straw again. Working vice squad appealed to his personality, but not his priorities because they'd changed. Holly and the farmstead sat above his professional career.

A guy in his forties wearing civvies and a lanyard with ID around his neck glanced up from the closest desk. "Can I help you?"

"Morning, I'm Grayson Brooks. Looking for Lt. Billings."

"You have a meeting with her this morning?"

"Reporting for duty. I've been transferred here from the Proactive Unit."

The agent rose and strode toward Gray. "I didn't realize we were bringing on new blood. I'm Sgt. Bill Thompson."

He shook the man's hand. "Yeah, came as a surprise to me as well. I only met the lieutenant Friday during an inter-agency meeting. By five p.m., I was transferred."

Bill's brow flexed. "You have previous experience?"

As a SEAL, he'd worked both in Little Creek and San Diego. Whenever he joined a new team, the best approach was to downplay his past. Get the lay of the land and read the team members first before settling in.

"A bit," he answered. "According to Billings, I was underutilized at the PU, and you're understaffed."

Bill flexed his shoulders as if loosening kinked muscles. "Not that I'm aware of. We're fully staffed. But welcome."

"Thanks. Where's her office?"

He pointed to the left. "Round the corner, but she's not in today. Capt. Baker came in earlier. Saw him go into her office."

Grayson stuck to the wall and passed a few empty desks. He found the lieutenant's office with the door closed.

After giving the glass a light tap, he heard, "Come in."

Behind the desk sat a gentleman in his fifties wearing a dark blue suit.

"Captain, I'm Grayson Brooks."

The guy with dark hair and a ruddy complexion pointed at the guest chair. "Have a seat, Brooks."

"I was expecting Lt. Billings. Said she was going to give me a debrief this morning."

Baker flattened his beige silk tie and sat forward. "She's taking a sick day. I came in because there's been a change in plans. I've already called Lt. Kline to explain the mix-up."

What the hell? "Mix-up, sir?"

"You're not transferring to the DTF," he said with a gruff, matter-of-fact tone.

"I see. Any particular reason why?" Had Billings retracted her bogus reasons for fronting his transfer?

"We're always under budget restraints around here. The DTF is fully staffed. Lt. Billings thought you'd be an asset to solve the Clayton case. With your experience, I was willing to float a position to have you on the team. You have an impressive record."

Grayson hadn't heard the *but* yet. No matter the reason, the cancellation of his transfer was good news. "Thank you. Anything to do with the lieutenant feeling that I wasn't a good fit?"

The captain's brows shot up with surprise. "Actually, yes.

She said you have other commitments and felt you wouldn't be able to give this department the obligation it needed."

Wouldn't be able to service Billings was more like it.

"She's correct. I left San Diego vice to help my family in Bellingham. DTF work is round the clock." To cover his ass, he said, "My partner and I met Lt. Billings on Friday during a meeting on the Clayton case. After the session, Lt. Billings asked me out for a drink, which I refused. By five o'clock, she called and said I'd been transferred to this office and wanted me down on Fifth Street."

Slowly but surely, the captain's brow creased with concern. "Where the four men were murdered?"

"Yes. That's homicide's AOR. No reason for me to be there. No drugs at the scene. I asked her three times why she needed me to attend. Her response was to ask me out for dinner and drinks again. I made it very clear that I'm committed to cleaning the streets and bringing down the ring that's responsible for the thefts and assaults but not a personal relationship with her."

Baker's mouth assumed a definite scowl. "Are you intimating that Kate asked for your transfer for reasons other than work?"

Gray dug his hand into his front pants pocket and placed the GPS device on the desk. "I'll let you decide the answer to that, but by nine p.m. she'd rolled into the Neon Lights resort where I was visiting my girlfriend and hid this under the wheel well of my pickup." He paused for effect, then asked, "Is it normal practice in the DTF to track a fellow law enforcement officer without their knowledge?"

The captain's eyes glared at the GPS device, then bounced to Grayson's face.

When Baker didn't answer, Grayson said, "I'll keep the video I took of her hiding it on my vehicle for safekeeping. As well as the recordings of her asking me out. Unless, of course, you want a copy. She also showed up at my family's farmstead on Sunday. We have a July Fourth celebration for the community. She was caught trying to enter the family home and was denied access. Lt. Billings confronted my girlfriend, misrepresented herself and said she didn't know who I was, then asked for my whereabouts. Later, she tried to intimidate the woman I love into leaving me."

Captain Baker's mouth seamed into a flat line.

"If you have further concerns, and you probably should, contact Capt. Gordon in San Diego. Lt. Billings worked vice there before relocating to the Pacific Northwest. He'll advise you on the lengths Kate took to infiltrate his marriage, which ended in divorce. Lt. Billings befriended Gordon's wife without him knowing, then took video of the sexual activity between Gordon and herself and sent it to his wife."

Baker leaned forward and picked up the GPS device used by law enforcement. "That's a lot of investigative work between Friday evening and this morning."

This would all be swept under the carpet, but the seed was planted. At least Baker had a clear picture of Kate's motivations and who he had in charge of the DTF.

"If my transfer is canceled, I need to catch up with my partner at the PU."

The senior officer palmed the desk and rose to his feet. He gnawed on his lower lip for a few seconds, then looked Grayson in the eyes. "Det. Brooks, if you ever want a change of scenery from the PU, feel free to contact me."

"Thank you, sir."

Grayson left Baker to stew over the information and dispose of the GPS device as he saw fit. A few minutes later, he walked into the PU's office. He tapped Cole on the shoulder as he passed his desk.

"What the hell are you doing back here?" he asked, following him.

Gray opened his laptop and signed in. "Home, sweet home, partner."

* * * *

Two hours later, Kline called from his doorway. "Brooks, Sterling, in my office."

Cole lifted his hand, indicating he'd heard their boss.

Gray grinned at his partner. "What do you say to throwing back a cool one after work?"

"Are we celebrating?" Cole asked, sitting on the edge of Grayson's desk.

Gray checked his phone and saw a text from Holly. "Yup, we sure are." He hadn't told his buddy about Billings' conduct, although Ivy probably had. "I'll give ya the dirty details at Roosters. Lead the way."

He followed Cole toward the lieutenant's office while reading Holly's text.

Morning, handsome.

He quickly replied.

Missed waking up next to my sweetheart. I have good news. Call u later.

Grayson's commitment to Holly brought an overwhelming sense of contentment. He never imagined he could feel this good.

"Have a seat, gentlemen. There's been some developments on the Clayton case," Kline said closing the door to his office.

"We getting closer to a green light for a bust?" Cole asked as their lieutenant sat behind his desk.

Lt. Kline shifted his gaze to Grayson. "Yes, very close. I spoke with Capt. Baker a few minutes ago. The men murdered at Purple Orchid were identified as part of Rory Hannigen's group. Rob Downing is one of the victims."

Gray thought he'd recognized Downing when he'd attended the scene. "The young guy from Hermes Coffee mentioned Downing as part of the theft ring."

Kline shoved a few sheets of paper across the desk. "The Hermes kid's name is Dean Jeffries. Unfortunately, his brother was one of the victims."

"Hmm," Gray shook his head. "They definitely pissed somebody off."

Cole handed him the rap sheets and he scanned them. The victims had all looked young to Gray when he'd seen them propped up against the bathroom wall with a bullet in each head. He'd been right. Looking at their records, mostly B&E's and theft, they ranged between the ages of eighteen and twenty-three.

"Highly doubt they all took a leak at the same time," Cole stated. "You think this is a result of us charging Rory Hannigen?"

Kline rocked back in his office chair. "Possibly. If that's the case, they'll be looking to change the stash house locations. It might mean we'll have to start hunting all over again."

Grayson dumped the rap sheets onto the desk. "In my experience, this is likely an internal issue or a rival gang."

Kline listened, then said, "There's not enough time for vice to infiltrate the ring with an undercover agent. DTF wants to nail them with a shipment at the warehouse. We'll see how it plays out. In the meantime, I want you to do some surveillance on the other stash houses and Purple Orchid. We know there's five houses, but likely more."

Cole shot a glance at Grayson. "Looks like night shifts are back on the table."

Gray shrugged. "Nature of the beast, but the weekend is off limits. Holly and I have plans."

The lieutenant chuckled. "You spending the weekend in Canada? Cheaper to take her out to dinner," he joked, referring to the currency difference in the dollar.

Kline had dropped by the July Fourth celebration with his wife and three kids. He'd already met Holly, but that afternoon Gray introduced her as his girlfriend.

"Nope. I booked a room at a historic inn on Orcas Island. We've got a full schedule: walks on the beach at sunset, visit the brewery, nose around the farmer's market and the town of Eastsound. I'm going to wine her, dine her, and make her come as many times as humanly possible before Sunday when she crosses that fucking border."

Both Cole and Kline laughed.

"My wife and I used to do things like that before the kids came along," the lieutenant said. "Now we camp with a thirty-foot pull trailer and two dogs. Enjoy it while you can."

Grayson grinned. "Plan to."

"Just out of curiosity, when exactly did your interest in a victim of this case turn into something more?"

Gray cleared his throat. "Officially or unofficially?"

Kline grinned. "I'm not busting your balls, Brooks."

"Unofficially, the second I saw her back in May."

"I knew it!" Cole spouted.

Grayson slid his partner a *shut the hell up* look. "Officially, a week ago."

"Well, she's a nice woman. Wish you the best of luck." The lieutenant eyed Cole. "I'd like a word with Brooks in private."

"Sure, Lieutenant." Cole exited the office and closed the door behind him.

Lt. Kline waited for Cole to leave before he forked his fingers on the desk and put his attention on Grayson.

"Capt. Baker told me that Billings won't be leading the DTF on the Clayton case. Apparently, as of this morning, she's on leave. Guy by the name of Bill Thompson is taking her place as acting lieutenant."

"Met him this morning. Seems like a decent guy."

Kline crooked his jaw and raised an eyebrow. "Not sure if I want or need to know how you ended up on the DTF for a sum total of thirty minutes before you were reassigned back to the PU."

Grayson cleared his throat and fixed an extremely benign expression on his mug. "Apparently, I wasn't a good fit."

"Uh-huh. Ten years in the SEALs and five in San Diego Vice, but you're not a good fit."

"Evidently."

"Right, well—Captain said you have some video and

audio recordings in your possession, and he's decided he wants a copy."

Gray had to wonder whether Kate's speedy escalation to the position of lieutenant had anything to do with Capt. Baker. The rise from detective to lieutenant in six years wasn't the norm. Maybe Baker had fallen prey to Kate's tactics like Capt. Gordon had, but this time she'd used her leverage to scale up her pay grade. With the information Grayson held, Baker could even the score indirectly.

"I'll send him what I have."

Kline didn't appear overly concerned. Curious at best. "Do I need to know more?"

"No, sir."

"All right then, we'll leave it at that. Good to have you back."

* * * *

Holly set her cell aside after sending Grayson a text. The glow of the weekend spent with him at the farmstead had kept her in good spirits. About to head to the lab to view the tablets from Cairo that arrived late Friday afternoon, a knock landed on her open office door.

"Hello." Grayson's old teammate grinned at her.

"Mr. Larkin. Hi. Come in." She'd expected him to contact the university before dropping by.

He chuckled. "Think I'd be more comfortable if you called me Dirk."

"Of course."

"I had some time to spare. Do you have a minute to discuss the tablets from Jerusalem?" he asked, sitting in the guest chair.

It was a little difficult for Holly to ignore the image of this man and Grayson having sex. Both retired SEALs were extremely attractive and with her overactive imagination and Gray's descriptive explanation of their past, her natural curiosity was piqued. Regardless, she hoped Dirk wouldn't step over professional boundaries with her.

"When it comes to ancient texts like the tablets you discovered, I have an open schedule. Why don't you follow me to the lab and we can talk there."

"I was hoping you'd say that. Lead the way."

Like Grayson, he had rugged, weathered features. There wasn't anything polished or pretty about him. His dark hair enhanced his fascinating green eyes. Dirk's strong masculine jaw and air of confidence created an electrically charged aura. All that sensual energy directed at a woman would be difficult to resist.

As they walked the carpeted hallway on their way to the lab, he said, "What's your gut telling you?"

She glanced at him. "I have a different theory than the summary reports I've read."

"I like the sound of that."

They reached the entry to the new transition lab in the museum building. There were numerous labs for different studies. Students, faculty, and visiting researchers were all welcome to use the facilities.

"The tablets you unearthed don't originate in Jerusalem."

"Interesting," he said. "I came to the same conclusion but so far, you're the only ancient text researcher who's made that claim."

Holly used her ID pass to unlock the door and Dirk pushed it open. The lab was temperature controlled, extremely clean, and segregated into research bays. She donned a pair of gloves and recovered the tablets from the repository of artifacts and placed them on an empty examination table, then turned on the overhead camera linked to a nearby computer that magnified the stone slabs.

"These symbols," she said, pointing at the third row of lines and shapes on the screen, "At first, I thought it was a dialect of Tamil we haven't seen before, but then I remembered an excavation from thirty years ago." With a few keystrokes, she split the screen and brought up another artifact found in India. "These symbols here." She pointed to five, which were identical.

"They're the same," Dirk murmured.

"Deciphering the origin of the tablets is one mystery, linking them to a known root language gives me a clue as to whether it's plausible to validate the connection. If I'm correct, what you found is about four thousand miles away from where they should have been located."

Dirk's interested gaze swung from the monitor to her. "And that leads to even more questions."

She nodded. "Exactly. Deciphering this marvelous find isn't just about the text, it's about the tooling, the tablets' structure and if the origin of the stone has been cataloged before. While my job is to research the script, identifying other components helps me narrow the search."

His head tilted a little and his gaze swept across her face. "How did Gray end up with a woman like you?"

The question blindsided her and she chuckled. "I'm not sure what you mean."

"I mean a woman of your caliber. That's not the Grayson I remember."

Holly put her attention back on the monitor. Archaic languages, she understood. Falling for Grayson so quickly was something she couldn't explain.

"If you're confused why a man handsome as Grayson is attracted to a Plain Jane scientist like myself, I'm not sure how to answer that."

Dirk loosely crossed his arms. "The Grayson I knew wasn't concerned with a woman's intellectual assets. How long have you two been together?"

"Not long." She'd met Grayson in May, but telling Dirk they'd officially been a couple for one week sounded lame. "Tell me more about where you found the tablets."

Dirk explained in vivid detail about the dig site. By the way he spoke, she could hear his dedication and enthusiasm were genuine. Dirk asked about her education and experience and shared his own path to working with his father in the field of archaeology, which led to her divulging her dream of being part of an actual dig one day.

Before she knew it, three hours had passed and there was no end to their conversation or mutual appreciation on the topic of anthropology.

Dirk turned his wrist and checked his watch. "Damn, look at the time." He offered her a captivating smile. "You know what, I'm changing my plans. Where's a good place to have lunch around here?"

"Sage restaurant has fantastic food and ocean views. I think you'd like it."

"Great," he said. "Then let's go."

"I'm sorry, what? With me?"

"Yes, with you." His brow curled as if her surprise didn't make sense to him. "We got sidetracked. I want to hear more about our tablets."

Holly did have a few theories, but she didn't have time. "I'd like that too, but I have a faculty meeting in twenty minutes."

Dirk dug his cell from the back of his jeans pocket. "Then let's exchange numbers and you call me when you're done for the day. Dinner's on me."

Charismatic and innocuous, Holly didn't see any reason why they couldn't have a working dinner. "Sure."

They parted company and Holly headed back to her office. She'd just settled behind her desk when Grayson called.

"Hey, sweetheart, how's your day going?"

She so loved the sound of his voice. Somehow, he managed to wrap her in an invisible, soft blanket of contentment.

"I had a visitor."

A long pause ensued where she heard muted birdsong and road traffic in the background.

"Sonofabitch," he growled. "Sure didn't take him long, but I didn't expect it would."

She snorted. "I didn't say who it was."

"Okay, fine. Tell me it wasn't Dirk."

Holly laughed at him. "Yes, it was Dirk. He just left."

"Yeah, and when's he coming back to pick you up for dinner?"

How the heck? "Um, when I'm done for the day," she answered honestly.

"Holly." His timbre dropped to sub-zero. "You're not going."

How could she be angry? Grayson's streak of possessiveness was flattering. If she were in his boots, she'd be pissed too.

Using a calm, lighthearted tone, she said, "Yes, I believe I am."

"Nooo, you're not."

"Grayson. This is about the tablets he and his father found outside of Jerusalem. He's interested in my research, nothing more."

"I swore to myself I wasn't going to be a domineering prick. I trust you, sweetheart, but I don't trust him."

"Good, then we can move on from this topic. You said you had good news. What is it?" Her intern appeared in the doorway. "I'll be finished in a minute, Juliette."

"Okay, I'll wait out here."

"Sounds like you have to go," Grayson said, his tone terse.

"Faculty meeting. So what's the news?"

"Billings is off the Clayton case. She's been replaced at the DTF. Apparently, she's on leave."

"That is good news. Then again, maybe she's taking leave to stalk you full time," Holly teased. After their standoff at the celebration, Kate didn't strike her as a woman who'd back down.

"I'm back at the Proactive Unit. DTF is fully staffed. I spoke with the captain of vice this morning. Gave him the tracking device and sent him the video and audio recordings of Kate. I have a feeling he strongly suggested she take the leave."

It didn't surprise Holly that Grayson had covered his ass. "You're not only hot, but extremely intelligent." He hummed and the sound vibrated straight to her core because he made the same sound when his shoulders were pinned between her thighs and his tongue teased her lady bits.

"Graaayson," she warned. "I'm at work."

He chuckled. "So am I, but it's getting mighty uncomfortable behind my zipper. Call me tonight after your date."

"It's not a date!"

"Sorry, work-related dinner. By the way, what's Dirk's number?"

"Why?" She knew why but asked anyway.

"Because we need to catch up."

"No, you want to warn him to keep it in his pants. It's sweet that you're jealous, but I'm telling you, it's all above board."

"Sweetheart, I'm sure it is," he said amiably. "Now give me that prick's damn number!"

She couldn't help but laugh. "Don't be mean to him." She gave him Dirk's number. "I'll call you later tonight, if you want."

"Yes, I want. Preferably when you're in bed."

"Are we going to have phone sex?" she asked innocently and grinned.

"Ever done that before, babe?"

"Nope. Never. Guess you'll have to give me private lessons."

"Holly, my old man reminded me yesterday that ya never know what will happen tomorrow, that's why I need to tell you that I love you today."

Her heart melted a little more around the edges. Before long, there'd be nothing but a bubbling puddle of goo. "Gray, I feel like I need to pinch myself when you say things like that."

"You don't believe me, do you?"

Sadly, she had reservations. "I'm not sure. When it comes to *my* feelings, I'm trying to be sensible, but you make that very hard to do." Juliette leaned in the doorway and tapped her wristwatch. "I'm going to be late. I'll call you later for my first lesson."

Grayson chuckled. "Looking forward to it, sweetheart."

* * * *

Sitting behind the wheel of his Ford in the PU's parking lot, Grayson disconnected the call. His finger rolled through the contact list until it highlighted Dirk's number. If he called the guy, he'd have a hard time not laying down a warning. Holly's specialty in ancient languages and Dirk's archaeological artifact put them on a collision course. Was this coincidence or karma?

After a few seconds of deliberation, he dialed Dirk's number.

"Hello."

"Chief, it's Grayson Brooks."

He heard the low hum of conversation in the background. Maybe a restaurant.

"Gray. Hey, man, how ya doin'?"

"Doing fine, Dirk. We didn't get a chance to talk at the celebration, thought I'd give you a call. Did you drop by to say hello or was there a particular reason?"

Once Dirk had left the teams, which was about two years before he retired, Gray never heard from the guy.

"Give me a second." The background noise dulled, then the sound of vehicle traffic increased as if he'd stepped outside. "Glad you called. I just spent the morning with Holly. Amazing woman. Her hypothesis about the tablets we discovered is impressive."

If he spent the morning talking with her, why did he need

to have dinner with Holly? "Yes, she is. Holly loves her work. Quite the coincidence how all our paths crossed."

"Life's full of 'em, Gray. So, when are we all going to get together?"

Gray's gut tightened, his instincts kicking into high alert. "When you say '*get together*', hope you're referring to having a few drinks."

After a lengthy pause, he asked, "Did you divulge our past with her?"

"Did I tell her we used to fuck the same women? Yeah, I did. When you showed up at the farmstead, I didn't have much of a choice, especially since you both have a connection through archaeology."

"Wanted her to hear it from you first, huh?" Dirk chuckled. "Those were good times."

Was he fishing, Gray wondered? "Yeah, while they lasted."

"I asked Holly how long you'd been together, but she avoided answering the question. I'm guessing that means not long. She's not exactly like the women who used to warm your bed."

"No, she's not. Holly has my undivided attention and I'm not sharing, if that's crossed your mind."

"Relax, Gray. I'm not going to steal your girlfriend."

Responding with *doubt you could*, would only give Dirk a reason to test Holly's commitment. His former platoon chief loved a challenge. He thrived on it. Least, that's the man he remembered.

Instead of doubling down on a threat, he used a different tactic.

"Hope not. So, when you take her out to dinner tonight, do me a favor and keep the flirting to a minimum."

"Wow, you guys must be tight. Is that the real reason you're calling? A warning to keep my dick out of your girl."

Even though he was jesting, Gray gritted his teeth. Dirk always had a boatload of charisma. When it came to the fairer sex, his confident but disarming personality touched women on a subconscious level and steered them straight into his bed.

"Holly was seriously burned by her first husband."

Two lines Dirk never crossed, though he was into every sexual experience one could imagine, were messing with a married woman or a woman who'd been a victim of any kind of trauma. Even if the gal was willing, he'd avoided them.

Sex to Dirk equaled an artist's rendition of a masterpiece. He'd perfected his skill, fine-tuning the experience, applying touch and taste for extreme pleasure. And ultimately, kept his sexual partner floating in an erotic trance of ecstasy for as long as possible before allowing them to reach an explosive release.

"I see," Dirk said. The humor in his tone dissipated. "She didn't mention that."

"She didn't tell me either for the longest time. Those wounds are still fresh," Gray added.

Not exactly the truth, but hopefully enough to keep Dirk from testing the waters.

"Don't have to worry about me, old friend. Talking with her about antiquities is enough of a thrill. The woman literally lights up when she's discussing her work. You're lucky, Grayson, she's one of a kind."

A shot of jealousy ripped through his gut. He'd seen that as well and wished he could see it every day.

"I know. This is a first for me."

"What d'ya mean *a first*?" Dirk asked.

"My habit of avoiding long-term relationships has been pretty consistent over the years."

"You telling me that Holly is your first crack at monogamy?"

Until Holly, he didn't have a reason to settle down. "Like I said at the celebration, she burned my bachelor card. And she's not a test run."

"Whatever happened to that chick, Erika? Weren't you

two a thing?"

"No, we weren't a thing!" Grayson gave him the short and dirty version. He glanced at the time on the dash. "Listen, I gotta get back to work. Give me a call when you've got time. We'll throw a few back, Chief."

"Looking forward to it, Gray."

Satisfied that Dirk would probably behave, Gray had adhered to Holly's wishes and kept his temper in check. He stashed his cell and got out of the truck.

"Grayson, we need to talk."

He pivoted on his heel to see Kate Billings' blue-eyed gaze centered on him.

CHAPTER TWENTY-SIX

"For fuck's sake." Grayson slammed the driver's door closed. He sighed and reached in his pocket for his phone.

"Don't," Kate said and raised her hand. "You don't need to record the conversation."

"Lady, I don't know what your problem is—"

"Just hear me out." Kate lowered her hand. "I want to apologize."

Women like her could end a guy's career with some bogus rape claim. He'd seen it before.

Gray glanced at the video cameras on the exterior wall of the building. "Don't need an apology."

He headed for the entrance to the PU fifty feet away.

The blonde jumped in front of him, and he stopped himself from running into her.

"I fucked up, all right?" she said.

Grayson eyed the woman. "You fuck up when you sent Capt. Gordon's wife a sex tape, too? Give it a rest."

Her jaw flexed and her nostrils flared. "I'm attracted to you and underestimated your relationship with that Canadian. I made a mistake."

"You call attaching a tracking device on my vehicle a mistake?"

She clutched her hands as if in prayer. "My career means everything to me. Capt. Baker is out for my head. I need you to rescind your complaint."

"Lady, I didn't make a complaint." This chick had *crazy* as a middle name. "You probably screwed him over like Capt. Gordon, then blackmailed the guy to climb the food chain. Whatever you did, that's your problem."

"Grayson." She glanced around, then said, "What's going on at the warehouse has ties to my department. I need someone in my corner. Someone I can trust. I put a tracker on your vehicle to make sure you weren't involved."

Her assertions didn't equate with her actions. "Lying to Holly then confronting her has nothing to do with your claim that something dirty is going on in the department. Sorry, not buying it."

She shook her head. "You know how dangerous working DTF can be. Gang bangers hate us, and they'll target people we care about. You and I can watch each other's backs."

There was crazy, then there was relentless crazy.

"Grayson! Don't walk away from me."

He aimed for the glass entry doors. "You're three bricks shy of a load, lady. If I see you again, I *will* make a formal complaint. Get some help."

Leaving the lunatic behind, he reached the building and traipsed down the hallway to the PU's office. Grayson felt sorry for Capt. Gordon. The hell he'd gone through by sticking his dick where it didn't belong must have been immense. Over the years, Grayson had run into some clingy chicks, but never Billings' level of psycho. When he entered the office, Cole waved him over.

"Just got off the phone with a woman who lives in Clayton. She thinks there's something funny going on with the house next door. Says she's seen guys coming and going at odd hours. Could be another stash house that's not on our radar yet."

"Then let's check it out."

Within a few minutes, Gray had changed into civvies. "I'll meet you out at the truck."

When Cole hopped in the passenger seat, he asked, "How did you end up back at the PU?" He inserted the address of the caller into the truck's nav system, then buckled in.

Gray told him what Billings had done while they drove through the commercial area of town toward their destination, ending with the conversation he and Kate just had out in the parking lot.

"She's fucking certifiable," Cole said. "Maybe Holly should stay north of the border for a bit until you're sure Billings has stood down."

Parking on a side street a block away from the reporting party's house, he said, "Crossed my mind, but she'll be with me when she's down here. She'll be safe."

As far as Holly knew, Billings was out of the picture. He wanted to keep it that way so she wouldn't worry.

Standing outside the truck, Gray surveyed the street. The front yards were in reasonably good shape with mowed lawns. Some of the homes needed a new coat of paint but otherwise, they were well kept.

Under the hot summer sun, he and Cole walked down a back alley to the caller's house. A mix of six-foot-high wood fences or chain link separated the roadway from the backyards. Gangs often hired or coerced neighbors to act as an early warning system. If they caught wind of law enforcement in the area, the bad guys scattered.

They reached the backside of the caller's home and peered over a thick wall of ivy. Grayson couldn't see directly into the backyard, but a one-story rambler with a pitched roof sat on the property. He and Cole used the detached two-car garage, accessed from the alley, as cover.

Gray signaled to Cole to hold his position when he heard the sound of bicycle tires on the gravel-surface road. Soon, two young boys passed their location, each with one hand on the handlebar and the other gripping a soda to-go cup.

Once they were gone, Gray led the way through a gate in the fence. A few feet inside the backyard, he halted. Two beautiful young women lay on lounge chairs, sunbathing in the nude. When the blonde caught sight of him, instead of grabbing the towel on the ground and covering up, a smile slid across the gal's mouth.

"Um, Cole, did you tell the caller that we were coming?"

"Yeah, I did," he said, standing on Grayson's right side.

The other woman, a brunette with an ample pair of breasts and slender waist, didn't seem concerned. Even bolder than her friend, she placed a foot on either side of the lounge chair, baring her slit.

"Hi, there," she said.

Both women wore sunglasses, shielding their eyes, but in order for Grayson to tell whether they were high, he'd have to get closer.

"Ladies," Grayson said, showing his badge. "We're from the sheriff's office. One of you called in a report to my partner."

The brunette slid the shades to the top of her head. "I did," she answered, then winked at Cole.

What the fuck was going on here? "How about you cover up, then tell us what you've seen at the house next door."

The brunette chuckled. "Why don't we not, and you come a little closer."

Gray scrubbed his jaw and shot a look at his partner. "You got a clue what's going on here?"

"Nope."

The blonde stood and wheeled around to stand behind the brunette's chair. "We saw you two at Neon Lights resort a while back." She leaned forward and glided her palms over the brunette's shoulders then circled the woman's areolas with her thumbs. "Don't be angry, but my friend and I always dreamed of having a little fun with two men like you. Law enforcement is willing to serve, right? We promise not to tell anyone."

Gray felt like he'd entered some pornographic episode of the Twilight Zone.

Cole chuckled and shook his head. "Sorry we can't accommodate, ladies," he said in an amiable tone. "To confirm, you don't have any issue with your neighbors."

The brunette pouted a little. "Oh, no, there's something funky going on next door." She swung her leg over the lounger and stood. "We see people coming and going from that place all the time. I think they belong to a motorcycle gang."

"Which house?" Gray asked.

The brunette pointed to her left. "They party in the backyard, and I've heard them talk about moving merchandise and drugs."

Cole crossed his arms over his chest. "Any strange smells coming from over there? Chemicals, cleaning products. Anything like that?"

"You mean a cookhouse? No. I don't think so. They smoke grass and what not, but I don't think they're making crack."

This had to be the weirdest interview Gray had ever experienced. Every time he made eye contact with the naked blonde with a killer bod, she tilted her head a little and smiled.

"What about the gang?" Grayson asked. "You know which one it is?"

"Werewolves," the blonde answered. "They're a scary-looking bunch, but they don't bother us." The woman threaded her fingers through her hair and held it on top of her head. "Maybe you should stick around for a while and see who comes."

Grayson couldn't help himself and laughed. At another time and place, he would have had her on her back after his shift. He reached into his pocket and pulled out a business card. "Sorry, honey. Appreciate the offer, but the woman I love doesn't like to share."

She shrugged. "That's a shame."

"Do us a favor," he said. "Keep a record of the license plates on the motorcycles you see parked out front and call me."

If a member of the Werewolves was a repeat visitor, it could mean they'd found another stash house.

The blonde took the card. "Drop by again."

Grayson nudged his head at Cole to get moving.

"Appreciate the call," Cole said. "Have a good afternoon, ladies."

Grayson didn't want to linger in the area. If there was a gang housed next door, it wouldn't take them long to identify law enforcement. A few minutes later, he and his partner were back in the pickup.

Securing his seatbelt, Cole said, "That is one call I'm not telling Ivy about."

He chuckled and started the truck. "Hot day. Hope they have plenty of sunscreen." Grayson headed for Fifth Street and the Purple Orchid for recon.

"Depending on who's coming and going from that place, we might have another stash house for the list."

Gray turned onto the main street and headed for the downtown core. "I'm sure the blonde will give me a call. If we can ID some key players visiting all the houses, we'll know there's a connection."

"I'm sure she will. By the way, were you just saving your hide back there by saying the woman you love doesn't share? Cuz at the backyard game on Saturday, you said Holly burned your bachelor card. Now you're spending another weekend with her. Thought you had a hard and fast rule about women and relationships."

Gray came to a stop at a busy intersection. "Past tense. I used to have a rule."

The old him wouldn't give a rat's ass that Holly's ex planned on camping out at her place on Wednesday. She said she could handle the guy, and she probably could. But he wasn't comfortable with the idea.

Cole unscrewed the lid from a bottle of water he'd brought and quenched his thirst. "You're jumping into the deep end of the pool pretty quickly. That's not your style."

"Sounds like you're trying to talk me out of seeing her. What gives?"

Cole gazed out the passenger window. "Not at all. Just being a realist."

His best friend seemed to be hedging. "Because she's Canadian?"

"No, buddy. Because she's way off course when it comes to your tastes. Those women back at the house are more your speed."

"Yeah, well, I hated Brussels sprouts when I was kid, but I love them now."

Cole placed the water bottle back in the console's cup holder. "All I'm saying is make sure this isn't some phase before you start using big words like love, especially to her. Holly's a nice lady."

"Jesus, Cole. Stop prancing around the subject. You've always given it to me straight. You obviously think there's a problem, so what are you trying to tell me?"

His partner looked over at him with a pinched expression. "I think coming home is a big change from your life in San Diego. You're adjusting and trying to do it too quickly by putting all your ducks in a row. Holly is one of those ducks. You chose her because she's the opposite of the type of woman that turns you on. I doubt it's going to last, which means you need to put on the brakes because when you dump her, it's going to hurt her a lot more than you."

The phrase *Tell me what you really think* came to mind, but that's exactly what he'd asked his friend to do. He wanted the truth and got kicked in the balls. His gut twitched with anger. But he wasn't sure if it was from Cole pointing out cold, hard facts or concerned that he might be right.

As his temper soared, he said, "So I better dump Holly now, huh?"

"Gray—"

"No. You know what? *Fuck you.* I was attracted to Holly the second I saw her. She's real, not some breast-augmented, Botox-pumped chick with ten tons of makeup and rice-paper-thin morals. She excites me. Intrigues me. I feel whole when I'm with her and empty when I'm not."

Cole gnawed on his bottom lip, then nodded. "Yeah, of

course. Sorry."

Grayson stewed in his friend's opinion all the way to the Purple Orchid. When they reached the bar, he got out and slammed the driver's door. Cole rounded the front of the truck and stepped in his way.

"Gray, you asked for my opinion."

"Guess I did. I just didn't realize how low it was."

He glared at the front window with *Purple Orchid* printed on the glass. Nice name for a shithole.

The homeless wandered the streets. One guy in tattered jeans staggered past, muttering to himself. Two chicks hung out by the corner in miniskirts and tight blouses, peddling their trade. This part of town reeked of tragedy.

His partner exhaled a sigh. "It's not a criticism of you or Holly, it's an observation. The people who love you see how your time with the teams left its mark. You're not the same guy who left this town fifteen years ago, Gray. And no one expects you to be. Take the time to transition."

A senior with silver stubble coating his face and a sour smell permeating his clothes shuffled up to them on the sidewalk. "Excuse me, sirs. Could you lend me some change?"

Gray dug in his pocket and pulled out a couple ten-dollar bills. "Get something to eat, old timer."

"Thank you, sir. Thank you." He took the money and stuffed it in his torn pants pocket and quickly departed.

Grayson wondered if Cole had the same concerns as Ivy, that he'd pack his bags and head back to San Diego at a moment's notice.

He gripped his friend's shoulder. "I appreciate the pep talk, but I didn't leave the teams yesterday. Granted, it took five years to get my shit together. If you think I regret coming home, I don't. Holly might not be what *you* picture as the right woman for me, but she's *exactly* who I've been waiting for. Did I jump in with both feet? I sure as fuck did. Holly sees herself as a geek and a nerd. And I admire every sweet, geeky, nerdy, sexy part of her. That woman is mine to love, respect and honor, and I know it with every fiber of my being."

A slip of a smile pulled at Cole's lips. "Does she feel the same way?"

Grayson lowered his hand. "I think she's fighting it. She's being careful."

He chuckled. "So, you're full ahead with Navy SEAL determination and she's thoughtfully reviewing the evidence."

Gray gnawed on his bottom lip. "Fair assessment." He didn't want to fuck this up. "I'm prepared for the day when she accuses me of being an insensitive jerk, and I'm telling you right here and now, I'll get down on my knees and beg for her forgiveness. I respect Holly and what comes from her very kissable lips as truth."

Cole snorted and smacked his arm. "Better get kneepads, buddy. If I know you, you're gonna be down there a lot."

* * * *

Holly glanced at her watch, surprised to see it was already eight-thirty p.m. She and Dirk had hammered out some viable hypotheses in regard to the tablets, then continued to discuss anthropology until the crowd in the restaurant had thinned out considerably.

The server brought Dirk another whiskey and refilled her water glass.

"You know, Grayson called me earlier," he said. "Warned me to keep things professional."

"Oh, dear. I'm sorry."

Dirk's sexy grin went into overdrive. With the low lighting of the restaurant, the SEAL-turned-archaeologist's handsome features and blistering green eyes were easy to look at.

"You don't have to apologize," he said. "Gray and I were close at one time. He knows me."

Holly's cheeks heated, remembering Grayson's

description of their sexual play with women.

Dirk tilted his head in query, the creases around his firm lips deepened with a muted smile. "By the blush on your face, he told you everything."

"He kept it brief, but yes, I know."

His eyes glittered under the pendant light hanging over their table. She didn't voice her thoughts but if she wasn't mistaken, Dirk remembered those times with fondness and it wasn't toward the women they pleasured, but the man he still desired.

Relaxing in the chair, he said, "Gray told me you were married once, and it wasn't a good experience. I'm sorry you had to go through that. If there's one thing you can count on with Grayson Brooks, he'll always tell the truth, whether you want to hear it or not." He picked up his glass and downed the amber-colored whisky.

Her phone beeped with an incoming text.

Be home in twenty. Your date finished?

Dirk chuckled when she twitched her nose. "Guess my time is up and Grayson wants his girlfriend back."

Holly grinned. "He's jealous for some reason."

She typed a quick reply.

On my way in a bit. Call u when I'm home.

Dirk caught the server's attention and asked for the check. "I'd say you're a good reason and Gray is a lucky man."

"Hey, do you know why his SEAL team name is Bone?"

Dirk broke into a healthy laugh as he retrieved his wallet from his pocket and gave the server a credit card. Still chuckling, he said, "Yes, I know."

When he wouldn't explain further, she said, "Awww, come on. Tell me. Does it have something to do with him being a medic?"

He scrubbed his jaw and hitched an eyebrow at her. "How long have you two been dating?"

She wondered what that had to do with anything. "We met in May, but he kissed me for the first time last week."

Dirk's eyes rounded a little and he blinked. "I see." He added a tip to the receipt, slid the card in his wallet, then leaned back to shove the wallet into his front pocket. "After Gray finished his Qual training, he was assigned to my platoon. Guys like us have a tendency to kid each other. Living in close confines, we see each other's junk—a lot. The new guy on the team always gets razzed. Not to put too much detail in the story, we'd hit the showers after a training session and I said, *'Hey, Brooks, you better watch who you bone with that thing.'*"

Like a complete moron, she leaned closer. "Because?"

Dirk's mouth opened, then closed, then opened again. "Holly, um, not to pry but have you two…?"

"Been intimate? Yes. Why?"

Dirk's shoulders bobbed with laughter. "I think I'll stop there, but you are one sweet lady."

The lightbulb came on. "Oh, you're referring to his size," she whispered.

Still grinning from ear to ear he stood. "Yes, that's what I'm referring to. From that point forward, the team guys referred to him as Bone."

She and Dirk left the restaurant and walked toward the well-lit parking lot on the right side of the building. "The only other man I've known in that fashion is my ex-husband."

Dirk escorted her to the Audi and waited while she unlocked the door.

"Mm-hmm, think I figured that much out. Not many men have Gray's attributes and he sure knows how to use it. Consider yourself blessed."

She laughed. "All right, I'll do that. Well, it was a pleasure talking with you about your exciting archaeological find and also getting to know one of Grayson's old teammates."

Holly held out her hand. Instead, he stepped closer and palmed her shoulders then placed a kiss on her cheek. "It has been my pleasure, Holly. I'm heading back to Jerusalem in a couple days. Let's keep in touch."

Like a gentleman, he opened the driver's door for her. "Take care, Dirk."

Twenty minutes later, she flicked on the kitchen lights and placed her laptop and purse on the counter. A knock landed on her front door, which made her leery at nine-thirty at night. She turned on the porch light.

What the heck?

Holly opened the door and Grayson's towering form stood on her stoop, his eyes smoldering.

"This is a surprise. What are you doing here?"

He came at her like a wave of molten masculinity. His arms wrapped around her waist, and he thrust her backward with a punishing kiss. Standing in the small foyer, he kicked the door closed, swung them one-hundred and eighty degrees and pinned her to the door with his massive chest.

His hands coaxed the lightweight sweater off her shoulders and let it fall to the floor. Instead of answering her question, his lips assaulted her mouth and his tongue darted against hers while he loosened the buttons on her silk shirt, then unlatched her bra.

Silent but deadly, his mouth laid a trail of blazing-hot kisses down the side of her neck, over her collarbone, then seized her tight nipple and sucked, causing a sharp ache between her legs. He put one knee on the tile floor and made quick work of removing her pants.

Naked and pressed against the front door, she writhed as Grayson's tongue lapped her clit. His calloused hands gripped her hips and his mouth drove her into a frenzy, suckling her sensitive nub with little tugs. Moisture coated her sex, and her knees weakened with the onslaught of sensations.

God, she loved when he did this to her.

Grayson stopped his sensual assault before she climaxed. He stood, kissed her while releasing the buttons down his shirt then unzipped his jeans and turfed them to the side.

When he gave her a second to breathe, she asked,

"Aren't… aren't you going to say hello?" She gripped his thick biceps, dizzy with need.

The feral look in his eyes told her he didn't want to talk. Gray clenched her wrist and led her into the living room. He planted her hands on the back of the couch and her pulse pounded with the way he handled her.

Grayson palmed her spine and urged her to lean forward. From behind, he slid his fingers back and forth over her slick clit.

"Phone sex is overrated when I can have you in my arms, Holly. But right now, I need to fuck you."

The heat of his hips warmed her ass, and the crown of his cock teased the entrance to her channel. She pushed back, needing his fullness, but he retreated.

"Did he try anything?" he growled.

His warm hand crawled up her stomach and palmed one breast, rolling her nipple while his other hand strummed her clit.

"No, of course not."

Shaking with impatience, she spread her feet wider and tilted her ass upward. Her heart thumped madly. Fire streaked through her blood and her fingers clenched the couch as his thick cock surged into her needy channel.

"Fuck." He groaned, buried inside her.

His shaft slowly pistoned in and out with deep thrusts. The tempo made her pant and beg him to go faster.

His raspy breaths shallowed. "You have any idea what the last five hours were like for me?"

Oh, God, he felt good. "No."

"Fucking torture."

Her body's lubrication drizzled down her thighs, his thick shaft filling her channel, stroking all the right places and driving her mad. "I'm sorry."

"Never again, Holly."

He withdrew his cock from her vagina. Was this punishment?

"Grayson, don't leave me this way."

His hands palmed her breasts. "Your body is mine to pleasure. Not his. Do you understand me?" He eased his erection into her channel.

"Yes." Sighs and gasps kept falling from her lips.

His rhythm increased, plunging faster and harder. Every thrust drove her closer to release. So close. Every nerve in her body sparked. When he slowed his pace, instead of retreating from the edge, raw lust tore her apart.

"You're close, babe."

His warm breath on her skin raised goosebumps all over her body.

She slammed her eyes shut, teetering. "Yes."

Gray's thumb strummed her clit, unleashing the orgasm that rolled through her, and she moaned with pleasure.

"Jesus, I love when you come on my cock." He groaned and yanked his erection from her heat.

Shocked that he didn't chase his own release, she looked over her shoulder. "Why did you stop?"

He laid a line of kisses down her spine. "I'm not wearing protection."

Holly pivoted. With his shirt unbuttoned, her gaze slid over the taut muscle of his tanned pecs and abs. She pressed her palms against his chest and steered him into the lounger adjacent to the couch. As he sat with a plunk, she kneeled and eased her mouth over his mushroom crown and gripped his thick shaft.

Grayson's fingers dug into the armrests, and he hissed. She traced his head with her tongue and sucked, pumping his erect penis with her hand.

"Oh, shit." He roughly threaded his fingers through her curls. Grayson's stomach muscles cinched tight, and his hips thrust upward. "Fuck, that's hot."

His guttural moan warned he was close. He'd never come in her mouth. At the last second, he tugged on her hair, and his head rocked back against the chair as warm cum fountained against her breasts.

She leaned forward and eased her mouth over his shaft, licking him clean, causing him to shudder and jolt. Finally, he opened his eyes and looked down at her.

Grayson gripped her under the arms, and she straddled his lap, easing his softening cock into her core. He palmed the nape of her neck and pulled her to his mouth.

"I love you, Holly" he said against her lips, then kissed her. "I had every intention of going home and waiting for your call, but I couldn't. Don't ever do that to me again."

She wallowed in the warmth of his possessiveness. If he didn't care, he wouldn't be here. "It was a business dinner."

His blue eyes blazed with emotion. "Doesn't matter," he said brusquely.

She gently pressed her lips to his, feeling closer to Grayson than any man she'd known. "I don't know how long this will last, but you make me feel special. I want to remember that. Don't be angry with me."

He fingered a curl of hair from her cheek. "Sweetheart, I'm *not* angry and you *are* special. Call me a possessive asshole if you want. I had to come."

"Are you better now?" She squeezed her vaginal muscles, causing him to twitch.

An irresistible smile spread across his lips. "Yeah, I'm better." He placed a gentle kiss on her mouth. "So…here it is, full disclosure. I crossed the border because I had to make sure you were home and not in his bed."

"Grayson, shame on you."

"Sweetheart, I'm telling you, that guy has a way of seducing someone that's almost inhuman."

"You're giving him too much credit. He's just a man and our relationship is strictly business."

"Are you pissed at me for being a jealous asshole?"

"No. I'm flattered, but don't let it go to your head."

He grinned. "Promise I won't." His gaze surveyed the living room while he stroked her back. "Nice place. Small but comfortable."

"I used to love it here, but I hate it now."

Gray's thumb slid through the semen on her breast and then brushed her nipple in lazy circles. "I have an easy answer to your dilemma."

"Don't say it." There was no way she'd leave her career and immigrate to the US.

He quirked a brow at her. "Too soon?"

She rolled her eyes. "I'm not moving to Bellingham."

Grayson's warm chuckle made her grin.

"Well then, let's get your stubborn Canadian ass in the shower."

"Are you going to put me to bed?"

Gray clutched her hips and stood up, carrying her toward the stairs. "Hmm, that and much more, babe."

For the first time in years, her townhouse didn't feel empty anymore. Although Gray had stormed through her door like a caveman, his presence warmed her heart. She felt loved but couldn't resist teasing him.

When they reached the top of the stairs, she said, "I should go out with Dirk more often."

The edges of his mouth pulled downward. "Not funny, Holly."

She grinned. "Second door on the left, Detective."

CHAPTER TWENTY-SEVEN

H olly reviewed the last page of Juliette's internship research paper. Her data was accurate, her arguments clear, and her conclusion offered a sound resolution.

"What do you think?" Juliette asked from the doorway of Holly's office as if she'd been hanging out in the hallway the whole time.

"For a first draft, I think this is very good, Juliette. I've made some suggestions in the margins. Consider them before submitting the final copy to Professor Carlson." She held out the ten pages of Juliette's blood, sweat, and tears.

The intern accepted the sheets and hugged them to her chest. "Thank you for reviewing the paper, Holly. I can't tell you how lucky I feel to have worked with you and this department."

"It's not over yet. There's another two months before your internship ends."

Holly glanced at the time. Close to three o'clock. She closed her laptop and collected her purse. "I'm going to call it a day."

Kevin said he'd be at her place around four o'clock. Holly wasn't looking forward to this evening, but she'd promised her ex he could spend the night since his sentencing was first thing tomorrow morning.

"Anything you'd like me to do in the lab?"

"We're expecting a delivery from Cairo tomorrow but if it happens to come in today, make sure there's no shipping damage and secure it in the repository."

Juliette nodded. "Will do."

Twenty minutes later, Holly arrived home and drove into the single-car garage of her townhouse. Kevin sat on the white ladder-back chair next to the front door. She'd made him return the house key before he'd left last time, which he hadn't been pleased about.

He strolled into the garage.

"Hey, Hol," he greeted as she got out of the car.

The deep shadows beneath his eyes were gone and he was smiling. "You're here early."

"I have good news and I wanted to share it with you."

Unless he'd won the lottery and booked a hotel room, she couldn't imagine what news he considered good with tomorrow's sentencing hanging over his head. She unlocked the door between the garage and the house while Kevin hit the button to close the garage door. He followed her through the small utility room where the washer and dryer were located and into the kitchen.

Holly set her purse and laptop on the granite kitchen counter while Kevin dropped an overnight bag by the foot of the stairs near the front door. He unzipped the bag and took something out.

When he returned to the kitchen, he revealed a bottle of white wine from behind his back. "Your favorite Pinot."

"That was thoughtful. You look well, Kevin."

She watched as he retrieved two glasses from her china cabinet, then dug out the corkscrew from a drawer near the sink and uncorked the wine. Kevin remembered where everything was and moved around the kitchen as if he'd never left two years ago.

"They bumped up my internal review to yesterday. It was intense, Holly. I thought for sure I would lose my job, but because of my excellent service record and the fact I was at the legal drinking limit but not way over it, things swung my way. Plus, the extenuating circumstances worked in my favor. The guy I hit was speeding at the time and had run a red light." He poured the wine and strode to the living room. "I wasn't fired. My lawyer thinks this is going to have a significant impact on the sentencing tomorrow." Kevin held out a wine glass for her to take. "Thought we'd celebrate early."

Holly took the wine she really didn't want and sat on the couch. Instead of sitting in the chair, he settled next to her.

"What does that mean?" she asked.

He tipped the rim of his glass to hers in a casual toast. "It means, I will probably receive a fine, but no prison time. I can put my life back together again."

She took a polite sip and set her glass down. "I'm glad to hear that."

"Holly." His eyes raked across her face. "I've done a lot of soul searching over the past few months. Not just because of the accident and conviction but what I did to you. The affairs. You came up a lot during my sessions in therapy."

That surprised her. "You took therapy?"

"Still taking it," he said. "Didn't want to at first, but it was a requirement by the department. Talking with a psychologist helped me discover the root of my infidelity, among other things."

Holly leaned back against the couch that now held a sexy memory. Grayson had stayed the night and left early yesterday morning.

She tucked her right leg under her thigh. Before Kevin decided to share his reasons for cheating, she said, "That's good. Maybe your next relationship has a chance of survival."

Kevin picked up her glass from the table and handed it back to her. "I don't want a new relationship. I'm sure this is going to be difficult for you to believe, but I was happy when we were together."

"You had affairs with three women. Probably more. You might have been happy with me, but you weren't satisfied. I was an afterthought, Kevin. You were pretty straight forward when you left."

He pursed his lips, then knocked back a deep swallow of Pinot. "You were my wife, Holly. You should have been my first priority." Kevin fingered a strand of curls from her cheek. "I look around this place and I remember the good times we shared."

It was also likely that he'd learned from Natalie, and if Holly allowed him back into the townhouse and her life, he could walk away with a healthy chunk of change after one year. "It's water under the bridge now, Kevin. You moved on and so did I."

He traced her shoulder with the palm of his hand. "Hol, I want to come home. I'm not asking you to forget. I know that's not possible. I'm asking for you to forgive me. Now that there's a good chance I won't have to serve time, the first thing I want to fix is us."

The doorbell rang, saving her from patiently listening to Kevin's bid to move in before telling him he could shove that idea up his ass.

He stood up. "I'll get it, honey."

Holly rolled her eyes when she heard a familiar voice. "Afternoon, you must be Kevin."

"Yeah, what can I do for you?" Kevin's tone shifted into his cop voice, a recipe of authoritative with a tablespoon of edginess.

Grayson's throaty chuckle drifted inside from the doorstep. "You can't do anything for me, except maybe step aside so I can see my girlfriend." The silence that followed was broken when Grayson said, "Holly home yet?"

"I'm home, Grayson," she said loud enough for him to hear as she stood. "Come on in."

He rounded the wall separating the front entry from the living room. "Hey, sweetheart."

Grayson crossed the carpet, sucking all the oxygen from the room. The man was just too damn handsome wearing a blue button-up shirt, casual black leather jacket, and jeans. And being the confident demi-god that he was, he wore a cocky grin.

"Hello, Detective," she said with a chipper greeting.

Grayson had perfect timing. She'd told him to stay away

but now that he was here, she was grateful he didn't listen to her.

"Missed you, Holly." Grayson made his dominant position known by drawing her tight to his body and laying a knee-quivering kiss on her lips.

"You're in trouble," she said under her breath.

"It's been a day and a half. Think it's you that's in trouble."

Her ex returned to the living room and stood stiffly, waiting for an introduction.

"Kevin, this is Grayson Brooks."

His eyes flickered with dislike. "You called him detective. Are you a member?"

"Member of what?" Grayson asked.

Kevin gave him a once over. "Are you RCMP or city police?"

Grayson kept one arm around her shoulders. "Neither. Skagit County Sheriff's Department."

"American? Huh." He glanced at Holly. "I didn't realize you were dating."

That, she thought, was because the world revolved around him.

Grayson's genuine chuckle drew Kevin's attention back toward her lover. "I'd say we're a long way past dating."

"Gray worked five years in San Diego vice after he left the Navy SEALs, then moved back to Washington. That's where we met."

With a clenched jaw, Kevin asked, "Can I get you something to drink?"

"No, thanks. Don't drink and drive."

Damn, Grayson, that's harsh.

Without missing a beat, Kevin said, "Holly and I are celebrating. You should join us for one."

If her ex foolishly pushed Grayson's buttons, this situation wouldn't end well. This was her home. Gray belonged here, Kevin didn't.

"The beer Grayson likes is in the fridge."

Kevin sniffed. "Isn't that convenient," he said, and headed for the kitchen.

Holly poked her lover in the chest. "I told you I can handle this."

Grayson's disarming smile blocked her irritation. "Border had a longer wait time than I expected. Guess you didn't make a dinner reservation."

"On the contrary. I had a feeling you wouldn't listen to me, so yes, we have a reservation."

He kissed her sweetly. "Good, because I made one too."

She blinked with surprise. "For dinner?"

"Nope."

"Here's your beer," Kevin said, setting the bottle on the oak coffee table.

She and Grayson sat on the couch.

"Thanks, appreciate it. Holly told me your sentencing is tomorrow and you're planning to stay here tonight."

Her retired SEAL took the reins, and she had a feeling he wasn't going to mince words.

"Not planning, I am staying the night."

Kevin sat in the lounger. The same lounger that Gray sat in on Monday when she'd made him moan with pleasure and come on her boobs. There was a little irony somewhere in all this.

Gray's eyes and mouth curled with a distinct sardonic expression that Holly read as *Nah, I'm gonna be nice for about five more seconds, then I'm kicking your ass.*

"She has a kind heart. Too kind." Gray's voice gathered grit with each word. "We're going to head out for dinner. When we come back, I doubt we'll get past this living room before I make love to her. Don't think you're going to want to be around for that." Grayson reached inside his leather jacket and slid a piece of paper across the table toward Kevin. "I hear you're a little hard-up for cash. Because you're a cop, I'm gonna do you a favor. That's a reservation at the Wingdom Hotel in Vancouver. Convenient location. A block from the

Supreme Court."

Kevin's mouth curled downward as he picked up the slip of paper and tore it in half. "Appreciate the professional courtesy, but no thanks. Probably a better idea if you use that reservation yourself because you're sure as hell not staying in this house with my wife."

"Ex-wife, you mean. The same woman you left two years ago for Natalie."

Kevin put his attention on her. "Holly, you're making the same mistake all over again."

She calmly got to her feet. "Mistake? Why do you say that?"

Kevin got up as well and his face twisted with a sarcastic smile. "If I got bored fucking you after a couple years of marriage," he said, "you sure as hell don't have what it takes to keep *him* satisfied."

Ouch. "Kevin, I think out of the three of us, the only person who got fucked and deserved it was you."

Grayson broke into a hearty laugh. "Fire in the hole, babe."

Kevin tossed them a stormy glare. "Guess this means you're not interested in trying to work things out."

"No, Kevin, I trusted you once. Forgave you multiple times. I'm not interested in letting you move back in then sue me for half the equity next year. I'm not a complete fool."

He shook his head as if totally disgusted. "Yeah, well, it was worth a try. It would have been tough putting up with you for three-hundred and sixty-five days."

Kevin headed for the front entry, stopping to clutch his overnight bag. She followed, and for the first time saw Kevin's deceptive character clearly. He didn't love her. The only reason he wanted to move in was to screw her over. He thought she was an easy mark.

Kevin opened the front door, stepped out onto the stoop, and turned. "He's going to fuck you and dump your homely, boring ass, Holly, because you're pathetic and it's easy to do."

Holly felt her detective's presence flare behind her like a safety net.

"Thanks for dropping by Kev," Grayson said, placing a hand on her left shoulder. "Gotta say, it was interesting meeting the stupidest prick on the planet." His strong fingers gripped the door and slammed it closed.

The confrontation had her heartbeat racing. Grayson swept the hair from her neck and his warm lips kissed her pulse.

"He took one in the nuts, sweetheart. He's talking trash."

"No, he's probably right, but I don't care." She sighed and turned around to face the man she trusted.

Gray's brows knit together. "Holly, come on. His parting shot was a blow beneath the belt and a complete lie. You know that."

"Before you arrived, he tried to convince me that he still loved me and wanted to move back in."

"Maybe he does but too fucking bad for him." He eased the side zipper of her skirt open. "Only way he's getting to you is over my dead body. You can take that as gospel."

Agitated because she hated confrontations, she stopped Gray's hand and gave him a stern look.

"Sweetheart, he's gone. You showed his ass to the door for the last time. That fucker doesn't deserve you. He *never* did. You handled that all on your own. I was just here as your defensive line."

She grinned and slid her arms over his strong shoulders. "You're here because you've got a possessive streak a mile long."

Gray dipped his head. "Want me to stop?"

"Undressing me or being possessive?"

Her skirt pooled on the ground at her feet. One side of his sexy lips lifted as he unbuttoned her blouse.

"Do I have to choose?"

"Detective, if I didn't know better, I'd call this a strip search."

With her shirt open, he made quick work releasing the clasp at the front of her bra and sweeping his palms across her bare breasts. The man's blue eyes literally shimmered.

"If you want an honest answer, then neither. So, you better lead me to the bedroom quick, or I'm taking you right here—again." He palmed her jaw and pressed a heated kiss on her mouth.

It didn't take long for Grayson to make her wet and quivering with excitement. "Are you going to fuck me or make love to me?"

He grabbed the back of her thighs and hoisted her against his firm torso, his brow wrinkled with humor. "Sweetheart, is that pottymouth of yours my fault?"

"Completely your fault."

Grayson chuckled. "I brought my handcuffs."

"For my wrists or yours?"

His gaze slid across the tops of her breasts that were pinned to his chest. "Your call, babe."

"We're going to miss dinner."

"I sure hope so," he said, carrying her up the stairs to her bedroom.

* * * *

On Friday afternoon, Holly sat on a wood bench in the US border services building. A wide, oak-stained visitor's counter ran from one side of the room to the other. Behind the counter, US border guards went about their business. It wasn't out of the ordinary for the agent at the toll booth to direct a vehicle to be searched, but she'd been sitting here for thirty minutes. Four other people had come and gone.

The exterior walls were made of glass, allowing her to view the activity outside. From where she sat, Holly could see her vehicle. All four doors were open, and so were the trunk and hood. An officer with a dog circled her vehicle, then he prompted the animal to jump into the Audi.

She'd been randomly selected before, but the process hadn't taken more than ten minutes and she was on her way. This time seemed quite different.

"Miss McNeela," a man with a deep voice called.

She turned her attention to the border guard, and he waved her over. The guy stood well over six feet.

"Yes," she said approaching the counter.

"A female officer will be arriving shortly to conduct a body search."

"I'm sorry, what?" Confused, she shook her head. She caught movement to her right and saw Bob Sagle. "Bob, what's going on?"

The tall agent's brow rose as Bob spotted her and strode over to join them.

"Hi, Holly."

"What's happening? They're tearing my car apart and now this gentleman says they want to conduct a body search."

Bob glanced at his fellow officer. "The department received a tip, Holly. Said you're running drugs across the border. We have to follow protocol. Even if there's nothing in the vehicle, if you resist a body search, you'll be denied entry, possibly for a five-year term or longer."

She gasped and her blood chilled. "What? This is crazy. I'm an ancient language researcher, not a drug runner."

"Ma'am. Put your purse and any other personal belongings on the counter," the big guard said.

Her nerves tightened and her fingers shook. Was Bob responsible for this because he had a chip on his shoulder over Grayson?

She handed the guard her purse. "Can I keep my phone?"

"No. That will be searched as well."

Tears welled in her eyes even though she tried to hold them back. She turned her attention to Bob. "Is a football game this important?"

Sagle's expression creased, but with sympathy not anger.

"No, Holly. This wasn't me. Honestly."

Another officer wearing a dark blue uniform joined them.

"Ramsey," Bob greeted the guy. "Holly, this is our shift supervisor."

"I don't understand what's happening. There has to be a mistake."

Ramsey gave her a hard stare. "Sagle, you know this woman?"

"I do. She's dating Grayson Brooks. He's a detective with the sheriff's office. He and I went to school together."

Ramsey's dark eyes glared at her, then flicked toward Sagle. "Follow me, Miss McNeela. Sagle, you come too."

Holly was seated in a small room she suspected was used to interrogate people. A claustrophobic space with white walls and a small table.

"You cross the border a lot," Ramsey said, closing the door while looking at a sheet of paper in his hand.

It wasn't a question, so she kept her mouth shut. The supervisor sat on the other side of the table, and Sagle remained standing.

Ramsey removed his cap and tucked it under his arm. "Border Services received a call a few days ago. The caller said you're running cocaine across the border. My agents haven't found any evidence or even trace evidence in your vehicle."

She sat quietly with her hands clasped in her lap to stop them from shaking.

The supervisor laid the paper down on the table. "It was a credible source."

Holly's eyes slammed closed. A credible source! Was this Kevin's doing or Kate's? If she accused the wrong person, this would only get worse. Kevin was an asshole, but she'd never known him to be vindictive. She had to be very careful how she presented her case.

"A woman has been stalking my boyfriend. Her name's Kate Billings. She was the lieutenant of the Skagit Drug Task

Force."

"Was?" Ramsey asked sharply.

"Yes. As I understand it, she was suspended earlier this week. I only met her once, but she threatened me. Told me to stay away from Grayson or there'd be trouble. Other than her, I don't have any enemies."

Bob stood behind his supervisor and nodded, then winked at her.

Ramsey sat back in his chair. "Have you ever been charged in Canada for any offense?"

"Never."

"Can I confirm this information about Kate Billings with someone other than your boyfriend?"

She tried to recall the name of the captain Grayson had mentioned. "Yes, it's um, Capt. Baker. I think he's in charge of the Drug Task Force."

Ramsey stood. "Sagle, stay with her."

"Yes, sir."

When Ramsey left the room, Bob took his seat. Holly covered her face and tears spilled out.

"I'm sorry, Holly. It was Kate who called in the tip. When a detective from DTF gives us intel, we take it very seriously."

"I understand." The tears worsened, scared of what would happen.

"Do you want me to call, Gray?"

She shook her head, knowing his temper. "No. H-he'd be furious," she stuttered. "Kate is crazy. She put a tracking device on Grayson's truck. And she confronted me at the farmstead's celebration last weekend."

If Capt. Baker wouldn't divulge Billings' suspension or why she'd been suspended, border patrol would restrict Holly from entering the US. Of all the scenarios she'd imagined that could end her and Grayson's relationship, she'd never expected something like this.

"Guess Gray and I both have tempers," Sagle said, leaning back in the chair. "I'm not exactly proud of my actions at the football game on the Fourth. I let an old grudge get the better of me. It's high school shit."

Holly, numb with worry, stared at the Arborite tabletop but appreciated Bob's honesty. "You and Grayson are both strong men. It's natural for you to compete. Throughout human history, warriors stepped forward to prove who was the fastest and strongest."

He sniffed and scrubbed his jaw. "Yeah, I guess so. Truth is, Gray's one of those guys who always succeeds. My old man was a bastard. He used to lay the boots to me when I screwed up. When Gray made QB and I didn't, I took one helluva beating."

"Did Grayson know?"

"Nah." He shook his head. "No one did."

"That's not right. I'm so sorry, Bob."

He shrugged. "The old man's dead. Went to the grave angry at the world. Guess I got a little resentment to work through because I sure as hell don't want to die like him."

She smiled, even though butterflies flapped non-stop in her belly. "Gray would understand. He'd take you out for beers and listen without criticism. Although the psych department at my university would probably disagree, sometimes all you need is a friend to vent the pressure."

"Maybe. Gray and I were good friends before my old man thought I should be the quarterback."

They talked for thirty minutes before Holly said, "It's taking too long. Bob, if I have to submit to the body search, I will. Anything to prove I'm not carrying illegal drugs."

The door burst open, and Grayson filled the entrance. Wearing his uniform and deep lines etched in his brow, his gaze zeroed in on her.

"Holly."

She leaped from the chair and rushed into his arms, resting her cheek on his firm chest. She didn't know if she was up shit creek or not, but his presence filled her with relief.

Ramsey stood behind Grayson and said, "She's free to go. There'll be no record of this incident attached to her passport or vehicle."

"Thank you," Grayson responded, his thick arms holding her close.

Bob got up from the chair. "Hey, Gray. Sorry about this, man."

She tipped her head to look into his eyes. "How did you find out?"

"Capt. Baker called me as soon as he spoke with Ramsey. You're shaking, sweetheart."

"Just nerves. Bob stayed with me while his supervisor investigated."

Grayson held out a hand. "Thank you, Bob. Appreciate it."

He nodded. "You're welcome. Come on, I'll walk you out."

Holly collected her purse and other possessions. The agent behind the counter returned her car keys while Bob and Grayson spoke by the entrance. She hoped Bob took the opportunity to make amends. They were friends once and probably would be again if they cleared the air.

She joined the men, ready to leave and find a quiet place to drink alcohol. Gray's arm slid around her shoulder and tucked her to his side.

"Drop by the farm next week, Bob. We'll sit on the porch and put a few back," Grayson offered.

They shook hands.

"I'll do that." He glanced at her and smiled. "Thanks, Holly."

She and Gray exited the building. Holly handed the pink slip the agent at the counter told her to give to the officer outside. The border guard checked it and told her she was free to go.

Standing next to her car, Grayson palmed her jaw. "That bitch is going down for this. Ramsey said he'll gladly testify on behalf of the US Border Services. There's nothing they hate more than wasting time on a false claim. Monday, I'm filing an official complaint. Kate won't be suspended, she'll be fucking fired."

"Gray, remember when I said I only drink under certain circumstances?"

"Yeah."

"This is a circumstance."

A sympathetic smile washed across his expression. "You got it, babe." He placed a gentle kiss on her mouth. "I have to drop off the cruiser. I'll meet you at the farmstead. We have a whole weekend to look forward to. Just you, me, room service and walks on the beach. Okay?"

There was a possibility he might think she was a huge wimp, but faced with the prospect of never seeing him again based on a lie had scared her to death. She nodded, kept her fears to herself, and hugged him.

Grayson squeezed his muscled arms around her body and exhaled a deep breath. "Aw, baby, you've had one helluva week, haven't you?"

She didn't want to let go, and he must have sensed it because he didn't push her aside, leap into his cruiser and drive away.

"I don't know why that scared me so much."

He palmed her jaw and gently tipped her chin so she'd look at him. "Because you still see yourself as alone. But you're not, sweetheart."

****

Once Holly calmed down, Gray followed her on the I-5 until she took the turn-off for the farmstead. He couldn't shake the moment when she'd literally leaped from the interrogation chair and clung to him. His sense of protection struck the moon and rocketed back to earth.

He'd rescued plenty of women during his service in special ops and law enforcement. Those incidents were far more serious, but none had marked him like the last half hour.

Holly had needed him. The idea filled him with a crazy sense of pride. He wanted to be the man she depended on, no matter what. If backed into a corner, he'd stand in front of her. If she could handle the fight, he'd watch from the sidelines and cheer her on. Gray had no problem accepting a partnership where she was the brains and he was the brawn, but he'd destroy anyone who tried to hurt his girl.

And he would start with that fucking bitch Billings.

Continuing south on the highway to drop off the cruiser and pick up his truck, he was thankful Kate hadn't hidden any narcotics in Holly's Audi. It would have been a helluva lot harder to convince Border Services she was innocent. He owed Capt. Baker a debt of gratitude, and told him so. Baker relayed enough information to Ramsey to prove Kate was unhinged and wasn't representing the DTF when she'd called in the tip.

When Capt. Baker called, Gray was on the north end of Bellingham, interviewing a guy on the Clayton case. Took him seven minutes in the patrol car to reach the forty-ninth parallel.

The whole incident concerned him. Millions of people crossed the US/Canada border in both directions each year, but he knew things most civilians didn't, the concept of freedom nowhere near as stable as the good citizens thought it was. Shadow governments orchestrated both of their countries. It was a dangerous time that most people were blissfully ignorant about.

If something caused that border to close, he and Holly would be disconnected, like pulling a plug from its socket. Video calls and emails wouldn't cut it. Every second he'd spent with her convinced him that he'd found the woman he'd build a white picket fence for. Cut off from Holly would be like losing part of himself.

She was it.

The one for him.

No question.

The team guys said the first part of a relationship was the most exciting. And it was, but if he didn't do something, there was a risk of losing her. Gray wanted to hear Holly say fifty years from now, *"Remember when we...."*

Gray pulled into the secured area at the PU and parked the patrol car. About to unlock the door to his pickup, he received a text.

Holly's out of the picture. Meet me for a drink.

The ID showed it was from Kate. He could block her number but instead, he was going to let her hang herself.

Why would u think Holly's out of the picture?

Rumor has it she can't enter the US.

How do u know that?

If Kate believed her false accusation had worked, Holly would be safe for a while. If the psycho was trailing him, she'd eventually figure it out.

Meet me and I'll tell you.

Did you tell border patrol Holly was trafficking drugs?

Will u be angry if I did?

Did u?

His phone rang, but he didn't answer. Instead, he repeated the text.

Did you try to incriminate Holly on a false accusation?

It's our time. Meet me.

Don't contact me again, Kate.

Between the PU and the farmstead, his phone beeped ten more times with incoming texts. Parking in front of the old Victorian, he saw Ivy and Holly sitting on the porch. Monday morning he'd deal with his stalker. This weekend, Holly would have his undivided attention.

CHAPTER TWENTY-EIGHT

A mountain breeze fluttered the sheers on the open balcony window of their hotel room and cooled the sheen of sweat on Gray's heated skin.

Holly's body arched with passion. Her snug vaginal walls like a silky massage, squeezed his shaft and her soft moans drove him insane. Every deep thrust rippled through his body with sublime pleasure.

Gray's desire raced toward the point of no return. Tonight, she was too hot and wet for him to resist. Normally, he wore protection. But sometimes, like now, exercising immense willpower, he avoided a condom.

"Baby. Oh, shit. I gotta retreat." Wound too tight, he couldn't hold back.

She sucked on his bottom lip and gripped his right hip. "Please, Gray. Don't stop."

Her soft, sexy plea catapulted him toward the edge. Every thrust was pure erotic bliss. "Fuck, you feel amazing."

He palmed the mattress on either side of her shoulders and crested a massive wave of raw pleasure. His cum spilled into her hot core, and Holly cried out with her own climax. Her inner muscles spasmed around his pulsing shaft and felt so damn good.

The release rolled through his limbs and kept coming. Jesus! His eyes snapped shut and he slammed his hips against her body, his cock buried to the hilt.

She hummed with satisfaction, a sweet signal he liked to hear.

"You make me see stars, sweetheart."

She smiled at him. "I've got a big crush on you, Detective."

Gray rolled onto his back and chuckled. Stress wasn't a

word in his vocabulary anymore. If a man could say his life was almost perfect, he could. The only thing missing was the opportunity to hold her every day.

It had been a long, busy week since they'd seen each other. As summer marched forward, they'd found a routine. When they were apart, they texted first thing in the morning and talked on the phone before bed.

Twice, they'd done a video chat, but the minx had worn that damn black negligee. The little show she'd put on for him last night blew his mind. She'd teased her clit with a vibrator. Fucking hottest thing he'd seen but absolute torture to watch. His cock had thickened and pre-cum bulbed on his crown. Yet, she had a little sadist in her because she threatened to stop if he touched himself.

He obeyed. Begrudgingly.

When Holly arrived at the farmstead this afternoon, he was wired tight. Their weekend destination was only a three-hour drive, but it had nearly killed him. He'd considered parking at a deserted rest stop and making love to her in the truck but instead, he held her hand and enjoyed the scenery while he broke the speed limit. The second they dropped their bags in the hotel room, he was all over her.

Every weekend through July and the first part of August, he and Holly had experienced a new adventure. They'd investigated Orcas Island. Kayaked the Olympic Coast National Marine Sanctuary, Kalaloch. Spent a weekend in Seattle. Stayed in a cabin at Discovery Bay in Port Townsend. Camped at Lake Chelan with a side trip to Winthrop, where she'd dragged him through every tourist shop.

With their full schedules, the five days between their visits felt like starvation to him. The first thing they did on Friday evenings when they reunited was make love.

He and Holly had talked about so many topics, he couldn't remember half of them. But they also spent time in each other's arms as they watched the logs in a fire burn to hot coals without saying a word.

Each time they were together, the harder it was to see her leave. Out of respect, Holly never stayed overnight at the farmstead. The *End of Summer Blast* celebration was on August 27th, three weeks from now. He'd talk it over with the family, but he wanted Holly to stay at the farm that weekend.

She rolled onto her side. "What happened at Kate's internal hearing yesterday?"

He figured she'd ask. Gray had followed through, filing a complaint against the lieutenant in July.

After Holly was detained at the border because of the bogus drug claim, Billings' obsession for him intensified. Between then and the hearing yesterday, Kate had kept sending texts and showing up unexpectedly. He kept documenting, knowing it would only cement his claim.

He rolled onto his side. "Her union rep was good. She might have gotten away with it, except for her false report to Border Services. She couldn't back it up with evidence. Capt. Gordon flew up from San Diego as a witness that she'd stalked him too and what happened in his case."

"What was the final decision?"

"Kate lost her badge. I filed a protective order, and it was approved by a judge back in July."

She perched her head in her palm. "You didn't tell me that."

"Didn't tell you a lot because I didn't want you to worry. The order prohibits her from communicating with me or interacting with me in person. She's violated that order many times. Now she's been charged with a Class B Felony. Kate could face a prison term."

"She needs professional help."

"Hope they lock the bitch up for what she did to you."

He'd been so close to decking the psycho when Kate ambushed him in a parking lot, especially the first time after Holly's detention at the border. He and Cole had gone to Roosters for a brew, and she'd been waiting outside when they left the bar. Kate didn't care that Cole was standing right beside him, but it was a good thing he was.

Holly pressed a chaste kiss on his shoulder. "You're a hot ticket item, Detective. Hard to resist."

He'd already put the whole affair behind him. The more important issue at hand was gently teasing Holly's nipple between his thumb and index finger.

"When it comes to obsessions, I've got an untreatable addiction for my girlfriend."

Her tawny-colored nipples pebbled with his touch. He knew her body inside and out. Lately, her breasts seemed firmer and her hips a little curvier, which was fine by him.

She grinned and snuggled closer. "You have to be bored by now."

"Never." He dipped his head and suckled a tender peak, then said, "Be right back. Don't move."

He returned from the bathroom with a wet cloth and cupped the moist warmth against her sex.

"That feels nice," she said.

Gray loved that Holly's modesty in the bedroom had vanished. He washed the excess moisture from her skin, then dabbed her with a dry towel at the same time kissing her, an act he'd never done with any woman. But like everything else, his actions and intentions regarding Holly were hallowed ground, only meant for her.

She hooked her arm around his neck, her kisses like whispers against his cheek. There was something different about her. He sensed it.

Gray tossed the towels onto the guest chair next to the bedside table, then sat on the mattress. "Sweetheart, are you okay?"

She smiled but tears welled in her eyes.

"Hey, now. What's going on?"

She sat up and hugged him, resting her cheek against his chest. "Nothing," she whispered.

He caressed her back and stared at the salmon-colored

wall behind the headboard. Holly was more cuddly than usual this weekend, not that he minded. He loved holding her.

"It's getting harder, isn't it, babe?" Gray kissed the top of her head. "On Friday nights, I'm already thinking of having to watch you leave on Sundays."

She tipped her chin to look in his eyes. "It's worse today for some reason. It'll pass."

Holly sat cross-legged and he laid across the bed in front of her, then propped himself on one elbow. If honest, he didn't want it to pass. He wanted her to love him so badly, she couldn't live without him. Because that was the way he felt about her.

Gray trailed his fingertips over her breast, down her ribs, then thumbed her clit with tender, lazy strokes.

"I miss you," he said, brushing her perfect little bud. "I get home from work, change my clothes and do chores around the farm. But I think about you. I wonder what you're doing. Our weekends together are amazing, but when we're apart, it feels wrong."

"Me, too," she said quietly. "When I'm at home, sometimes I turn around, expecting to see you, but you're not there."

Holly untangled her legs and parted her thighs. She leaned back, propping herself up with straight arms. He loved her innocent sensuality. She was an open book and accepted him, flaws and all, exactly how he was.

"Is it wrong that I love it so much when you touch me?" she asked.

Slick cream coated her sex and stirred his cock back to life. He grinned. "No. Truth is, I can't get enough. You're so damn irresistible."

He sat up and shifted onto his knees, then laved her firm nipple. She inhaled sharply and her soft hand clasped his thickening penis. Gray leaned forward and kissed her. Their tongues met and teased each other.

"Roll onto your stomach, babe."

"A massage? Yes, please." She grinned and did what he asked.

He chuckled. "No, sweetheart. That live video performance last night was torture. You gotta know I'm not letting you get away with that."

Holly laughed. "Oh, come on. You loved it."

"You bet I did."

She gasped when he spread her legs and eased two fingers into her slick pussy. This was her favorite. She lost her mind when he finger fucked her while she lay on her stomach.

Holly had admitted her sexual experiences had been bland until they'd met. Of course, Kevin had been the sole source and too fucking stupid to realize what he had.

Thank God for that.

With her shyness long gone, she loved to experiment. He'd done things to her body she'd never expected but enjoyed immensely.

When the first whimper erupted from her mouth and her fingernails curled into the sheets, he grinned. His cock was too thick for her anus, but he'd upped their lovemaking by covering his thumb with her body's lube and strummed her little star when she was losing her mind, like now.

He kissed her butt cheek, then reached under the pillow where he'd stashed a new toy.

"I promised that once your knee healed, I'd show no mercy." Gray pulled a small, stainless steel butt plug from its hiding place.

"Is that—?"

He reached for the lube he'd left on the bedside table, then gave her sweet ass and the plug a liberal dose.

"Grayson, I'm not sure."

He brushed the slender tip against her star. "I'd never hurt you, babe. You know that, right?"

"I know, but—"

"Then on your knees, because this is going to blow your

mind."

She did as he asked.

Teasing the small, tapered toy at her entrance, he eased the tip inside, rocking it as he inserted. He coached her, not rushing the process.

Gray praised her when the plug was in all the way and strummed her clit with his thumb.

"Feels full," she said.

Gray clicked a button on the edge of the jewel-topped end and the vibration made her gasp. He gently palmed her ass. "You're beautiful. Does it feel good?"

"Yes," she gushed.

Sinking his erection deep in her core was his first thought, but Holly was so damn responsive she'd come in seconds. Instead, he used one finger in her vagina with a slow rhythm.

She pressed her forehead against the mattress and lifted her ass in the air. "Oh, yes!"

If he was going to make her come, he wanted her to fly apart. Gray rolled onto his back and slid between her parted thighs. He tucked a pillow under his head, then slowly lapped her sensitive clit before inserting three fingers.

"Shit. Shit. Shit." She moaned and rocked her hips.

"Mmm, nice."

Holly's cries got closer together. He loved edging her. She hated him for doing it but loved when he finally let her come. He teased the tip of his tongue along her slit with generous pauses in between.

"Not fair," she breathed.

He sipped on her sweet sex and swirled his tongue.

She groaned and gasped her pleasure. "Gray, make me come."

"Not yet, baby."

Teasing and tasting her firm nub stiffened his cock. He coiled his hand around his erection. Flattening his tongue, he lapped her sweetness and fingered her with the same cadence he stroked his dick.

She uttered a series of wispy "ohs."

A knot formed deep in his spine. On the verge, he squeezed her firm bundle of nerves between his lips and suckled.

His pulse thudded, but his hand wasn't enough to get him there. "Holly. Ride me, babe."

She shimmied down his body and eased her blistering hot core over his shaft.

The vibration from the plug and her tight channel was fucking incredible. Holly pistoned her hips, milking the hell out of his cock.

"Gray. Oh, God. So good."

He thrust his hips upward to meet each silky plunge. The buzz from the plug made the tip of his dick ultra-sensitive. Holly slowed her cadence, finding the sweet spot, and they drifted in the ecstasy.

"Shit, babe. Yeah. Just like that." He swept his thumb back and forth over her clit.

Holly grasped his shoulders and cried out, her body shaking with release. Cum exploded from his crown in hard pulses, and the nerves in his body roared with satisfaction.

After catching his breath and his heart rate eased, he slid his hand up Holly's thigh and palmed her hip. Her nipples grazed his chest as she leaned forward to kiss him, and he gently removed the plug.

She rolled onto her back and closed her eyes, looking extremely satiated. He'd tuckered out his sweetheart. Gray clicked the button on the toy and set it aside. When he lay on his back, she snuggled into his side and kissed his chest, then his shoulder.

Jesus, could he love this woman more than he already did?

"Next time, it's your turn," she said in a sexy tone.

Yes, he could love her more. He didn't fuck everything on two legs like Dirk, but it was through the experiences with him that he'd learned orgasm by teasing the prostate had a deeper penetrating release. But with Holly, he wasn't missing out.

He grinned and touched his nose to hers. "I'm all yours if you want to play with me."

"You're kind of turning me into a naughty girl."

He sighed and gently nibbled on her bottom lip. "Then all my hard work paid off."

"Do I make you hungry?"

Yeah, he was starving too. "You ready for some good Bavarian food?"

"And a huge mug of icy cold, malt beer," she added.

This weekend they'd decided to stay in Leavenworth, a replica of a Bavarian village with tons of little shops filled with knickknacks, which—*groan*—she loved. Wasn't easy to get a room in the popular tourist town.

He lifted his wrist. Six o'clock. "Let's put some schnitzel and booze into you."

"Sounds good. I'll take a shower."

"'Kay, be right behind ya."

She scrambled over his legs, and he watched her stroll toward the bathroom, her long, black hair raining down her back. *Homely, my ass.* She was fucking beautiful, and she was his.

"Hey."

She stopped and turned a look over her shoulder.

"I'm a lucky man."

Holly blew him a kiss then entered the bathroom.

Gray's cell rang. He swung his legs over the side of the bed and stretched to reach his jeans on the chair.

Caller unknown. Huh. If this was Kate phoning from the county jail, she'd just wasted a fucking quarter.

"Hello."

"Hey, Bone. How are ya, man?"

Took him a second, but then the voice gelled in his brain. "Anson. How the hell have you been?"

"Good. Listen, I was talking with Checkers the other day. He told me you'd left the teams and joined the sheriff's department."

Gray kept in touch with a few guys he'd served with. Checkers, aka, Rod Bradner, was one of them. He'd just talked with Check last week.

"That's right. Five years, now. I keep tabs on you. Hard not to."

"Yeah, well that's why I'm calling. I'm lining up a new season of videos for the channel. We want to do something different, focusing on life after the teams, especially guys like you that went onto other careers like law enforcement. Checkers also told me you finally settled down with a lady named Holly. Think I got that right."

"Yeah, you got that right."

"We'd like the Frogs we're inviting on the show to bring their significant others."

"Holly and I weren't together when I served."

"Doesn't matter. She's with you now and her perspective counts," he paused then chuckled. "So, says my wife. What d'ya think. Interested?"

"Let me talk with Holly and get back to you. When is this going down?"

"We film here in Texas, but I'm juggling two other couples as well. I was hoping next week."

Whoa. That was short notice. "Holly works at the university as an ancient language researcher. I don't know if she can swing that, and I'm collecting intel on a warehouse we're going to bust. If we came, it would have to be a quick in and out."

"No problem, Gray. Talk to Holly, and I'll pencil it in for the weekend. We're not going to be in the studio this time. Just hanging around the fire pit at my ranch. Fly in Saturday and extract Sunday. I'll arrange the tickets and the hotel."

"Tempting. Who else is coming?"

"Check is bringing his wife and, believe it or not, I've got

Admiral Austen and his wife, Kayla, on the hook."

"You're kidding. Did the admiral retire?"

"No, but he's not Commander of the West Coast Chain any longer." Anson chuckled. "If he's available, I'm not missing the chance to have him on the show."

"What's he doing now?"

"No one really knows, but you can bet its top-level shit. Kayla has her own story, of course, and I think viewers will be interested to hear how they met."

Gray snorted. "Fuck, yeah. I was at N.A.B when that went down. Ghost certainly went the distance for her."

"No shit. I've gotta run, but call me after you talk with Holly. Really love for both of you to be on the show."

"All right. Talk soon."

Holly came out of the bathroom with a white towel wrapped around her body while drying her dripping hair with another towel.

"You leave me any dry towels?"

"Nope," she chirped.

"Woman, you're crossing the line."

She wrinkled her nose at him. "You don't scare me, big guy."

He strode across the carpet, yanked the towel from her body as he passed, and draped it over his shoulder.

"Grayson!"

Midway through the shower with his head tilted back, washing soap out of his eyes, the wicked wench ambushed him.

"Fuuuuck!"

Holly hit him with a bucket of freezing ice water and scampered from the bathroom, laughing her head off.

"You just earned yourself one helluva spanking!" he shouted.

* * * *

By seven p.m., they were seated at one of the many restaurants in Leavenworth. The server planted two mugs of icy, dark beer on their table. They ordered, and Gray lifted his sweaty mug. Holly used two hands to lift hers.

"Thanks for falling in love with me, beautiful."

Thinking she wasn't going to say anything, he took a huge swallow of malt beer.

"Thanks for the butt plug, honey."

Caught off guard, he laughed and sucked the beer down his windpipe. Holly giggled while he coughed up the remnants. What the hell could he say to that?

After clearing his throat, he reached across the table and held her hands. "I got a call from an old teammate while you were in the shower. He has a popular channel on social media and asked if we'd like to be on the show."

Holly's eyes rounded. "On the show? Wait, you said, 'we.'"

"That's right. You and me."

"Who is this person?" she asked as the server delivered a basket of rye bread with slabs of cold butter on the side.

Gray picked up his phone and Googled Anson, then turned the cell so she could see. Holly's mouth draped open like the rear hatch on a C-5 Galaxy.

"Are you fucking kidding me? That Anson?"

He barked with laughter. Holly never swore. It certainly packed a punch when she did.

"Problem?" he asked innocently.

"But that's...he's...I mean...Grayson, are you pulling my leg?"

"Sweetheart, if I'm going to pull on anything, it's not going to be your leg. Truth is, he's not the most famous guy who'll be on the show with us."

"He isn't?"

"No, Admiral Thane Austen will be there. You probably never heard of him, but to guys like us, he's a legend."

After filling Holly in on the admiral's service to his

country, Holly sat back looking stunned.

"Um."

There was that cue. Whenever she was shocked or unsure, her vocabulary shrunk to one word. "Anson is footing the bill for us to fly out there and stay one night. It would be a quick turnaround."

"Where's *there*? And when?"

Their meals arrived. Huge, oval plates covered with Jaeger Schnitzel, red cabbage, and spätzle were settled on the table.

The twenty-something server wearing braided pigtails and a pinafore dress, pointed at his empty. "Another beer?"

"Sure. Why not."

She collected his mug and hustled to a table of new guests.

"Texas," he said to Holly. Her jaw stopped chewing. "Saturday."

"Next Saturday?"

He sawed a piece of schnitzel drowning in mushroom gravy. "You got it." He shoved the food into his mouth while he had the chance.

"Why would they want me there? I'm not a SEAL wife."

The food hit his stomach and gurgled with happiness. Damn, this stuff was good. "I'm a retired SEAL and you *will* be my wife."

The response shot out of his mouth without taking a second to stop at the crosswalk before rushing across the street. The clank of cutlery forced him to look across the table.

Holly swallowed and blinked at him.

Her eyes so round, they reminded him of an owl. *Shit!*

He slowly lowered his knife and fork, suddenly feeling as if he was traversing a field of land mines. Her gaze bounced around the restaurant and finally came to rest on him.

"Grayson, that's never going to happen," she said in a soft voice. "Kevin's right. I am...mundane. Sooner than later, you'll send a text telling me it's been a slice, but you've found someone else. I'm prepared for that."

"What?" She floored him. He saw in her beautiful grey eyes that she actually believed what she'd just said. "How many times have I told you that I love you? You...you think I'm lying?" he choked out.

"No," she said calmly. "But saying or even feeling that you love someone doesn't mean you won't be drawn to some incredibly beautiful woman who catches your eye one day."

His pulse beat at a frantic pace. "You really believe that, don't you? That sonofabitch you married didn't just burn you, he scarred you for life."

"I'm not scarred." Her gaze dropped to her plate, staring at the mound of food. "By now, you know that I'm a pragmatist. There are facts and assertions. One doesn't necessarily make the other truth. Sitting on an aircraft, passengers rely on the assertion that planes rarely crash. But when it's lying in a mangled, burning heap on the ground, the facts prove otherwise."

He had two choices: Walk straight out the doors of the restaurant to cool off and figure this out or make this the hill he died on.

"You made my point perfectly. Not every marriage ends in a crash, Holly. Millions of times, it goes from Point A and lands sixty fucking years later at Point B with matching headstones and your kids laying flowers at your grave. Like my parents."

Holly's face collapsed with distress. "Oh, Grayson, I'm sorry. I didn't mean to—"

He held up his hand for her to stop talking. "You didn't. I did. Do you actually think that with my past, I would entertain a future with you if I thought for one second I could be lured by another woman? Or is it probable my mind is made up? That a guy like me, who's screwed what's equal to a small country of women, doesn't know how special you are."

"I—"

"No," he said sharply before she tried to veer off course. "Answer the question."

Holly's gaze jumped to the nearest tables, but no one paid attention to them. He saw her hesitation. Her doubt. He was three weeks from executing what he'd planned to the last detail. If that weren't the case, he'd drag her back to the hotel room and make her repeat *"I believe you"* until she damn well did, then ask her to marry him.

"Holly, I have never, ever, uttered those words to another woman. No one can steer me away from you." Around her neck, she wore his Trident. As far as he knew, she'd never taken it off since the day he'd given it to her.

Then he got an idea. "Those books you used to read. What's the one theme they all have in common?"

Her smooth brow wrinkled. "A happily ever after. The playboy or hard-to-crack SEAL finally falls in love."

"And does he vow that he'll love her?"

"Yyyes."

"And is she his 'it' girl, the woman he can't live without?"

"Gray—"

"Is she?"

"Yes."

"And even if he's had a questionable past, does she find the strength to stand beside him and trust him?"

Holly's grey eyes welled with tears.

"Yes," she whispered.

He leaned back against the cool leather chair and crossed his arms over his chest. "Then you can stick your assertions up your ass because the fact is, I want you, I love you, and I'm keeping you."

"Excuse me, dear."

Both he and Holly turned their heads toward a woman in her seventies, sitting at the next table with her husband.

The senior citizen smiled warmly. "If I were you, honey, I'd keep him too. That's the sweetest proposal I've ever heard."

Her husband, a man of the same vintage said, "Linda, mind your business. It's a lover's quarrel, not a proposal. They'll work it out. Besides, look at those tattoos on his arm. He's served this country. Easy to see he won't give her up without a fight."

"Thank you," Grayson said, somewhat vindicated. "And you're right, I'm not giving up." He shifted his gaze to Holly. "If you want to introduce me as your *boyfriend* when we're eighty, be my guest."

Holly rolled her eyes. "You told me from the start, those books were bullpucky. Eat your dinner, it's getting cold."

Damn, he hated when his own words bit him in the ass, but he'd gotten his point across. Gray winked at the old woman. Her soft, weathered skin tightened with a shy smile, and she turned her attention back to her husband.

An hour later, they strolled down the main street, peering in the windows of the closed shops.

"I have to come back to this place tomorrow when it's open," she said, holding a hand to the glass and checking out the specialty Christmas decorations store.

Holly said that with practically every shop on the main drag. The one thing she avoided talking about was their previous conversation. He wasn't entirely sure she wouldn't bolt across the border Sunday night and go dark.

"Woo, look!" She pointed at a sign hanging over a store. "Ice cream."

He grabbed her hand and steered it to his lips, kissing her knuckles. It was time to rip off the bandage. And there was a very good chance he'd bleed to death.

"Holly, if you're going to break my heart, then do it now. If you actually think I'm not committed to you and too weak to resist temptation, then you need to end this."

Calling her bluff wasn't the smartest thing he'd done, but she had to face the truth, or her fears would fester.

Her pretty eyes gazed up at him. "I don't know what you

want me to say, Grayson."

Across the street was a small, grass-covered area with a large gazebo. Couples and families moseyed about. Some watched as their children romped around. Some folks walked their dogs.

"Choices, Holly. Right now, we're standing on this side of the street." He pointed at the park. "But I want to be over there with you, like those people. Committed to each other and watching their children play." Gray flattened her palm over his heart. "The only roadblock between here and there is your faith in me. Until today, I never realized I'd lost it."

"You didn't lose it."

"Then I never had it." He clenched his jaw against the thought. "You and me, Holly. We're the real deal. You need to accept that."

Her shoulders drooped and her eyes strayed toward the park. "May I think about it?"

"No, you may not," he said briskly, and hid a grin.

"I love you." She brushed an open hand down his arm. "But that's not enough, is it?"

Three young women strolled past, wearing shorts and tanks, their eyes glued to him. Two of them turned their heads to survey Holly.

One of the girls whispered, "Oh my, God, he's hot."

Her friends giggled and they swaggered down the street, high on youth and having a good time.

"Is love enough?" he repeated. "With you? Not even close."

She narrowed an eye. "Are you saying this is an all-or-nothing deal?"

He gazed over her head at the quaint town with tree-capped mountains in the background. "That's what I'm saying."

"Is that a dare or a proposal, Detective?"

He clenched his teeth. Don't do it! He had a plan and was sticking to the plan.

"I don't beat around the bush, Miss McNeela. When I propose, you'll know."

Holly's slender arms slid around his waist and a mischievous twinkle shone in her eyes. "So, if I bared my soul and admitted that I'm scared but willing to risk it all on you, then you'll love me until the end of time, and I have nothing to worry about."

Was that sarcasm he smelled in the air? "Exactly."

"And I should trust you because," she paused and raised her eyebrow, "Oh my God, you're so hot, and no woman is going to put the moves on you," she said, emulating the girl who'd walked by.

He snorted. "Are you questioning my morals?"

"No, but I really want to go back to the room and make you come with our new toy."

Playful, she snuggled closer. Holly totally disarmed him when she did that. "Don't try to distract me with an orgasm. I want an honest answer and a promise."

"I promise to give you an honest answer if you're foolish enough to propose."

Jesus H. Christ. This was the problem with falling in love with a woman packing intelligence and wit in her toolbox. They'd reached a stalemate and he had to suck it up.

"Are we going to Texas?"

"Yes, we're going to Texas. Can I have ice cream now?"

She'd polished off her entire dinner. How did she have room for ice cream?

"You can have whatever you want, sweetheart." He lowered his head and kissed her nose.

"Oh, one more thing."

She usually had a punchline, so he waited, but by God, he was gonna have the last word this time.

"Grayson Brooks." Her hands roved up his chest and curled around his neck. "I've thought about being on the other side of the street with you too, but we're like two cars on a double-lane freeway with different destinations."

"I know, sweetheart. But once you believe that I love you, we'll be in the same car."

He buried his fingers in her luscious curls and laid a languid, sensual kiss on her pillowy lips. The kind of kiss that declared he loved her above all else, because he did. Always.

CHAPTER TWENTY-NINE

T he Houston airport hummed with activity. Holly held Grayson's hand as they walked through the terminal and bypassed the luggage carousel surrounded by passengers from their flight. They'd packed light, each carrying one overnight bag. People reminiscent of ants, zigged and zagged, hugged and waved.

She and Grayson exited through the arrival's level and without pausing, he hung a left. The moist heat hit Holly square in the face. It had to be over a hundred degrees.

"Have you been here before?" she asked.

"Long time ago."

They strode past a line of people waiting for cabs. An endless stream of cars and hotel shuttles rolled by the terminal.

A distinct whistle, almost like bird song, made Grayson stop and scan the area. Looking across three lanes of traffic, he lifted his hand to signal he'd seen someone.

"He's over there."

Anson had said he'd pick them up from the airport. A break in the traffic allowed Holly and Grayson to navigate the roadway in a way that resembled a Pacman video game.

When they reached the other side, Grayson's old teammate grinned. "Bone, you ugly sonofabitch."

"You got fat, Frog."

Anson laughed and the men clasped hands with a thunderous clap and then did what Holly called the man-hug with a slap on the back.

To say she was nervous would be an understatement. When Anson turned his brown eyes on her, he reminded her of a Teddy Bear with a beard, not a deadly warrior who'd become a global phenomenon when Hollywood released a movie based on this man's fight to survive during a military operation.

"Anson, like you to meet Holly McNeela."

He clasped her hand for a gentle shake. "Glad you came, Holly. My wife, Beth, and the other wives are looking forward to meeting the gal who managed to put a collar on this guy."

"It's an honor to meet you, sir."

He raised his hand. "Ho, no. I'm no *sir*. You can save that for the admiral."

"Are we the last to arrive?" Gray asked.

"Yep, Checkers and Ghost came in on the same flight about four hours ago. Let's get on the road. It's a forty-five-minute drive to the ranch."

When they reached Anson's black SUV on the second level of the parkade, she scrambled into the backseat, certain Gray and their host had plenty of reminiscing to do. Anson got behind the wheel and turned a look over his shoulder, just as Gray leaned forward and kissed her.

"Holly, why don't you take the front seat?" Gray suggested.

"I don't mind. I'm sure you have plenty to talk about."

He took the seatbelt buckle from her and clicked it into the latch at the same time kissing her again.

"This should be fun," Anson said in a baritone voice. "Bone, you sure you don't want to sit back there and make out for an hour? I promise not to look."

He chuckled. "You can kiss my ass, Frog."

Gray winked at her and closed the rear door.

There'd been a change of plans. Instead of a hotel, Anson had invited them to stay at the ranch. It made life easier for their host and them. Grayson told her that Anson and his wife owned a large ranch with cabins to house their guests.

For Holly, the experience of listening to the men talk was enlightening. She had zero exposure to the military until she'd met Grayson. The men's terminology and acronyms were one thing, but they communicated in the same fashion with quick, decisive speech patterns. They talked about places she'd never heard of, people she didn't know, and combat equipment she'd never set eyes on.

Though both men had retired from Special Forces, their training made them brothers for life. What she'd perceived as harsh and edgy characteristics, were common in both men. They operated on a different frequency than civilians without military backgrounds. Witnessing their reunion, she surmised that their training and missions had carved a *never quit* attitude deep in their psychological character.

From the airport until they drove down a long gravel drive lined with oaks and ash trees, Anson and Gray never paused for a breath.

The topography was different than what she'd expected. Instead of a sea of flat, barren ground, Anson's ranch boasted hay fields and watering systems. They drove by a herd of horses nibbling on lush, green shoots in the front pasture.

They'd made it to the ranch by noon and on schedule.

As they neared the house, two yellow Labs and a Shepard ran alongside the SUV, barking. Anson parked near a two-story home. Not more than a hundred paces away were ten small cabins. Planted in the lawn in front of the accommodations was a tall pole with a large American flag flapping in the breeze.

Holly stepped out of the vehicle and the dogs sniffed her legs while Grayson lifted the back hatch and retrieved their luggage.

"I'll take ya inside to say hello and then show you where you're bunking," Anson said.

As they approached the front door, it swung open and a guy much lighter in frame than Anson and Gray vaulted from inside.

"Bone! Bring it in." The guy whose arms were covered in tats like Anson's surged forward for a big, no-holds-barred hug on Grayson.

"Been too long, Check!"

Checkers wore a green ball cap and an Army-green t-shirt. Built with lean muscles and standing about six feet, he exuded the same aura as the other men; raw male testosterone.

Another man exited the front door of the home and she unintentionally held her breath. Somewhere in his mid to late forties, Holly instinctively knew this was the type of man who ate lightning and crapped thunder. His stride wafted with confidence. Like Grayson, he had sharp, brilliant blue eyes and trimmed, dirty-blond hair. What Holly couldn't ignore was the man's aura, which pulsed with bold authority.

Grayson saw him and his shoulders straightened.

"Admiral," he greeted.

"Petty Officer Brooks, been a long time."

The man's strong timbre fitted his stature.

"Yes, sir," Grayson said, extending his hand.

Unlike with Anson and Checkers, complete reverence saturated Gray's tone when he addressed the admiral.

Gray backed up a step and wrapped his arm around her shoulders. "Gentlemen, like you to meet Holly McNeela."

The admiral stepped forward. A wicked scar, although years healed, ran down the man's cheek and onto his jaw. Although extremely handsome in the same rugged, weathered way as Grayson, the scar made him look dangerous.

"Hello, Holly. It's a pleasure."

"Mine as well, Admiral Austen. I'm certainly pleased to be here."

"Admiral is fine for these characters, but please call me Thane."

"Respectfully, sir, Grayson told me about your dedication and years of distinguished service to the United States. Admiral is most appropriate."

In mid-shake, he paused and cocked his head slightly. He glanced at Gray then back at her, and a slight grin lifted his mouth, exchanging his intimidating presence to, dare she say, heart-stopping handsome.

"My wife, Kayla, was born and raised in Canada as well."

Her mouth formed an "O" of shock. "How?"

Gray shook his head. "How is it everyone has that figured out but me?"

Admiral Austen's lips stretched into a broad smile and caused her pulse to beat faster.

"Her accent," he answered.

"No disrespect, sir, but there's no fucking accent."

The admiral and Holly both laughed at Gray's puzzlement.

"Believe me, Brooks, when she gets pissed at you, you'll definitely hear the accent. Mademoiselle, parlez-vous francais?"

"No, unfortunately my French is sadly lacking, Admiral."

"My wife made it a point to teach both our children. They're fully bilingual."

"How old are they?"

"Our son, Adam, is nine, and our daughter, Sloane, is seven."

"I have nieces and nephews Sloane's age."

Checkers winked at her, then said, "Are ya gonna hog her the whole time, Admiral, or do I get to say hello?"

She got the feeling he sported a sense of humor and healthy dose of cockiness. "Nice to meet you too. Should I call you Rod or Checkers?"

He palmed her shoulders. "Holly, you can call me whatever you want." As if they'd been friends forever, he stepped to her side and draped his arm over her shoulders. "Look at her. You see it, right?"

The admiral shot Gray a conspiratorial look.

"I'm sorry, I don't understand," she said.

One of the admiral's monstrously broad shoulders tipped

upward. "Yes, I see it, Checkers."

"Huh." Gray nodded. "Now that you mention it, Check, yeah, I guess I do too. Just going by memory though. It's been a long time since I've seen Kayla."

"Well, she's inside and waiting to say hello," Admiral Austen stated. "We left the kids at home. Marg Cobbs is babysitting."

Holly didn't know who Marg was but saw the other men nodding in a solemn fashion.

No one explained what Checkers referred to when he asked the other men if they *saw it*, but she wasn't left to wonder long.

Inside the modern, southwestern-decorated home, more hellos were exchanged, and a woman with raven-colored curls, identical to her own, stepped forward.

"Hello, Holly," she greeted. "I'm Kayla Austen."

Although Kayla's eyes were so brown they were almost black, the similarities between herself and the admiral's wife were too many to ignore. "Nice to meet you, Kayla."

She was introduced to Beth, Anson's wife, and Tammy, Checkers' wife.

"Lunch is served," Beth announced, and they all gathered around a massive, rustic pine table to break bread together.

* * * *

After lunch was finished, Grayson and the other men got to their feet.

Anson shoved his chair under the table. "I'm taking the guys into town. Shouldn't be gone more than a few hours."

Gray walked around the table large enough to feed twelve people to stand behind her chair and put his mouth to her ear. "Sweetheart, I'm going to stow our bags in the cabin first. Anything you need from town?"

"Nothing I can think of."

He kissed her on the cheek then whispered, "I love you,

babe."

She turned her head to face him, and Gray placed a very long and heated kiss on her mouth.

"See you soon." When she glanced at the women, they all smiled.

The men scattered and Holly rose to help clean off the table. Kayla, Tammy, and Beth all seemed to know each other. She was the odd man out. Throughout the conversations during lunch, she'd gleaned that all three women had been with or married to their SEALs during their service years. In essence, Holly felt like a runner-up because she didn't know what that was like. The books she'd read described the independent nature these strong women possessed when their warriors had deployed.

Once the dishes were done and leftovers put away, Beth, a lovely woman in her thirties with a gracious smile and gorgeous brunette hair, announced, "Time for us to have a little fun. Follow me, ladies."

Beth led them to a large metal garage and opened the twenty-foot-high door, revealing several ATVs.

After a crash course on how to operate the machines, they donned their helmets and headed out on a well-worn trail. Rolling hills melted into flat plains under a crystal blue sky. They stopped often to enjoy the vistas. Beth toured them through the thousand-acre ranch. Three hours later, they returned to the house and retired to the patio for drinks.

During lunch, Tammy and Beth had mostly talked about their kids. Kayla, however, seemed to bounce between the men's conversations about team business and the women's conversations about family. The admiral's wife seemed to understand the unique military linguistics the men used, as if she were familiar in a professional way with the SEALs' operations.

Holly and the other women settled outside under a covered patio with cold refreshments. Thirty feet from the house, a large fire pit and Adirondack chairs sat on a circular-shaped brick patio. Grayson had mentioned the video would be filmed in a casual atmosphere around the fire. There was also a large, rectangular swimming pool that looked truly inviting in this heat.

Kayla sipped on a dewy glass of lemonade, then said, "Checkers looks like he's doing better."

Tammy, a woman with dazzling red hair, nodded and sat back in her chair. "Our trip to Mexico was amazing. The difference in Rod is night and day. Almost like I've got my husband back."

Beth reached across the wooden tabletop and gripped her hand in a squeeze of support. "It takes time and patience, right?"

Tammy's sympathetic green eyes glistened with a sheen of unshed tears. "Thanks to you and Anson. You helped him take that step. It probably won't last, but I'll take what I can get."

Holly sat quietly, observing. Burrowing into their personal affairs didn't seem appropriate.

Tammy shifted her gaze across the table toward Holly. "Rod was an explosives breacher in the teams. After fifteen years, he finally got out. But he has microscopic tears in his brain tissue due to the heavy blasts during combat."

"I'm sorry. I assume there's no cure for something like that," Holly said.

Tammy shook her head. "No. But awareness and more research are needed. My husband isn't the same man I married. Military personnel often experience physical and emotional issues. Headaches, difficulty sleeping, trouble concentrating, irritability and memory problems. Rod has all those symptoms. But his character changed dramatically in the last couple years of his service and steadily got worse. It almost ended our marriage."

Holly could only imagine how difficult that must have been on their family. "And there's a treatment in Mexico?"

Beth refilled her glass with ice water. "Yes. The treatment

uses Ibogaine, an alkaloid extracted from the root of a plant native to Africa. It's an illegal substance in the US but our medicine wasn't helping. Anson went through the therapy with remarkable success. We've been sharing our experience with others. It's not a cure, but I don't give a rat's ass what the medical bureaucrats with bloated bank accounts tout from their gleaming offices. If there's a therapy that stops the torment my husband endures, we'll do it."

Holly heard the unwavering determination in Beth's voice. "The therapy sounds promising."

"Anson and I also host weekends here at the ranch where families who experience post-service issues can share their problems and discuss treatment options. The worst thing is to suffer in silence."

Holly could tell by the way Beth and Tammy spoke that the men they loved weren't the indestructible heroes fiction often portrayed. But the women certainly proved that a SEAL wife bravely stood by her warrior.

Kayla said, "Beth mentioned that your and Grayson's relationship is relatively new."

"It is." She set her glass of lemonade on the table. "We met in May. I often visit a resort just across the border from where I live. Gray and his partner, Cole, were investigating a slew of thefts that occurred at the resort. We crossed paths by accident a few times. Then in June, I was attacked while leaving the resort. Grayson attended the incident and helped me."

"Did they catch the guy?" Kayla asked.

"Gray and Det. Sterling arrested and charged the man, but they haven't brought down the criminal ring he's associated with."

Beth grinned. "Sounds to me like you skipped over an important part of the story."

Tammy gave her a friendly swat on the shoulder. "Don't be nosy."

Although the women were friendly, Holly felt out of

place in their presence. Since Beth and Anson hosted the show they'd be filming later, she swung her attention to the brunette.

"I was thinking that maybe I should excuse myself from the video tonight. You're all a very unique league of women. I can't imagine the strength it took to navigate your husbands' time in the teams and their challenges with medical issues." She gnawed on her lip for a second. "The truth is, Gray and I live in different countries. We both have responsibilities and careers that aren't likely to change. I look ahead and I can't see a future where our paths will cross." Holly paused, wondering how much she should reveal to these women who were, in fact, strangers. "Grayson admitted that he isn't a long-term relationship kind of man. Personally, I think he's going through a phase, and I just happen to be part of that."

Tammy grinned. "The way he kissed you earlier didn't look that way to me."

Beth nodded. "And I'm pretty sure I heard him say he loved you. That's not a phase. It's a commitment."

Kayla leaned forward, resting her forearms on the table, and forked her fingers. "Holly, all of us have a story. When I met Thane, he was my commanding officer. A relationship between us was strictly forbidden. I was pregnant with our son, Adam, when the brass found out Thane was the father. My career was on the chopping block. Thane told the brass he'd leave N.A.B so I wouldn't lose my job. He was so valuable to the Special Forces they promoted him, but the new position was in Hawaii. He'd proven over and over again that I could trust him. Yet, the hardest thing I ever had to do was have faith in him, but I chose Thane."

Tammy laughed. "Now look who's leaving a huge part of the story untold." She looked at Holly. "Ghost—that's the admiral's team name—tracked a serial killer who'd put his sights on Kayla. In the end, he killed the guy when the bastard took her hostage."

Stunned, Holly gaped at the admiral's wife. "A serial

killer? Really?"

Kayla nodded. "My point is, I used to think my career defined me, and it did at one time. I fell for a man who was committed to dying by the sword and viewed women like Grayson did—a brief reprieve. When we met, Thane changed, and so did I. If I hadn't taken a chance on him, I wouldn't have my beautiful children and a life I'd never trade." She smiled and a sympathetic notch settled on her brow. "Men like ours are extremely focused. When faced with an emotion like love, some of them see it as a distraction. Believe me, the warrior inside them puts up a fight."

Tammy nodded. "How is Grayson doing?"

Holly wasn't sure how to answer. With the wives educating her on combat trauma, she wondered if Gray had walked away unscathed from his time with the SEALs like he thought he had. She also got the distinct feeling that she didn't know Grayson at all. He'd never spoken about his time in the Special Forces.

"Why do you ask?"

"Rod's concerned. He keeps in touch with Grayson. Most SEALs go through some kind of separation anxiety after leaving the teams. Gray didn't. He jumped right into another career."

"And that's uncommon?" Holly asked.

Beth refilled her glass and said, "Depends on the man. Gray got out after ten or so years, but he chose another challenging career in law enforcement. That's not uncommon. Plenty of team guys get into private contracting or shift to the CIA or Homeland Security. Others choose a completely different route."

"I met Dirk Larkin recently," Holly said, trying to shift the conversation away from Grayson.

Kayla's brows rose. "Chief Larkin? How's he doing?"

"Finished his Archeology Degree and works with his father. I'm currently researching two tablets they discovered in Jerusalem."

Tammy chuckled. "Now that guy was a player. He ever settle down?"

Holly shrugged. "Not that I know of. Beth, can I use your washroom?"

"Of course."

She excused herself and used the facilities but instead of rejoining the women, Holly walked out the front door and strode across the gravel driveway, wandering toward a large pond surrounded by a manicured lawn. She stopped to watch three colorful birds near the water's edge, pecking at the moist mud. Summer bugs created a synchronized buzz in the hay field to her right. She strode toward the wood fence and propped her arms on the top board.

Holly didn't hear Grayson approach until he stood right next to her.

"Everything okay?" he asked.

She nodded. "How was the trip into town?"

"Good."

Holly watched the tall grass sway in the wind. In truth, she felt out of sorts after speaking with the women.

Gray cleared his throat and assumed the same pose with his forearms perched across the fence board. "You're unusually quiet."

"I hope you understand, but I excused myself from the video this evening."

Gray gently gripped her shoulder and urged her to turn and face him. "Why?"

"The women asked me how you were doing. I have nothing to compare to and you've never talked about your service. The show is about moving forward after team life. There's nothing I can offer that's of value."

He nipped at the edge of his lip and turned his gaze toward the field. "I served and I retired. I told you why I didn't sign up for another term."

She didn't want to make a big issue out of this. "You did. And that's fine. I find it especially heartbreaking and unfair that Beth and Tammy endured the hardships of marriage to a SEAL, only to be faced with daunting medical issues once their husbands retired."

Grayson's blue gaze crisscrossed her face. "Yeah, I know. Check had a hard go there for a while, but he's doing better. We keep in touch."

"Apparently, he's concerned about you too. But I'm not clear on why that is. Maybe mental or emotional issues. I don't know."

The Lab trotted to the pond, nose down, sniffing his way around the circumference and chasing the wild birds into the air.

"Holly, some Frogs get a little lost when they leave the teams. I chose a new direction. Law enforcement suited me and helped me transition. I have a supportive family and I'm in a good place."

She glanced toward the house and saw the other three men head in the front door. "I get the feeling that you're hiding something from me, but I'm not concerned."

"I'm fine."

Then why did her instincts say otherwise? "Okay."

"No, not okay. I can see there's something wrong."

"Nothing I can put into words except to say that right now, I feel like I don't know who you are."

A sympathetic smile crowned his mouth, and he slid his arms around her waist. "Aw, sweetheart, that's not true. But —maybe there is something we should discuss."

She eased out of his grasp. "As in?"

Gray's chest expanded with a deep inhale and his eyes surveyed the landscape behind her for a few seconds. "It wasn't something I wanted to share when we became a couple."

She didn't like the sound of this, but she nodded for him to keep going.

"Guess I should just tell it to you straight and hope that it doesn't give you reason to doubt me."

Holly crossed her arms over her chest and prepared herself for whatever he had to say. "Go on."

Grayson nodded and stared at the ground between their feet. "You questioned me once about why I never married, and I told you that I'd avoided relationships because of my job and bad choices." He cleared his throat. "That's not the whole story."

"Are you sure you want to tell me?"

"I do. I get the sense that you keep building fences between us."

"Grayson, that's not my intention at all. If there's something you think I need to know, then I'm listening. But if it's none of my business, then don't."

He eyed her for a long moment, then Grayson squared his shoulders. "All right, then. Something happened when I joined the teams. Something in the wiring." He pointed to his head. "Up here. At first, I didn't notice it, because I was young and one-night stands were the norm. Plenty of gals wanted to crawl into my bed but some women wanted more."

Holly figured there must have been dozens of women who hoped Gray would fall in love with them. "By more, you mean a relationship."

"Exactly. After I had sex with a woman, my emotions evaporated. Literally went dark. It was like pulling a plug and my feelings vanished. I started noticing it more and more. Even if I thought I liked the woman, the second I left her bed, I wanted her gone. If she tried to see me again, I got angry. Agitated. Didn't matter who they were, I cut them off with zero regrets. Eventually, I stopped questioning and accepted that this was who I was. If I needed to ease my carnal pressure, I only chose women of like mind. I picked them up in bars, mostly. I fucked them and forgot them."

Holly's jaw loosened with shock. "For ten years?"

He shook his head. "No—for fifteen." His gaze pinned itself to her. "Until I met you." Gray shoved his hands into his front jean pockets. "That's the real reason I kept myself distanced from you initially. I was afraid if I made love to you, my brain would disconnect from my heart like it always did."

That definitely explained why he hadn't married. "Why did you change your mind?"

A muted smile lifted his sexy lips. "Holly, the risk of losing you far outweighed my concerns."

She processed his explanation in clinical fashion because doing anything else would send her down a rabbit hole. "Emotional detachment is a psychological disorder. But in your case, it only manifested itself with your sexual partners?"

He blinked a couple times. "Yeah. It wasn't a conscious choice. It just happened."

"Clinically speaking, and of course I'm not a psychologist, there are numerous reasons why that occurred. Anything from traumatic experiences to nurturing issues, abandonment issues, but I don't think any of those apply to you." Grayson hadn't escaped his years of service completely unaffected. "Psychological issues are rarely singular. I have two theories."

"I'm listening."

"Some people fear commitment because of trust. In particular, revealing their weaknesses. Allowing someone to get close enough to see your imperfections wasn't tolerable and short-circuited your emotions. The other reason is perfectionism. Although you avoided attachments, you were looking for the perfect partner. You set unattainable standards that were purposely impossible to find. You said this began in your early days of service?"

He nodded.

"The women you chose, were they always beautiful? I mean, extremely beautiful?"

Gray's brow held a permanent crease. "Yeah. Most."

"Then there's a plausible answer. Somewhere along the way, your intense training as a SEAL, which doesn't allow for failure, transitioned not only into your work ethic but your emotions. Those high standards ingrained themselves into every aspect of your life. You chose the most attractive women, seeing physical perfection, but found fault with other aspects and immediately disengaged after serving your carnal needs. When they tried to initiate a relationship, you detached, because it meant revealing yourself. No one is perfect, but for you, that translated into weakness."

"Um..."

She chuckled. "Um? Not exactly the response I'd expect from a domineering, alpha male."

He scowled at her. "Not funny."

"Yeah, it kinda is. The ugly girl gets the unbelievably hot guy for a while because of crossed wires."

A storm of anger blew into Gray's eyes and he swiped at the air with his fist. "That's not fucking true, Holly. You're not ugly. There might be some shrink who agrees with you, and there might be some merit to your theory, but I think the answer is a helluva lot simpler."

She puzzled at his sudden anger. "Yeah," she drawled. "What's your hypothesis?"

He pointed a finger at her. "Listen, I might not have a degree in my back pocket, Miss High and Mighty, but I'm not scared of showing you my underbelly. I told you I have flaws."

"You did. But you also know deep down that no man who looks like you would want me. There's no threat."

Gray's mouth flattened with anger. "No."

She nodded her head. "Yes."

"You're not unattractive," he said at double the volume he normally spoke.

"Not a ten, either. But I'm a scientist and your subconscious is willing to accept that as a sufficient substitute."

Her lover's expression was so tight with anger, he looked like he could shit nails. Instead of arguing, he stomped away from her. Holly shook her head, still puzzled at his reaction.

It was just a theory, but it made sense to her. He'd calm down eventually.

Grayson stopped abruptly, then did an about-face and strode toward her like he was going to attack. She took a step back.

"You want honesty?" he shouted. "I'll give you honesty."

Something in their conversation had lit a fuse. "Start by asking yourself why you're so angry."

"I'm angry because what you're inferring is that I fell in love with you because you're sub-standard and our relationship is only temporary until some hot chick winks at me, and I'll vamoose. What the hell is the matter with you?"

In a calm voice, she said, "Grayson, I'm not saying I'm right, but there is—"

"No, there isn't! There isn't a speck of goddamn truth in your theory. I'm not the one with trust issues. You are."

Although Grayson was smoking under the collar, she wasn't mad at all. She'd found her center of balance when Kevin broke his vows and dumped her.

"Kayla told me that her career used to define who she was, but she gave it up for the admiral. I'd never give up the career I worked so hard to achieve, especially not for something as unpredictable as love. Look where I'd be if I'd trusted Kevin with my life."

Gray's blue eyes darkened. "That's a pretty tall fence for me to jump over, Holly."

Disappointment formed a lump in her throat. She swallowed her sorrow and prepared to face heartache head on when Grayson realized she was right.

"There's an ounce of truth to my theory, Gray. I know you see it. Maybe I'm the last piece of your transition. If you can accept a relationship with me, you can find one with anyone."

Better to end this now before she was completely devoted to him. Her detention at the border had proven she was getting dangerously close to the point of no return.

His jaw clenched and he shook his head, his eyes simmering with emotion.

Here it comes, she thought, and clenched her hands.

He gripped her upper arms and wrenched her against his firm chest. "Nice try, sweetheart."

The kiss he slammed against her mouth seemed like punishment at first, then softened into a sensual assault.

Holly didn't understand. This wasn't the correct response. Her chaotic heart beat with confusion. Gray's warm palm slid down her spine, pausing at the sway in her back. He tilted his head and weakened her defenses by easing his tongue between her parted lips and inhaling as if he wanted her inside of him.

When he finally ended the erotic overload to her senses and backed away, she gazed up at the warmth and depth in his eyes. Somehow, he'd managed to chastise her in the most caring but meaningful way. Or maybe this was how he ended his connection with every woman.

Gray cupped her jaw, brushing his thumb against her cheek. "The one thing—the most important thing—I learned during BUD/S is that you put the team in front of yourself. Every man who successfully earned his Trident learned that lesson. The video tonight is about life *after* our service. I want you beside me because you are my team and the best part of my life."

Holly closed her eyes and felt her world shift another step closer to Grayson.

CHAPTER THIRTY

S parks from the burning logs crackled and danced into the night air. Four couples sat in an arc with a video camera rolling. Holly listened, sitting next to Gray, as Anson introduced them all for the show. He explained, for the benefit of his two million subscribers, the focus of the interview.

Grayson held her hand and gave it a little squeeze.

Tammy and Checkers, along with Anson and Beth, spent most of their airtime promoting health and awareness for warriors with combat exposure. Checkers described his medical issues, as did Anson, and the negative impact on their families by ignoring the symptoms.

Holly was surprised to hear that it was Kayla, not her husband the admiral, who lived with complex PTSD from traumatic events in her childhood and her first marriage. She explained that counseling gave her the tools to coexist with the symptoms, but it was the admiral who refused to give up on her that saved Kayla's life.

The men spoke about their new ventures as civilians, except for the admiral, who still actively worked with the government. Which department and what he did wasn't brought up in the conversation.

Between the serious subject matter there was also good-hearted bantering among the men and a few humorous stories thrown in.

Anson turned his focus on Holly and Grayson. "Gray, you've been out for five years now. What was the biggest hurdle you faced leaving the teams?"

Appearing completely calm, Gray's rugged good looks were intensified by the flames that cast a warm glow. The man had a confident, magnetic charisma just sitting relaxed in a chair. Holly wondered how many gorgeous women would message Anson, looking for Grayson's number after the video released.

"Biggest challenge for me was losing my sense of purpose," he said. "You've got that in spades when you're a frogman."

Mumbles of assent came from the other men.

"So, you found a career in law enforcement and bridged the gap," Anson said.

Gray thought about it for a moment. "I used to think that was the case. I joined the sheriff's department because it emulated certain aspects of team life, like my commitment to helping people, taking illegal narcotics off the street, and working with like-minded officers who hold the same goals. As a SEAL, duty and purpose are the same. A hundred percent focus pinned on training, the next deployment, and missions. That's why we succeed. But that's not the case as a civilian."

All eyes were glued on Grayson as if he was cracking some ancient mystery wide open.

"My duty still exists, but it terminates at the end of a shift. No matter how many bad guys I arrested, I still felt detached. Trying to fill that emptiness is what leads to unhealthy habits and abuse."

Holly listened as intently as the other guests, impressed, if not proud, at how well Grayson deciphered his transition.

Anson nodded. "Did you find your purpose?"

Gray's broad shoulders lifted when he chuckled. "I did." He pressed Holly's hand to his mouth and kissed her knuckles. "She's sitting right beside me."

The wives crooned at his answer and Holly felt her cheeks heat.

Checkers adjusted his ball cap and grinned. "You're one smooth talker, Bone. Ya always were."

"Might sound that way but it's the truth." He shifted his

gaze to the admiral, who wore an expression as if impressed with Grayson's hypothesis. "Holly pointed out earlier today that my training ingrained itself so deeply into my sub-conscious, I wasn't able to form an emotional relationship with a woman while I was in service because I saw it as a threat. A distraction. To a certain degree, she's probably right."

The admiral grunted in agreement and shot a look at Kayla.

"My initial response to her theory was anger. Not at her, but the thought that I wasn't in control of my actions. I left the teams five years ago, but I still couldn't connect with a woman on any level except physical. That changed when I met Holly."

Beth, who held her husband's hand, asked, "Do you know what made her different from other women?"

Grayson's handsome grin tightened his jaw. "I didn't at first, but I do now." He paused and turned his head to gaze at her. "She's strong, if not stronger than I am. When life throws a curve ball at us, we'll face it together. Holly doesn't need me, but I sure as hell don't want to live my life without her."

Holly's heart executed multiple backflips, Gray's reason scoring a perfect ten-point-oh landing.

Kayla piped up. "I might know someone like that too."

Admiral Austen chuckled. "She straightened me out pretty quickly then dragged me through something akin to one year's worth of Hell Week, back-to-back."

The guests all laughed.

Kayla rolled her eyes. "It wasn't that bad."

"It sure as hell was."

"Well, you deserved it," she fired back.

The admiral scowled at his wife. "Stubborn as a goddamn mule. If you'd just believed me from the get-go, we wouldn't have gone through hell and high water before you let me put a ring on your finger."

Beth cracked up. "And here they go." She looked at the

camera. "We're gonna refresh our drinks and let them get this out of their systems, and we'll be right back."

Anson strode over to the camera and paused the filming.

Holly watched as Kayla and the admiral continued to spar.

She leaned toward Grayson. "What's happening?"

He laughed. "What usually happens. You should have seen them go toe-to-toe back in the day."

"So, Admiral Austen was like you? He didn't have long-term relationships?"

"Yeah, he was a card-carrying bachelor until Kayla started working at Base Command. She was hired as a civilian liaison. When it comes to tactical analysis, she's a savant. The admiral never had a problem getting a woman into his bed, but Kayla kept her focus on the job. The more she dug in her feet and resisted him, the more it drove him crazy."

Holly grinned because Kayla and her husband kept firing shots at one another. "But they love each other."

Gray picked up Holly's water bottle from the ground. "Oh, yeah. Tightest couple I know. He respects and loves Kayla as much as I respect and love you."

Holly's heart swelled even though she found it hard to believe.

"More water?" he asked, then kissed her.

"Thank you."

After watching Kayla and her husband's verbal duel, which Holly thought they both enjoyed, she decided to intervene.

"Excuse me, Admiral," Holly said, causing an abrupt cease fire. "If you don't mind me asking, what was it about Kayla that made her different from other women?"

The other couples standing at the beverage table Beth had set up outside of the camera's view, paused what they were doing and looked over their shoulders, waiting to hear the answer.

Admiral Austen shifted his attention to his wife as the

fire crackled under a perfect Texas night sky filled with thousands of stars.

"The answer to everything I wanted was in her eyes."

Kayla leaned forward and placed a languid kiss on her husband's lips.

Grayson returned to his seat and handed Holly the refilled water bottle. "Couldn't have said it better myself."

The taping resumed and within an hour, they finished. The couples called it a night except for Kayla and the admiral. Holly was tired but enjoyed sitting by the fire and gazing into the heavens. Their flight didn't leave till noon tomorrow. Not having to get up at the butt-crack of dawn was great.

Admiral Austen broke the silence. "Special Forces lost a good man when you left, Brooks. Not to mention a non-commissioned officer, which I'm sure you would've become if you'd stayed."

"Thanks, Admiral. I appreciate that. Lt. Cobbs was pushing me to take the leap before I retired. I seriously considered it."

Austen nodded. "Yeah, Pat sure knew how to spot a warrior with leadership qualities."

Grayson placed his empty beer bottle on the ground near his chair and put his attention on Holly. "Lt. Cobbs died on a mission. He was Alpha Squad's lieutenant."

"That must have been very hard on all of you. Were you in Alpha Squad?" she asked.

"No. Delta, but Lt. Cobbs was one of those men everyone respected." He glanced at the admiral and then back to her. "He was the admiral's best friend and swim buddy. They were in the same BUD/S class."

"I see. I'm so sorry for your loss, Admiral. I suppose the longer you serve, the more that happens."

Kayla squeezed her husband's hand and nodded. "It does. Too often, but we can't dwell on it. Drive ourselves crazy if we did, especially the spouses. I won't lie. I'm extremely relieved that Thane isn't actively involved in combat anymore. But law enforcement isn't without its dangers, so I understand how you must feel, Holly."

Grayson didn't work in vice any longer. She hadn't even considered the risks he faced in his current role. She'd assumed they were very low.

"The Proactive Unit is relatively safe, right?" she asked, gazing at Grayson.

"Sure."

The admiral raised a brow. "Brooks, take it from me, they can smell a lie a mile away."

"Gray, tell me the truth."

"What?" He cocked his head at her. "Nothing to worry about, sweetheart. I mean, you only live in another country. I'm sure you'll make it to the hospital before I expire."

Holly thrust herself forward in the chair to sit up. "That's not funny."

Kayla winked at her husband. "He's probably right. When Thane was seriously wounded, I had to fly from San Diego to Germany. Worst eight hours of my life. I had no idea if he'd be alive when I got there."

Holly swallowed a large knot of worry, but it only shifted into her belly.

Kayla stood, and the admiral joined her. "All I'm saying is that I didn't have a choice because Thane's mission was thousands of miles away from home. If I were in your shoes, I'd seriously consider dual citizenship. A man doesn't look at a woman the way Gray looks at you if he doesn't love her."

Admiral Austen wrapped his muscled arm around Kayla's slender shoulders. "My wife has a point, Holly. Wouldn't be a bad idea."

Holly narrowed an eye at all of them. "I see what this is. Grayson, did you tell them I have no intention of immigrating to the US?"

A complete look of innocence coated his expression. "Who, me?" He yawned and stretched his shoulder. "I'm beat. Time to get some shut eye, sweetheart."

"We are not finished with this discussion."

"Okay, you can yell at me while we walk to the cabin." He gave the admiral a two-finger salute. "Night, sir. Ma'am. Been a pleasure."

"Petty Officer Brooks, when you and Holly visit San Diego, make sure our house is on the itinerary."

"Will do, Admiral."

Grayson shone the flashlight on the gravel driveway as they walked toward their accommodations.

"That wasn't a planned ambush," he said.

"I know. They're your friends and care about you."

"No. They're *our* friends." They reached the cabin and Gray paused before opening the door. "Holly, will you do something for me?"

"I suppose, but I draw the line at hunting Great Whites off the Barrier Reef."

A handsome grin coated his expression that never failed to soften her heart.

The porch light attracted a myriad of bugs that ticked against the glass shield protecting the bulb. She hoped he made this quick because the Texas mosquitoes loved her blood.

"Guys like us don't ever expect to go off the rails. If we do, we're the last to admit it. I don't foresee that happening with me, but if it does, I trust your judgement and want you to say something." Gray placed a chaste kiss on her cheek. "But the one thing I refuse, and will always refuse to accept, is what we have is temporary. I brought you here so that you could meet the people who are part of my past. And I wanted them to meet you because you're my future."

Gray opened the door then swept his palms down her bare arms, held her hands, and stepped backward into the cabin. The accommodation was a cozy space with a queen bed and small bathroom, the décor in shades of white and burnt orange. Gray closed the door and steered her to the bed.

She sat on the mattress while he started to unbutton his

shirt. "You certainly make it hard for me not to love you," she admitted.

"You told me from the start that trust and time were your stumbling blocks." His grin dissolved, replaced with a sincerity in his eyes that she'd never seen before.

"I did."

"So, here's some tough love that I think you need, because no matter how many times I tell you, your past keeps getting in the way."

Grayson loosened the last button, and rolled his broad shoulders, removing the shirt and revealing his contoured chest.

Shock made her blink. Her mouth parted but no words came out.

Until this morning, Gray only had tats covering his right arm. At some point this afternoon that changed. A three-dimensional dagger pierced the center of a blooming red rose centered over his left pectoral. The workmanship was outstanding. The knife penetrated his skin at the top of his pec and the tip of the dagger appeared again below his heart. *Holly* was tattooed along the silver blade.

She palmed her chest and her gaze strayed up his throat, over his rugged features to connect with his eyes.

"I—I." She couldn't think. Didn't know what to say.

Dumbfounded. Blindsided. Stunned.

Gray leaned over, his firm lips a whisper's breath from hers. "The answer to everything I've ever wanted, I see in your eyes."

She clamped her arms around his neck and yanked him forward at the same time falling back on the bed, taking the full brunt of his weight on top of her. He quickly propped himself up with his muscular arms. Holly's fingers couldn't move fast enough to loosen the button at his waist and release his zipper.

She wanted her man naked. Her man! Her partner.

Her lover.

Gray rolled onto his back, and she roughly jerked the pants from his legs as her body temperature rose from hot to volcanic.

Gray seemed amused with the gratified smile on his lips, but his eyes heated as she ripped the tank top over her head and shoved her shorts off her hips to the floor. Holly was desperate to be skin against skin with the warrior who'd marked his body with her name over his heart.

She straddled his hips, her palms on the bed beside his broad shoulders. Gray's large hands palmed her waist, and she slid his thickening cock against her sex. Shaking with impatience, she centered his crown at the entrance to her channel and assaulted his mouth.

Making love to Gray always made her wet, their passion intense and hungry. Tonight was different. She needed to ride him hard.

"Babe."

She kissed him.

"Condom."

She shut him up with another kiss and eased his thick head into her aching core, swaying her hips back and forth.

With slow, deep lunges, Gray's erection filled her channel, stoking her need.

"Oh, fuck yes." He groaned and his eyes closed. Gray palmed her ass and lifted his hips, meeting every erotic plunge.

The more turned-on he got, the wetter she became. Gray cupped her breast and suckled her nipple, sending sparks through her veins.

Her breath shallowed and she spoke in shallow gasps.

He was being gentle with her. She wanted savage.

Holly straightened, perched on her knees. "Fuck me, Gray. As hard as you can!"

He didn't hesitate and powered his cock in and out of her channel, every thrust meant to penetrate and possess her. His chest, shoulders and biceps molded into rock-hard muscle.

"Holly!" Restraint pinched his expression. "Oh, babe, you're so hot and goddamn perfect. *Shit.*" His gaze dropped to where their bodies connected. Each thrust more frenzied. Gray clenched his jaw. "Fuck, I wanna come deep inside you."

She loved the raw need when Gray reached this point. It always got her off and now was no different. The way his thick shaft stretched and filled her body detached her from reality. He lifted her into an erotic ecstasy that only had one end.

Holly squeezed her inner muscles. "Don't stop, Gray. You feel so good."

The release rolled through her body and sent him racing over the edge, too. Throaty moans of pleasure erupted from the man she loved, and a sublime warmth filled her core.

He palmed the back of her head, threading his fingers in her hair, and slammed his lips against her mouth as she continued to ride his shaft with a lazy glide. His onslaught of kisses didn't subside. If anything, they increased. What he didn't know was that every kiss had seeded her heart from the very first time.

Gray retreated from her mouth, and he gazed in her eyes. "Wow, babe. You've never loved me like that before." One side of his mouth tipped upward in a smile. "I liked it. A lot." He gnawed on his bottom lip for a second. "It felt like I had all of you." His gaze shifted back and forth between her eyes. "Do I have all of you?"

Holly tipped her head and gently kissed the edge of the clear wrap that protected his new tat. She made a promise to herself. She'd never doubt his word again.

"Every last bit," she whispered against his lips.

CHAPTER THIRTY-ONE

B y three o'clock Sunday afternoon, Grayson dropped his overnight bag on the suede couch in his bedroom. The flight from Texas to Seattle had gone off without any delays.

A roast Ivy had put in the oven hours earlier infused the old Victorian with a delicious aroma. He'd tried to coerce Holly into staying for dinner, but she had an early start at the university tomorrow.

As he watched the Audi disappear around the bend in the driveway, he knew their weekend in Texas had been a success in more ways than one.

While they'd been at the ranch, Checkers had made an appointment to get a new tattoo. The therapy he received in Mexico had been life-changing for his old teammate. Anson drove Gray and the other men to the dime-sized backwater town a few miles away and hung out, watching the artist add more ink to Checkers' arm.

Admiral Austen had noticed Gray clocked out of the convo. At the time, he'd been thinking about Holly. She'd been relatively quiet while listening to the other women talk during lunch after they'd arrived. She'd met Dirk, but this was her first real exposure to people from his previous life in special ops.

"She's fine, Brooks," the admiral said, surprising him. Austen had an uncanny ability to read people's thoughts.

"Yeah, I'm sure she is." Anson and Check stopped their conversation about a gnarly mission in Syria they'd worked years ago to listen. "Holly's out of her element. If you want to talk about hieroglyphics on a sarcophagus, she'd be right in there, but her only exposure to the military was the romance books she used to read."

Anson snorted. "Those friggin' things are a joke."

Gray shrugged. "Yeah, some are. Some aren't." That got an eye raise by all the men. "All I'm saying is that this is a part of my life I haven't shared with Holly. I convinced her to come this weekend, but I think she feels that she doesn't belong here."

"Never spoken about your service with her?" the admiral asked.

"No, sir. Talking about my past might lead into dangerous territory, especially my track record with women. Convincing her that I want a shot at growing old together isn't easy when I've never had a relationship that lasted more than a few hours. I've been upfront about that, but didn't exactly tell her the whole story."

Anson ran a hand through his short-cropped, dark hair. "You gotta come clean. Does she know you received the second-highest honor for bravery?"

Gray shook his head. During the last deployment prior to his retirement, his squad had come under fire while protecting an Afghani village that agreed to let US troops use it as an armament. Around zero-two-hundred hours, the attack began. Their lead breacher was the first to fall. Standing in the open, he took a few rounds from an enemy sniper. During live fire, Gray had launched himself over his teammate's wounded body. While rocket-propelled grenades landed all around them, he dragged the LB to cover. Every time one of his teammates took a bullet during the fierce firefight, Gray put himself in the open to recover the man. After two hours of exchanging rounds, he saw five Taliban soldiers breach one of the Afghani homes where the villagers were hiding. Ten years of training and experience fueled his limbs. It was a bloody fight, most of it using hand-to-hand combat, but he'd saved the lives of the civilians inside.

Anson's brows popped with surprise. "She doesn't know about the Navy Cross?"

"No. Didn't see any reason to tell her. And to be honest, I don't think I did more than any of the other men."

Checkers shook his head in what looked like disagreement. "I was there, Bone. Never seen a SEAL do what you did. It was like you were everywhere at once and no bullet could bring you down. You saved a lot of lives that night."

Gray looked over toward the admiral, who was one of the few men who'd received the highest award in the Armed Forces, the Medal of Honor. "Don't you feel the same way?"

Austen nodded. "I can tell ya that it makes zero difference to my wife. She orders me around at home like I'm a seaman recruit."

The men chuckled and mumbled their assent.

Gray's gaze slid over the hundreds of images tacked on the far wall. From skulls to mermaids, the artist working on Check was extremely gifted. His ability to ink in 3-D was pretty rad. "Aside from living in different countries, deep down I don't think Holly sees a future with me. It's because of her first marriage. The guy was an asshole."

The admiral set his empty bottle on the side table. "She'll come around, Brooks. Count yourself lucky that she's not as hard-headed as Kayla. My wife didn't cut me any slack." He grinned and cleared his throat. "In hindsight, I didn't deserve any. She held her ground and I crawled through the mud to reach her. She threw up smoke screens and diversions, thinking I'd back down, but it all stemmed from her traumatic past."

Gray figured that must have been the case, from what he'd heard through gossip. He'd been on N.A.B's dock the night the admiral caught and killed the Blood Shark. The fact that Kayla had driven a knife into her own body in order to allow the admiral to take out the serial killer was badass.

"Your situation was a little extreme, Admiral."

"Different circumstances, yes, but one action makes all the difference. Something you do finally clicks. Big or small, doesn't matter. The key is trust and respect."

Check sat in the chair, the artist's tool buzzing as the retired Marine shop owner worked on his arm.

"Tammy deserves a medal for puttin' up with me, that's for sure. What did you do that clicked?" Checkers asked the admiral.

Austen rose and opened the lid of the cooler Anson had packed for their jaunt, then returned to the well-worn leather tub chair.

"To this day, I have no fucking clue." The admiral cracked the top off the cold brew. "I knew Kayla loved me. She was pregnant

with Adam. But to tell you the truth, when I stood beneath her balcony and proposed, I didn't know whether she'd say yes or yell, 'Get the hell outta here before I call the cops.'" He broke into a hearty laugh. "Alpha Squad was with me in full dress uniform. She thought I was making a grand gesture. But really, I was giving myself a tactical advantage, hoping she wouldn't shoot me down in front of the squad."

Gray kept scanning the artist's work. "No matter what I say to Holly, she doesn't believe I'm in love with her." He wandered to the wall, his attention drawn to a particular image at eye height. It was a drawing, not a picture, of a tat.

Caleb turned off the tattoo machine and cleaned Checkers' new ink. He looked up and said, "I drew that the other day."

Gray turned to face the men. "Maybe I need to stop telling and show her instead."

"You sure, buddy?" Anson asked when Gray instructed Caleb to ink the name Holly on the silver blade of the tat.

Hell, yes. "As sure as I was the day I stepped on the Grinder and knew I wanted to be a SEAL."

He removed his shirt and lay on the tattoo bed while Caleb changed his gloves and set up.

Checkers took a seat in the chair Gray had vacated, then popped open a beverage. "Yeah, man, but you left and became a fucking cop."

"I'm not a fucking cop, I'm a goddamn detective with the sheriff's department. How many times do I have to tell ya there's a difference, dickhead?"

His old friend lifted his beer. "To Holly, may she have the patience of a saint and nerves of steel to put up with you for the rest of her days."

Gray gave Check a one-finger salute as the needles punctured the skin over his heart.

The tat took two and a half hours to complete, but the finished product was outstanding. Holly's response when she saw the ink confirmed his suspicions. She had to see his commitment with her own eyes in order to believe him. What he didn't mention was that he'd asked Caleb to leave the cross-guard empty because one day he'd add their children's names to the space.

* * * *

Feet thudded on the steps leading upstairs.

"Gray." Cole stepped into the open doorway of the bedroom. "Just got a call from Kline. DTF got wind of a shipment. The bust is going down."

Finally! Gray opened the closet doors, brushed aside his shirts and unlocked the safe, then withdrew his service weapon. He donned his concealed carry shoulder holster and secured the buckle as he walked across the room. Passing the desk, he swiped his dark blue nylon jacket from the chair.

"Does Kline want us to meet him at headquarters, or is he bringing the weapons and body armor?"

"SWAT has the warehouse covered. Kline will meet us along with four DTF members at the Werewolves' stash house on Epsom, like we planned."

He and Cole had found three more houses during July. The place on Epsom was heavily guarded by gang members. Gray figured it was where the local dealers exchanged money for drugs. The modern, large home was situated in a middle-income neighborhood. One of the CIs working with DTF said the president of the Werewolves lived there.

"Lead the way."

"Where are you two going?" Ivy asked, standing near the open dishwasher in the kitchen. "Dinner's ready in an hour."

Cole detoured and laid a deep kiss on her lips. "Don't wait for us."

Her hand strayed over Cole's chest, then she lifted one side of his jacket to reveal his weapon. "Okay," she said softly and bit her bottom lip.

Cole winked at his fiancée. "Keep a couple plates warm."

She nodded. "Be careful."

Gray had seen the same fear in the SEALs wives' eyes when they said goodbye before deployment. A poignant moment when reality hit. They knew the danger their husbands faced and the risk of never seeing them again.

Cole headed out the front door.

Ivy stood stiffly watching her fiancé leave. "Gray, is this the big case you've been working on all summer?"

He smiled at his sister. "It's probably gonna be a long night, Ivy."

Her brow creased tight. "Promise me you won't let anything happen to him."

Gray couldn't do that. He knew it, and so did she. When it came to experience in these situations, he had a helluva lot more than his best friend, but Cole was a good detective.

"I know it's hard, sis. You're marrying a man who takes down bad guys. You gotta send him out the door with confidence that he's gonna walk back through it in one piece, okay?"

Jackson skidded around the corner from the hallway into the kitchen on stocking feet. "Where ya going, Uncle Gray?"

"Gotta put in a couple hours at work, buddy. Give your mom a hand with the dishes tonight."

His nephew was getting older and wiser. He glanced at his mother and saw her tight expression.

"Okay." He ran to Ivy's side, squeezing his arms around her hips. "Cole going to work too?"

Ivy swallowed and nodded her head in a jerky fashion.

Gray needed to go but took the extra second to hug his sister while wrapping a hand around his nephew's slender shoulders as well.

"Ivy, it doesn't get any easier, but you'll get stronger, I promise. See you two later."

Gray jogged down the steps and slid into the passenger side of Cole's Mustang. The tires spit gravel out the back wheels as his partner tore down the driveway.

* * * *

The senior officer for the Clayton case multi-task force raid ordered the operation to go ahead before nightfall. Lt Kline, three detectives from DTF, four Federal DEA agents, Cole, and Grayson waited for Lt. Bill Thompson of the DTF to give the word. Thompson was located at the warehouse on the Bellingham waterfront. As planned, the raid would happen at each site simultaneously.

From behind a cedar hedge, Gray watched the house. He'd seen movement in the second-story window and reported through the comm set they all wore to communicate.

Cole was situated in the alley at the back of the property with two DTF detectives and two feds. Gray, Kline, and the other officers waited out front.

"There's six motorcycles parked in the rear driveway," Cole reported. "One of the plates belongs to Cage Martin, president of the Werewolves."

With the warrant approved, they patiently waited. If this was where drugs and money changed hands, they'd have plenty of weapons inside the house.

Lt. Kline had sole communication with Lt. Thompson.

Not more than five minutes later, Lt. Kline said, "Green light, Brooks. Go, go, go."

Gray hopped the fence and ran toward the house, carrying a thirty-two-pound ram. He hammered on the front door with his fist.

"Sheriff's Department. Search warrant." Gray knew that inside they were busy flushing evidence or setting up a trap. Only giving the occupants a few seconds, he used the ram to break the lock. On the fourth blow, the latch busted, and he kicked the door open. Kline, DTF, and the feds were close on his tail.

Weapons drawn, they flooded the entrance shouting, *"Search warrant! Show yourselves!"* Downstairs, all the blinds were drawn to darken the rooms.

Gunfire erupted from a landing at the top of the stairs, peppering the tile floor and wall in front of Gray. He thrust himself backward for cover behind the entry wall.

"Got a shooter at the top of the stairs," he reported.

Another volley of rapid fire came from somewhere down the hallway ahead of him, probably the kitchen. Glass shattering and shouting from behind the house meant Cole and the other agents were engaged.

Leaning around the corner, he surveyed the arched, open stairway that led to the second floor. A guy in leathers appeared at the top of the stairs.

"Drop your weapon! On your knees!" Gray ordered.

The response was an AR-15 spray of rounds. Kline and the other officers took cover in the living room. The shooter upstairs paused. Gray rounded the wall and fired. The guy at the top of the stairs stumbled and fell to the floor.

More gunfire erupted from the opposite side of the house.

The feds took the stairs to the second floor, weapons drawn.

Kline stood behind a wall in the living room, but in Gray's line of sight.

"Lieutenant, active shooter in the kitchen," Gray said into the mic. He motioned with his hand that he would proceed toward the back of the house.

Gray kept his back to the hallway wall. More shouting and then a blast of gunfire erupted from upstairs.

Up ahead, Cole shouted, "Put your weapon down! On the ground!"

Gray reached the end of the hall and peered around the corner of the kitchen cabinets.

Jesus Christ! Cole was face to face with Cage Martin, both with their weapons pointed at each other. No more than eight feet separated them.

"Put your weapon on the ground!" Cole ordered.

The biker aimed the .44 magnum handgun straight at Cole's chest.

This was bad.

Gray only had one option. "On the ground, Cage!"

The fucking guy didn't even turn around. The next few seconds ticked by in slow motion. Gray watched the leader of the Werewolves squeeze the trigger. Gray emptied his weapon a split second before Cage. As the bastard's body bucked from the bullets entering his back, the sonofabitch squeezed off two rounds.

He and Cole wore bullet-resistant soft armor, not the thirty-pound vests with plates like SWAT. Gray watched the body of his partner and oldest friend jolt, taking both rounds, and falling onto the tile floor.

"Officer down! We need an ambulance at 4411 Epsom Street!"

He leaped across the kitchen and kicked Cage's weapon across the floor. The gang member didn't move. Gray quickly checked his pulse.

Dead.

He scrambled to kneel next to Cole, who lay still with his eyes closed. The rounds had entered the upper left chest area. Gray worked quickly, tearing apart the Velcro tabs securing the vest. Cole's shirt was soaked in blood. A kitchen towel lay draped over the edge of the counter next to the sink. Gray tore open Cole's shirt and used the towel to cover the wound and applied pressure.

"What's the ETA on the ambo?"

Kline responded in Gray's comm set. "EMTs have been dispatched, Brooks." The lieutenant ran into the kitchen. "Rest of the gang is secured or dead upstairs." He dropped to his knees beside Cole. "How bad is it?"

"Open your eyes, Cole." Gray checked his carotid pulse. Weak. "Ivy is waiting for you at home, buddy. Hang..." No more pulse. "Kline, find some plastic wrap."

Gray located the bottom of Cole's breastbone, placed the palm of his hand at the base of his sternum and started CPR compression.

Kline flung open cabinet doors and drawers. "Found some."

"Put it over the wound and keep pressure on it."

In the distance, Gray heard a siren and prayed it was the ambulance. It wasn't the first time he'd dealt with this type of wound. He'd lost count during his missions.

But this was different. His best friend and the love of his sister's life *had* to live.

"Come on, Cole!"

Fifteen minutes later, Gray stood in front of the stash house as the ambulance turned on its lights and sirens then raced toward the hospital. The EMTs had restarted Cole's heart but he was in serious condition. TV station vans littered the street and reporters jostled to get a story but were held back by patrol units. The reporters yelled at Lt. Kline to make a statement as he stepped up to Gray's right side. Neighbors gathered across the road on the sidewalk, huddled together, watching with concern streaked across their faces.

"Brooks, we can take care of the clean-up here. Go to the hospital," the lieutenant said.

He nodded solemnly. "I have to call my sister before she sees the news."

Kline's hand squeezed his shoulder. "I can call her if you want."

"No. I'll make the call but do me a favor, don't mention Cole's name when you talk to the reporters."

"I won't. What about his parents?"

"Cole's old man deserted them when he was nine. His mom lives in Bellingham. I'll give her a call once I'm at the hospital."

Numbed by what he had to do, Gray headed for Cole's Mustang. He slid inside and shut the door. Leaning back against the headrest, he closed his eyes for a second. Goddammit, what the hell had Cole been thinking? He'd left his cover to face off with Martin.

Gray fingered the cell from his jacket pocket at the same time he started the engine. Scrolling the contact list, he highlighted Ivy's number. His sister had already lost one husband. If Cole didn't make it, she'd be devastated. Gray was glad he was home to hold her hand and let her lean on him if the worst happened. He slid his thumb over the call button and centered himself.

* * * *

Holly spent a long, boring hour inching her way to the border before crossing into Canada. Once she'd unpacked her suitcase, she heated a bowl of mushroom soup and sat in the living room. According to the time on the TV, it was six o'clock.

She flicked through the channels, looking for the news. A video of an urban neighborhood with state police and sheriff cruisers amassed out front of a home caught her eye. Along the base of the video, the banner read *Skagit County drug raid*. Holly pressed the volume button to increase the sound.

A male reporter stood in front of a two-story house while a deputy sheriff leading a K-9 crossed the lawn, heading toward the home.

"From what we've learned so far, the raid that took place at this home behind me was part of a multi-agency task force collaboration. Hiding among this appealing middle-income neighborhood was one of several locations used by the Werewolves motorcycle gang, a well-known group responsible for criminal activity in Skagit County."

Werewolves? Wasn't that the gang Grayson had mentioned?

Our sources tell us the president of the gang used this unassuming residence to house drugs for local dealers. Neighbors reported a massive shootout when the sheriff's department and federal drug enforcement agents entered the home."

The video shifted to a clip of a stretcher being loaded into the back of an ambulance, then flashed back to the reporter.

"A few minutes ago, I spoke with Lt. Kline of Skagit County Sheriff's Office. One detective was critically injured during the standoff between law enforcement and the occupants in the house. Although not confirmed, we believe Cage Martin, president of the Werewolves, was killed during the raid."

Holly's heart ticked with unease. This had to be the case Grayson and his partner, Cole, were working on. She'd left the farmstead around three o'clock. Was he involved in this? Who was on that stretcher?

Shaking all over, she ran to the kitchen and retrieved her phone from the counter. Swallowing her fear, she called Grayson.

It's not him. It can't be him.

One ring.

Two.

Three.

Her heart thumped with dread. Kayla's voice echoed in

her mind. *"When Thane was seriously wounded, I had to fly from San Diego to Germany. Worst eight hours of my life. I had no idea if he'd be alive when I got there."*

Four rings.

Holly slammed her eyes shut and clenched her hand. *Please answer!*

"Hey, sweetheart," Grayson said when he picked up.

She burst into tears of relief. "Are…are you all right?"

He hummed low in his throat. "You saw the news. Guess that means you made it home."

Her pumping adrenaline eased. "The news said an officer was critically injured."

"It's Cole."

"No. Oh, no. Are you at the hospital?"

"Yeah, I'm here with Ivy. We don't know anything yet. Doctors are still working on him."

She'd be losing her mind if she were in Ivy's position. "What about your dad and Jackson? Are they with you?"

"No. Think it's better they stay at home until we know —" Gray sighed. "Until the doctors tell us how long it'll take before Cole's on his feet again."

Surely Ivy was sitting beside Gray and he was trying to remain optimistic. He must have been there when Cole was shot. As a former medic, he had to know the severity of the injury.

"What can I do?" she asked.

"Nothing but pray, sweetheart."

She swallowed the knot in her throat. "Of course."

"Lt. Kline just walked in with some of the other detectives. I better talk with him."

"Cole is going to recover. I feel it in my bones."

"I hope you're right. I love you, babe."

"I love you too."

How the hell could he be so calm? Inside, Grayson had to be feeling a thousand pounds of worry but remained collected for his sister. Holly disconnected and her gaze drifted toward her purse and car keys.

CHAPTER THIRTY-TWO

Well past midnight, Grayson parked in front of the old Victorian and shut off the engine. The surgeons had successfully repaired the damage caused by the rounds striking Cole at close range. Literally less than an inch had made the difference between Cole's survival and a gravestone.

Ivy remained at the hospital, wanting to stay close to her fiancé.

Sapped but relieved, Gray blinked, noticing the red Audi parked under the oak tree.

Holly?

He ran up the front steps and opened the door.

The sight that greeted him dissipated the angst in his heart and he smiled. Amber coals glowed in the massive living room fireplace. Dad slept in his favorite La-Z-Boy recliner, a newspaper draped over his lap and his reading glasses skewed on his nose. Holly leaned against the overstuffed armrest of the turn-of-the-century couch, her eyes closed and her arm across Jackson's shoulders, who slept soundly with his head on her lap.

He'd called Dad earlier to let him know Cole survived the operation. The old man hadn't mentioned Holly had returned to the farmstead.

Gray quietly crossed the room and gently squeezed his father's shoulder. "I'm home, Dad. Everything's gonna be fine. Go to bed."

His father snorted and opened his eyes, then fumbled with his glasses and shoved them in his shirt pocket. "Ivy?" he asked in a gritty voice as he gripped the lever on the side of the chair and dropped the raised leg rest.

"She's with Cole. We can all visit tomorrow. I'll put Jackson to bed."

His father nodded and clumsily got to his feet. Dad rubbed the heels of his hands over his eyes. "Holly said she'd stay until you got home. Jackson stuck by her side all night. She kept both of us entertained with stories about mummies and ancient curses. She's a good woman, Gray."

"I know that, Dad."

His father headed for his bedroom and Gray lifted Jackson into his arms.

The kid woke but barely opened his eyes. "Is Mom home?"

Gray mounted the stairs leading to the second floor. "No, buddy. She's staying with Cole, but he's going to be fine, and you can visit tomorrow."

"I was scared, Uncle Gray."

He walked down the hallway and nudged open Jackson's door with an elbow and entered the big bedroom, the walls covered in movie posters and superheroes. An obstacle course of clothes and toys were strewn over the floor.

"I know, kid. We all were."

He pulled the top sheet and comforter aside and laid his nephew on the bed.

"Holly told me Cole is a hero. He caught the bad guys."

Gray grinned and covered the boy with the Superman blanket. "He did. Sometimes heroes get hurt, but men like Cole never give up. Get some sleep."

Jackson rolled onto his side and closed his eyes.

Gray shut off the nightlight. When he turned, Holly stood in the doorway with her head tipped against the frame. She stepped back into the hallway so he could close the bedroom door.

"Everything okay?" she asked quietly.

He nodded and palmed her jaw. "Thank you for watching over him."

She smiled, her eyes glazed with exhaustion. "You're welcome. I'll call you tomorrow."

Call? Did she actually think he'd let her drive home now? He clasped her hand and led her down the polished wood floor of the hallway and into his bedroom. The moon cast a soft glow through the tall, arched window.

Her eyes rounded as her gaze panned the room. "This is quite the bedroom. Massive. Masculine but comfortable. Not what I expected. It reminds me of a wealthy lord's chamber."

"They built the rooms big back in the day."

"They certainly did. Thanks for the tour but I'm really tired, Gray. I need to get on the road."

"So am I." He unbuttoned her shirt, unlatched her bra, and then eased the straps down her arms. "You're staying here tonight."

Gray released the button and zipper on her pants, but Holly finished undressing herself.

"Thought we agreed it's not appropriate." She stepped out of the pants pooled at her ankles.

He collected her clothes and placed them on the large, leather-topped bench next to his desk.

"I don't want you driving when you're exhausted." After taking off his own clothes, he led her to the big king bed and lifted the sheets.

Holly slipped under the covers. "When I saw the news, I don't think I've experienced that depth of fear before. It was paralyzing."

He joined her in bed, and she snuggled into his side, tucking her head under his chin.

"We're all still breathing. That's what counts."

"I wasn't sure if I should come or not, but I knew Jackson was probably scared to death and your dad could use a little moral support."

He kissed the top of her head then rolled onto his side to face her. "Sweetheart, you're part of me, which means you're part of this family."

"How's Ivy?"

"Still shaken, but relieved. Cole opened his eyes for a few

seconds once they'd moved him into ICU. He knew she was there and squeezed her hand."

"Will it be a long recovery?"

"Actually, no. Surgeon stitched him up and the rounds missed Cole's heart. He's got a broken rib, but that was because of me doing compressions. Fuck, he was lucky."

Holly's soft hand trailed down his pecs. "Sounds like he was lucky you were there if you had to perform CPR." She placed a soft kiss on his shoulder.

Gray caressed her back, his knotted nerves releasing with Holly's warmth next to him. "It makes a difference."

"What does?"

"Knowing someone loves you. For the last fifteen years, I never wanted anyone to need me. Didn't seem to matter." He trailed his thumb along her jaw. "When I saw Cole look into my sister's eyes, I knew he wanted to live because of her. It reminded me of you and how much you mean to me. Holly, I —love that I belong to you."

She slid her warm palm over his hip. "Close your eyes."

He grinned, reminded of the night she'd been attacked and how he'd done the same thing to let her know he was there.

Hours later, somewhere between dreams and reality, Holly's soft lips brushed a trail of heated kisses down his chest. Her silky hair tickled his thigh. When her hot mouth eased over his erection, he floated in a languid, sensual state. Gray moaned but didn't wake. His body relaxed, suspended in bliss. Her tongue circled his tip, and she sucked his shaft with a tempered, seductive pace. Unsure if he was dreaming, he threaded his fingers through her soft curls. This had to be real, but he didn't want to wake. His heart drummed and his breathing shallowed as her mouth made him writhe with pleasure.

Gray had no idea whether seconds or minutes passed but carnal flames crept through his veins the way she played with his cock. He reached above his head and gripped the iron rods of the headboard.

"Sweetheart, I love you so fucking much."

Holly lured him into a place where every muscle in his body was rock-hard. His back arched and he thrust his hips to meet each sweet, moist plunge of her mouth.

He clenched his jaw against the rising wave but when she rimmed his anus with her thumb, a powerful ripple washed through his spine.

"Oh, babe, I'm gonna come." The hot walls of her mouth twisted him into an erotic mess. She hummed her approval and the vibration tipped the scales. "Fuck, Holly. Aw, sweet Jesus."

Engulfed in a series of endless quakes, the release rocked him to the core. Euphoria rushed through his blood, her little tongue licking him clean, making him shudder with aftershocks.

She placed a chaste kiss below his navel then slid up his body, her soft breasts pressed against his side.

"I love you so much my heart aches," she whispered next to his ear. "I'm afraid to face the day when this all ends."

He slid his arm around her slender waist and held her tightly. Half asleep, he couldn't be sure if his mind wasn't just making shit up.

"There's no end to us. I'd never let that happen."

When Gray opened his eyes, light streamed in the window and roosters crowed outside. He tipped his head to the left, but Holly wasn't beside him. He blinked, wondering if last night had been a dream. Maybe she'd left early.

Throwing his legs over the side of the bed, he sat up and ran his fingers through his hair. Someone was up because his stomach rumbled with the delicious aroma of breakfast wafting in the air. He quickly washed and headed downstairs but paused on the last step.

Holly glanced up as she set a plate of food in front of his dad, who sat at the kitchen table. He hadn't been dreaming last night, this was the dream. Seeing her here with a demure smile on her lips.

"Don't stand there gawking like an idiot. Tell her you love her and come eat breakfast," his old man said. "She made us both an omelet and they smell great."

He heard his father, but his gaze didn't waver from his raven-haired girlfriend. The closer he got, the more her cheeks tinted with a gorgeous hue. He swept his arm around her back and tugged her to his chest, then tilted his head but halted before kissing her, his eyes sweeping across her pillowy lips.

"Did you have sweet dreams? Because I did."

She bit her bottom lip and grinned. "Yes, I slept well, thank you."

A rumble of contentment rolled around in his chest, and he kissed her like he wanted to kiss her every single day.

"Good morning," she said sweetly and stepped out of his grasp.

They sat down and his father held up the newspaper. "Front page, son."

Both he and Holly leaned closer.

Shit.

Holly's eyes widened. "You're on the front page, Gray."

The image of him standing in front of the house they'd raided must have been taken while he'd watched the ambulance pull away with Cole. The byline read, *"Sheriff's office means business and won't stop until the streets of Skagit County are safe."*

"What does the article say?" Holly asked.

The article explained that millions of dollars' worth of narcotics, weapons, and stolen goods were seized at a warehouse and seven stash houses in the county's largest multi-agency raid in history. Fourteen gang members were killed in shootouts between law enforcement and the criminals, including Cage Martin, president of the deadly, one-percenter Werewolves gang. One detective from the sheriff's department was critically injured and two members from the drug task force sustained minor injuries. The community owes these officers gratitude for their bravery and commitment.

Kline had put two deputies on security duty outside the ICU, just in case the Werewolves sought retribution.

Holly didn't wear an expression of pride, it was pinched with worry.

"I'm glad the ball cap shielded most of your face," she said. "This gang will want revenge, won't they?"

"Probably." He decided not to sugar-coat the truth. "Depends on who takes Cage's place. He might order a cool-down period, or he might be bent on revenge. This type of hazard is part of the job, Holly. We always keep our eyes open."

Her brow furrowed. "I want you to keep breathing too. Maybe you should retire and work full-time here on the farmstead."

"Holly," he said in a low timbre. "Your first husband was a cop. Did you ask him to quit?"

She narrowed her eyes at him. "No, but as you pointed out, Mr. Brooks, I didn't love him like I love you."

Dad's eyes ping-ponged between them.

"That's not fair."

"You want me to quit my career and immigrate to the US. Is that fair?" she asked.

"Holly, I didn't ask you to do that."

"No, but that's what you want!"

Of course, that's what he wanted. "I can easily support both of us, and I know you can find a job here."

"Grayson, I don't want a job. I worked hard to establish myself as a reliable and respected ancient text researcher."

"Then establish yourself here," he said, piercing the air toward the table with his finger.

"Should I contact Dirk and ask him?"

His temper flared at the thought. "No!" he said sharply.

"The farther he stays away from you, the better."

Dad cleared his throat loudly and they both ceased fire. "You remind me of two billy goats butting heads. You're not going to solve this argument today. All of our nerves are singing because of yesterday. Y'all just need to give it time."

Holly sighed and picked up her fork. "You're right, Samuel. My apologies. Breakfast is getting cold. Let's eat."

Gray dug into his omelet without another word. He didn't want to fight with Holly. After breakfast, his father went outside to get some chores done before taking Jackson to the hospital to see Cole. Gray told Holly to leave the dishes, he'd clean up, but she rinsed and stacked them in the dishwasher anyway.

He had to leave for work. Holly had to do the same. They were always going in opposite directions.

Stiff silence defined the tension between them. Gray stared at the wood grain of the old family table for a moment before turning his head to see Holly standing at the sink, her arms stiffly extended, gripping the edge of the counter.

He got up and skirted the island. "It was a helluva day yesterday, but I'm thankful for the time we have together," he said, wrapping his arms around her body and leaning his chin against her soft curls.

"Me too," she said quietly, still facing the white backsplash behind the sink.

"There's no easy answer to our dilemma. I realize that now, Holly, but I love you and that's not ever going to change."

She pivoted and hugged him around the waist, resting the side of her head against his chest. "I'm sorry I even brought up the subject of you retiring from law enforcement. It's fear talking."

"I know. Believe me, I understand."

Holly smiled up at him. "Our situation isn't perfect, but we'll manage. I better go. I have a faculty meeting this morning."

As much as he didn't want her to leave, he had no choice. She collected her purse and Gray walked her outside.

"Tell Ivy and Cole I'm thinking about them," Holly said, opening the driver's door. "If you need help with anything, please ask."

"Okay." He gripped her upper arms, stopping her from getting behind the wheel. "I need help sleeping, so come back after work."

He placed a deep, slow kiss on her lips.

She grinned. "You're incorrigible."

"Sweetheart, when you make a man come like you did to me last night, expect a full-scale, show-no-mercy attempt to keep you as long as I can. I'm not going to apologize or back down. I want to wake up every morning and see you beside me."

Her nose twitched and she raised a brow at him. "Because of one epic orgasm," she teased.

Gray traced her bottom lip with his thumb. "No, because I love you and we belong together."

"You know, for a hard-ass, you're kinda romantic and sweet."

They hugged and as always, he didn't want to let her go, but stepped back so Holly could get in the car.

He waved as the Audi drove away. Again. She needed to maintain her independence and career. Even if Holly opted for dual citizenship, the commute from the farmstead to the university was over an hour and a half drive, not including wait time at the border that could exceed two hours. Even with a Nexus Pass, she could run into long delays. Gray considered contacting Dirk. He had to have connections in Holly's field. Maybe he could help her find a job here in the US.

Much as Gray disliked the thought, Dirk might have the solution to their problem.

CHAPTER THIRTY-THREE

S itting at his desk in the PU on Monday afternoon, Grayson's cell rang.

"Charlotte," he said, greeting his realtor from San Diego.

"Good news, Grayson. We got a solid cash offer on your townhouse."

"For the asking price?"

She chuckled. "Would I be calling you with anything else?"

He grinned. "Okay, when do they want possession?"

"After they get the inspection. We'll sign the documentation and close. They'd like to move in by the beginning of September."

"Sounds good. Does Erika know?"

"I told her a few days ago that someone put an offer on the house. I dropped by today, but it looks like she's gone."

He didn't have a lot of furniture, just the basics. "I'll try to hunt her down. She can have my furniture if she wants. Either that or I'll have Goodwill pick it up."

"Great. Let me know if you need a hand with that. Talk to you soon."

He sat back and grinned. Selling the townhouse wrapped up his life in San Diego. Time for the next big step. A huge step!

Checking the time on his phone, it was close to four o'clock. Cole had spent a week in the hospital, recovering in record time. He'd have to take it easy, but the doctor said he could leave today. Ivy was making a big dinner to welcome him home.

By six o'clock, the family sat on the back patio, enjoying

homegrown corn and fresh nugget potatoes. A colorful platter sat in the center of the table with a savory pork loin Ivy had slow-roasted all day.

With everyone in good spirits, Grayson said, "I heard from my realtor today. My place sold in San Diego."

His family spouted congratulations and lifted their glasses in the air for a toast.

"Next weekend is the August celebration here at the farmstead. I was thinkin' that I'd invite Holly to spend the weekend at the farm."

Holly hadn't stayed overnight at the farmstead again. This past weekend, he'd crossed the border and stayed at her place Saturday night and came home Sunday.

Ivy nudged Cole with her elbow as if they'd had some secret bet going on. "Woo-hoo, giant step, big brother!"

Dad's silver moustache twitched with a smile. "Think that's a great idea, son."

Grayson waited for *I told you so* from the old man, but he just winked.

Jackson piped up. "Holly can have my room. She doesn't have to stay out in the shed. I'll bunk with you, Uncle Gray."

The adults chuckled.

"Thanks, buddy," Grayson said, "but you don't have to move out of your room."

The kid shrugged a lean shoulder and pierced a juicy chunk of pork roast.

Dad scratched his jaw. "You know your mother and I loved this land. After your grandfather passed and I left the rodeo circuit to take over the farmstead, we knew we'd never leave. We wanted to raise you kids here. Since I see some big changes happening around this place,"—he opened the folded newspaper to reveal a small stack of sheets stapled at the top—"I figure you're going to need this."

He handed the paperwork to Grayson.

Gray glanced at the top page and shook his head. "Thanks, Dad. I don't know what to say."

"What is it?" Ivy asked.

He handed her the documentation showing ten acres subdivided from the farmstead and his name on the title.

"Oh, wow. That's fantastic," she crowed, showing Cole.

Gray got up and hugged his old man. "Love you, Dad."

Samuel Brooks rarely got emotional, but a sheen appeared in his eyes. "I'm glad you're home, son. Not to put the cart before the horse, but I'm guessing there's a reason you're asking Miss McNeela to stay the weekend."

His father was just too on the ball. "Yeah. There's a reason."

Cole piped up and said, "Guess this means you're head over heels in love with Holly. Millions of women in the US, buddy, and you fall in love with a Canuck."

As the family started teasing the hell out of him, someone cleared their throat. They all turned to see a woman standing next to the flower planter, gripping a suitcase, but it wasn't Holly.

Shock thread its way through Gray's veins.

"Hey," she said brightly. "No one answered the front door." Erika swept forward and threw her arms around his neck. "Hi, baby. I've missed you so much. Where's your room? I'll put my bag in there and join you all for supper. I'm so excited to meet your family."

Everyone at the table was dead silent until Ivy said, "Um, Grayson. Who is this?"

Dumbfounded as to what the hell Erika was doing standing in his backyard, he didn't answer.

Erika, wearing a low tank that allowed most of her tits to spill out, screwed her brows together. "What do you mean, who am I? I'm Grayson's girlfriend." She dismissed Ivy and said, "I have so much to tell you, baby. When I heard your place was selling, I jumped on a bus."

Was this some kind of fucking joke?

"Excuse us for a second." He led the way into the house, and Erika followed on his heels.

"Where's your room?" Her gaze roamed the large living room. "God, I love this place. It's like a turn-of-the- century mansion. That kitchen is enormous." She spun on the spot, taking everything in. "This place must be worth a ton of money."

"Erika, what the hell are you doing here?"

She sauntered over to the big river rock fireplace, checking out the framed pictures on the mantle. "Gray, I kicked the booze and drugs. I'm clean." She turned and smiled, as if this was news he'd been waiting to hear. "You've always been there for me. It's my turn to be there for you. Here, I mean. You can teach me everything there is to know about farming."

"Erika, we—"

She strode over to him. "I love you. I've always loved you. I've been a mess, and I understand it's my doing. Every time I screwed up, you were there to pick me up. That's not ever going to happen again."

Ivy opened the patio door, her expression tight with anger. "Excuse me," she said, with a definite bite in her tone. Then marched across the room. "This is a family farm, not Grayson's bachelor pad. I don't know who you are, but you've got some nerve appearing on our doorstep with your luggage and think you're going to take roost in this house."

Erika blinked with surprise. "I spent my last dollar to get here. I have nowhere else to go. We're a couple. Of course, I'm staying."

Ivy was obviously plenty pissed by the hard glare she aimed at him. "Grayson, family meeting!"

Erika clung to his arm and looked beseechingly up at him. "You sold the townhouse. It's probably enough to buy a home in these parts. We can leave and get a place of our own."

He urged her to sit on the couch. "Wait here."

Gray followed Ivy outside and before he could open his mouth, his sister thrust her hands on her hips. "Who the hell is that woman? She looks like she just finished her shift at a strip club." Even their father raised his brows at that one. Jackson snickered. "Young man, go feed the birds. Now!"

"Yes, ma'am," Jackson said, and left the table.

Finally catching his bearings, Grayson addressed his confused family. "I did not invite her here, Ivy."

"She showed up like she has a right to be here. Is she your girlfriend or not?"

He gripped the back of a chair then sat because his legs felt unstable. "We met when I was serving in the Forces. It was casual."

"You mean sex. She was your fuck buddy when you were in town!"

Cole cleared his throat. "Ivy, let the man talk."

Grayson eyed his sister. "Yeah, she was one of many, but she kept coming back. Erika had a rough upbringing. She liked to party and became addicted to drugs and alcohol. In the last five years, whenever she got into trouble, she had me on speed dial."

"And you took her in," Ivy said. "Because you love to rescue birds with broken wings, or is it because she looks like she strutted off the pages of a Victoria's Secret catalog?"

Ignoring her jibe, he explained, "When Erika sobered up, she'd leave. Recently, she needed a hand. I let her stay at my place while I listed it because she was homeless. When I left San Diego, I left her too."

Ivy crossed her arms over her chest. "She's sober and has nowhere to go, so she lands on our doorstep and expects us to take her in? What about Holly? I'm not stupid, ya know. You've always kept your private life private, but you've changed since you met her. You're happy, Gray. That permanent scowl on your face is gone. Are you gonna toss Holly aside for this slut?"

Cole slid his arm around her shoulders. "You need to calm down, honey. Gray knows what he's doing. He'll handle it."

Ivy swept her hand through the air. "Never mind, not my business. What is my business is what you intend on doing with that woman squatting in our living room."

Good question. Ivy nailed his character by saying he had a weak spot for rescuing the helpless. Tossing the woman out on her ass to fend for herself wasn't in his nature. They had history, even though it was fraught with an unhealthy, one-sided dependency.

His family all stared at him, waiting for a response. "She can stay in the suite for a couple of days. I'll figure this out."

Ivy gnawed on her inner cheek. "You're making a *huge* mistake, Grayson. If you can't do it, then I'll drive her to the bus station and buy her a ticket back to San Diego."

He knew Erika's tenacity. She wouldn't get on the bus. Instead, she'd hitchhike back to their place and try again. "It's my problem and I'll fix it."

Erika stepped up to stand beside his chair. "It's pretty clear Grayson never told you about us." She turned her focus on Ivy. "I'm sure everything's going to work out fine. Grayson would never abandon me." She placed a hand on her stomach. "Or the baby."

His entire family's mouths gaped, as did his.

"Whaaaat?" Ivy screeched.

He held his hand out to signal his sister to calm down. "Ivy! No. It's not my kid."

* * * *

Grayson planted Erika's bag next to the bed in the suite, then threw open a window to air the place out.

"Are we staying here?" She came up behind him and wrapped her lean arms around his waist.

He pried himself from her grip. "No, I'm not staying here."

"Grayson, please," she whispered. "I want to stay with you in the house. It's just temporary until we find a place of our own. I'm sure your sister will understand."

He led her to the suede couch, pointed for her to plant

her ass, and took a seat in a chair across from her. "If you're hungry, I'll bring you some dinner."

Her lips curled upward in a smile. "I'd love to have dinner with you."

"That's not what I said. I said I'd bring you dinner."

"Don't be angry with me, Gray. I've missed you so much and I know you've missed me."

Had she actually stopped the drugs? Because it sure sounded like she was hallucinating. His cell rang, and he pulled it from his pocket. It was Holly. Instead of answering, he let it go to voicemail.

"I let you stay at my place because you needed a roof over your head. A chance to find your feet and get a new start. That was the whole point, Erika."

Her lips curved into a sultry smile. She got up, pulled the tank over her head, and dropped it on the coffee table. Stepping in front of him, she straddled his legs and sat on his thighs, her firm breasts and tight nipples front and center.

"I did, and that's why I'm here. If your family doesn't want me to stay, then let's move. I'll find a job. But first, before we discuss anything else, make love to me."

The woman had a body that drew men over cliffs—his included—but for the first time, he wasn't losing his mind.

Her fingers trailed down his abs and went for his belt. Gripping her hand, he stopped her from going further.

"We've taken this lap too many times, Erika. Put your clothes on and take a seat over there so we can talk."

Without showing an ounce of resentment at his rejection, she swept her shirt from the table and pulled it over her head.

"We're at the finish line," she said and plopped down on the couch. "If I have to prove it to you, I will."

He leaned forward. "There's nothing to prove, Erika." If she had sobered up, it was a start. He didn't want to send her into a tailspin. "What I left at the townhouse in San Diego is yours. You need to prove to yourself that you can fly solo."

"I don't like being alone. You know that. I'm not going to fall off the wagon again, Gray. I can't throw our relationship away. And neither can you."

"It wasn't a relationship. It was physical. Supply and demand," he stated flatly.

If Erika used her zeal toward something like a job, which she'd never had, she'd probably be a CEO.

A steady diet of memorable moments with Holly taught him the difference between satisfying his dick and a relationship. He and Holly made love. That was for sure, but they also spent hours talking and enjoying each other's company in complete silence. The only thing he hadn't shared with Holly was his past with Erika. At the time, he'd been certain she *was* the past and there was no reason to bring her up.

"You've changed," she said, eyeing him. "But so have I. I don't think San Diego was good for either of us. I'm excited, Grayson. For the first time in a long time, I can tell that our future is going to be incredible."

Maybe she had changed. There was literally no way of knowing.

"Listen, get some rest. I have work to do."

She jumped to her feet, grinning. "Then introduce me to the cows."

He laughed. The only place she'd seen a cow was on TV.

Erika swaggered over to him in a familiar way, usually before she'd kneel, unzip his fly, and ease her wet mouth over his heavy cock.

"I love seeing you smile." She placed a hand on his chest. "All those years ago, when I first saw you in the bar, you were laughing with the other team guys. I fell in love with that smile. I know my friends were there to hook up with a SEAL, but I didn't care what you did. You were the hottest guy I'd ever seen. Sex was the only thing you wanted, but with time, I hoped you'd fall in love with me." Erika ran a finger across her bottom lip. "I think you did, but I was set on self-destruct.

Angry at my horrible upbringing, I used booze and drugs to stop the pain. I'm so sorry, Gray."

As always, her apology resonated with the ring of authenticity. "I appreciate your honesty, but I don't love you."

Even with all the abusive habits, her beautiful, blue eyes and pretty features never tarnished.

"I know. You've told me that over and over again. I also know in my heart it's not the truth. All I'm asking is for a little time to change your mind. Let me offer an olive branch to your sister."

He didn't want Erika to fall off the wagon, but her truth and his were very different. "I left you in San Diego because I wanted to cut ties. I'm not going to change my mind."

Erika's brow creased with hurt. She stepped back and covered her stomach with a palm. "You'd abandon us?"

"Not my child, Erika." Did she actually think another man's baby would make him change his mind? "Where's the father? Why aren't you on his doorstep?"

Worry etched her face. "He didn't want us." Her eyes welled with tears. "Gray, I need your help."

* * * *

Holly ate, slept, and worked through four days without hearing from Grayson. She'd left several messages on his phone, but he hadn't called back. Not even a single text.

Thursday afternoon she stood next to her bed, looking at her open but empty overnight bag, unsure what to do. She was supposed to spend the weekend at the farm. The entire Brooks family put in long hours to prepare for the celebration at the farmstead.

Worry kept burrowing into her gut. Had something bad happened?

Just before five o'clock, she couldn't stand it anymore and called Brooks Farmstead Store. Arlene answered. She said hello, then asked for Ivy.

471

A minute felt like an eternity until Ivy picked up.

"Holly."

Ivy voiced her name with so much weight it scared her.

"Hi, Ivy, I'm so sorry to disturb you. I know you're super busy getting ready for the celebration."

"It's okay. Glad you called."

"The summer went by so fast. I can't believe it's the end of August," she said, instead of peppering Ivy with questions about Grayson and making herself sound too desperate.

"Yeah, summer always goes fast with so much work around here."

Ivy didn't sound very chipper, and Holly wondered whether she might be angry because Grayson had spent the weekends away from the farm with her.

"I feel a little guilty. Gray should have probably worked more on the farm instead of spending time with me."

"He worked plenty. Don't feel guilty, Holly," she said in a sober tone. "Grayson's been a whole new guy. When he'd come home on Sunday nights, he'd be whistling. My cranky-assed brother never whistles. You made him happy."

She said "made" not "make." Holly's veins thinned with concern. "How's Cole?"

"Recovering quickly."

"That's good. Listen, I don't want to keep you, but Grayson asked me to spend this weekend at the farm. I haven't heard from him in four days. I just...want to make sure nothing bad has happened."

Ivy snorted. "Guess that depends on what you mean by bad. If you're asking me, it's bad."

Her heart galloped. "Is he hurt?"

Cole had nearly died during the take-down at the stash house. Had the Werewolves come looking for revenge?

"No, he's not hurt," Ivy said briskly. "My brother's an idiot. A big-hearted idiot, but an idiot, nonetheless. I should let him explain."

"He's not answering my calls. Explain what?"

Ivy sighed. "His girlfriend from San Diego landed on our front porch on Monday. A shock to all of us, since he'd never mentioned her before. She's a piece of work, let me tell you. If it were me, I'd have sent her packing the same day, but he wouldn't let me. Then Erika dropped the ultimate bomb and told him she was pregnant."

"I see." Holly bit her bottom lip to stop from tearing up.

A rooster crowed in the background. "I don't know what to say, Holly. Are you still planning on coming for the weekend?"

The bedroom walls seemed to sway, and a heavy weight hung in her chest. "No. Please tell Grayson there's no need to call me back. Thanks for letting me know. Sorry for disturbing you."

Holly disconnected the call and zipped her suitcase closed, then stored it in her closet. There was no reason to cry. Why bemoan a relationship that was doomed to fail?

She sat on the edge of her bed and stared at the delicate pattern in the cream-colored carpet. They had both set aside the truth. Although they lived close enough in miles, there was a border that separated their lives. But a pregnant girlfriend severed all hope.

It was over.

Holly laid down and pulled the throw blanket over her legs and rested her head on the soft pillow. Lying on her side, it was easy to imagine Grayson facing her, his firm, bronze chest covered in a light sheen after they'd made love, and the way his eyes always spoke to her.

She'd believed him when he said he'd never had a relationship with anyone but her. No matter how many times she'd warned herself that Grayson would probably dump her, she never thought it could hurt this badly.

She took solace in the memory that he'd loved her enough to tattoo her name on his chest. Obviously, he'd thought his relationship with this *Erika* was over.

But with a baby on the way, it had only begun.

Loneliness seeped into her veins with a familiar chill, but so did anger. He'd just shut her out. Not even a phone call to explain. No goodbye.

Oddly, her familiarity with loss gave her strength. She'd survived this before when she hadn't been enough to keep her husband.

Losing Grayson was a different kind of emptiness...the crippling kind.

CHAPTER THIRTY-FOUR

J ackson handled the tractor like a pro, but Grayson supervised and loaded the bucket with hay bales that his nephew moved to the barbeque site near the store. Gray waved, signaling to the kid that he had a full load, and Jackson turned the tractor and headed down the driveway.

He grinned, remembering when he was Jackson's age. All he wanted to do was drive the farm equipment too.

Ivy walked into the hay shed. "Dinner's ready in fifteen minutes, Grayson."

"Thanks. We're getting close to the finish line."

"Where's your baby-mama?"

He scowled at his sister. "I told you already, not my kid. She hasn't been feeling well, so I gave her a couple of extra days."

Ivy crossed her arms over her chest. "More opportunity to convince you to take care of her and some other man's baby forever. I love you, brother, but you're one stupid shit. She's manipulating you. I don't know why you can't see that."

"Throwing someone like her on the street is a recipe for disaster. Erika's vulnerable. Once she's found her confidence, she'll leave. She always does." Ivy didn't understand how volatile sobriety was for someone like Erika.

"Newsflash, Grayson. No woman is confident with a baby growing in her belly. At least not one with any sense. In the past, Erika sobered up and left, but the situation has changed. She's carrying a child. She doesn't have a roof over her head. No job. No one to support her except you. If you think she's leaving any time soon, you're nuts."

Grayson gripped the twine of a square bale and shifted it off the pile for Jackson's next load. "Jesus Christ, Ivy. Lay off. I've contacted a friend from San Diego who operates a homeless shelter. They have space for Erika. It's arranged. AMVETS is cleaning out my condo in San Diego. My old life is terminated. Finished. I want it clear and unburdened before I take the next step."

Ivy shook her head and looked at him as if he were a lunatic. "Typical man. Life doesn't fall in sequential order just because you want it to. You're juggling one ball and all the rest are on the ground being run over by a tank."

"What the hell does that mean?"

"While you're forging ahead with your master plan, have you spoken to Holly? Been up-front? Told her what's happening?"

He closed his eyes and exhaled deeply. "No. I don't want her involved."

"Oh." Sarcasm dripped from Ivy's tone. "So, she hasn't heard from you or has any idea what's going on with Erika."

Instead of backing off, Ivy was full speed ahead, giving him a bad time. This was the downside of living with family.

"I already explained myself. I want a clean slate."

Ivy rolled her eyes. "Didn't you invite Holly here this weekend?"

Shit. He pulled his cell from his pocket.

"Don't bother, Grayson."

If Holly showed up, Erika would make a scene. Back in the day, she showed her claws to a chick in a bar who'd wandered up to talk with him while Erika was in the restroom. She'd gone from calm to psycho in seconds, which made no goddamn sense, since Erika knew he fucked other women. She just couldn't watch another chick come on to him.

"I don't know how Erika would react. Badly, I'm guessing. Holly doesn't need to be part of that."

"My God, Grayson. Do you hear yourself?" She tsked, then said, "Don't worry, she's not coming."

A feeling of unease curled up his spine. "How do you know that?"

"Holly called the store yesterday. You'd invited her this weekend, then shut her out. She wanted to make sure you weren't hurt."

"Let me guess, you spilled your guts."

"No, I spilled yours." Her eyes narrowed with anger. "To save Holly from prolonging the heartbreak. Erika is never getting on a bus. She's inching her way back into your life. She's using the baby as a weapon and you're letting her do it." Ivy glared at him with pure disgust. "I really like Holly. She doesn't deserve to be treated like this, especially after she faced off with that bitch, Kate, and didn't back down."

Kate? Billings? "What do you mean?"

"July Fourth. I told you Holly had face time with that crazy cop. Billings wanted to sneak into the house. Holly wouldn't let her in. Kate threatened her and told Holly to pack her shit and leave. I don't remember the whole convo, but when Kate said she liked a challenge, thinking she could intimidate Holly with a badge, Holly went for her throat. Told her you weren't some rookie cop and Holly wasn't Mrs. Gordon. She tore strips off that bitch and said if Kate liked a challenge, she better be ready for a fucking nightmare. Billings tucked her tail between her legs and took off."

Thunderstruck, it took him a second to process Ivy's story. "She didn't tell me that."

"Holly bared her teeth to protect you, Grayson. And now another stray female wanders into her territory and what do you do? You just shoved her aside to lick Erika's wounds." Ivy shrugged as if she'd given up on him. "I don't know why you'd choose a woman who will always be on a path to destruction, but you'll be on that path with her if she stays."

Growing up, Ivy had gotten mad at him plenty of times, but he'd never seen this depth of rage. "What did Holly say when she called?"

"She said goodbye, Gray. Stop making promises to her you won't keep."

He ground his jaw to stop himself from saying something

he'd regret. "You think I'm afraid of commitment?"

"No. Not at all. You're committed to that *fucking* train wreck bunking in the suite. Soon she'll lure you into her bed. You think Holly will forgive you for that?"

"I haven't slept with Erika in years. I sure as hell won't start now. I don't expect you to understand—"

"No, I don't!"

"Jesus, Ivy, calm down. I'll call Holly and straighten things out."

"And tell her what, Grayson? The same bullshit you're feeding me? She won't believe you either. It's too late to drag her into your mess and expect her to wait. Damage is already done."

"You're the one who told her Erika was here. If you'd kept your nose out of my damn business, I wouldn't have to explain my biggest fucking mistake."

Oh, shit. As soon as the words were out of his mouth, he snapped it shut. But it was too late.

A look of utter triumph slathered over his sister's face. "Exactly. Covering your tracks is more important, isn't it, Gray?"

"Holly will understand."

"That what? You lied to her. Deceived her. You have no clue what it takes to trust a man after what Holly went through." When he raised his eyebrows with surprise, Ivy said, "That's right. We talked, and she told me about her first marriage. Not only was he unfaithful nearly the entire time, but he was a cop, Gray. You're the first man since her husband walked away that she's trusted, and you betrayed that trust by protecting Erika and yourself."

"Ivy, I'm not protecting Erika. She's leaving."

"Yeah, right." Ivy turned her back on him. "I'll keep a couple of plates warm. You can pick them up and feed your *stray* in the suite. She's not eating with the family."

He watched his sister stride toward the house then he gripped a bale and hurled it at the metal wall. Frustration made him pace the dirt floor. On the tenth revolution, Erika strode into the shed.

"Hey, baby. You okay?"

"Yeah, why wouldn't I be?"

She swaggered up to him wearing a pair of low-slung shorts that showed off her mile-high legs, and a half-length tank revealing her narrow waist and tanned skin. "I heard most of that. Guess your sister has made her mind up about me. And I take it you've been fucking some chick named Holly."

"I'm not *fucking* Holly."

"That's good."

That's not what he meant, but he let the subject drop. Gray sat down on a bale and thrust both hands through his hair. "How are you feeling?"

"Still nauseous and weak." She smiled sweetly at him. "I'm not the monster your sister thinks I am. You know that. I'm never gonna *use* again. I have this baby to care about." She sat next to him. "You might think I'm a mistake, but I'll never stop caring about you."

She laid her hand on his thigh and he abruptly stood up. He was only half listening. Mostly, Ivy's words echoed in his head that the damage was already done. Holly was a reasonable woman. She'd understand why he was doing this when he explained himself.

"Grayson."

"What?" he said sharply.

Erika stepped behind him, and her fingertips slid up his back and massaged his shoulders. "You worked all day. You're tired. Fighting with your sister is pointless. Why don't you grab those plates, and we'll have a quiet dinner together? I know you hate drama, and you've had your fill."

He closed his eyes, his anger subsiding. Although her fingers felt good, he turned and faced the woman who had come and gone from his life for far too long.

"I'm not playing house with you, Erika."

"Oooh, don't be grumpy," she said, as if ignoring his warning. "I've been cooped up all day. I could use some fresh air. Let's take a walk. It'll be good for both of us."

"Getting some fresh air is a good idea. Probably help with your nausea. It's going to be a long day tomorrow, and I've got at least another two hours of work tonight."

The lie rolled off his tongue easily. He needed some space and to throw back some cold ones at Roosters.

She shrugged one shoulder and grinned. "Then I'll wait."

He sighed and palmed the back of his stiff neck. "Erika, you've always waited for me. It's time you stopped."

She laid her palms on his chest. "There's been a lot of bumps in our road, but the truth is, I'd do anything for you. I *have* done things for you I didn't want to do because it made you happy."

He'd told Holly the truth about Dirk, but he hadn't mentioned Erika. She'd been one of the many women they'd shared. "I didn't force you to do anything."

"Hey, I know you didn't." She smiled. "You always took care of me."

Holly was attractive but not stunningly beautiful like Erika, yet his heart pointed in one direction—north of the border. He, like most men, noticed a woman's physical attributes. In his younger years, that's all that had mattered. Obviously, he'd changed somewhere between San Diego and here. He finally understood the term "better half." Holly was the woman he couldn't live without.

Erika's arms slid around his neck. "I missed you, Gray. I took the time to get clean for me, but you as well. Even though your sister hates me, I'm glad we're together now."

He gripped one of her wrists and unhitched her grip. "We're not together, Erika. You showed up on my doorstep pregnant with no money in your pocket. Because of our history, I didn't park your ass at the end of the driveway and tell you to leave. But that doesn't mean my feelings have changed or will change."

The smile evaporated, and she glared at the ground. "You're only saying that because you don't trust me. I love it here on the farmstead. Give us some time, Gray. You won't regret it, I promise."

The more he thought about what Ivy said, the more he realized he'd done something incredibly stupid. *"You shoved Holly aside to lick Erika's wounds."* He'd always been honest with Holly but hadn't told her about Erika. Why?

The answer existed between wanting Holly to feel special and not wanting her to think he had a weak spot for Erika. But that's exactly what Ivy had accused him of.

"I called an old friend in San Diego. When you're ready to travel, she'll have a place waiting for you at a shelter that supports expectant moms. They have doctors on staff and cover all the medical bills. You'll be safe."

She palmed her stomach. "I'm not ready to go anywhere." Tears rimmed her eyes. "Go, do your work. We'll talk later."

She strode out of the shed without a backward glance.

Within forty-five minutes, he'd showered, dropped off Erika's dinner and jumped in his pickup. By the time he reached Roosters, he'd called Holly three times. Each time it went to her voicemail.

Sitting in the gravel parking lot, he tried once more, but this time he left a message.

"Holly, I know you spoke with Ivy, and she told you Erika showed up. Please, I need to explain."

* * * *

Holly sat in her office at ten past six on Friday evening. Another notification sounded from her cell. She didn't have to look to know it was a missed call from Grayson. Tomorrow, Brooks Farmstead would be teaming with visitors, minus one. Her.

With her chair swiveled to face the wall behind her desk, she stared up at the three framed images. Crystal clear, close-up photos of ancient glyphs carved into clay tablets. The holy grail of a mysterious language from the Bronze Age and still undeciphered by researchers like herself. The lines and shapes were pieces of uncharted territory in human history.

Concentrating on the left image instead of her bleeding heart, her work acted like a healing balm.

"Knock-knock."

Holly rotated the chair to see Dirk Larkin leaning in her doorway. "Hey, what are you doing here?"

He tipped his head as if in question. "Is this a bad time?"

"No." She straightened in her chair. "Come in."

Dirk was an extremely good-looking man. He wasn't as muscular as Grayson, but he carried himself with confidence. Wearing a pair of jeans and a creamy-white, button-up shirt with the hem untucked, she watched his easy stride cross the low-pile carpet.

"Are you sure you're all right?" he asked, sitting in the guest chair.

She bit the inside of her lip to stop from tearing up. "Not really." She cleared her throat. "So, what brings you to the university?"

Dirk gazed at her for a few seconds, then got up, rounded the desk and crouched next to her chair. "Good news, but I can see something's upsetting you. Why don't we talk about that first?"

Her personal issues weren't anyone's problem but her own. She shook her head.

"Okay." He stood, cupped her right hand and sat on the edge of her desk. "Holly, I don't need many guesses to figure out this has something to do with Grayson. It's the *Last Blast* weekend celebration and you're sitting here instead of at the farmstead. What's happened?"

If she opened her mouth, words wouldn't come out, but tears certainly would fall. She fought hard against a wave of sadness. When she looked into Dirk's compassionate gaze, tears overflowed her determination to keep them hidden.

"He—his girlfriend showed up at the farmstead. She's... she's pregnant." Holly shook her head as if she could rid herself of the truth. "Grayson lied to me. He told me he'd never had a relationship before. I knew that was highly unlikely, and I don't know why I believed him."

Creases formed at the edge of Dirk's eyes as he squinted. "Was it Erika?"

Her stomach clenched and dove into a pit of remorse. "You know her?"

He shrugged. "Sure. They've been together off and on for nearly fourteen years."

She clutched her chest as if someone drove a dagger into her heart. Jesus, he hadn't just lied about some woman he'd had a fling with, he'd been with this woman far longer than her marriage lasted.

Dirk squeezed her hand. "I'm sorry, Holly. I don't know what to say."

"I don't either." She felt numb and betrayed. "Is she beautiful?"

He shifted his butt on the desktop and made a clicking sound with his tongue. "Yeah, she's a stunner. But what difference does that make?"

"None, I suppose."

"Look, Grayson has always been a favorite with women. When it comes to the male population, he's extraordinary. Two people like Erika and Gray are bound to connect."

"I feel so foolish."

"Don't," he said. "I know this must hurt terribly. Nothing I say will take that pain away. Grayson has a way of getting under your skin. It takes time."

She shook her head. "No, it doesn't. Not for me, anyway."

Dirk slid off the desk, rotated her chair, and balanced on his haunches. "What does that mean?"

She briefly told him what happened in her first marriage. "I knew what Gray and I had was just a fairytale and wouldn't last." She plucked a tissue from the box on her desk and dried her eyes. "Anyway, why are you here?"

He smiled, gripped both her hands, and urged her to stand. "I might have something that will cheer you up, and it's right up your alley. I just spoke with your department head and he's in agreement."

Although her heart felt like a block of ice, she was curious. "What is it?"

"We found a new cave, Holly. In Qumran. It's a scroll cave, I'm sure of it."

She gasped. "Are you serious? That would be—"

"The thirteenth," they said at the same time.

Dirk nodded. "One hundred percent sure, and I want you there when we start the dig."

"Me?" To see ancient manuscripts revealed from where they'd laid for two thousand years would be the biggest milestone of her career. "Dirk, I don't know what to say."

"You better say yes." His tanned features creased with a smile. "We don't have a lot of time. They're clearing the entrance to the cave."

"How much time do I have?"

"I talked to my team on site this afternoon. They should clear the entrance within two days."

"My intern, Juliette. Would you allow her to come as well? She's incredibly bright and talented."

Dirk slid his hands to the tops of Holly's shoulders. "Of course, she can come. So, is that a yes?"

Holly couldn't help herself and hugged him. "Thank you. I can't believe this is happening. I've dreamed about this all my life."

His large hands settled on her waist as his gaze wandered to the photos. "The Vinča Scripts."

"Amazing, aren't they?"

Dirk hummed his assent. "We won't find those in the cave, but we will discover other important antiquity. I'm excited about this dig."

"How long do you expect we'll be there?"

Holly's phone rang, and they both glanced down at her desk.

"Going to answer?" He raised an eyebrow. "Maybe it's a misunderstanding and you should."

As the phone rang, identifying Grayson as the caller, she said, "No. There's no misunderstanding. You're right, I was supposed to be there this weekend, but five days ago he just cut me off. I got worried something happened to him and called his sister, Ivy. She explained what had happened. I didn't know he'd been involved with Erika for that long. Ivy probably told him I'd called. I don't need to hear him tell me it's over between us. I know it is."

Tears welled in her eyes, and she slammed them shut.

Dirk hugged her and rubbed her back. "Hey, look at the adventure we're about to embark on. It's going to be incredible, Holly." He palmed her shoulders and leaned back. "Plan for six months."

She smiled and swept the tears away. "I can do that."

"Tell you what—we'll fly to Israel together. Think you can coordinate everything by Sunday night?"

She nodded. "Not sure if Juliette can."

"Find out and let me know. I'll arrange a later flight for her, if necessary."

Maybe things hadn't worked out with Grayson, but because of him, she'd met Dirk, and he was giving her the opportunity of a lifetime. "I better get moving. I've got a lot to do."

"Sounds good, but you need dinner first," he said. "Let's grab some and I'll tell you how we plan to execute the dig and what we've discovered so far."

She hadn't really eaten in two days. "Okay."

Though her heart ached, Holly had a reason to smile again.

* * * *

Saturday morning, Grayson groaned and swung his legs over the edge of the couch. His head thumped because he'd put too many beers down his throat at Roosters and ended up calling Cole to come get him. Ivy came too but didn't get out of the car. She dropped Cole off and headed home.

He palmed his face, then scraped his fingers through his hair.

"Coffee is on, man. Get your sorry ass off my couch," Cole said, stepping into the archway between the kitchen and living room.

He shoved himself to his feet, and the room did a three-sixty. "Yeah, I could use a coffee."

Grayson strode into the kitchen and dropped into a chair at the spindly wood table.

Cole dumped a plate of buttered toast and a bottle of ibuprofen in front of him. "You sure were talking a string of shit last night."

The hot java felt good on Gray's throat. "I'm sure I was, but I don't remember what I said." He unscrewed the cap and downed two pills.

"Most of it was alcohol-induced babble." Cole opened the fridge and retrieved a short carton of cream. "Ivy filled me in."

He snorted. "I bet she did. If she'd just kept her mouth shut, I wouldn't be in this mess."

Cole stirred some cream into his coffee. "This isn't Ivy's fault. I think everybody sees it, Gray, except you."

He sighed and leaned back in the chair. "Sees what?"

"You can lay down a hundred excuses for taking the soft approach with Erika, but she's taking advantage of the opportunity. No matter what you decide, you've lost Holly and have nobody to blame but yourself. Maybe it's better to leave things the way they are."

He gaped at his friend. "You think I should sever my ties with Holly and let Erika stay?"

Cole shrugged. "Holly's a scientist with a career she loves, and she's Canadian. Your life is here. You've got a long history with Erika and obviously care about her, or you would have cut her off a long time ago." He spread some strawberry jam on a piece of toast. "The evidence is pretty clear. Listen, if you really gave a shit about Holly, you would have called and explained."

Grayson emptied his cup and walked across the kitchen to get a refill. "Your evidence is bullshit." He returned to the table, topping up Cole's mug.

His friend looked him in the eyes. "You want some straight talk?"

"As long as it's you talking and not my sister."

"Is it possible that deep down you love Erika? She's definitely a beautiful woman, and I'm guessing pretty fucking hot in bed. You've always had high standards. I think you never put a ring on her finger solely because she's like the women we arrest. Erika ended up as an addict. Holly, on the other hand, you obviously respect, but I have my doubts you can keep your eyes off other women."

Holly had blamed herself for her ex's adultery. Total crap.

"Not a bad hypothesis, but you're dead fucking wrong. I severed my ties with Erika when I left San Diego. No," he said emphatically, "I never loved her. To all of you, it might seem like I'm hedging, but that's not the truth. Before I left San Diego, we had a heart-to-heart. She knew I wasn't coming back, and she wasn't coming with me. I've been thinking about it, and it doesn't make sense that Erika got on a bus for Washington."

Cole brushed the crumbs from his fingers over the plate. "Guess the pregnancy made her change her mind."

Grayson shook his head. "I don't buy that excuse. She's a tall woman and I don't know how pregnant she is, but there's no baby bump yet, from what I can see."

His buddy downed his coffee and set the mug aside. "You think she's lying about the pregnancy?"

"I'm only certain that she's here. Erika has been extremely amiable. Not to mention relentless at tempting me into her bed."

Cole's brows popped. "Takes a strong man to resist a woman like that."

He snorted and got to his feet. "Not at all difficult when you're in love with someone else." He checked his watch. Seven o'clock. "Thanks for letting me crash on your couch. I better get home and shower. It's gonna be a long day."

Cole collected the dishes and put them in the sink. "I'll be right behind ya."

About to leave, he paused and turned to look at his best friend. "You know, every time we've talked about Holly, you always suggest I let her go. You point out our differences or say things like, you doubt I can keep my eyes off other women." Cole's jaw clenched, and he crossed his arms over his chest. "I don't know if that's you being hard-core practical, but sometimes it feels like you want our relationship to fail, or maybe you just want me to fail."

Cole's brow notched together. "No, man. I don't think it's possible for you to fail. You're a decorated combat hero. Dedicated son and concerned brother. One helluva detective. You saved my life."

"Then why would you tell me more than once to bail on Holly? She's the one—" A knot swelled in his throat. "I fucked up. I know that. But she's the one person who's ever made me happy."

"Gray, I believe you, but your actions this week say something else. That might sound like I'm beating you over the head with your mistake. I'm not. We all like Holly. Sometimes two people can love each other, but circumstance puts them on roads that never cross. It's not what you want to hear, but it's something you need to consider."

He'd considered every option, from the mundane to the insane.

"I'm not willing to walk away from Holly. Not ever."

CHAPTER THIRTY-FIVE

T he Last Blast celebration brought flocks of people to the farmstead. Erika tagged along at his side for most of the day, offering to help. Grayson ignored the questioning looks from friends who'd expected to see Holly and seemed confused about Erika.

Around six-thirty in the evening, he stood manning the barbeque station and having a beer with a few old buddies from the football team. Erika strolled up and slung her arm around his shoulders.

"Baby, I'm gonna take a shower before dinner." She eyed the guys watching and grinned. "Feel free to join me."

She'd been doing shit like this all day, especially with friends who'd dropped by to say hello, and he was getting fucking sick of it. Erika sauntered away and his buddies glued their eyes to her five-feet-ten hourglass figure and perfect ass.

Dave lifted his beer. "That's some upgrade you got there, Gray."

He slammed the long-handled fork on the mobile cart, catching the edge of the sauce bowl and splattering the contents. "Not an upgrade, Dave. She's pregnant and a recovering drug addict, but have at 'er, buddy. She doesn't belong to me."

Cash, who'd played left tackle in school, said, "She's been attached to your hip all day. We just figured you and Holly broke up."

"We didn't break up," he growled. "She's—" The guys waited for an answer he couldn't give. "She couldn't make it. Erika's from San Diego. She dropped by for a visit."

Dave chuckled. "Yeah, um, I'd say she wants more than a

visit. But, hey, none of our business." He shrugged. "If it were me, I'd take a bite out of that."

Grayson ripped off some paper towels from the roll and cleaned up the mess he'd made. Holly should be here, not Erika. He'd called at least twenty more times, but she refused to answer. Monday, he'd call the university and explain everything. If she hung up on him, then he would get in his truck and cross the border. He'd had something big planned for tonight until everything fell apart, but that wouldn't stop him.

An hour later, their guests and friends settled down to eat dinner. Erika returned wearing a peach-colored see-through summer dress with just enough modesty to hide her tits. Her blonde hair was curled, and every guy's head turned to take a second look.

Grayson was doling out beef ribs when Wendy stepped up with her plate. "Hey, gorgeous. I'm starving, so lay it on me."

He chuckled. Wearing her signature straw cowboy hat, a red and white checkered top tied with a knot in the middle of her taut belly, shorts and boots, she truly was the picture of country cute.

"How ya doin', Wendy?"

She leaned toward him and winked. "Think I've had one too many. But don't tell Daddy, he thinks I'm pure as the driven snow."

Laughing, he put ribs drenched in whiskey sauce on her paper plate. "Your secret's safe."

"Graaay." Erika strolled up and snaked her hand around his upper arm. "Who's this?"

Wendy's bright smile withered, and she gave Erika an up-down look, then dismissed her. "Grayson, where's your girlfriend, Holly? I haven't seen her all day."

Oh, boy. Ivy had been talkin' with Wendy and the adage, *enemy of my enemy is my friend,* came to mind.

"She couldn't make it."

"Ooooh," Wendy cooed. "I was thinkin' of arranging a

girl's night out. I wanted to invite her." She flipped her hand in the air. "I know, I know. I was a little jealous at first, but I can see you love that woman to death. Tell her we're gonna kick up our heels one night real soon."

He grinned. "She'd like that, Wendy."

His neighbor's brilliant smile reappeared. "So"—she cocked her head and put her gaze on Erika—"who might you be, and why are you draped over my friend's sweetheart?"

"I'm Erika, and I think you're a little confused. Gray and I have been together for years. We've always had an open relationship, but that's over now. Your friend was just his last fling before we settle down."

Wendy let out a loud bark of laughter. "Yeah, right. Good luck with that, honey." And she strutted away.

"That woman is delusional," Erika snarled.

He was still chuckling over Wendy's antics. "How so?"

Erika raised her sleek eyebrow and rolled her eyes. "First of all, I don't see anyone named Holly around here. Secondly, you don't do girlfriends and you've never fallen in love, except with me."

She tilted her head forward to kiss him, but he dodged her attempt then closed the lid of the large smoker.

"Sorry, but Wendy isn't delusional. My girlfriend's name *is* Holly."

Erika's forehead crunched into a field of creases. "Grayson, I've never been possessive of you, but that time is over. Whoever this chick is, she's not here because you didn't invite her. And we both know you didn't invite her because I'm here. Now," she said brightly, "I'm starving. Let's grab some dinner."

It wasn't Wendy who was delusional. "Go ahead and eat. I'm still serving."

A couple who frequented the farmstead store wandered up with their twin boys.

"I hear those ribs are fantastic," the husband said.

Grayson opened the smoker. "You'll be back for seconds."

The family thanked him after he'd doled out the ribs and they wandered toward the buffet table loaded with side dishes.

"Gray, it's a beautiful, balmy evening. Why don't we enjoy it together?" Her hand slid down his arm and onto his ass. "Baby, we don't have to make things complicated."

"My ass doesn't belong to you." He scowled, not because she dropped innuendo, but because his cock responded with muscle memory. With Erika's tendency to create a scene, he kept things low key.

A knowing grin slipped onto Erika's glossy lips when her gaze dropped to his crotch. "Your ass and you belong to me." Instead of pressing the matter, she stepped back. "Guess I'll keep myself company for a while until you're finished." She headed toward the buffet.

He yanked his cell from his pocket and called Holly. When it went to voicemail, he said, "Holly, you're turning me into a textbook stalker. I get that you're pissed off, but what I don't understand is why you won't let me explain. You should be here. With me. With the family." He rubbed his forehead. "Answer the damn phone, woman."

He disconnected and exhaled his frustration. Holly could run, but she couldn't hide. This wasn't the end. No way.

The evening waned on. The band Ivy hired jumped onto the wooden stage he and Cole had hammered together and started playing for the guests. The booze flowed. People kicked up their heels, dancing and having a good time.

Grayson kept to the shadows and watched Erika. She was never alone, flirting with guys who wandered up to talk with her. Every once in a while, she'd look over at him. She was playing a game, mistakenly thinking he gave a shit.

Around ten p.m., she abandoned the men trying to score with her and wandered over to where Gray stood next to a column at the front of the store. She held a hand over her stomach and grimaced as if in pain.

"Grayson, I'm going to lie down for a while. I'm not

feeling so great."

His first instinct was to help and ask questions about her discomfort, but instead, he nodded. If it was serious, she'd tell him.

"Night."

Once she was gone, he wandered through the crowd to a picnic table where Cole sat nursing a beer.

"Another success," Cole said, tipping back the brown neck.

"Always is." Ivy was dancing up a storm with Jackson and Wendy. "Why aren't you up there with your future wife?"

Cole's profile remained stoic, his eyes glued to Ivy. "Because she just told me I'm going to be a father and my legs are shaking so bad, I don't think I can walk."

"What?" Grayson clanked his bottle against Cole's brew and threw an arm over his buddy's shoulder. "Congratulations, man. That's fantastic."

Cole chugged the rest of his beer. "I never thought it would happen this fast."

Grayson chuckled at his partner. "Do Dad and Jackson know?"

"Not yet. We're going to tell them tomorrow morning." He bowed his head. "Holy shit, I'm going to be a father."

"Aww, stop freaking out. This is great news. Are you tying the knot before or after the baby's born?"

"We talked about it. I'm happy either way, but it's up to Ivy."

"Maybe that's why my sister blasted the shit out of me yesterday afternoon. Hormones."

"Could be, but she's seriously pissed off at you."

A commotion on the other side of the crowd attracted his attention.

Gray stood to get a better look. "Aw, Jesus. It's Dave and Tim."

Cole stood as well. When fists started flying, they ran toward the disturbance. The guys were already on the ground exchanging blows. A crowd formed around the men. Gray and Cole shot a look at each other and dove in, separating the men.

Grayson grabbed Dave by the back of the neck and one arm, then yanked him off Tim. Cole snagged Tim and held him back.

"Let me go, Gray," Dave barked, and tried to lunge out of his arms.

Dave didn't get far. Gray had a loose choke hold on the guy. "Settle down, Dave, or you're going night-night," he warned.

"Fine. Fuck." The muscles in Dave's shoulders relaxed.

Grayson dropped his arms and shifted to the guy's side, just in case. "You two fucking idiots need to settle this shit once and for all. Seriously, how long are you gonna hold this grudge, Dave?"

Tim shook out his shoulders when Cole let go. "I'd like to know that, too. Gemma and I have been married for thirteen years. Get over it."

Dave's speech slurred when he said, "Fuck you. She never would have married you if you hadn't knocked her up."

Tim's eyes narrowed. "Yeah, well, I knocked her up three more times, just for you, asshole."

Dave made another sloppy lunge and Gray swept Dave's legs out from under him. The guy went down hard. He kept the unruly drunk pinned face to the ground. Cash, Dave's best friend, stood close by.

"Cash, take him home and put him to bed."

Cole put his arm out to stop Tim from doing something stupid. "Don't say another word," he warned.

With the fight curtailed, Cash and another friend picked Dave off the ground and shuffled him toward the parking lot.

Tim's wife, Gemma, a woman with honey-blonde hair who Grayson remembered from high school, stepped out of the crowd of onlookers.

"Grayson, I'm so sorry about that." She turned an angry

look at her husband. "And you didn't help matters."

Tim's face split into a cocky grin. "Honey, I was fighting for your honor."

Grayson chuckled when Gemma rolled her eyes and grabbed her husband's hand. "Time to find the kids and go home. You've had enough fun."

As she dragged her husband off, Tim said, "You wouldn't have been happy with him, babe, he has a little dick."

"Timothy, shut up!"

Cole and Grayson stood with their arms crossed and both broke into a laugh.

When a text beeped from Grayson's phone, he whipped the cell out of his back pocket, thinking it was Holly.

Gray, can you come to the suite? Something's wrong.

Yeah, be right there.

"Was that Holly?" Cole asked.

"No. Erika. She says something's wrong. Guess you're policing the party by yourself for a few."

"No problem."

* * * *

Leaving the party behind, Grayson walked down the driveway until he reached the suite at the rear of the equipment shed.

He knocked on the door, but Erika didn't answer. Unlocked, he opened the door and walked in to find the lights off, but candles burned on the TV, coffee table, and a small bookstand.

"Erika?"

"Grayson," she answered, stepping into the bedroom doorway.

With the flickering candles as the only light, they cast a glow against her tanned, silky skin. She stood naked except for red high heels on her feet. Erika stretched her arms above her head and gripped either side of the door frame. Most men would buckle at her pornographic perfect body. He couldn't argue that the woman was extremely fuckable.

"Glad you came." She gave him a demure smile. "It's true, ya know. When a woman's pregnant, she gets very horny. She ran her teeth over her bottom lip and tipped her head to the side.

Ivy's words echoed loudly. *"Soon she'll lure you into her bed."*

His sister was right. Erika had no intention of leaving.

Ever.

He took a step closer. Erika lowered her arms and pinched her peaked nipples. "I remember how you love to suck on these. Makes me wet just thinking about it. I'm not asking for forever, Gray. No strings. I just want you to fuck me like you used to."

It wasn't easy looking away, since he remembered clearly what sex had been like with her. "Suppose I don't need a condom since you're already pregnant?"

She smiled. "Course not. Can't get pregnant twice. Believe me, baby, I've always wanted to fuck you bareback, but you never let me. No worries now."

Erika strode across the room like she was walking the catwalk toward a stripper pole. And he was the pole she wanted to ride. Her fingers slid to the button on his jeans, but he gripped her wrist. Pushing what she thought was her advantage, she placed her other hand on his erection and massaged, her lips parting slightly.

"Grayson, you want me. So, take me."

Her hand had a tactile effect on his cock, but not his heart.

"I want..." He swallowed his anger, but it was more like rage burning in his belly. "I want you to pack your bag tonight."

Shocked, she shook her head. "What? No."

"Tomorrow, first thing, I'm taking you to the bus station. You're going home."

"Grayson—I don't feel well enough to travel."

"Cut the shit, Erika. I'm not responsible for you. If you're pregnant, which I fucking doubt, it's not my burden. I'm sorry, but we've been around the block too many times for me not to see where this ends. I don't even know why you're here. We said goodbye in San Diego."

She stepped back, not as beautiful with a pinched expression. "I knew this was a fucking mistake."

"Then why did you come?"

She turned her back on him. "Because of that stupid asshole I ran into."

"What? Who?"

She swished her arm through the air. "I don't remember. One of your old teammates. Two weeks ago, I had a relapse and got hammered. He was at the bar, and we reminisced about the old days. You came up, and I told him you'd left San Diego and I missed you. He convinced me I shouldn't quit." She choked out a laugh. "Your motto, right? Never quit? He gave me the bus fare and told me to do whatever it takes."

He'd love to know who that fucking jerk was. The team guys were always playing pranks on each other. Guy probably thought it'd be funny.

She turned and faced him. "You're right, I'm not pregnant, but I love you, Grayson. I want a family. With you. Don't send me away."

Manipulative bitch. So, she'd hoped he'd fuck her and get pregnant with his child. He wasn't angry anymore, he was fucking furious.

"Here it is one last time for clarity. I am in love with Holly. She's the only woman I want as my wife. If I'm lucky, she's going to say yes, and we're going to live a long and happy life together. Tomorrow, I'll get you to the bus station. You can put your deceitful ass on it or not. I don't give a shit, but I don't want to see your goddamn face again."

The color drained from her cheeks. "You ruined my life!"

"No." He shook his head. "No, Erika. You did that all by

yourself."

She rushed toward the bedroom and slammed the door.

Grayson dug his wallet out of his front pocket and sighed. Last time, he thought. He laid three hundred bucks on the kitchen counter and left.

In the wee hours of Sunday morning, he heard a car roll down the gravel drive. He didn't have to get up and look out the window to know Erika was gone. Obviously, she'd found the money he'd left on the counter.

He reached for his phone, the display casting a focused light into his dark bedroom. No new messages or texts. Sunday would be spent on the clean-up at the farmstead, but as soon as Monday morning came, he'd call the university and convince Holly to see him and then drive over the border after work.

Everything was going to be fine.

CHAPTER THIRTY-SIX

G rayson was at his desk early on Monday morning. The other officers employed by the proactive unit arrived, going about their routines and filling coffee cups.

The moment eight o'clock showed on his cell, he dialed Holly's office at the university.

"Hello, you've reached Holly McNeela, Office of Ancient Languages. I'll be away from the office for six months. If you have any questions, please direct your call to Professor Carlson, Department Head at 555-2234. Have a good day."

His heart thumped while scribbling down the number. There had to be a mistake. Did she mean six days?

Grayson dialed the number.

After the third ring, a man answered. "Good morning, Department of Anthropology, Professor Carlson."

"Good morning, this is Detective Grayson Brooks from the Skagit County Sheriff's Office. I'm looking for Holly McNeela. I called her office number, but the message said she's away for six months. Is that a mistake?"

"No. No, it isn't, Detective. Holly's been invited to take part in a very important archeological project."

An uncomfortable numbness crept into his chest. "I see."

"Detective, are you calling with regard to her assault case?"

"Yes," he lied. "I have some further questions. Where's the dig?"

"A little out of your range, I'm afraid. The West Bank. Qumran Caves. We're all eagerly waiting to hear what they unearth."

Israel. Jesus, woman.

"Did she leave yet?"

"I'm not entirely sure, Detective. Is this an urgent matter?"

Urgent to him, but he didn't want Carlson to call Holly. "No, not at this time."

"It's quite possible she's at home," Professor Carlson said. "This was very short notice. She's probably still preparing to leave."

"Thank you. I'll try to contact her at home or when she arrives in Israel."

Grayson disconnected. Holly had to have listened to his calls. Why would she leave without giving him a chance to explain?

Maybe she hadn't left Canada yet. Gray booked off work and raced back to the farmstead. He'd change, grab his passport and head to the border.

Coming to an abrupt stop in front of the old Victorian raised a plume of dust. When he hurried into the kitchen, Ivy was preparing some canning jars, the same big metal pot their mother had used, simmering on the stove.

"You're home early. Like, way early," she said.

Now that Erika was gone, so was Ivy's anger. "Came home to get my passport."

She pointed at the island. "A registered letter arrived in the mail addressed to you. Probably something to do with the sale of your townhouse."

He'd received all the documents through email. Grayson picked up the cardboard mailer. "What exactly did you say to Holly when she called?"

Ivy gripped the edge of the island. "I'm sorry, Grayson. I shouldn't have said anything. I was just so pissed off."

"*What did you say?*"

"Um, she asked if you were okay because she hadn't heard from you. I told her you weren't hurt. Initially, I said she should talk to you, but she sounded worried. I said Erika showed up unannounced at our door, then dropped a bomb, saying she was pregnant."

His blood pressure went from zero to a thousand. "Did you *fucking* clarify the baby wasn't mine?"

As if she hadn't made the connection between what she'd said and how Holly might perceive the meaning until this very second, his sister's eyes rounded. "Well. Ah. No, she..."

A sound he recognized came from the cardboard mailer. He tore open the strip and shook a small manila envelope into his palm. He ran his finger under the glued flap, then tipped the package. His chain and Trident clattered onto the stained wood counter.

A cold, creeping finality consumed his heart. He peered inside the envelope and saw a Post-it note stuck to the interior. With the tip of his finger, he coaxed the yellow paper out and turned it over.

It had been a long fucking time since he'd felt the crippling emptiness of loss. On that day, he had said goodbye to an important woman in his life: his mother. With the return of his Trident, Holly had made a decision. The note held her conclusion.

Goodbye.

A stuttered exhale escaped his throat. He'd shut Holly out the second Erika showed up, trying to isolate her from his past. Too late, he understood that hiding a truth was the same as a lie. It didn't matter that Erika's baby wasn't his. Didn't matter that Erika meant nothing to him. Without an explanation, from Holly's perspective, a pregnant girlfriend showed up from San Diego and he didn't return her calls.

Ivy was right. The damage wasn't only done, but permanent.

Until his injury completely healed, Cole remained on medical leave. He wandered into the kitchen and assessed the room.

"Why are you crying?" he asked Ivy, then wrapped an arm around his fiancée's shoulders.

"I made a mistake." Ivy clapped her clutched hands to her

mouth and her eyes squeezed shut.

With his thumb and index finger, Grayson lifted what should be around Holly's neck and drizzled the chain into his palm. He looked at his sister, her brow crumpled in apology.

"No, I did. Fourteen fucking years ago. And I kept making it." He crushed the note in his other hand and dropped the balled paper into the garbage can. "I had a chance to explain my history with Erika before this all happened, but I didn't."

Ivy shook her head. "Grayson, no. This is my fault. If I hadn't lost my temper, I would have realized what I'd said. Let me call Holly. I'll explain my mistake. Everything will be fine."

He made a fist, the Budweiser clenched in his hand. If he'd known Ivy had told her about Erika's pregnancy, he would have clarified the child wasn't his in one of the many messages he'd left.

"It's not fine. Holly's gone."

Ivy swiped the tears from her cheeks. "What do you mean, gone? Gone where?"

"The West Bank. Israel. For six months."

Ivy clapped a hand over her mouth again and pressed her face into Cole's chest.

"Is she on the plane yet?" Cole asked.

He shrugged. "I don't know. Probably."

"If you're not sure, what are you standing around here for?"

* * * *

An hour later, Grayson pulled into the short driveway at Holly's townhouse. Nicely treed and landscaped, the neighborhood had a comfortable urban feel.

He walked up the path that cut through the tidy yard with a small, manicured lawn to her front door. Why hadn't he dropped everything and come Saturday night or Sunday?

He knocked on the dark blue door, then stepped back.

Open the door, Holly. Please be home.

He waited, then rang the doorbell.

"Can I help you?" a woman said from behind him.

He turned to see an elderly woman standing on the other side of the metal picket fence dividing Holly's property from her neighbors. The woman wore a colorful smock, a visor to keep the sun out of her eyes, and gardening gloves. Grayson retraced his steps.

"I'm looking for Holly. I'm Detective Brooks from the Skagit County Sherriff's Office."

"I see. I thought you boys caught the man responsible for Holly's attack?" she said, crossing her arms.

It was a beautiful, late summer day, the sun warm on his shoulders, but inside he felt cold. "I did. You're Mrs. Norman."

Holly's neighbor picked up a pair of trimming shears. "You're very thorough, Detective."

"I need to speak with her. The professor at the university said Holly was invited to the Middle East. I thought I could catch her before she left."

The senior eyed him for a second. "You missed her, dear. She left Sunday night."

Although he expected this, it didn't hurt any less. As much as his heart ached, he wondered how Holly must feel.

"Thanks," he mumbled. "Have a good afternoon, ma'am."

When he turned to leave, Mrs. Norman said, "You know, I tried to talk her out of it. It's crazy for her to be halfway around the world in her condition."

Holly was lucky to have a kindly neighbor.

"She's a smart woman." He'd been to the Middle East many times during his years with the teams. The topography was pretty rough, but she'd handle it. "Her knee isn't that much of an issue. She's had two months to heal."

"Knee?" The woman grinned. "No, dear. I guess I'm old-fashioned. I just think it's wise to stick close to home with your first pregnancy. Things can go wrong, you know."

The ground under his feet turned to quicksand.

"Pregnancy," he repeated. A white hum in his head blocked out the birds twittering in the trees, and his world rocked side to side.

She smiled at him. "I had four of my own. The first one is always a little scary, but Holly? That young woman is fearless."

Grayson swallowed thickly. He didn't have a single doubt the baby was his, but he asked anyway. "And the father?"

The old woman cocked her head, her aged skin wrinkled with a sympathetic smile. "I used to tease Holly that one day she'd meet her soulmate, just like I did. She'd tell me she didn't believe in unicorns, either. But this summer she met someone. That girl was so in love. When I asked her about the father yesterday, her eyes filled with tears, and she said he had other commitments."

Grayson stood at the end of Holly's walkway, shell-shocked, angry, and out of his mind with joy. He didn't think it was possible to feel that many emotions all at once.

"Thank you, Mrs. Norman."

"Son." She paused and snipped a small branch from the top of the boxwood hedge. "Do you have other commitments? Because it looks to me like you're as heartbroken as she is."

He bowed his head with a grin. Seniors. People didn't give them enough credit. "It was a misunderstanding, but my fault."

"My husband and I had a few misunderstandings over the years too, but we always agreed on one thing. We loved each other, and there wasn't anything we couldn't fix."

Holly didn't want to give him that chance. She'd put oceans and continents between them.

* * * *

Holly stepped from the cool air of the Qumran cave into the blistering sunlight, the West Bank's arid landscape in complete contrast to the dense, deep green of home. She rubbed the back of her hand across her brow, removing an exfoliating layer of fine grit and sweat.

Gazing at the limestone cliffs and the Dead Sea in the distance was a dream come true. Hundreds of caves had been found since the 1940s, but this was the thirteenth referred to as a scroll cave. A monumental discovery, and Holly was part of the team of researchers.

Fifty scrolls at first count, were located inside pottery jars. The condition of the artifacts appeared exceptionally good. Other caves in the region had produced thousands of scraps and whole decipherable texts that shed invaluable light on early Judaism and Christianity. She couldn't wait to see what these scripts revealed.

"Holly!" Juliette called from the base of the slope.

She waved.

The intern put a hand to her mouth and shouted. "You're needed at base camp. Someone here to see you."

"I'm coming down."

Holly was expecting a representative from the Hebrew University of Jerusalem today. Determining the authenticity of the parchments wouldn't happen at the site. The pottery jars remained at the entrance to the cavities where they'd been discovered. The process of documenting the cave and removing the jars took time and great care to preserve their precious contents. Initially, an internal wall had collapsed, likely from past earthquake activity, and blocked access to the cave. By the time Holly had reached the Middle East, the soil and rock had been removed.

As her eyes scanned the scorched beauty of the land, she flattened her palm against her stomach, struck with bittersweet joy. Grayson was never far from her thoughts. If he hadn't reunited with his girlfriend, she would have shared this experience with him. Holly had no choice but to view their relationship as a summer love.

Intense pleasure and joy filled her memories. Confident,

sexy, and definitely bossy, he'd swept her off her feet. She imagined he'd have disliked the idea of her being here, but she would have come anyway because by next April she'd be a mother, her priorities and life forever changed.

Eventually, as the pregnancy progressed and there were no complications, she'd let Grayson know about the baby. His girlfriend wouldn't be happy, but Gray had a right to know he was going to be a father—again. In time, when all the emotions became a dull roar, she certainly wanted their child to know the Brooks family.

Holly worked her way down the long, sloping base of sand and coarse rock that encompassed the cliffs. Dust particles created a hazy layer in front of the falling sun and heatwaves performed a slow shimmering dance on the horizon.

The camp's canvas canopies billowed in the wind on the valley floor. A figure stood next to Juliette. As Holly descended the slope, a large man wearing camo pants and a moss green shirt took shape.

Gripped by an odd sense of familiarity, her feet stopped. The man turned and broke into a jog, his thick arms pumping as he ran up the incline.

It had to be a mirage.

Less than eight feet apart, the man stopped, his forehead creased and his carved jaw taut with concern.

Was she dreaming? Had she somehow tumbled down the steep slope and lay unconscious?

"Holly?" The mirage spoke, sounding and looking exactly like Grayson.

"What are you doing here?"

The breeze toyed with his hair and his unforgettable blue eyes focused on her as he took a few more steps.

"You didn't answer my texts."

She shook her head. Considering where they stood, it was the craziest answer she'd ever heard. There was no logical reason for him to be here.

This felt hauntingly familiar. Similar to when her ex had unexpectedly shown up at her door with his life in tatters. That couldn't be the case with Grayson. He had a wonderful family, a satisfying career, and a pregnant girlfriend Holly hadn't known about.

"I'm speechless and have no idea why I'm looking at you," she said.

His gaze panned across the rocky clefts behind her.

"There are no terrorists up there, Grayson. Only a cave with an incredible discovery."

A weak smile slid onto his rugged features. "I know. You've dreamed of being part of an archaeological dig your whole life. It must be exciting."

She opened her mouth to agree then hesitated, recognizing their small talk as out of place as Grayson standing a few feet away. "I don't understand. You don't belong here."

His shoulders straightened and his worn military boots crunched on the coarse ground to bring him closer. "You left, so I followed."

Holly crossed her arms and set her eyes on the blue water of the Dead Sea, a stark difference from the surrounding desert and desolate ground. "I returned your Trident. I hope it arrived."

"It did, but it belongs around your neck."

"Not anymore." Seeing him now swept away her rational thoughts, her raw and tattered emotions too fresh. "I wish you hadn't come, Grayson."

"Sweetheart, Ivy led you to believe that Erika is pregnant with my baby. That was a mistake my sister is extremely sorry for."

Holly shrugged. "I didn't know you had a girlfriend you'd left behind in San Diego. You invited me to the August celebration, but then I didn't hear from you. You wouldn't answer my calls. Not even a text." Anger stirred in her belly. Hadn't she at least deserved a fricking text? "I only called Ivy to make sure nothing bad had happened."

"Something bad did happen," he said. "Someone I thought I'd never see again showed up. Turns out she wasn't pregnant, but even if she was, the baby couldn't be mine." He exhaled and stared at the ground. "I should have told you about Erika."

"You don't need to explain, Grayson. My focus is on this incredible discovery. I'm not wallowing in grief that you've reunited with an old flame. I've heard these types of justifications before…and *I don't care.*"

His lips tightened and curled downward at the edges. "I'm nothing like that dirtbag you married, and I haven't reunited with anyone."

"I don't think there's any good reason for me to stand under the scorching sun, listening to this. You said you'd never had a relationship before. That's not the truth. I'm not going to whitewash everything you told me as a lie, but it's a waste of energy to debate the details. I don't want to talk about it."

Grayson shot out his muscled arm to stop her from heading down the slope.

"That's not a lie, Holly. Erika and I hooked up fourteen years ago when I served in Special Ops. When I left on deployment, she'd crawl into some other guy's bed. But the second I returned, she'd find me. Young and foolish, I was all too willing to spread her legs. As the years went by, Erika used her body to keep a roof over her head, but not my roof. We never lived together."

"I wasn't born yesterday, Grayson. Whether or not you want to admit it, you and Erika had a relationship. You told me you only made love to a woman once. If she wanted more, you left her. You lied to me!"

Grayson's scowl deepened. "It's more complicated than that."

Anger trembled through every cell in her body. "Fuck you!"

Gray blinked and jerked his head back as if shocked she'd use language like that. He swallowed thickly. "Just...hear me out. Please."

He'd wasted a plane fare to do this, so whatever. "Fine, get it off your chest. Let's hear the excuses."

Gray snapped his eyes closed for a second and cleared his throat. "Eventually, Erika started using drugs. When she got into trouble, she'd call me, and I came to the rescue."

"You were her knight in shining armor. Easy to see how that happened. She wanted a life with you."

"She did, but I didn't, and she knew that. When I returned to Washington, I let Erika crash at my place in San Diego because she had nowhere else to go. I told her she could stay until I'd sold the townhouse. With me out of the picture, she put herself through a rehab program. When my place sold, I never expected her to show up at the farmstead."

Holly crossed her arms over her dusty short-sleeve shirt. "There's always an explanation with men like you. I seriously don't care, Grayson. Go home. If you want, we'll talk in six months when the dig is finished."

He took a few more steps until he was close enough for them to be eye to eye on the incline.

"I care, Holly. I haven't slept with Erika for five years. Prior to that, the only thing we ever shared was sex. When she showed up at the farmstead with no money in her pocket and said she was pregnant, I couldn't kick her to the street. That's not how I'm made. Ivy warned me that Erika was playing a game, and I fell for it. My sister wasn't happy, and it was after that when you called."

"Did you take care of her?" Holly asked while processing the information.

"If you're asking if I slept with her, the answer is no. I gave her some cash and told her to leave because I was in love —with you."

Holly rubbed her bare arms. The sun burned her shoulders but didn't do much to melt the ice from her heart.

"You must have felt like a great big hypocrite when I told you about Kevin and you kept your lips sealed about Erika."

His gaze flicked toward her feet. "It crossed my mind, but in my defense, I sincerely didn't think she'd resurface. Erika is gone. She's not coming back. Ever. I called you. And kept calling you. When you didn't answer, I contacted the university. Your department head told me you'd been invited to the dig. I thought I could catch you before you left and drove to your place."

"This." She raised her arms. "Is a once in a lifetime opportunity. As far as being dumped for someone else, I've walked in those shoes before. It gets easier the second time around. You and I never made sense." She paused, deliberating her next words. "But I don't regret a second of our time together. That's the memory I'm keeping, but I'm not keeping you."

Gray shook his head. "I didn't dump you, Holly. Nothing is over."

Rehashing the details wasn't helping. "Maybe not, but you shut me out when your other girlfriend showed up. For five days, Grayson! Erika wasn't just a one-night stand, she was part of your life for years. Don't insult my intelligence by trying to tell me you didn't care for her."

She could tell he didn't enjoy discussing the subject by his rigid stance and tight jawline, but sweeping it under the carpet wouldn't help.

"I told you I'd made bad choices in the past," he explained. "Erika was my worst. For a long time, I—I felt responsible, in part, for her addictions. She wanted something from me I couldn't give, and she spiraled. That's why I kept catching her before she'd hit rock bottom."

Holly wasn't really shocked that Grayson swooped in to help Erika. Or take some of the blame for her actions. Nobility and a firm set of principles were part of his nature. His career with the SEALs and law enforcement had only sharpened those values.

"And when she spirals again, she'll be back. Obviously, she loves you. Maybe you should try to love her back."

Grayson's mouth seamed, and he shook his head. "I understand why you're angry."

Holly dug her toe into the loose gravel and sand. "I would hope so."

"Even before we met, Erika had issues. Pretending to love her would only cause more harm. Holly, I didn't come all this way to analyze her problems with you."

"You didn't need to come all this way at all." Thirsty, she needed water.

Grayson put his sizeable body in her way when she took a step to go around him. "I spoke with your neighbor, Mrs. Norman."

Mrs. Norman liked to gossip. Holly's stomach somersaulted, and she was sure it wasn't the baby.

Grayson rested his hands on his hips with his feet apart, a stance that made him into an impenetrable wall. "I know I hurt you, Holly, but I wasn't unfaithful. We're standing here navigating our first argument. You have every right to be angry with me, but I'm not leaving until we move past this."

"It's not our first, it's our second argument." She didn't like wallowing in a wasteland of useless pessimism either. "We both knew our relationship would eventually end. There's nothing to move past."

Grayson gnawed on his bottom lip. "I had a big surprise planned for the August long weekend. Then everything went sideways."

She nearly snorted. Her surprise was a helluva lot bigger. "Yeah, I had one too."

"You go first," he blurted.

She narrowed a suspicious eye at him. "You're not going to like it."

"Try me," he said, his focus like a laser beam.

"You said you spoke with Mrs. Norman."

The most ridiculous smile she'd ever seen exploded on

his face. A crazy cross of boyish excitement and a *caught with a hand in the cookie jar* expression.

"I did."

"You're a detective with experience interviewing people."

"Some. Yes."

"Then you already know my secret."

His muscled chest inflated. "I do."

"Just to clarify, you're going to be a father and I can assure you, it's yours."

Grayson's smile was absolutely blinding. "I'm happy, Holly. So fucking happy."

When she'd taken the pregnancy test and seen the results, she'd been filled with utter joy. After talking with Ivy, she was prepared to raise the baby on her own.

"You said you never wanted children."

"I said I never wanted children until I met you." He lunged and trapped her in his arms. "Forgive me, sweetheart. I'm an idiot. I can't control everything, even though it's in my nature to do that. I thought I could clean up my mess. That's all I wanted, but I should have never shut you out."

She reached up and threaded her fingers through his hair. "If you want to be part of the baby's life, we'll figure it out. But you didn't have to fly halfway around the world to tell me you're an idiot."

"Nope. Could have sent that in an email." He backed up a step and slid his callused hand down her arm, stopping at her wrist and turning her palm up. "But I couldn't send this in an email."

He rooted around in his camo pocket, then placed a white box in her open hand.

She cracked open the container expecting to see his Trident, but a gold band sparkled with diamonds in the sunlight.

"Holly McNeela, will you take a chance on a retired SEAL and dedicated detective who cherishes the ground you walk on?"

"This was your surprise?" she asked, stunned.

Holly had met Grayson at the end of May. Fallen in love during June. Was pregnant by July. Thought she'd lost him forever by the end of August, and now he was proposing. So much for taking things slowly.

The boyish grin still plagued his rugged features. "You always made sense to me. This isn't exactly where this was supposed to happen, though."

"I never expected this to happen at all." He'd discussed marriage, but she set the idea aside because it meant sacrificing her career.

"Do you remember that spot by the creek on the farmstead, the one with the natural clearing?"

She remembered it well, especially from one evening when he'd brought a blanket and a bottle of wine and made love to her under the moonlight. "It's beautiful there."

"That's where I wanted to propose. It's part of the ten acres my father subdivided from the farm and gave us to build our new home."

Her jaw slackened and Grayson leaned in, stopping a breath away from her lips. "Holly, I know I promised that neither of us would give up anything to be together, but I can't walk away from you. I want forever, sweetheart. When you're done here, come home and marry me."

She tipped her forehead to his. "Everything inside you wants to toss me over your shoulder and take me home right now, doesn't it?"

"Yup," he admitted, before bestowing her with a very long, healing kiss.

When he finished ravishing her mouth, she said, "I'm not leaving, Grayson. I don't care how many times you kiss me."

"I respect that. But I had to look in your eyes when I admitted that I'd fucked up. I don't know why I can't convince you that we're a perfect fit. I see it so clearly. But I won't stop trying. Maybe when we're eighty years old, surrounded by our grandchildren, you'll believe me."

He seemed so sincere. "Are you going to wait until Christmas for me to come home?"

Grayson squinted. "Hmm, more like a month before I fly out here again, if I can last that long. But after we decide on the house plans, I'm breaking ground. By the time you come home, we'll have just enough time to finish the interior before the baby's born." Grayson flattened his warm hand on her stomach. "Sweetheart, I know I'm asking a lot, but we have so much to look forward to."

"I'm still angry and probably will be for a while. I have no reason to trust you."

"Yes, you do."

She highly doubted it. "There isn't a single reason I can think of."

In that handsome, sexy stare he used like a weapon of mass destruction on her heart, he said, "Because you make me all warm and squishy inside."

She couldn't help but burst into laughter, hearing a man like Grayson utter words like that. "That's my line."

Her detective brushed a soft kiss on her mouth. "I played the field for a long time, Holly. You're the only woman I want with me in the end zone."

"I'm still mad at you."

"I know you are. I'm still angry at myself." He swept a strand of hair from her face. "I never loved Erika. I swear to you that's the truth. If she ever shows up again, I'll let you answer the door."

"I'm not saying yes to your proposal, but I want our child to have a happy home." She had to be crazy but... "In light of that, I have four hundred and fifty thousand American dollars, thanks to the resort, you can use to hire contractors."

Grayson kissed the end of her nose. "It wouldn't be a home if you're not there, sweetheart. I have more than enough to get the job done. I'd rather you use some of that money to hire an immigration lawyer to speed up the paperwork." He grinned. "As for the rest, college costs a fortune. We might as well start saving now."

She liked the way he thought. "You have this all figured out, but I haven't accepted your proposal. Nothing has changed."

He drew back, one eyebrow raised in playful anticipation. "I screwed up. I know that, but I'm prepared to make you milkshakes for the rest of your life."

"Holly!" Juliette jogged up the hill, stopped halfway, and bent over. "Woo, I'm out of shape." She straightened after a few panting breaths. "Everything okay?"

"Uh-huh. Juliette, this is Grayson. He just flew halfway around the world to admit he was wrong and ask me to marry him."

Juliette's mouth gaped, and she shoved her dark-rimmed glasses up her nose. "Wow. Did you say yes?"

Grayson wrapped his arm around Holly's waist. "She's teaching me a lesson in patience, so I'll pretend she isn't going to."

"Nothing is decided. Grayson's American. I'd have to leave the university," she said.

Juliette's honey-colored ponytail swung like a metronome as she ascended the last few feet to join them. "Oh, you lucky duck. Do you know how many more opportunities you'll have in the States? And with your experience"—she waved her hand—"you'll find a job in no time."

Holly adored Juliette's optimism. "If I'm gone, chances are very good the university will offer you my position."

"That would be amazing, but I'm nowhere as talented as you, Holly."

Two guards ascended the slope. Right on time, they switched shifts at six in the evening. His eyes tracked the men, and the energy around Gray stiffened.

"What's wrong?"

"Private armed security," he stated.

"Yes. The university who is hosting us hired them to keep

the dig safe. Why?"

Gray turned his attention back to her. "Because there's something invaluable at this site."

Holly held the stray curls the wind loosened from her bun, out of her face. "Two-thousand-year-old manuscripts. I'd say they're invaluable. Looting is common practice around here."

The guards passed by on their climb to the cave, neither man giving them much notice.

"Holly, I'm not talking about biblical scribble, I'm talking about you."

Juliette sighed. "That's so romantic."

Grayson grinned. "Juliette, where can I find a Bedouin priest or rabbi?"

Holly laughed. "What do you want with one of them?"

"To marry you. How about a cave-dwelling juju man? I don't give a shit. Let's tie the knot."

"Grayson Brooks, you're crazy. How about a private tour of an archaeological dig instead?"

Grayson's thick arms wrapped around her middle. "Sure, but after that, we're heading to my hotel. Room service. Silk sheets. Balmy breeze off the Dead Sea blowing through open patio doors. Setting sun. I think you get my drift."

Juliette giggled. "Think I'll leave you two alone." She trotted a few feet down the slope. "Oh, I almost forgot. Dirk needs to talk with you, Holly."

"'Kay." She turned her attention back to Grayson, not expecting the look of utter shock coating his face.

"Dirk." His brow twisted into a tight accordion of creases as he released his grip. "Dirk is here," he said, pointing at the ground.

"Yes. It's his discovery. Why?"

Gray's eyes erupted in a fiery blue as if his internal temperature was hot enough to weld metal. "He's the one who invited you?" His jaw sharpened into chiseled granite.

Why was he so angry? "Grayson, I'm an ancient biblical

text researcher. Why shouldn't I be here?"

His biceps knotted, and he clenched his fists. "Did he know?"

"Know what?"

"About the baby. Did he know you were pregnant with our child?"

She shrugged. "Eventually, I told him. Yes."

"You told him about Erika, and that you and I were over, didn't you?"

Was that wrong? "He visited the university. I was still coming to grips with what Ivy said. I was upset. So, yes, I told him."

"Where is he?" he demanded, his tone deadly.

"Probably at the base camp."

He took off at a run down the slope, a cloud of dust trailing behind him.

"Grayson, wait! What's going on?" She chased him toward the line of billowing canopy covers.

CHAPTER THIRTY-SEVEN

D irk stood under a white canopy behind a portable table covered with trinkets and tools the excavation team recovered from the cave. When he looked up and saw Grayson stampeding toward him, he took a step back.

Holly wasn't far behind and saw Gray grip the eight-foot-long table and toss it into the air, scattering all the relics onto the sand. The table cartwheeled, then landed upside down.

Dirk threw up his hands as if to ward off the attack. Grayson hauled his fist back and hammered the archaeologist in the face, sending the man toppling to the ground. The other researchers, shocked by the aggressive display, quickly stepped back, giving the men space.

"I should fucking kill you!" Gray roared.

Dirk shook his head, rolled onto his knees and staggered to his feet. "Why?" He swiped the blood from a busted lip. "She's where she belongs."

"You set us up. You set it all up!" he shouted. "You're the one who gave Erika money to buy a bus ticket to Washington. Then invited Holly to this dig. Why?"

Dirk gnawed on his inner cheek, glancing at her. Anger slanted his eyes. "It's pretty fucking obvious, Gray. Holly's a decent woman and you broke her heart, just like you destroy everyone who falls in love with you. I'm protecting her— from you."

Grayson took another threatening step toward his old teammate. "What was the plan, Dirk? Give it some time. Play the game, then lure her into your bed? She's pregnant with our baby, and you fucking know it."

Dirk bent to retrieve his sunglasses from the sand. "People change. I changed. Holly and I have common interests. She lives and breathes discoveries like this," he said, sweeping his arm at the landscape. "Just like I do. You, on the other hand, don't love anything. Look what you did to Erika. At one time, she was a vibrant woman. You screwed her, then shared her with me. For years, she believed you loved her, and then you tossed her aside. The same way that you left me."

Holly clutched her chest. She'd been right. Dirk loved Grayson. At least he *had* loved him.

Grayson shook his head, seemingly unwilling to accept Dirk's reason. "You executed this plan to hurt both of us. This isn't about saving Holly, it's about revenge."

Dirk swept his gaze across the other archaeologists and researchers who witnessed the stand-off.

"No, Grayson, it's not," he said solemnly. "I just know what you're going to do. It's what you've always done, and Holly is your next casualty." He exhaled and shifted his attention to her. "Gray's correct. I convinced Erika to seek him out, and he did exactly what I thought he'd do. He pushed you aside and took care of her. And he always will, even if he tells you it's over. It will never be over between those two."

She tensed, expecting Grayson to go into a rabid attack, but he didn't. Instead, he turned to face her, his expression stiff. Holly couldn't deny that Dirk's words struck the most vulnerable parts of her. If Erika returned, would he shut her out again? She clutched the engagement ring in her fist, uncertain and unable to veil her concerns. Had she forgiven him too quickly? Trusted him, only to face something worse down the road.

Grayson didn't come closer when he said, "Holly, if we'd never met, I'd still be the man Dirk is talking about. But I'm not. He makes it sound like I turned my back on you. I didn't."

She swallowed thickly. "You did, Grayson. You turned your back on me when she showed up."

He closed his eyes as if in pain. "Listen, I know that hiding my mistake from you, which is what Erika is, *was* the biggest error in judgment I've ever made."

She swallowed, her throat dry. Holly held her clenched hand out to him. "Maybe you should take this ba—"

"No," he said brusquely. "I don't have doubts. I never did. July Fourth, Holly."

She wasn't following. "What about it?"

"Our baby. That's when we conceived him or her, isn't it? I've never taken a chance before. *Never*. I could have stopped myself that day, but I didn't because I already loved you."

* * * *

From Holly's ragged expression, Gray was almost certain she believed Dirk. She might not walk into the archeologist's arms, but the guy's reasoning destroyed Gray's credibility.

She glanced uncomfortably at their audience. "I think this conversation should resume in a private setting."

Dirk righted the table Gray had overturned. "Sorry for the show, folks. Gerry—" He addressed a young man wearing a red bandana around his forehead and oval sunglasses. "Please recover the artifacts."

"Yes, sir."

Dirk glanced at Grayson. "Follow me."

They wound their way through a clutch of smaller white canvas tents. Under the shade of an enormous cliff, they reached their destination. A desert tent, large enough for twenty people. Holly waited, allowing Dirk to enter first. Gray followed them inside and saw a desk, a table with four chairs, and a separate sleeping area piled with brightly covered pillows and blankets.

"Have a seat," Dirk said as he closed and secured the canvas flap.

Holly sat at the table, but Gray needed to pace.

Dirk joined her, then jumped right in with a defense. "My motivations were to protect you, Holly."

"Bullshit," Gray stated sharply, continuing to walk off his anger.

"Grayson, please sit down so we can talk this out," she asked.

"I'll sit when I don't want to kill the son of a bitch." He glared at Dirk. "Seriously, man. What the fuck were you thinking?" At one time, he'd respected Chief Larkin. Looked to him as a mentor. "Holly is pregnant with our baby. You really have balls if you think for one second, I'd let you raise my child or seduce the woman I love."

"That's not what this is about." Dirk shook his head. "Maybe I took it too far involving Erika."

Grayson slammed his fists on the table, cracking one of the horizontal slats. "Maybe?"

Holly jolted, her eyes rounding.

She sat to Dirk's left, and he clasped her hand as if to console or protect her. "You're pissed. I get it."

He pointed at the guy who used to be his friend. "Get your goddamn hands off her." Dirk inhaled deeply, but Gray glared at him until he released her hand. "I'm not pissed. Pissed is when a car breaks down on a deserted highway. Pissed is when the TV goes to shit before a big game. I'm not pissed, you fucking cocksucker, I'm seeing red!"

Dirk shot to his feet. "Listen—"

"Sit...the fuck...down, or I'll put you down."

He rolled his eyes but sat. "Jesus Christ, you and your goddamn temper." He leaned toward Holly. "And this isn't even at the highest volume. Believe me, I've seen worse."

Her expression churned with worry. Gray was scaring her and had to tone it down. "You went to great lengths to drive a wedge between Holly and me."

"I swear to you, Gray, it wasn't revenge. And I certainly didn't mean to hurt you, Holly."

"Yeah, you did," he hurtled at his old teammate. "You wanted her broken so you could sweep in and pick up the pieces."

It became obvious that Dirk had a deep-seated respect for Holly, but his interest went far beyond her ability to read ancient scripts.

Gray stood behind the empty chair across from Dirk and settled his hands on his hips. "You and I haven't had contact in years. You spent one day with my girlfriend, then purposely sought out Erika. And you're trying to tell me this isn't about revenge? You fucking dangled this opportunity in front of Holly, knowing she couldn't refuse. Did you honestly think I wouldn't follow her to the ends of the earth to get her back?"

Dirk's green gaze coursed across the table, then landed on Gray. "No. I didn't think you would. That's the Grayson, I knew. All he cared about was a piece of ass and once he'd had it, he left."

Gray yanked back the chair and sat. "I used to look up to you. You had a strict set of morals. Confidence. Skill. I trusted you. How many missions did we run together, and you always had my back." Dirk's betrayal didn't just make him angry, it gutted him. "Hell, you practically taught me everything I know about pleasuring a woman in the bedroom."

Dirk's chin dipped. "Yet, you left mine."

Holly had been right, and he'd been blind. All those years ago, when he and Dirk shared women and experimented with each other, it wasn't just physical for Grayson's teammate.

Loss and regret emanated from Dirk's green eyes.

"Are you trying to tell me—?"

"That there was more? Yeah, there was."

Holly sat quietly, acting as an arbitrator. She slid her delicate hand over Gray's fingers and squeezed, a signal he interpreted as her wanting him to listen. Understand. Absorb Dirk's admission and sympathize with the guy's fucking feelings.

The wind rippled the canvas walls of the tent,

interrupting the silence. After some substantial soul-searching, Gray looked across the table at the man who'd literally had a hand in shaping his life.

"Dirk. I didn't know and didn't hurt you on purpose."

Even though his apology carried a brittle edge, it seemed his old friend had been waiting all this time to hear it, and his broad shoulders dipped with relief.

"I know you didn't. Telling you how I felt wouldn't have changed anything. I knew that too."

Had he missed the signs or chosen to ignore them? "You're right, it wouldn't, but you opened my eyes. I don't have any regrets or shame if that's what you think made me pull away. It was a phase for me. You knew that much. So, explain why you orchestrated a plan to destroy my and Holly's relationship."

It took a while before Dirk spoke. Gray needed answers and wanted Holly to hear them too.

"All those years ago, I watched you evolve," Dirk said. "You didn't just walk away from me, you didn't connect emotionally with anyone." He shrugged. "Sure, you'd fight. Fuck. Joke with the guys, but something went AWOL in you. I figured it was permanent. Team life does that to some guys."

Gray took a deep breath and exhaled slowly. "Yeah, there was an issue, but it wasn't permanent."

He glanced at Holly, who watched with little to no expression. Since they were spilling their guts all over the table, he might as well dive right in. In Texas, he'd told her the reason he'd never had a relationship before. But there was one thing he hadn't admitted and should have.

"I often look at you, sweetheart, and ask myself, if I would have walked into a bar while I was still in the teams and seen you, what I would have done." It had been more than *often* that he'd questioned himself, literally hundreds of times. "I keep coming up with the same answer."

She shifted to sit a little taller in her seat, her hands tightly clutched together.

"I would have fallen in love with you back then, just like I did in May. Because it's not about where I was in my life, it's about you. I'd have selfishly asked you to wait for me. As a SEAL's wife, you'd have gone through years of hell. I'd have hurt you. Disappointed you. Scared you. But I would always love you, Holly. I know in my heart that when we met, no matter when that happened, there was no more room for anyone else."

Tears welled in Holly's eyes and leaked down her cheeks.

Dirk crossed his arms over his chest. "Jesus, Gray, I had no idea. I guess that's on me. When I spent the day with Holly, I saw how much she cared about you, and how naïve she seemed. We talked non-stop for hours about our shared interest in anthropology. She's an engaging, intelligent woman. The more I thought about her, the more I didn't want her to experience the pain I went through."

Gray understood Dirk's motivations, but it didn't excuse his actions. "Admit it. Your fondness for Holly goes far beyond saving her from a prick like me, and you fully intended to cross the professional line with her."

Dirk shifted in his chair. "You know me. It's not about gender, it's about the person."

He wouldn't let Dirk slide out of this. "In other words, yes. You wanted me out of the picture. Your mistake was thinking I'd choose Erika over Holly."

The archaeologist turned his gaze on Holly. "Gray isn't going to forgive me, but I hope you can. I admire your talents and I'd like you to stay."

That might have been mostly true except Gray recognized the heat stirring in Dirk's eyes, not only when he looked at him, but at Holly, too. It was carnal. The man hadn't changed as much as he professed.

She couldn't see it. Her gentle nature and willingness to forgive blinded her.

"You're not—"

Holly lifted her hand. "Grayson, please. He addressed a

question to me, and I will answer it."

"Sorry."

Dirk's eyebrows arched with surprise, then notched together with amusement before turning his attention to Holly.

"Dirk, I'm willing to stay as long as the reason I'm here is authentic. If asking me to take part in the excavation was purely to get in my pants and hurt Grayson, then I need to know the truth."

He tsked and shot a perturbed glance at Gray. "I respect your talents. Your research is impeccable. Dedication like yours is irreplaceable. I truly think we could discover great things together." He paused, as if deciding whether he should continue. "Do I wish I found you before he did? Yeah, I'm pretty sure I do."

Gray leaned forward on his elbows. "The truth, Dirk. I see it stirring in your eyes. Tell her the truth."

The man sighed and narrowed a look at Gray, probably pissed because he couldn't hide his intentions.

"You know what I think's got you on edge, Gray?"

"I don't give a fucking shit what you think."

"Whether you'll admit it or not, you're afraid that if I had met her first, she'd be in love with me, and that scares the shit out of you."

Gray's pulse beat with a thready pace and he clenched his jaw.

When he didn't answer, Dirk didn't gloat and refrained from smearing an expression of smugness over his face, convinced he was right.

"To answer your question," Dirk said, and put his attention on Holly. "Was I going to try my damnedest to get closer to you on this dig? No question, but it doesn't mean I don't respect your talent."

Holly relinquished a sigh. "I'm still mad at Grayson. He knows it, and I'm sure you do too, but I also love him. Only him."

Dirk nodded and folded his hands on the table. "I can see that."

She unfurled her clenched fist to reveal the engagement ring. "He proposed today." Gray watched with a thumping heart as she slid the ring on her finger. "And I accept."

Any residual fear or anger washed away but he was concerned because she'd answered while looking at Dirk, not him. What Gray had done was a fresh wound on an old scar of mistrust. The question was, how long it would take to heal.

Dirk gnawed on his bottom lip. "Remember when I told you that Gray would always tell you the truth? That still stands. If he says he wants to be with you for the rest of your days, he means it."

In a tender voice, she said, "But you still want Gray, don't you?"

Dirk's masculine features morphed into a wistful smile. "Holly, you're a sweet woman and this is a concept I'm sure you can't comprehend, but I want both of you."

She sat back in her chair and calmly sized Dirk up.

Because she didn't object immediately, a flicker of cautious hope crossed Dirk's face.

"Once," he added.

Still caught in the afterglow of Holly agreeing to marry him, Grayson's head drew back sharply. *Say what, now?*

* * * *

Near sunset, lying in the hotel room with Holly's smooth, warm body nestled in his arms, they watched the brilliant orange globe slide into the horizon, and he rationalized what had happened earlier. She wasn't only intelligent, the depth of her empathy was bottomless, and her curiosity endless and innocent.

Gray understood Dirk's reasons for a threesome. They all belonged to a different generation. One that was more open and accepting of physical pleasure. If it had been any other woman sitting in the tent with them, Gray knew he would have agreed without question. Instead, he proved he was nowhere near liberal as he thought he might be. Sharing Holly with Dirk was where he drew a line deeper than the Grand Canyon in the sand.

The fact that Holly hadn't quickly objected to Dirk's suggestion taught Grayson a hard truth: the bittersweet taste of sharing someone you love, which he'd forced Holly to experience when Erika reappeared, literally carved a lesson in his soul. The heart didn't care whether the conduit was physical or emotional, it grieved either way.

"Holly."

She tipped her head back to look at him.

"I'm sorry I hurt you. I understand what happened this afternoon when you considered Dirk's offer as part punishment and part curiosity. Call me old-fashioned or a dominant, selfish prick, but I won't share you. Not ever."

Holly sat up on her haunches and placed her folded hands in her lap. "I can't share you either." A naughty little grin sculpted her lips. "But you have to admit, it would have been kinda hot."

He chuckled and snagged her around the waist, yanking her on top of him. "Jesus, you're a sexy little minx, and you're mine."

Holly's soft cheek brushed against his jaw. "Was he right, Gray? Are you concerned that I would have fallen in love with Dirk if I'd met him first?"

His heart raced with the thought. He thanked God it hadn't happened.

"Only you can answer that, babe."

She eyed him, then straddled his hips. "Grayson Brooks, you have never avoided answering a question until now."

He grunted and glanced away from her inquisitive eyes. "He's your perfect mate, isn't he?" Gray lifted her left hand and ran his thumb over the engagement ring on her finger.

"You would have explored the world, excavating your next ancient treasure, wearing stupid Tilly hats and fucking like rabbits on Persian silk sheets while loving every minute of your life with him."

Sickened by the truth, the idea knotted his stomach. A primitive growl of possessiveness wedged in his chest.

Holly traced the tat on his chest with her finger. "That sounds like a great *Indiana Jones* sequel, but it's not the truth. Although, I do hate snakes."

He smiled, despite feeling like he couldn't give Holly a life of adventure.

"I love *you*," she said. "I want to wake up in soft cotton sheets to the sound of roosters crowing and cattle calling in the field. I'm just as happy digging up weeds and worms in a garden as long as you really love me."

Gray couldn't tell if she said that to make him feel better or not, but his heart expanded to the point of bursting. He placed his palm on her belly. Holly's body was so familiar, he could detect the smallest change. He'd been right about the July Fourth weekend. She was two months pregnant. They'd created a new life that Saturday afternoon.

"I need to tell you something."

She tipped her head to the right. "Is there another Erika in the wind?"

He grinned. "No. But it's something I need to get off my chest. It's about our baby."

"Okay," she said warily.

"The first time we made love without protection, I didn't just *think* you could get pregnant." Man, was he really going to admit this? As bad as it was going to sound, he had to. "I purposely touched and teased you, hoping you wouldn't tell me to stop. It's been weighing on me all this time." He licked his lips and forked his fingers through hers. "It was a combination of lust and love, but I still feel guilty because I wanted—aw, shit." He shook his head. "Yeah, so—I'll just fucking say it. I remember feeling a savage need to plant my seed in you like I'd never experienced before. There it is. That's the truth." He closed his eyes and exhaled. "It doesn't matter that I was desperate to make love to you. I know it wasn't right."

"Grayson."

He opened his eyes and etched his way up her body to her face. "Yeah."

"When we started dating, did I go on birth control?"

"Not that I know of."

Her index finger slithered down the center of his chest. "And you never suggested it. Not once."

True, he hadn't. As time went on, the reasons became clearer and made him feel worse. It wasn't only because he wanted a connection with her, it was because she wouldn't budge on moving to the States. Maybe starting a family would break the stalemate.

"You said you were ready to become a mother, and I'd told you I'd be there every step of the way. I should have admitted at some point that every time you let me come inside you, I hoped a baby would be a good enough reason to cross that damn border for good."

Holly leaned forward and placed her palms beside his shoulders, not a stitch of resentment or anger on her expression. "You were a little lackadaisical about wearing a condom. Not just once, but often. With your history, I was pretty sure I knew what you wanted."

"Compiling information and analyzing results," he teased, remembering the first hint she'd given him about who she was when they'd met.

"No more latex raincoats for you, mister."

Relieved that she wasn't angry, he raised his head, and she met him halfway for a kiss. "I love you, sweetheart. You have no idea how lucky I feel."

She wore the cutest, excited smile. "We're having a baby."

There were times in his life when he'd known what pride felt like, but nothing compared to this.

"I can't wait to hold you both in my arms."

CHAPTER THIRTY-EIGHT

G ray made sure Dirk kept his word and visited the Middle East once a month until the end of the dig. His old teammate and Holly had created a platonic bond and dove into the mysteries they discovered in the Qumran Cave. According to Holly, Dirk occupied his downtime by showing Juliette there were more than Seven Wonders of the ancient world behind the flap of his tent.

When Holly finished the excavation just before Christmas, Gray rendezvoused with her in Nova Scotia.

Kayleigh, Holly's mother, was a friendly woman, and he finally found the source of his fiancée's unique grey eyes.

Those Cape Bretoners were like no other folks he'd met before. Warm-hearted people with a hearty sense of humor that took real concentration on Grayson's part to understand what they said at times.

At first, he figured they couldn't remember his name because they kept calling him Buddy. Turned out, everybody was *"Buddy"* to an East Coaster. Buddy down the road. Buddy at the post office. *Didja* hear Buddy's on pogey? Gray asked for a translation on that one.

When it came to the consumption of alcohol, he thought his teammates could drink. No SEAL could keep up with her kin. Holly had laughed her head off, dragging his sorry, staggering ass to bed more than once when he'd made the mistake of trying to match her uncle's whiskey consumption, ounce for ounce.

Holly's parents lived in a modest, two-story home on ten acres. The kitchen always smelled like freshly baked bread in the morning. Before everyone got up, her mom had four loaves in the oven.

They were salt of the earth-type people. Every blanket and quilt handmade by an auntie or grandmother. Tablecloths crocheted by a friend. Canning jars lined the kitchen's walk-in pantry.

Holly's father was a mariner through and through. Gray had hit it off with her old man from the start, a jovial guy who never missed an opportunity to pinch his wife's ass when he passed her in the kitchen or steal a kiss when she cleared the plates.

Being six months pregnant, Holly didn't want a wedding until after the baby was born. Grayson wasn't willing to wait and mentioned that to her sisters, Paige and Raegan, on Christmas Eve. That's when he learned if you want something done, well Jeezus B'y, a Cape Bretoner will make it happen.

By New Year's Eve, the McNeela women had wrangled a preacher and slapped his ass in a suit. Gray had his dad Express Post the wedding ring from Washington to Nova Scotia. With the help of a magical phone tree and a flurry of activity, he married Holly in a Baptist church filled to the gills with people he didn't know, twelve minutes from where she'd been born.

A potluck dinner followed in a hall called *The Hall*. Someone knew someone who had a band, and there was no doubt the Celtic culture ran through these people's blood. With a fiddler whose bow was on fire, the shoes came off and the women step-danced up a storm with his beautiful wife in the middle.

He and Holly agreed that once the baby was born, they'd have a big party at the farmstead, but nothing would top their Cape Breton wedding.

During January and February, they finished construction of their two-story home with five bedrooms, a reading den and an office, while juggling calving season. Sleep was a rare commodity around the Brooks farmstead, but they worked in shifts and hired temporary ranch hands. By the middle of

March, they'd added one-hundred and ten calves to the herd.

April bloomed in the Pacific Northwest. The tulip bulbs popped their heads from the soil and cherry trees boasted fat, pink blossoms. When the OB-GYN said Holly and Ivy would deliver within days of each other, everyone had a feeling fate would bring both new additions to the Brooks/Sterling family on the same day.

* * * *

April 11th

"Ho, boy!" Ivy groaned while holding her belly. "Launch time."

Grayson's eyes flashed between his sister and Holly. He would have laughed at the irony, except Holly had just clenched her jaw through her own strong contraction.

Cole stood next to him in the old Victorian's country kitchen. "This is really happening. They're gonna have the babies on the same day."

By Cole's slightly rounder than normal eyes and stiff stance, the guy looked terrified.

Dad sat reading his paper at the kitchen table. "Yep, and if you two idiots don't get moving, my daughter and daughter-in-law are giving birth in the living room." He dropped the newspaper and looked at Jackson, who ate a bowl of cereal. "Meanwhile, Jackson and I are gonna take care of business around here."

Ivy's son kept his eyes on the table. He didn't like seeing his mom go through the contractions and he'd been extremely quiet all morning.

"Jackson, come here, sweetie." Ivy waved her son over, and he got up from the table and ran across the kitchen to her. "Cole's going to come back and get you once the baby is born."

He tucked his face against Ivy's belly, staring up at her. "I'm sorry, Mom. I wouldn't have asked for a sister if I knew it would hurt so bad."

She smiled and swept her fingers through his hair. "It's a good kind of pain, honey. You give Grandpa a hand and before you know it, Cole will be back to get you."

Grayson rounded the island and gently palmed Holly's stomach. He was ready to coach her through this incredible milestone in their lives. He'd been timing her contractions with mounting excitement.

"They're six minutes apart. By the time we get to the hospital, we'll be right on time, sweetheart."

Holly nodded and took a few deep, calming breaths. "Okay, get the truck."

His sister's contractions were five minutes apart and lasted for a solid minute. Gray kept track since Ivy's fiancé couldn't count past three right now.

Cole took the stairs two at a time, then returned with Ivy's overnight bag and set it by the front door.

He plucked her white jacket from the hook. "All right, let's do this."

Grayson laughed at his normally calm and composed buddy. Ivy kissed their father on the cheek and waddled to the door, then slipped her arms into the jacket.

"Cole, are you sure you want to be in the delivery room?" Ivy asked. "This isn't my first rodeo."

He opened the front door and a rush of sweet spring air washed into the house. "A herd of stampeding bulls couldn't keep me out. I just hate seeing you in pain."

She kissed him on the cheek. "You haven't seen nothing yet, baby."

Dad stood with a grunt and strode over to Holly. He squeezed her hand, then kissed her forehead. "I'm gonna call your ma and let her know."

"Thanks, Dad," she said and smiled at him.

Holly's parents were flying out from Nova Scotia for a month once the baby was born. Grayson knew they'd be booking their tickets within an hour of his father's call.

With Ivy and Holly in the pickup's backseat and him and Cole in front, Grayson drove to the hospital.

An hour later, Jackson's baby sister arrived. Grayson popped in to check on Ivy. She was doing fine, and Cole was one proud father.

Standing in the hallway outside of Ivy's delivery room, Cole said, "I gotta tell ya, man. That was incredible. How's Holly?"

"She's getting there. I don't want to be gone long."

Cole held out his hand. "Gray, thank you. Seriously. I don't think I'd be standing here, feeling like I do, if it wasn't for you."

He clutched his hand for a shake. "Not sure I had much to do with that, but you're welcome."

Cole got the joke and laughed. "Ya know, between you and me, I'm a little relieved the baby finally arrived. I'd prepared myself for Ivy's emotional ups and downs. I also thought sex would be off the table for months. But near the end, her libido went through the roof. I could barely keep up."

Gray laughed. "Yup, that happens to some women. Hormones and increased blood flow. Holly and I had an agreement. If she *needed* me, I'd get a text that read *Mommy needs a hug.* I deleted about thirty of those off my phone in the last two weeks."

His buddy coughed out a laugh. "Okay, so I'm not the only one."

"Definitely not. I'm looking forward to finally eating something when I go home for lunch," he joked. "Have you decided on a name?"

A bittersweet expression eclipsed his friend's features. "Yeah, sure did. We're going to name her Kira."

A lump formed in Gray's throat. "Mom would have liked that."

"Wish she were here today, Gray. Not just for Ivy, but for you too."

He ran a hand through his hair. "She's here in spirit,

looking over her grandchildren and all of us."

"Ivy told me your mom always worried when you served in Special Ops. Guess after today we're going to learn what parental concern is like. I hope I don't suck as a father."

Grayson placed a hand on his friend's shoulder. "You're nothing like your old man, Cole. You got no worries there. Give Ivy a kiss for me. I'll check back with you guys later."

"You bet."

Holly, experiencing her first labor, took longer. The nursing staff were incredible, with non-stop encouragement and reassurance. By six p.m., Grayson had coached her through some fierce contractions, kissed her, held her hand, and reminded her the pain would be over soon, but he was getting concerned. She was tired.

The doc arrived and gave the green light.

"Grayson." Tears streamed from Holly's eyes.

He saw the fear and exhaustion. "Almost there, sweetheart. You got this."

The two nurses coaching Holly wouldn't let her quit either.

Grayson sat right there, right by her side, when his son came into the world. Never, as long as he lived, would he forget the moment.

The nurses performed the afterbirth care, cleaning, checking the baby's airway and mobility, weighing and measuring. Holly's cramping wasn't too severe as the rest of Mother Nature followed through.

Finally, they returned their son to Holly's bare chest for skin-to-skin contact. Grayson laid his palm lightly against his son's back. His boy had a healthy head of silky, dark hair, and his heart swelled when their son opened his eyes to reveal brilliant, blue peepers.

He'd watched and read enough to help their baby get a good latch on Holly's breast. The nurse turned around just as he eased his finger over his son's top lip to incentivize him to open. Like a champ, he started to feed.

"Well, you don't see that every day," the nurse said.

Holly grinned. "I'm pretty sure you're not talking about breastfeeding."

The brunette chuckled. "No, I mean a father with those skills. I'll come back in a few and check on how you're all doing."

After hours of activity, they had the delivery room to themselves.

"How ya doing, sweetheart?" he asked as Holly watched their son nurse.

"Exhausted. Sore." She smiled and raised an eyebrow at him. "Are you jealous?"

"Maybe just a little, but our boy needs that gorgeous breast of yours more than I do right now."

With his role in the SEALs, Grayson had an interest in the subject of medicine and read more pre and post-natal books than Holly. He watched, completely at peace, as his wife bonded with their son as only a woman can do. It was a moment of pure beauty.

Their son didn't nurse for long, but that was to be expected.

"So have we decided on his name?" she asked, wrapping their son in a soft, blue blanket, then shifting him into Grayson's arms.

"Hey, buddy. I've been waiting a long time to hold you." Cradling his baby in the crook of his arm was surreal. He kissed his son's forehead. "What do you think? Would you like the name Ronin?" Holly told him it meant little seal in Celtic.

He glanced at his wife, who watched him while wearing a beautiful but tired smile.

"My life is perfect," she said.

"Thank you, Holly. I realize what you gave up for us. You loved your job at the university."

She tipped her head to the side. "Think I love you more."

With his son asleep, he gently placed Ronin back in his

wife's arms. "Guess I should call Dad and your parents, then find Cole and Ivy."

The nurse returned to check on Holly and the baby's condition. Grayson waited to make sure there were no complications.

Holly's nurse finished her checks and nodded. "Everything looks fine. We're going to move you in a few minutes, Mrs. Brooks."

"Thanks." The nurse left the room and Holly said, "Mom and Dad are going to want pictures."

He hadn't even thought about that and pulled the phone out of his back pocket then snapped a few shots, sending them to the family. One went to Lt. Kline so he could share with the other detectives, a couple photos went to Checkers, and one for his old partner in San Diego. He paused, then scrolled through the list of contacts and highlighted Dirk's name. Gray wasn't certain whether sending him a pic was a dick move, rubbing their happiness in his face, or whether he was saying *you're our friend, so don't be a stranger.* Guess he could decide for himself. Gray thumbed the send button.

He leaned over and pressed a gentle kiss on Holly's lips. "I'll be back soon."

Memories from the past year flooded his mind. An unexpected spike of adrenaline slithered through his veins. The kind you get with a bullet's near miss and realize how lucky you are.

He'd told his sister that after leaving the teams, he needed time to acclimatize to civilian life. Staying in San Diego and working vice had been a crutch, not a cleansing. The endless string of women like binging on empty calories.

After coming home, he could have easily slid into that lifestyle again, except for one chance encounter with a woman who'd crossed the border and whose beautiful eyes kept him awake at night. Holly had seduced him with her intelligence, wit, and sincerity. She'd peeled away the layers of his past with every moment they'd shared. The feeling of dread rested in the question of what would have happened if their paths had never crossed.

"Grayson, are you all right?" she asked as he reached the door.

Too many men like him burned out, addicted to an adrenaline-fed lifestyle. They sacrificed their relationships when temptation knocked. Instead of sharing a life with someone, they needed to control every decision. If he'd walked down that road, it would have led him *away* from Holly, not *to* her.

When he turned to answer and saw his wife holding their newborn son, Grayson couldn't imagine his life without them.

"I'm a lucky man, Holly. If anyone needs to get on his knees and thank God, it's me."

Her brow creased with an amused expression. "You could do that, or you could grab your best friend and get a drink. You've had a tough day."

"*I've* had a tough day? You just spent hours in labor and delivered a ten-pound baby from your body."

"Yup," she quipped. "That's the price you pay giving birth to a future quarterback."

The woman never failed to put a smile on his face and lighten his heart.

"I hope you realize I love you in a million different ways, Holly Brooks. Cole is my oldest friend, but *you're* my best friend."

She smiled at Ronin. "It won't take until we're eighty and surrounded by grandchildren to accept that we're a perfect fit. I believe you now."

Her words echoed what he'd said to her in the Middle East, and his heart swelled for the umpteenth time today. He realized he was a lucky man, not because she'd crossed his path, but because she'd crossed a border and fell in love with him.

The End

MESSAGE FROM GRAYSON

Hey, folks. Grayson here. Want to extend my thanks for spending time with the cast of Bordering On Love. We all hope you enjoyed your visit to our corner of the Pacific Northwest.

Holly and I run out of daylight before we run out of chores here on the farmstead. Cole, Ivy, and Jackson have their hands full too. Dad's been doing plenty of babysitting, but he loves spending time with his grandkids. We heard from Dirk. He and Juliette are on a new dig in some remote part of the world. Knowing my old chief, he's showing her more than one new wonder of the world.

As for Natasza, she's juggling balls and writing books. With so many talented authors to choose from, she's grateful that you spent time with her characters.

Natasza is always looking for trusted ARC readers. Drop her an email.

From all of us here at the Brooks Farmstead,

88's

Grayson

ACKNOWLEDGEMENT

To those who have supported my crazy endeavor of writing romance novels, I thank you.

ABOUT THE AUTHOR

Natasza Waters

Writing books with a cup of romance and a twist of steam, Natasza's been penning characters that readers love since 2011. Action, suspense, and romance are the trifecta you'll find in her steamy novels. After publishing twenty-plus books and being honored with three awards for her military romance series (A Warrior's Challenge) and a heartwarming tale that proves love is more than skin deep in His Perfect Imperfection, Nat is still wearing down the letters on her keyboard with more adventures for readers who adore angst and passion.

Whether you're a fan of series or standalones, her novels feature unforgettable characters. Who can resist a book vacation with an eye-popping hero on the road to happily-ever-after?

Visit my website at http://nataszawaters.com/
Follow me on Amazon, BookBub, Goodreads, and Facebook for new releases.

BOOKS BY THIS AUTHOR

A Cup Of Romance With A Twist Of Steam.

A Warrior's Challenge Series
Code Name: Ghost (Book 1)
Code Name: Kayla's Fire (Book 2)
Code Name: Nina's Choice (Book 3)
Code Name: Luminous (Book 4)
Code Name: Forever & Ever (Book 5)
Code Name: Redemption (Book 6)
Code Name: War of Stones (Book 7)

A Warrior's Passion Series
Cricket Under Fire (Book 1)
Dixie Under Siege (Book 2)

Contemporary Romance
Unquenchable Cravings: Gamble on Love (Book 1)
Unquenchable Cravings: Last Chance on Love (Book 2)
Unquenchable Cravings: Wager on Love (Book 3)
His Perfect Imperfection
Twila's Tempest
Committed to Chase
Sealed With a Weekend
Bordering on Love

Paranormal Romance
Legend of Spiralling Cedars
Vyro Creek Series
Arizona Lightning (Book 1)

Arizona Thunder (Book 2)

www.ingramcontent.com/pod-product-compliance
Lightning Source LLC
Chambersburg PA
CBHW020624020726
47494CB00001B/34